"*vN* fuses cyberpunk wi[...] something wholly new. There's a heavy kicker in every chapter. Zombie robots, vampire robots, robots as strange and gnarly as human beings. A page-turning treat."

Rudy Rucker, author of the Ware Tetralogy

"*vN* is a clever book with a wonderful ending by a writer who is well versed in AI technology, who can evoke sympathy with a few well-turned phrases and tells a satisfyingly complex story."

The Guardian

"Will AIs be objects, or people? Caught between the category of human and everything else, we can't think about the very real entities that inhabit – and will inhabit – the excluded middle. Madeline Ashby's done more than just think about that territory; she's made it her home. Person; object; we need new words for things that are neither – and in *vN*, Ashby provides them."

Karl Schroeder, author of the Virga series

"*vN* is a strikingly fresh work of mind-expanding science fiction."

Charlie Jane Anders, iO9

"*vN* is a striking debut, one part tech thriller and one part adult fairy story… The best sci-fi not only entertains but also educates and informs, and vN manages all three effortlessly."

The Eloquent Page"

BY THE SAME AUTHOR

iD
ReV

Company Town

MADELINE ASHBY

vN

THE.FIRST.MACHINE.DYNASTY

ANGRY
ROBOT

ANGRY ROBOT
An imprint of Watkins Media Ltd

Lace Market House,
54-56 High Pavement,
Nottingham,
NG1 1HW
UK

angryrobotbooks.com
twitter.com/angryrobotbooks
The fourth law

First published by Angry Robot in 2012
This edition published 2017

Cover by Martin Bland/Spyroteknik
Set in Meridien by Epub Services

Distributed in the United States by Penguin Random House, Inc., New York.

ISBN 978 0 85766 542 3
Ebook ISBN 978 0 85766 263 7

Printed in the United States of America

9 8 7 6 5 4 3 2 1

For Caitlin Sweet, who loved Amy first,
and
Peter Watts, the Giant Squid who lent me
an island when I rebuilt myself

PROLOGUE:
GIVE GRANNY A HUG

Jack had lived through this same moment before, with human women.

Before meeting his wife (he insisted on referring to her that way, despite their lack of legal standing) at a tech show in Las Vegas, he had spent most of his dating life in what he called the Relationship Academy of the Dramatic Arts. Through a combination of patience, politeness, punctuality, and other qualities curiously absent from most of his competitors, he managed to attract the most volatile women in his available pool. They were the kind who called you in tears at 3am, two years after the breakup, when their latest "performative bio-political modification" art project got infected. He offered these women the opportunity to calm down and sort things out. Things their moms had said. Things their dads had never said.

Charlotte was different. Charlotte was vN. She had no hormones to influence her decision-making, no feast-or-famine cycle driving dopamine or serotonin. She didn't get cramps or headaches or nightmares or hangovers. She didn't need retail therapy or any other kind. Her "childhood" was difficult – her mother abandoned her in a junkyard – but her spirit was as strong as the titanium sheathing her graphene coral bones, her personal integrity as impermeable as the silicone skin overlaying the polymer-doped memristors embedded there, her wit as quick as the carbon aerogel currents wafting through and shaping the musculature of her body.

Charlotte was a self-replicating humanoid. Charlotte didn't do drama. Until now.

That morning he'd found Charlotte in the same place he'd found her all week, curled up beside Amy, in the hammock their daughter used for defragging. Their faces echoed each other: heart-shaped, with narrow little elfin chins and high cheekbones, delicate ears, couture eyebrows just as fair as the hair on their scalps. Depending on how much and how often they fed her, Amy would eventually grow to her clade's default size and shape. At that point, she and Charlotte would be indistinguishable. Jack worried about that, sometimes. What if one day, years from now, he kissed the wrong one as she walked through the door?

For the past month, Jack had gone to bed alone. He only felt Charlotte slip in beside him in the dimmest hours of the morning. He always rolled over to hold her for the last few seconds before her body went completely still, untroubled by snores or twitches. That perfect stillness took some getting used to. At first, it felt like holding a corpse. Now he suspected he'd find human women too warm, too loud, too mobile.

When he'd asked last week, Amy said her mother

spent most of her time looking up potential clademates online and mapping their locations. She had shared access to the map with Amy, but not Jack. The clusters glowed throughout the American southwest. The Border Patrol sometimes found them helping migrants across the desert. It was the failsafe, Amy said. They had to help, even when helping was illegal. With a flick of her wrist, Amy and the projector had put him down inside the canyons where the sightings took place, walking him down the blazing paths his wife had traversed only hours earlier. Amy had snagged the images from drones the Border Patrol shared with the public, but confessed to having already played them in an epic weekend game of Capture the Frag.

"You're not supposed to play violent games," he'd said. "They could trigger you."

Amy ignored him and changed the subject. "Mom's been away from her mom and her sisters so long, she doesn't know how big the clade is. They don't even know she's replicated."

"Iterated," Jack corrected her.

Amy shrugged her mother's shrug. Then she asked: "Dad, what's an r-selector?"

Like most mixed families, Jack and Charlotte and Amy kept their kitchen carefully organized. Although the labelling had improved in recent years, it was still easy to mistake vN food for human food, especially since all the brands now seemed to manufacture the equivalent of their most popular products for vN. The majority of the pantry was dominated by whatever vN food they'd managed to find on special at the handful

of retailers licensed to sell it. Jack had gone on a spree
when he realized Charlotte was iterating. Now he
realized that they really didn't need that closet full
of vN products, not while they were keeping Amy
little. Were it not very illegal, and were it not for
the trackers embedded in each box, he might have
considered reselling the merchandise.

Five years ago, Jack had been tempted to speed
Amy's progress and get to the fun parts: theme parks,
concerts, bikes. He bought all the food to start that
process. But now he knew what life with vN was really
like, and he knew his daughter. She needed the time
to grow at an organic pace. She needed to understand
how she was different and why and what it meant,
from her lack of physical pain to her abundance of
opinion. She needed trips to museums and street
markets; she needed to ask about glistening roasted
ducks hanging in windows and why there weren't
any for vN; she needed to build her endless succession
of dream homes and secret lairs and impregnable
fortresses, each more elaborate and clever than the
last, in her multiple gaming environments. This time
– this sweet time, pulsing with rhythms he was finally
learning after years of moving too fast – was the gift
most vN never received. He was determined that
Amy have better – even if it meant adhering to a strict
child-sized version of the Ro-bento Rory diet, even if
it meant telling his little girl to go without meals.

"She stayed up last night."

Jack turned. Charlotte knotted the belt of her pale
blue bathrobe and pulled out a barstool from the
kitchen island. He watched her take note of the box

of vN pancake mix he'd pulled down from its shelf, and the spray can of special oil he needed to cook them with. Her eyes didn't lift from the products. "So you don't have go to all this trouble," she continued, "because she won't wake up for a while."

Jack persisted with his preparations anyway. He opened the box of pancake mix, nose wrinkling at the dried-blood smell of the rusty orange powder that puffed up when he ripped open the liner bag. "How late was she up?" he asked.

"Midnight."

Jack nodded. "Did she finish the ship?"

"Oh, she's never really finished with anything. You know that."

Charlotte continued staring at the box of pancake mix. Her gaze didn't move when Jack began measuring the powder into a bowl. She blinked at the proper intervals to simulate a human need for moisture, but her expression – default neutral – remained unchanged. Sighing, Jack retrieved a black tub of ionic gel from the refrigerator door, and set it beside the mixing bowl. He wouldn't open and emulsify the spoonful required by the recipe until Amy woke up, but he felt better just having it ready on the counter. He liked the integration of old and new in this kitchen – his humanoid daughter's advanced nano-particle meal formula sitting at home beside the chipped earthenware bowl and the scarred bamboo butcher block. He liked the life those things indicated. He wanted to keep that life.

"You've slept with her every night this week, Charlie."

He watched his wife's internal protocols negotiate for which expression to summon. Her face vacillated between embarrassed and indignant before settling again on neutral. "Amy can't play with human children. She needs a vN friend."

"I agree, but I need my wife, too."

Now Charlotte's eyes rose. "Is this some kind of test? Do you think that my feelings for you aren't genuine?"

Shit, Jack thought. Now he'd done it. He'd committed the one sin that no human partner of a vN humanoid should ever contemplate: he had doubted the reality of Charlotte's emotions. How many times had he unwittingly made that same mistake? Shame prickled across his skin. No wonder Charlotte was acting strangely.

"Charlie, that's not it–"

"You think I really am just a robot–"

A chirp from Amy's wrist-mounted design assistant interrupted her. Their daughter stood in the doorway, wrist held up in its habitual composition pose, perhaps articulating the bend of a banister or an arcade. Her hand dropped abruptly and she turned back down the hall. Her footed pyjamas made scuffing noises as she marched away. Jack dropped his measuring cup immediately and went after her. He caught her door on its track before it could click shut.

Amy's room was made to look like the interior of a treehouse. The knotty pine had cost them, but it was worth it, and the sheer number of nails meant that she never really lost anything because she could always hang it in plain view. She stood at her pegboard now, carefully reorganizing her shirts by colour. Her projector remained locked in display mode. The light from the projector hid her from him a little, and when he moved she moved, too, obscuring herself in the brilliance of last night's creation: an eighteenth-century pirate cruiser called *The Sun Queen*. He watched its walls peel away to expose the decks hidden within, and all the mates inside swabbing floors and tying down barrels and playing dice.

"How much did you hear?" Jack asked.

Amy shrugged.

"I was making pancakes." Jack tried to smile, just in case she turned around to see it. "I should know by now not to start a conversation with your mom before having any coffee. It's an organic thing, you know?"

Amy nodded. She must have heard this excuse any number of times, from any number of humans. He certainly offered it enough.

"This is a really cool ship, you know. You did a great job."

For a synthetic child, appeals to Amy's ego still worked fairly well. This time she did turn around. She twisted her wrist, and the display vanished. "Mom thought she saw one of her sisters last weekend," she said. "That's why she's being weird."

Jack nodded. He looked around for a cushion large enough to hold an adult, and sank into it. Amy joined him in his lap.

"Mom says our shell used to be popular."

"That's true," Jack said. "That's why she gets confused, sometimes. There are so many vN with your face running around, it's easy to make a mistake about seeing a clademate."

Amy nodded into his chest. "That's what she said, too." She fiddled with her assistant, sliding two fingers under the haptic bangle and wiggling them. "She said I'm not supposed to talk to them."

"You're not supposed to talk to *any* strangers, no matter who they look like."

Jack kept his voice light. No need to teach Amy his phobias. He knew other parents feared the same things: strangers, vans, promises of puppies. In their darkest moments they imagined their children kicking and screaming, wrestling against duct tape or blankets. What terrified Jack was the willingness with which Amy would allow herself to be taken by whatever human pervert came along. Her failsafe guaranteed that.

The angel investor supporting the development of von Neumann humanoids was not a military contractor, or a tech firm, or even a design giant. It was a church. A global megachurch named New Eden Ministries, Inc, that believed firmly that the Rapture was coming any minute now. It collected donations, bought real estate, and put the proceeds into programmable matter, natural language processing, and affect detection – all for the benefit of the few pitiful humans regrettably left behind to deal with God's wrath. They would need companions, after all. Helpmeets. And those helpmeets couldn't ever hurt humans. That was the Horsemen's job.

It all went to hell, of course. The pastor of New Eden Ministries, Jonah LeMarque, and many of his council members became the defendants in a class action suit brought by youth group members regarding the use of their bodies as models in a pornographic game. The church sold the licenses to vN-related patents and API rights to finance the settlement. They had risen in value over the years that Pastor LeMarque spent in the appeals process, but LeMarque insisted on keeping the failsafe proprietary. He claimed that this way, the vN could never be used to hurt human beings. The judge who sentenced him was the first to remark on the irony of this particular opinion.

"How come Mom has sisters, but I don't?"

Jack blinked himself out of his thoughts. He kissed the top of Amy's head. "Because your mom and I got it right our first try, sweet pea. We don't need anybody else but you." He pulled back a little to peer at her. "Would you like to have a sister?"

Amy twisted her assistant around her wrist. "I don't know." She furrowed her pale brows at him. "She'd be just like me?"

"She'd *look* just like you. That doesn't mean she'd *be* just like you."

Amy nodded. "Would you keep her little, or would you feed her a lot so she caught up to me?"

Jack considered how to reframe his daughter's question. "Well, I guess she would grow at a human pace, just like you." He smiled. "Would you like a little baby to help take care of?"

Amy looked genuinely perplexed. Then her face resolved into mock accusation. "Aren't you late for work, Dad?"

He laughed. "I'm taking the day off work."

Amy perked up immediately. She twisted in his lap to face him fully. "Oh yeah? Can I take the day off school?"

He lifted her in his arms and stood. "What? You can't take today off school; you'll miss your party!"

Amy rolled her eyes. "The party's going to be stupid. I bet they forget that I can't eat the cookies, like last time."

"Then you'll need your breakfast, won't you?"

Jack turned. Charlotte stood in the door, armed with a wooden spoon still glittering with ionic gel. "Pancakes are ready," she said.

Amy slid out of his arms, briefly threw her arms around her mother, and bounded off to the kitchen. Jack heard the clatter of cutlery a moment later. His eyes locked with Charlotte's and he opened his arms. Pursing her lips, she stepped inside them. Seven years later, her body still felt the same. Engineers and artists and experts of all sorts had worked to sculpt this form for human use, but Charlotte still felt uniquely fitted to him when she let him hold her like this.

"Are we OK?" he asked now.

She nodded. "Sure." She pulled away to look at him. "You're taking the day off work?"

"I decided my girls needed me more, today."

Charlotte smiled. "Thank you." Her head tilted. "Do you believe that I love you, Jack?"

Jack's eyes shut. He tugged her back to him, so he felt the brush of her eyelashes on his neck. Marriages like his operated on a different kind of faith. It wasn't the synthetics themselves that organics like him had to trust, but the emergent properties latent within them, the sum total of decades of research and design and prototyping. You had to know, deep down, that the expression of feeling was as valid as the chemicals that made all human feeling possible, that the story you read on your wife's mass production face was just as mysterious and meaningful as the ones gleaned from more wrinkled texts. Five years ago he had sworn by those words or something like them, not legally, but he had wept and so had she and that was all he needed to know.

"Yes. I believe."

His wife rarely spoke of her childhood, but Jack knew it involved a lot of hiding during the day and raiding junkyards at night. Her mother Portia had iterated her in a junkyard. It was one of the only places with enough raw materials available to trigger the self-repair mode into total self-replication. Charlotte was a glitch; because her clade did not stem from a networked model, neither she nor her mother had access to the clouds that might have regulated their iterative cycles. Now fully grown and far away from her mother, Charlotte craved both open space and solitude. Too many people made her nervous, but too tight an enclosure did the same. So on their dates, he often took her to Lake Temescal.

The first time he brought her here, she asked: "You're taking an artificial woman to an artificial lake?"

"It wasn't always artificial," he had said. "We pitiful humans just improved it a little, with our primitive damming technologies."

On that day, just like this one, Charlotte luxuriated in the sun. (Sunscreen had fast become the default accessory to their relationship.) She loved the night sky just as much, even during the peak power seasons when it glowed orange with light pollution. She loved hiding in fog and reaching out for the rain from the roof of their building. Charlotte couldn't fathom Amy's constant desire to stay inside – working on environments that would never exist – when there was so much outside, waiting to be explored. They fought about it, sometimes, in a completely logical and amicable vN way that nonetheless resulted in stalemates.

Despite the impulsive nature of his decision, Jack had chosen exactly the right day to take off. Clear sky, no bugs save the botflies keeping an eye on the tourists, the clammy fog of winter a distant memory. Others had gotten the same idea: milling around under the shade trees behind Jack and Charlotte was a group of high school seniors attempting to grill a brunch of maple sausage and English muffins on a barbecue with a mostly empty solar cell. It involved a lot of snide laughter and cursing.

The beach was also populated by other vN, both vagrants and min-wage workers standing patiently inside snack stalls. He could pick out the vagrants by the lumps under their skin; unlike the vN with enough money to buy the pre-fabbed food, they often resorted to consuming e-waste to survive. He watched one – with a rather bland square-jawed, broad-shouldered shell – seated at a picnic table, picking errant pieces of plastic from his skin and saving them carefully in a colourful pile between his legs. Jack watched him scoop the pieces into his palm and transfer them to a zippered pouch inside his shirt. He would probably feed them to depository later and earn some cash.

"It's good they have those machines, now." Jack glanced over to find that Charlotte was looking at the vagrant vN as well. She closed her eyes for a moment, then turned away to hug her knees. "We used to have to actually ask for the money, sometimes."

"We?"

Charlotte shrugged. "Just vN in general."

Jack nodded. "If it's still this nice tonight, I was thinking we'd take Amy to Lake Merritt after the graduation."

Charlotte winced. "With all the quake tourists?"

"It's either that or the zoo."

"I can't stand the—"

"*Fuck!*"

Jack twisted to look at the group of teens. A boy wearing a Raiders jersey staggered away from a picnic table beside the grill, clutching his hand. A cheap-looking knife and a half-skinned pineapple stood abandoned on the table, and when the kid turned Jack saw blood. He checked: Charlotte kept her eyes pinned to the grains of sand welling up between her toes, where she wouldn't see the injury or the pain it had inflicted; the vagrant vN hunched at his own picnic table, head hidden in his arms; the vN at the snack counter had shut their eyes.

"I'll see how bad it is," Jack said, and pushed himself up off the beach.

"I could help," Charlotte said. "My clade has a

healthcare plug-in."

"Yeah, a *deactivated* healthcare plug-in," Jack said. "No wife of mine is shorting out because some kid can't use a knife."

He jogged over to the kids at the grill. They had it mostly covered; the kid with the cut hand had immersed it in a cooler full of ice while his friends rifled their bags for skin glue. Botflies hovered over the kid; one settled on his shoulder and blinked greenly at him before alighting on the cooler itself. The kid held up his hand, pink now with diluted blood, and the fly blinked again.

"You OK?" Jack asked.

The kid turned. "I think so." He held out his hand. "Does it look bad?"

Jack looked. The kid had sliced into his fingers pretty deep; probably deep enough to chatter a doctor about it, but the glue would do the job in the meantime. "You're fine," he said. "Next time, slice the bottom off the pineapple before you trim the sides. That way you'll have a stable base."

The kid nodded. He returned his hand to the cooler. He looked over at Charlotte's hourglass shape, still sitting patiently on the beach. "Does she belong to you?"

Jack had corrected others on the matter of his relationship so many times that he could now summarize it in a single line: "She belongs *with* me, not *to* me."

"Sorry." The kid tried smiling. "I just wish they could, you know, help with this kind of thing."

"They help us with all kinds of things."

The kid gestured at his face with his good hand. Jack couldn't tell if the pink of his skin was sunshine or embarrassment. The kid said, "What's it like when you cut yourself shaving? Does she freak out?"

"I don't cut myself shaving, any more," Jack lied. "I'm not a fucking amateur."

They were washing off the beach in the shower together when a call came from Amy's school. It was her principal. Amy was in trouble, and her principal wanted a meeting.

"I'm sorry, but what did she do?" Jack watched the water meter under the showerhead slowly dialled into the red zone as their allotment swirled down the drain.

"She was in a spitting contest," Mrs Lindsay said, as though that explained everything. "She left a hole in the flooring, and I expect you to pay for the damage."

"Mrs Lindsay, if this is your idea of an end-of-term joke, it's not funny. My daughter is a humanoid, not a xenomorph."

"Pardon me? A what, now?"

"Whatever. We'll be there soon."

Jack and Charlotte had researched schools all over the city before finally selecting one where Amy might safely make human friends. They chose the one with the smallest classes and the youngest teachers and the best after-school programs. They conducted interviews and obtained references. They wanted her to grow up alongside organic children, to think of herself as a person first and a synthetic second. They showed Amy stories about vN actors, vN chefs, vN teachers and dancers and designers; they avoided news about expanding anti-vagrancy laws and the millions of angry, jobless humans replaced by synthetics. They hoped the world might be a different place for vN by the time she grew up. Things would harmonize, Jack thought, as they entered the schoolyard and made their way to the principal's office. His daughter would find her place, and she would be happy, and so would her own daughters. They just needed time.

Jack heard himself explaining all of this to Mrs Lindsay after the door to the principal's office clicked resolutely shut behind him and Charlotte.

"I understand that, Mr Peterson," Mrs Lindsay said. She was a small Indian woman who wore her black hair in a tight chignon and offset her rather plain suit with ornate enamel earrings in the shape of hummingbirds. "But the reality is that the lifestyle you have chosen for your daughter is having harmful side effects, and not just for school property."

Jack turned to Charlotte. "How many pancakes did she eat this morning?"

Charlotte shrugged. He was seeing a lot of that shrug today, and he didn't like it. "However many her diet said."

"This is the diet that retards her growth, yes?"

"It doesn't *retard* her growth, it gives her *time*–"

"Mr Peterson, your daughter is going hungry."

Mrs Lindsay laid her hands flat on her desk. Between her fingers, Jack saw a hot map of the school. It randomly leapt between classrooms, offering attendance stats and tiny windows of surveillance footage.

Mrs Lindsay's gaze slid over to Charlotte, who met it blankly, then back to Jack.

"I'm not certain why I need to explain this to you, but when vN children go hungry, their digestive fluids build up and permeate their saliva. That makes it corrosive, and very dangerous in an environment like this one."

Jack sat up a little taller in the too-soft chair across from the desk. "I'm well aware of my wife and daughter's physiology, Mrs Lindsay. What I don't get is what gives you the right to tell me how to live in my own home. Amy is a smart, happy kid–"

"No, she isn't, Mr Peterson."

He uncrossed his legs. "Excuse me?"

"Please don't feel badly about this. Children often hide these kinds of things from their parents. But Amy has no friends in her class. The friends she does have are teachers. She talks with them during the recess and gym periods."

"Only because you won't allow her to participate!"

"Accidents happen in those settings all the time, Mr Peterson. We can't risk her failsafe going off if a human child falls off the monkey bars and cracks his head open." Mrs Lindsay squeezed her eyes shut and took a moment before continuing. "We cannot fulfil your daughter's special needs *and* allow the other children to play normally."

"Then don't. Keep a closer eye on the organics, and let Amy play. It's not her fault if one of the monitors can't stop a fight fast enough."

"That's true. It's not her fault. But it is definitely her problem." Again, Mrs Lindsay glanced at Charlotte.

When Charlotte said nothing, Mrs Lindsay raised her hands in a conciliatory manner. "I'm going to recommend that we allow Amy to skip a few grades. Frankly, I was never fully convinced that she should start school in kindergarten. She is not a kindergartener, and has not been one for years."

Jack looked at Charlotte, expecting backup without knowing why. His wife had voiced the exact same concerns, back when they made this choice. Now he wondered how much of *their* choice it had been. Maybe Charlotte was just going along with it, waiting for him to see her brand of reason. He suddenly felt very alone in the room.

"So, what if we don't skip her ahead, or grow her bigger, you won't let her come back next year?"

"Please don't treat this conversation as a hostage negotiation, Mr Peterson. This is an inclusive school, and we simply want it to be a safe place for all our students, organic and synthetic." She steepled her delicate fingers. "But it's because this school operates from that ethic that I would be forced to report you to certain authorities if I found you unusually defensive about keeping your daughter prepubescent in appearance."

Fear opened up a void inside him. He knew why other men kept their synthetic little girls so little. He wasn't one of them. But Mrs Lindsay had the power to make the pedo squad think he was, and that kind of thing didn't just leave your record, even if it was only a simple search for the wrong kind of pornography. It could lose him his next job, and the one after that. He thought of the vagrant vN, their skin bulbous with trash, like serfs of the Dark Ages afflicted with plague.

Beside him, Charlotte stood. "I think we'll be taking Amy home now," she said. Somehow, Jack stood with her. He wandered toward the door. Behind him, he heard Charlotte ask: "How old were you when you reached your full size?"

"A year," Mrs Lindsay said.

Back at home, they ordered delivery from the nearest Electric Sheep location. Amy wanted to go in and sit down to eat like a grown-up, but the Sheep was a meat market. At least, their local was. Maybe the other franchise locations were different. But the last thing Jack wanted in this moment was for his daughter to watch organic men watching synthetic women. So he put his foot down, and Amy ordered a Folded Hands sandwich with Flexo Fries and an orange LCL punch, and hid in her room playing games until she was done. The meal itself was too big, far beyond her dietary limit, but she said nothing, perhaps having already guessed the things Mrs Lindsay had told them. Jack wondered, as he munched on his own potato version of the Flexo Fries, whether the principal had counseled her at all before meeting with him and Charlotte. Did they already have some sort of scheme going? Had she asked Amy to report anything unusual?

Jack finished his fries, put his GO Box in the sink, and stretched out in his chair. He watched Charlotte watching the scroll-style display above the trick fireplace. He'd bought the place solely for that fireplace; it was one of the last units in the city to be built with one. In every dream house Amy designed there was now a fireplace, sometimes with a display over it, but most often with a real brushwork scroll or tapestry or painting. With Amy safe in her room, Charlotte had lifted the usual limits from the feeds. Occasionally, the eye-shaped clockwork gear that indicated failsafe-triggering programming would pop up and the secondary limits kick in, delaying the signal and shuffling until something suitable was found. She flicked through the remaining content with one irritable, jerking finger.

"What's wrong?" Jack asked.

"Nothing."

"It's not nothing. Something's bothering you. What is it?" He hunched forward and tried to catch her eye. "Is it because you were right, all this time? That we should have grown Amy more quickly?"

Charlotte opened her mouth, then closed it. "No. That's not it."

"Then does it have to do with your clade? I know you've been tracking them. Do you miss your mother?"

Charlotte leveled him with a glare the likes of which he had never seen in a synthetic woman. It seemed to penetrate his every cell, as though she were watching him decay one picosecond at a time. She was silent for a full minute before whispering: "No."

Jack swallowed. His wife's eyes had never seemed so pale before. They were like jagged pieces of sea glass bleached by the abuse of sun and ocean. Despite the ageless skin surrounding them, they looked terribly old. "We've never talked about her, Charlie. Maybe we should."

His wife shook her head and returned to the feeds. "Nothing about Portia can be solved with conversation."

"Don't shut down on me now, I want–"

"Did you intend that pun, Jack? Or was it just a slip?"

Recognizing a no-win scenario when he saw one, Jack stood up and left.

In her room, Jack found Amy captaining a pirate ship and losing. A zombie virus had overtaken her crew, and she, the sole survivor, fired her limited weaponry from the crow's-nest. Her little body swayed with the rocking of the simulated cruiser projected at her feet. She had run out of bullets for her blunderbuss, and now mimed loading the thing with gold doubloons straight from her pocket.

"The gold melts too fast," she said, "but it leaves a nice big hole."

Jack poked a finger through one of the miscreants' sucking chest wounds. The creature cast him an affronted glare. "I thought zombies were weakened by salt."

"They are, but I lost my loyalty round, so my first mate rebelled and bought women instead of supplies."

"You should have hired a better first mate. Now you'll have to find another one."

Amy shook her head. "It's the ship I mind losing. I worked really hard on this one."

Jack watched the zombies shambling over his shins. He thought about what Amy's principal had said. "You don't mind losing a friend?"

"He isn't a friend, he's the game."

"How can you tell?" Jack let a peg-legged zombie crawl over his hand. An undead parrot alit on his wedding ring and started pecking at it. Bright green feathers the size of rice grains molted away as its head bobbed. They dissipated into smoke in the time it took to blink his eyes. "I'm sure his programming is just as complex as yours."

Amy rolled her eyes. "Dad, please. I know the difference between adapted and automatic."

Jack nodded slowly. "Oh."

Amy made a pincer gesture to freeze the game. "Are you trying to give me a talk about being in trouble? Or about being vN?"

He closed his eyes briefly. "No, I'm not. You're a person just like anybody else, Amy. You know that."

"And people get in trouble, sometimes."

"Yes. People get into trouble, sometimes."

Amy thawed the game. He watched her fight the zombies as nobly as she could, until they were crawling all over each other to climb the mast and attain her perch. She waited until she could see the pixels of their eyes, and then used an ancient ruby amulet won on her last quest. Jack recognized it from his many trips through her treasure chest. She had played for weeks to find it. The gleaming cabochon inside granted her power over flame. With its projection clutched delicately in her tiny fist, she held it to the in-game sun and watched the light refract red and hot on her enemies. Fire blazed within the stone's bloody depths. It ran down the red rays and caught and spread among the moaning hordes.

They gibbered and screamed and jumped ship. But the damage was already done, and the loss total: the fire had spread to Amy, too, and had run down her sleeve onto the mainsail and mast. The ship was burning. She was going down with it.

"Oh, Charlotte! Hello!"

It was Liz, one of the other mothers. Her son Nate had attended the same daycare as Amy. The boy had nursed a crush on Amy all year and given her a special synthetic chocolate heart last Valentine's. Now he sat beside Amy in the front row, with the gold star students waiting onstage for kindergarten graduation to start, staring at her openly. Amy pretended not to notice.

"It must be so nice to have a boy," Charlotte was saying. She had brightened since they got in the car. Jack suspected Amy's unexpected willingness to wear the pretty new graduation dress Charlotte picked out had something to do with it.

Liz laughed. "You didn't have to potty-train him!"

Gary, Liz's husband, looked Jack up and down. "You think this is it for you, Jack? No more?"

Jack defaulted to his usual answer: "If Charlotte wants another, we'll have one."

"Hey, that's pretty handy. No worries about accidents, right?"

"*Gary*," Liz said in her scandalized voice. She used it on her husband a lot. "Amy is *just like other kids*."

Liz was one of those really informed human women with a habit of sometimes sounding like a public service announcement. "Oh, there are Nate's grandparents." She gestured toward the door. "Are your parents coming, Jack?"

"My parents won't be coming," Jack said. "I've pretty much always been a disappointment, if you know what I mean."

"What, with a pretty lady like this on your arm?" Gary asked. "Come on, what father doesn't dream of a girl like Charlotte for his son?"

Jack made a mental note never to let Amy play at Nate's house under Gary's sole supervision.

"Oh, just ignore him," Liz said. "We have to go meet my mother, anyway. See you after!"

Together, Jack and Charlotte watched them leave. They sat on folding chairs and sighed in unison, though for Charlotte it was a simple motion of her shoulders. Jack leaned back and looked up at the vaulted ceiling. It was a good school. He kept telling himself that. It was a good school. Better than most kids got. Better than the insane military shit he'd been subjected to after breaking curfew for the umpteenth time, that was for sure.

"Hey." Charlotte slipped her cool hand into his. "It's my turn to ask you. What's wrong?"

He squeezed her hand. "Just thinking about my dad," he said. "How stupid he is to be missing stuff like this."

Charlotte smiled. "The important thing is that we found each other."

"Damn straight." He stretched one arm over her shoulders and pulled her closer. "Have I ever told you how smart you are?"

She shrugged. "All that graphene has to be good for something."

He kissed the top of his wife's head. He watched his daughter on the stage: her swinging feet, her eager wave. Her bright smile hit him in the gut, as straight and sure as if she had reached over the heads of chattering parents and bored siblings to deliver a finishing blow.

Amy's teacher, a willowy woman who wore her waist-length hair over a long denim dress, ascended the stage soon after that. She held the microphone with both hands in a white-knuckle grip. She swayed in place as though guided by some internal music. "Welcome to kindergarten graduation," she said in a thin, high voice. "This has been a very special year for all of us. We've learned a lot, and although we're sad to leave our class behind, we're excited for next year! On with the show!"

With that, the kindergartners shuffled out of their seats and sang a song complete with hand motions (guided from offstage by their swaying teacher), then herded back to their little chairs (with the name tags affixed to the backs), and fidgeted through a "commencement address" offered by the principal. She was wearing the goofy robes of her alma mater. Then it was time for the diplomas to be handed out.

"Amy Peterson," the teacher said, and Amy stood. She crossed the stage halfway, before pausing and squinting at someone standing among the other parents below the stage.

"Mom?"

A woman rose slowly to the stage. She wove unsteadily on her feet. Her clothes didn't quite fit; she'd buttoned her shirt wrong. She wore no shoes.

Her skin bristled with unshed plastic. Otherwise, she was Charlotte's exact replica.

"Come on, Amy." The vN's voice had the rough, hollow sound of real hunger. She held her arms out. "Give your granny a *hug*."

"Please God, no." It was the first time in Jack's memory that he had heard his wife invoke any deity whatsoever.

Onstage, Amy came no closer but did not back away. She spoke clearly and sharply. "I don't want to hug you. Leave me alone."

Charlotte's double lunged, but Nate's sly five year-old foot tripped her up. He looked directly at Amy. "Run!"

But Amy didn't run. She stared as the other vN's arm shot out across the floor and grabbed the boy's tiny ankle. Nate screamed as she yanked him off the chair, off the stage, and threw him like a discus into the crowd. His soft little body hit the linoleum and concrete face-first before skidding down the aisle. Blood smeared from his open mouth and smashed nose. In the gleaming trail, Jack saw a baby tooth. Then it disappeared, swallowed by the tread of a man's boot. Charlotte's hand left Jack's grip as the shrieking started. Her feet pounded down the aisle. She leapt high and crashed down on the stage piano in an explosion of wood and music.

Charlotte said, "Amy. Run. Now."

"Mom–"

"Do it!"

Amy hurried down the stairs. Now Jack ran too, trying to get to her, but he stumbled and fell to the floor. Now he lay eye to eye with Nate, level with the blood oozing from his open mouth with its two front teeth still missing. The boy was dead. Terribly, awfully, horrifically dead, his eyes still open and his hands still sticky with ketchup, a redder red than the deep dark fluid pooled around his ruined face. Jack roared. It was a sound he didn't know he could produce, something mighty and raw that tore its way up out of his gut and must have signaled his child, because Amy crawled out from the forest of folding chairs to meet him.

"Dad…"

Jack stood up in a flash, pulling her with him and shielding her eyes from the corpse at their feet in case her failsafe – *Why is that boy dead, how can that boy be dead, why isn't Charlotte's mother dead* – triggered and caused sudden memory corruption.

Now backing toward the nearest exit with Amy in his arms, Jack watched his wife battling her mother onstage: a blur of twisting limbs and hasty swipes, their arms and legs sweeping the air. Where did she learn to fight like that?

"You can't have her." Charlotte grabbed a mic stand. She hefted it across her shoulders. "She's mine."

Charlotte's mother laughed low in her throat. "She can be replaced."

Charlotte spun, swinging the stand foot-side out. It landed inside her mother's ribs. The other woman looked at it a moment before snapping it off and gripping the rest of the stand.

"You knew this was coming." More laughter hiccuped out of her torn body. "You can never outrun me, I'm your mother."

Charlotte screamed high and desperate. She charged. Her mother grabbed her by the collar and drove her head into the opposite wall. In his arms, Amy had gone perfectly still.

"Dad, Mom needs help."

He bent her head to his chest, kissed her scalp and stroked her hair. He was at the door now. He could feel its push-bar in the small of his back, already giving way as he prepared to make the final step. Shame shrank his voice into a rasping thing. "I can't, baby. I'm not strong enough."

"Oh." Amy hugged his neck. "That's OK." Then she slipped down his body and ran away.

"Amy, no!"

But Amy, whose body was ten times as strong as that of its organic inspiration, was already at the stage. Her little feet danced up the steps. Her voice came out bigger than her little body would have suggested possible: "Granny!"

Charlotte wailed. Amy evaded her frantic grasp and dashed toward the wretched, broken thing before her. She scrambled up it like a monkey on a tree. Charlotte's mother grinned triumphantly, clasping her arms around Amy's tiny body, pinning her flailing arms. And as though their reunion were a happy one, Amy darted down for a kiss.

For a moment, it was almost beautiful. Jack thought of his wife and daughter's kisses, thought of Charlotte's lips, warm and tingling with digestive fluid. You developed a taste for it, after a while. That sweet, distinctive burn remained in the mouth and on the skin for hours. He went to sleep with it every night and rolled over every morning just to get it back. But as Mrs Lindsay had pointed out, that very pleasure came from the acid bubbling behind their smiles, the kind that only came up if they were obsessive about their diets, if they were trying not to iterate or trying not to grow.

Muffled behind her melting lips came the sound of Portia screaming.

Jack had never enjoyed depriving his daughter of food. He firmly believed that for Amy to grow up right she had to grow up slow, and that meant growing up starved. She felt no pain. Her belly didn't distend. Her nails didn't weaken or her locks begin to fray. But watching her break the fast of her hungry years he sensed how long they must have felt for her. Her mouth opened wide, wider, until it unhinged like a snake's and sucked down the remnants of her grandmother's neck. She snapped a clavicle in her teeth. Black bone dust poured down her throat. Aerogel wreathed her face in a darkly glittering halo. It adhered to her skin in sparkling black streaks. She licked it off the heels of her hands and spat plastic like a hunter freeing buckshot from fresh-cooked game.

Amy's grandmother sank to her knees. Amy dug her fingers into the older woman's skin and pulled. Flesh flensed away from the ribs; aerogel piped out in a smokestack. It coated Amy's hair and hands and face. The ribcage shuddered and trembled in her grip before finally giving way with a groan. It was not hunger Jack witnessed, now. It was vengeance.

He tried to step forward, to intervene, to be the dad,

but there was a tide of frightened people streaming around him and he was, after all, only flesh. He watched as Amy's body lengthened – her limbs stretching and popping, her shoulders expanding, her waist narrowing, as her grandmother's body dwindled, faded, became a pile of glittering silicon or lithium or whatever was left. Amy stood, her pretty white graduation dress mere shreds over a woman's body, and wiped her mouth with the back of her hand.

"All gone, Mom."

Charlotte covered her face with her hands and slowly crumpled to the floor.

On the floor, Liz keened. She rocked what remained of her son's body on her lap. Amy hopped offstage and padded down the aisle to the mother and child. Liz scuttled away, whimpering. Ignoring her, Amy knelt beside her dead classmate. She stared at the blood, the broken limbs, the clear evidence of human suffering that should have tripped alarms all through her cognitive systems. Other von Neumann types would be twitching piles of carbon by now. In her calm face, Jack saw the collapse of his daughter's future and the beginning of what he had always dreaded. The failsafe had failed. The world had changed, and his little girl was no longer safe in it.

1: THE UGLY PARTS

Amy woke on the floor of a cage that hummed. She tried moving her legs and kicked the fencing nearest her feet, igniting a spark that jolted up from her toes to her teeth and left her so rigid even her eyes couldn't move. She hated being more conductive than organic people.

"Careful," someone said from outside the cage. "It's rigged."

The man wore a blue uniform and held a scroll-style reader between the thumb and first finger of each hand. Its anonymous blue glow made his expression hard to read. He looked organic; she could see his pores and the patchiness of his hair. Other clades had advanced plugins for differentiating humans. They used thermoptics or gait recognition or pheromone detection. Amy just looked for the ugly parts.

"Where am I?"

He didn't even bother putting down the scroll. "You're being detained."

Amy tried moving again. She had to do so carefully; her limbs were grown-up limbs now, and they were much longer and clumsier than the ones she remembered. Finally she sat with her knees to her chest and looked around. She sat in a kennel like at an animal shelter, a rectangle of white linoleum bordered by black chain-link. Across the room was another set of kennels stacked two rows high. In the centre aisle sat an empty cage, shaped more like a cube. Its floor was black.

In games, Amy had escaped far more challenging environments than this. In fact, she could have easily designed a more intimidating space, given the time and the tools. She checked for laser turrets or acid sprinklers, but found none. Maybe the whole room had a mutable magnetic field. It would certainly explain how they'd kept her asleep, and why they bothered with an organic guard. Without a helmet, he'd be vulnerable to the field and start seeing things. Did that mean the field generator was being reset? Were there other vulnerabilities in the system?

She decided to take stock of other resources. She wore a bright green jumpsuit. It didn't seem particularly sturdy, much less fire- or acid-proof. Far at the end of the kennels was another person in the same jumpsuit. She couldn't tell if it was a boy or girl just by looking, but it had a very big shape over which the fabric stretched tightly. It wasn't moving.

"Where are my parents?" She tried to think of something more intelligent to say. "They should be here. I'm a *minor.*"

This time the scroll did fall, and a hand strayed toward his taser. The guard's eyes had the dead, blank look of someone watching late-night shows. "I don't know how it is in Oakland, but where I come from, *minors* know how to behave themselves."

Amy had nothing to say to that. She looked at her new prison slippers. She had never thought of her mother's feet as big, but now that she was wearing them, Amy wondered how her mom got around without tripping. How had she never noticed details like this before? Where was her mother now? Was she still repairing the damage to her body?

"May I please call my parents? I think I get a phone call. People who get arrested get a phone call, right?"

Now the guard stood. He lumbered over to the kennel and leaned close without really touching it. This close his humanity was more obvious: burst capillaries in his nose, silver hairs sprouting from a mole below his left ear, sweat stains blackening the blue of his shirt. "I think you're failing to grasp the enormity of the shit you're in. Now if you know what's good for you, you'll sit tight and wait. It won't be long, now."

"It won't be long until what?" Amy asked.

He straightened up and pulled his shirt down where it had bunched up over his curling waistband. He wore a yellow gold wedding ring. The skin around it was puffy and red. He must have started wearing it years ago, when his fingers were slimmer.

"You didn't have to tell me about being young," he said. "It's already on your record."

"So you know I just graduated kindergarten?"

He nodded slowly. "Yup. So I figure maybe you don't know that all you vN were designed by a bunch of Bible-thumpers."

Amy shook her head. "I know. They wanted us for after the Second Coming, or something. To take care of everybody God didn't like."

"That's right. That's why you've got all the right holes and such. So people can indulge themselves without sin."

Amy's attention scattered over several simulated outcomes to this conversation. It cohered on the one in which he opened the cage to touch her, and she wove around him and got away, somehow.

As though he had run the same simulations in his own mind, the guard shook his head. He held up one hand. "Don't worry, kiddo. I'm a grown man; I don't play with dolls." He leaned down a little. "What I'm saying is, I don't know if they left behind some piety programming or what, but if they did you had better make peace with your god."

Amy's body remained very still, but her mind raced. They were going to kill her. She didn't know why. She had been trying to *help*. Her granny had been hurting people and Amy had stopped it. Maybe that was the problem – maybe her granny belonged to somebody important, and Amy had eaten her. That wasn't her fault, either: she'd only meant to bite her, but Amy's diet left her so *hungry* all the time. When her jaws opened all the digestive fluid came up, a whole lifetime's worth, hot and bitter as angry tears. It ate the flesh off her granny's bones. By then, Amy couldn't stop. The smoke was too sweet. The bone dust was too crunchy. And the sensation of being full, really full, of her processes finally having enough energy to clock at full speed, was spectacular. Being hungry meant being slow. It meant being stupid. It felt like watching each packet of information fly across her consciousness on the wings of a carrier pigeon. But her granny tasted like Moore's Law made flesh.

"I didn't know it was so bad," Amy said. "I really didn't. I swear. I just couldn't stop myself."

"I know," the guard said. "I used to work corrections before I got this job, and that's what kids in your situation always say, organic or synthetic."

Amy hugged her knees. She supposed organic kids wanted to curl up in a little ball in this situation, too. "There won't be a trial, or anything?"

"Of a kind. Tests, probably. Lots of tests."

"Tests?" That was something. She had to be alive, if there were going to be tests. "I get to live?"

He looked her up and down. "Part of you does, I guess."

Amy pinched the skin of her arms. If you couldn't brag in the brig, where could you? "I've got fractal design memory in here. Even if I'm cut up, my body remembers how to repair itself perfectly. I'll come back in one piece, no matter what."

"Oh, believe me, dollface, I know. I've seen it happen. You put some vN shrapnel in the right culture, and it grows right back. Like cancer." He snorted. "But whether what grows back is actually *you*? With all the memories, and all the adaptations? That's like asking how many angels can dance on the head of a pin."

Amy imagined her skin sliced thin as ham, suspended in the shadowy clouds of vN growth medium. Maybe she wouldn't even miss her mom and dad. Never once seeing their faces or hearing their voices or feeling their arms around her would probably hurt a lot less, if she were smashed into a million pieces.

Red lights washed the kennels in a sudden cough syrup haze. "Shit," the guard said. He thumbed off his scroll, rolled it shut, and stuffed it in one shirt pocket. Then he pressed open a panel over his shoulder and retrieved a shotgun. Frowning, he snapped it open and sniffed the rounds. Apparently pleased, he marched down to the kennel holding the other person.

"This your doing?" he asked. "Your boys know where you are?"

"...*chingada, cabrón.*"

"Yeah, same to you, pal. I know exactly what they're doing with you, later. They're gonna smoke your ass." He stared up at the ceiling. "Serial–"

Behind him, another door slammed open, knocking him forward. He stumbled, and the gun clattered to the floor. An alarm filled Amy's ears. She covered them. Now she watched three women walk in through the door. One aimed a can of spray paint at the guard; she misted him with it and he began to collapse. The woman caught him, and laid him down tenderly, arranging his limbs as though for sleep. It must have been some kind of drug in that can; Amy heard no screams and saw no blood. What she did see frightened her more.

Granny. Three of them.

Now Amy did skitter backward in her little kennel. She watched the three women walk forward, single file. They each wore her mother's face, but every other detail shouted *Wrong!* in Amy's head: the tightness in their shoulders, the alertness of their gaze, their mismatched clothes and the hungry way they looked at her. Up close, she saw the plastic embedded in their flesh. It poked up at odd points, black and pink and green just visible at the thinnest stretches of their skin. They peeled her door away; sparks hissed harmlessly off their thick gloves.

"You're coming with us," one said.

Amy whimpered. There was no way she could escape from all three of them. They were here to punish her. They had to be. She had eaten their mother. "Go away!"

One of them moved forward. "You have something we need."

"Leave me alone!" Amy pressed herself up against the wall. Her fingers, for some reason, were still in her ears. She was crying. They were staring. "I'm sorry, OK? I'm really sorry. I didn't mean to. Just please let me go home. Please, I just want to go home."

One smiled faintly. "You *are* home." And she reached out–

–and then her hand vanished, gone in a hot puff of wind that smelled vaguely of bile. For a moment, the other von Neumann woman watched her flailing stump of a wrist. Then the wrist disappeared, blazing away into blackly glittering nothingness that smoked from her disintegrating arm. She didn't scream. She didn't howl with pain or fear as a human would have done – she just watched as a large figure in a green jumpsuit loped down the hall carrying the guard's shotgun.

"I think you know what this is!"

Amy's fellow prisoner primed the shotgun again. He was hugely fat, and wore badly scorched prison slippers on his hands. Amy smelled burning cloth. The other vN women backed away, abandoning their sister, who cradled her disintegrating arm close to her chest. Now he stood at the ruined door to Amy's cage. He said, "There are three more puke rounds in here. The peroxidase in just one can eat carbon tubes faster than your repair mods can handle it. You're gonna die."

He pointed the weapon straight at Amy's head. "And now you're gonna let me leave."

Amy tried moving, but he was bigger and faster and he grabbed her arm and wrenched her upward. He pressed the gun into her back and nudged her forward. "Move."

Fight back, a voice inside said to Amy. *You can take him.*

But then the gun was prodding her again, and she stepped forward. The sisters followed her with their eyes. She kept walking. At the end of the hall stood a set of doors secured by a single steel bar.

"Open it," her fellow prisoner said.

Amy's fingers fumbled on the lock. Grimacing, she forced the bar up and over. It squealed a little as it slid down. She pushed open the doors–

–and almost fell into oncoming traffic. Her arms windmilled for a minute before a hand bunched up in her jumpsuit and yanked her back. Columns of headlights had gathered just a foot below them. Drivers honked and gestured at dashboard comms. Far away, she saw the blink and spin of police cars.

The kennel room wasn't a room at all: it was a vehicle.

"Hey, a mobile prison," said her new captor. "The chimps are getting creative." Then he pushed her.

Amy landed on her knees – atop a car. She winced and tried to apologize to the woman shouting in the driver's seat. Beside her, the other prisoner jumped down and grabbed her arm. He pulled her off the car and along the highway, out of the red glare of the mobile prison and into the rows of increasingly noisy cars. Amy looked back. The sisters stood high above in the mobile prison, watching. *They could still help you,* a voice inside said. *Do you want to be a hostage?*

"Out," said her kidnapper. He was tapping on the driver's side window of an old and dented blue sedan with the business end of the gun. The teenaged boy inside yelled something, and Amy's captor flipped the gun around and busted the window with it. "Out," he repeated. *"Please."*

The boy scrambled out of the car on the other side. He held his hands up. "You can take whatever you want," he said. "I mean, seriously, just take it, just let me go–"

"Start running," Amy's kidnapper said. The boy ran.

Her kidnapper reached inside the door via the broken window, and opened it. He pushed her inside. She crawled over to the passenger side and squeezed back against the seat as her hostage-taker reached across her and pulled the door shut. It slammed and she flinched. He gave her an odd look before shutting his own door and edging the car past the prison and into the flow of traffic. He could barely fit his bulk inside the driver's seat. He didn't bother with a seat belt.

"You see that?" he asked, pointing at the mobile prison as it blurred past. Outside, it looked like an ordinary eighteen-wheeler with the words ISAAC'S ELECTRONICS inscribed across its panels. "That's somebody's idea of a *joke*. It's fucking *sick*."

Amy said nothing. The gun sat between them. She wondered if she could grab it and use it. But where would she go? They were screeching through traffic. She couldn't drive. At least, not in real life.

"You could thank me, you know." He began ripping out peripherals and throwing them out the window.

"For taking me hostage?"

"For saving your ass!" He tossed a fistful of wires onto someone else's windshield. "You didn't want to go with them, did you?"

Amy blinked. She hadn't quite thought of it that way. "Well, no…"

"Who were they, anyway?"

Amy hugged her knees. "My aunts, I guess," she said. How much had he heard back there? "I, um… I sort of killed my grandmother." He said nothing, but she sensed the suspicion anyway. "She and my mom were having a fight, and I got in the middle, and–"

"Whatever. Family drama. Got it."

Amy's kidnapper had sort of a doughy face, olive-skinned and fringed with huge black curls on top and a scrubby beard across the non-existent jaw. He had very nice eyelashes, though, long and perfectly curled like in a commercial. He seemed to notice her staring, because he turned to her suddenly and said: "I'm Javier."

"I'm Amy. Amy Frances P–" She paused. Maybe giving out her name wasn't such a good idea. "Amy Frances."

"Was that your first time in jail, Amy Frances?"

"Uh huh."

He sped up. "Lucky you."

Amy watched the highway scrolling by. It looked like an old cartoon where the backgrounds were the same and just recycled on a loop: strip malls, streetlights, abandoned car dealerships full of desperate signs and black windows. The same everywhere, over and over, not like the unique shops her mother frequented – full of handmade things and loud music that Amy couldn't understand, but still danced to while waiting outside the fitting rooms. Even the trees were different: thin and bristly and spiky-looking, not like the broad, shady ones planted in sidewalks. She was very, very far from home. And she had no idea where they were headed.

"Are you hungry?"

Amy turned to Javier. "Not really." *Your granny did make a pretty big meal, after all.* "But thank you for asking."

"Seriously? I'm starving. Jail-breaking is hungry work."

"Do you do a lot of jail-breaking?"

"Define 'a lot'."

For some reason, Amy had assumed that this kind of bragging was confined to organics, and ended with boyhood. Men of this size, be they flesh or mech, weren't supposed to get dimples in their faces while hinting at their exploits. Then again, she hadn't met that many vN models. Maybe Javier's had add-ons for charm.

"I'm not used to eating very much."

Javier peered at her from the corner of his eye. "You're a dieter, huh?"

"I was. But a little while ago, I..."

"Fell off the wagon?"

She tucked her hands under her legs. "Something like that."

"Sweet." Javier licked his lips. He turned off into a tiny little strip mall full of For Lease signs. "Then I guess it's time to go shopping."

"What?"

He parked in front of a thrift store. LEAVE DONATIONS HERE read a sign in one wall-sized window. A giant arrow pointed downward at bulging black garbage sacks. Javier jumped out of the car and hurried over to one. He started ripping it open. He looked over his shoulder. "What's your shoe size?"

Amy looked at her new, grown-up feet. "I... I don't know..."

"Well, come on and find out!" He threw a pair of pink flip-flop sandals at the car.

Slowly, Amy left the car. She scoped the parking lot. Arc lights cast a dull orange glow over the whole place. Earthquakes had left dark lightning patterns in the concrete façade of each dead shop. Black mould grew there, now. She heard wind in the pines. It was the loneliest place she'd ever been.

"Isn't this stealing?" Amy asked.

Javier was wriggling into a giant black T-shirt,

faded grey now, with a picture of an old video game controller on it. BLOW ME, it read in peeling white letters. "No way," he said. "People donated this stuff already, right? They don't care."

Reluctantly, Amy started picking through the garbage bag. After a few tries, she found a *Sesame Street* T-shirt with the Count on it. The brand made her feel instantly at home, as though the little yellow and green street sign could act like a talisman and keep her safe with its promise of cheery songs and word games. "Found one," she said, holding it up.

Javier's brows lifted. "That's a kid's T-shirt."

"So?"

"Gonna be tight, is all I'm saying."

Amy looked down at herself. Maybe he was right. Still, it couldn't hurt to try. "Um, where do I try it on?"

Javier gestured at the parking lot. He was already pulling at the legs of his jumpsuit. Amy quickly covered her eyes, reached blindly, and ran around the side of the building, trailing old clothes behind her. She pressed herself up against one shadowed wall, near a door marked LOADING. She threw on the clothes as quickly as possible. She'd found track pants, the shiny kind with all the buttons up each leg, and without underwear they felt a little weird. But there was no way she was digging through somebody else's underwear and putting it on. *None*. Synthetic or not, some things were just disgusting.

Amy emerged from the shadows still wearing her prison slippers. They fit, and she had no desire to wear somebody else's socks or shoes. Her new pants made a slippery sound as she walked. Javier had retrieved an enormous pair of shorts – she couldn't tell if they were for swimming or just wearing – with a camouflage pattern and big pockets. She wondered suddenly if he did this a lot. He seemed used to it. He stared at her new clothes as he slipped on some old foam beach mocs.

"Uh, you might wanna roll those up."

"Excuse me?"

"Your pants. Roll them up."

Amy bent down. The ends were dragging, a little. She started folding.

"At the *waist*, I mean. Start rolling at the *waist*. So they don't fall off."

"Oh! OK." Amy started rolling. It took a couple of folds, but the pants did fit better. Javier threw a nubby old grandpa sweater at her, too, saying something about it being cold outside, as he shuffled off toward another store. Amy followed, rolling up her new woolly sleeves. Javier crowed, and ran across the parking lot to the store on the opposite side – a used electronics shop. Amy jogged behind him. He ran around the side of the building and started rubbing his hands together at the sight of a row of three dumpsters.

"Awesome." He tossed a chunk of asphalt at the nearest one. When it fell back to ground, he began opening its massive creaking lid.

"What are you *doing*?"

"Grocery shopping. Didn't I say I was hungry?" Javier leapt in. A moment later, out flew a positively ancient keyboard that clattered to the concrete and promptly lost a few dirty keys. "Plastics! In the trash! It's like they're just throwing money away!"

Amy tiptoed to the side of the dumpster. She stood on her toes to peer inside. It seemed mostly empty, aside from a few stray accessories. Rationally, she knew that other vN, the unlucky ones out there on their own, had to eat garbage sometimes or sell it to buy food. They didn't have to worry about diet plans like Rory's pinging their kitchens every time they opened the cupboards, because they were just scraping to get by. She'd just never seen or met one of them, before. Not until her granny.

"You take the other one," Javier said. "This one's mine."

Amy frowned. She hadn't asked to share his loot, but she moved on to the next dumpster anyway. Slipping her fingers under the lid, she pushed it up until it rested against a wall, and tried hopping in as Javier had done. He evidently had a lot more experience, though, because he had made it look easy, and she ended up slinging one leg over before teetering on the dumpster's lip and falling down inside. Like the other dumpster, this one was mostly empty aside from a few loose loops of frayed cable and discarded dongles, yellow and blocky like old organic teeth. She listened for rats, but doubted they would have much use for an electronics store dumpster; after all, there was nothing inside that they would want to eat.

Emptiness aside, Amy liked the dumpster just fine. It was surprisingly clean, and its faint rusty smell gave her only a little twinge of hunger. If she were still in a child-sized body, it would have made the perfect spot to play Scorched Earth. She had designed her own tanks in games, of course, and had bounced and careened over their perfectly rendered deserts blowing the middles out of everything from Nazis to djinns, but she had never really played that kind of game *outside*, with things she could actually *touch*. She wasn't allowed to visit playgrounds during the day when human children might be there, so when her parents took her to the nearest place with swings and slides and cargo netting and a crow's-nest, it was always after dark and the other kids were always gone. She would sit up there alone, or maybe next to her dad on the swings (her mom's arms were so much stronger that she always pushed them both), but inevitably they left before too long.

If they'd had a backyard, maybe she could have played those games there. But they weren't rich, so they didn't have one, so she didn't. She built her tanks and forts in-game instead, and her dollhouse's walls and chimneys had gone gluey and flexible with having been recycled and reprinted so many times. She wondered about the dollhouse, now. The week before graduation, she'd programmed some new designs – based on having looked up the word "caliphate" a while back. Maybe the panels were still there waiting for her in their tray; pale and thin like the bone cups she had seen in a museum once. When she got home, she could put all the pieces together.

"What's taking you so long?" Javier asked.

Amy looked up. Javier stood over the dumpster, clutching the old keyboard to his chest.

Amy looked around the dumpster. "This place

would make a great fort."

Javier frowned deeply. "Were you tased as an infant? Quit daydreaming and get out of there." He moved on to the third dumpster. Amy heaved herself out of hers, and watched him cautiously put down his bounty before propping open the lid. Looking inside, he laughed and patted his belly. "We're eating good tonight, that's for sure," he said, and jumped in.

The dumpster promptly closed around him. Amy watched the massive lid slam down on Javier's head. Locks sprang up, threading through bails that pinned the whole structure together. She heard nothing. Maybe he was too muffled in there. She took a hesitant step forward to listen, and startled as a sudden thud sounded against the walls of the dumpster. "Hey! Get me out of here!"

Amy ran the rest of the way to the dumpster. She ran her fingers over the lock; it zapped her and she flew backward. She skidded roughly over the broken asphalt. Her teeth sang. Her limbs refused to move. This was twice in one night. Locked inside her own body, she worried about permanent memory damage. Javier continued banging inside his new cage. And now there was an alarm, and it was speaking in calm authoritative tones over funhouse music: "LIE DOWN ON THE GROUND AND PUT YOUR HANDS OVER YOUR HEAD. POLICE HAVE BEEN NOTIFIED. LIE DOWN–"

"Amy!"

She tried speaking. "I… I can't…"

"AMY!"

She forced herself to stand. Her legs were slow. She

stumbled. "I'm coming…"

"Get me out of here!" The dumpster shook with the force of his kicking and punching. She saw dents. "The whole lid's electrified!" she heard him say, his voice muffled with garbage. "You gotta get me out from outside!"

"I…" She looked at her hands. "I'll try. Wait right here."

"Hurry!"

Amy staggered away from the dumpster. *You could just leave him, you know,* a voice inside said. *He's not your business. He kidnapped you at gunpoint.* Amy shook her head heavily. It would be wrong to leave him, if only because she had said that she wouldn't. She staggered forward toward the car, crossing the parking lot on traitorous feet. She opened the door with shaking hands. Thankfully, Javier had left the keys inside. Amy buckled herself in after two tries. She turned the ignition, and promptly rammed the sacks of old clothes. Wincing, she carefully switched to reverse, twisted in her seat to look behind her, and pulled away. Then she stopped with a jerk, and tried wrestling the car to her will. It was absurdly stubborn. She blinked and tried keeping her gaze straight. When it wandered, so did the car. It felt heavy and stupid under her guidance, like a clumsy prosthetic. Javier had set the seat way back, and she had no idea how to fix it. She had to keep stretching her legs just to brake in shaky fits and starts. She made a wide turn and put the dumpster in her sights.

"Hold on!" Crossing her fingers, Amy floored the gas and aimed straight for the dumpster. The impact threw her forward so hard her teeth clicked. A giant pillow exploded in her face, slapped there as though by an especially nasty girl at a sleepover. The alarm changed. She heard sirens, now. She wanted to sleep.

Someone wrenched the passenger side door open. The car sagged under sudden and massive weight. Javier. "Good thinking," he said. "You shorted the system."

"I crashed the car."

"Yeah, well, get moving, unless you want to wind up back in jail."

Amy looked up. She squinted out the shattered window. Police cars were filling the parking lot. "Oh, no…"

"Oh, yeah," Javier said. "Floor it." He held his stomach and grimaced. "I mean it. Move! Now!"

"Stop yelling at me!"

"Start driving!"

"Shut up!" Amy tried in vain to peek over the giant balloon in her face. "I can't see!"

"Pull back and go right," he said. "I'll talk you through it." He bent double in his seat.

"Are you OK? Did I crush you?"

"No. Just drive." He hissed air through his teeth. "Aw, damn. Not good. Not good."

"What's not good?"

"Just drive!"

Amy jerked the car into reverse, promptly rear-ending a police car, then peeled off across the parking lot. "Where am I going?"

"You're entering traff– You're there."

She heard horns.

"Keep going straight. Nudge yourself left."

"Nudge myself?"

"I don't know! Think left! Just do it!"

"I *hate* this. I *hate* cars. I don't understand why people actually *like* this."

"Those people drive a lot faster than you do."

Amy's foot fell. She leaned out the window. An oncoming car nearly took her head off, and she ducked back inside. The car filled with red and blue police lights; the sirens sounded much closer, now. "What do I do?"

Javier turned back to look at the police cars. "Uh… Go left."

"There is no left! There are *cars coming!*"

"Puta madre," Javier muttered, rolling his eyes and yanking the wheel from her grasp.

They roared across two lanes of traffic. The sound of Amy's shrieks filled her ears. Other cars swerved to avoid them. *Take your foot off the pedal,* something inside reminded her, but it was too late – she felt the ground give way beneath the car, heard a groaning creak as the vehicle tipped forward, then over, and began to fall.

Trees rushed to catch them.

Amy tried her door. It was jammed; she had to slip outside her seatbelt (it took a lot of awkward bending) and slide over to the empty passenger side. In the dark, she could only feel around in the dirt. Javier must have crawled away. "Javier?"

Nothing. Just distant road noise, and the occasional hush of air through the pines. Then the single chirp of a stopped police car. Turning, Amy saw two white vehicles parked at the place where the car had ripped through the guardrail. She didn't bother looking for humans; she scuttled away from the flickering rays of busted headlights and into the deeper darkness. She ran blindly. Rocks and raw roots tripped her twice, but she barely noticed. The important thing was to stay out of the light.

Her new long legs no longer seemed so awkward; they carried her a lot farther a lot faster than her old ones would have done. Ducking under a low-hanging bough, Amy paused to listen again – this time for machines. Right now, humans worried her less than other, lesser robots. It made sense that the officers parked on the embankment hadn't come down to look for her; two baseline humans simply could not outrun a frightened vN. But a drone could survey the entire forest with a single glance, and a botfly could zip in and out of the trees to seek her out, and both of them could give the police the information they needed to surround her. She listened again. But she heard no high-pitched cicada whine… just the quiet hiss of muttered swear words.

"Javier?"

"Not so loud!" he said.

He had hidden himself behind a tree a few yards away. She saw his foot, now, the only thing wiggling in the shadows. Amy scrambled over, her limbs twice as clumsy now, and leaned against the tree.

"Are you OK?"

He shook his head. He doubled over. "No." His lips pinched together and his eyes squeezed shut. "Jesus

Christ, you'd think this'd get easier with time."

"What's wrong?"

Javier almost laughed. It came out high and a little desperate. "Where did you grow up, a fucking *convent?*" He slammed his head against the tree and trembled. The vibration came from inside him, like someone had twisted his tendons taut one at a time until they shivered and sang. Under his eyelids, his eyes darted back and forth. He smelled a little sweet; his systems had started burning energy at a furious pace.

"You're scared," Amy said.

"Gold star, *querida*, gold fucking star."

"Hey, don't snap at me just because you're the one who's frightened. Don't you think it's a bit late for that now, anyway?" Javier continued shivering. His hands came up to cover his face. He rocked back and forth against the tree. Amy swallowed. and tried to think of something nicer to say. "I mean, you've already done some pretty scary things today, and you didn't seem frightened at all."

Hesitantly, she reached over and tried to pat Javier's hand. It burned hot to the touch, and shook under her fingers. He grabbed them and squeezed them; Amy squeaked and he let go, a little.

He spoke through gritted teeth: "This is different."

Javier placed her hand over the warm skin of his enormous belly where his shirt had ridden up. Beneath it, something moved. Javier's heels ground ruts in the dirt. He whimpered and kept her hand pinned to his body. "When you feel it start to rip," he said, "you just keep it open, OK?"

Amy looked into his damp and grimacing face. "What?"

"Better this way. Didn't want to do this in a cell." Javier's eyes opened. They seemed calmer now, focused. "It's the stress. The shocks. He's early."

Beneath Amy's fingers, something warm and wet oozed up from Javier's navel. It glistened in the dark. She pulled his shirt up the rest of the way. A seam opened, bubbled, split across his skin. Javier curled his fingers under the tear and pulled the skin back slowly.

"You gotta help me," he said. "Baby's coming."

2: LUCKY NUMBER THIRTEEN

Javier's baby popped free of his father's body like a shiny coin from an old rubber purse. He emerged head-first, his wrinkled body wreathed in glimmering smoke, and blinked once at Amy before vomiting everywhere. Then he lifted up his arms feebly.

"Pull him out," Javier said, holding his giant wound open with trembling hands.

"What?"

"Careful. He'll be slippery."

Javier was right. Sticky threads black as obsidian covered his son, and they stretched like melting candy as Amy lifted him, leaving wisps of themselves curled around the surrounding trees and their needles. Amy had to wind the baby around a few times, like collecting noodles around a fork, before finally pulling him free. She tried to wipe him off (and succeeded only in coating her arms up to her elbows in Javier's goo), but Javier tugged the hem of her shirt.

"Don't," he said. "It's good for him. Raw materials. Growth medium." He pushed at the flabby skin of his belly, trying to close the wound. It oozed out all over his hands. He curled in on himself like a human boy who'd just been kicked. "He needs the sun. Find a clear spot."

Amy looked down at the baby in her arms. He had his father's perfect eyelashes and head of shiny black hair. The goo had already dried into a fine crust there, and it crackled all over Amy's arms and hands. He regarded her with calm, still eyes. "Don't you want to hold him?"

"No. Go. Now." When she didn't move, Javier slit one eye open. "Please. Just gimme a minute. I'll be there."

"Are you sure? Because–"

"Will you get going, already?"

Amy stepped back. "Fine. Sorry." She turned and started walking.

"Hey."

She whirled. "Now what is it?"

"You're OK, right?" Javier swallowed. "You were sounding a little crazy, before."

"Excuse me?"

"Talking in your sleep," Javier said. "After we crashed." He tapped his temple. "Thought you were booting wrong."

Amy frowned. "I'm fine. And I *don't* talk in my sleep."

Javer grinned. "How would you know?"

Rolling her eyes, she carried Javier's son into a little empty place where she could watch the sky paling into blue from an old stump. She and Javier must have crawled further away than she'd originally estimated, because from here she couldn't see the wake of

destruction their stolen car must have left behind.
When dawn finally came, she saw how alone they
were – the trees stretched on for miles, their progress
broken only by jagged lumps of rock. Water streamed
between a few of them, forming dark ribbons that
whispered down a mountainside ringed by other,
lower mountains, all blanketed in a patchwork of
alternating bald earth and spindly pines. Amy had
never been anyplace this green before. There were
fewer resources for vN in out-of-the-way places, her
dad had told her. Cities were better. More shops sold
vN food and the humans were friendlier, less afraid. It
was safer, he said, to stay urban. Now they were lost
in the middle of nowhere.

The baby grabbed her hair insistently. "I've never
seen anybody give birth, before, especially not a boy,"
Amy told him. "At least, not in real life."

She had seen it happen a lot in dramas. They always
got humans to play the part of vN. The actors always
glowed with real sweat and real tears and they always
tried really hard to make it look like they had only a
handful of facial expressions, until the baby came and
the actor got to look human for a few minutes while
he smiled tiredly into the camera. Her mother used to
say that it was a little unfair how humans won awards
for playing robots, but robots never won anything
for playing humans. Amy hadn't really understood
what she meant at the time. She had asked about it,
but they were in the middle of Friday movie night
at home and her mother had said something about
getting the vN pizza out of the oven. Amy had gone
to follow her, but then her dad decided to play tickle

monster and soon they were rolling around on the floor. Amy wished she had told him the truth: that it wasn't his dancing fingers that made her laugh, but his smiling face. Maybe other vN were ticklish, but not her. It wasn't in her model's original programming. She wondered if her dad knew. She wondered where he was.

Again, Javier's baby tugged her hair. Javier had said that stress made the baby come early. Maybe she had triggered it somehow; maybe she had seriously injured him when she drove the car into the dumpster. "I didn't know," she told his son. "Honestly, I swear, I didn't know. I was just trying to *help*."

Look what happened the last time you tried helping, a voice inside said.

"I'm sorry." Amy no longer knew whom she was saying it to. She shut her eyes and held the baby tight. "I'm really, really sorry. I'll try to be more careful next time–"

"He can't understand you, you know." Amy flinched. She scrubbed her eyes with the back of her hand, and turned around. Javier had shed his shirt, and his fat had melted back inside him, leaving only vague hints of itself in loose skin that hung over his suddenly-baggy shorts. His belt curled away from him, now, cinched tight enough to leave slack. When Amy squinted, she saw the shining scar across his stomach. Already, it had begun to fade. Javier threw himself to the grass at her feet. "All my kids default to Spanish." He tickled the air with his fingers. "Give him to me."

Amy handed the baby to Javier. He proceeded to unwind him from the sweater and check his hands, his feet, and between his legs. He nodded once, satisfied. "All mine." He laid the child stomach-down on his chest.

"But you speak English," Amy said.

"I learned it. My father taught me." Javier rested a hand across his son's back. "We – my boys and I – stem from a clade based in Costa Rica. They were re-forestry specialists. That's what my father was doing before he left and iterated me. He was bringing back the rainforest."

Amy tried picturing life in a rainforest, with all the animals. She imagined birds bright as jewels swooping past, and lazy, lethal cats sleeping in the boughs of giant trees. "Why did he want to leave?"

"He didn't," Javier said. He stood his son up on his chest, now, holding him with hands that shook only a little. "You got kids?"

Amy shook her head. "I'm…" *I'm too little,* she wanted to say, but that wasn't true, any longer. "I'm not ready," she said instead, because it was something her mom's human friends said when the subject came up.

Javier nodded. "Me, I got twelve."

"Twelve?"

"Yup. This one's lucky number thirteen."

Amy couldn't help but stare. She knew that technically, vN could iterate as many times as they wanted, as long as they ate enough and didn't get hurt and no one interfered. But who would want to have twelve babies? And where were they, now?

"Are they all grown up?" Amy asked.

He nodded, lifting his son and letting him go

horizontal, as though he were flying. "Oh yeah. They're all big, now. I had six last year."

"*Six?* In a *year?*"

"What can I say? I'm the last of my clade. I gotta spread my seed. Literally."

"But…" Amy did the math. "But that means you forced them to grow up early, right?"

"What's early?" Javier asked. "vN grow at the speed of consumption. I fed them. They grew. The end."

"But… where are they?"

"Here and there," Javier said. "Wherever I left them. Wherever they choose to go. They're independent guys. *I'm* an independent guy."

Amy didn't quite know what to say. Her own dad said that a man who didn't spend time with his family could never be a real man, but he also said that came from a movie, and it was a movie that came with a failsafe warning so she couldn't watch it. "But on the inside, aren't they still little? When you… abandon them?"

Javier put his baby down and pushed himself up on his elbows. "I don't abandon them. I teach them stuff. Like English, and how to get food, and stuff like that. They can take care of themselves by the time I'm gone."

She pointed at Javier's new baby. "So you're just going to leave this one behind, too, once he's bigger?"

"That's the plan. Then he'll have his own iterations, and do the same with them. And then they'll repeat the process. Exponential growth. Survival of the species."

Amy's mouth fell open. "But he didn't do anything! You've got no reason to leave him behind!"

"Sure I do. Once he's grown, he'll iterate more. We'll grow the clade from San Diego to Vancouver." Javier lifted the baby again. "This size, he's just a little parasite."

Amy snatched the baby up off the ground. "That's a terrible thing to say! I can't believe you actually think of your own baby that way! *My* parents never called *me* a parasite!"

"Doesn't mean you weren't." Javier stretched. "I mean, you sucked up a lot of their resources without giving anything back, right? Like electricity and water and clothes and all that prefab vN food. That shit costs money, and you were just using it up like nobody ever worked for it. Right?"

Amy regained her stump. "I... I guess so... I never really thought of it that way."

"No shit." He sat up. "How old are you?"

"Five."

It was Javier's turn to look surprised. "You're *five*? Do you even know how *old* that is? You should be, like, a *grandmother* by now!"

"But five is when you go to kindergarten," Amy said. "I was in kindergarten. And then I... grew up."

Javier's eyes narrowed. "You're one of those slow kids, huh?"

"I am *not!* I always do well on–"

"Not like that! Like, human speed! *Slow.*" He made it a whole hand gesture, his flat palm stroking the air.

"Mom and Dad said it would be good for me," Amy said.

"When you say *Dad*, you mean the human your mom lives with, right? Humans always think up crazy self-justifying bullshit. They totally retarded you."

"I'm *not*–"

"I didn't mean *you* were retarded, I meant that they *retarded* you. They slowed you down. That's what the word means. It means delayed. You know, *tardy*?" He shook his head. "You're like a bonsai tree. You kept growing and they kept clipping you." He made a *snip* motion with one hand.

Amy squared her shoulders. "Well, at least they never left me behind."

Something changed in Javier's face. His eyes went dark and flat. He snatched his baby from her. "Iterating isn't something most of us do because we feel like it, or because we're ready, or even because we want to."

Amy straightened. "Then why do you do it?"

"Because I can't stop," Javier said. "It's what I'm programmed to do. I'm an eco-model. I was made for helping trees. But I'm also a big fat carbon sink, and so are all my boys."

He seemed to come back to himself. Suddenly his grin reappeared. "You know, the more babies I make, the cooler this planet gets."

Amy had only just graduated kindergarten, but had watched enough media to know a line when she heard one. "I'll bet you say that to all the girls."

He nodded, and winked. "All the boys, too."

They didn't speak much after that. A morning spent in the sun helped Javier feel better, though, and soon he was tying the old sweater around himself like a sling in which to carry his son. He pushed vaguely north, claiming that he'd been headed that way before being arrested for "serial iteration," which Amy hadn't known was illegal in California.

"I didn't know, either, till recently," he said. "It's to preserve resources or something. They know we have to eat a lot to keep iterating, and the trace metals cost money. That's why they jack the price up on the reprocessed crap."

Amy happened to enjoy the reprocessed crap. She didn't like having to stick to the diet plan Rory sent her parents each week, but she liked the cute shapes each piece of feedstock was moulded into, and the smart offers on the wrappers, and the prizes that came with them, and the way she and her mother would save up for days and days just to binge on bigger meals later in the week. Her mom was trying to avoid having another baby. To do so, she had to monitor her diet very carefully. Her portions were only a little bit bigger than Amy's. But Javier didn't seem to have that problem. Now that she'd eaten the first big meal of her life, Amy could understand the draw.

"Were you really going to eat all that garbage behind the old electronics store?" she said.

"What the hell else is it good for? Better in my belly than a landfill."

"Isn't it all that metal bad for your teeth?"

"What, you've never broken a tooth before? They grow back the next day."

Javier picked out trails much faster than Amy did; he seemed to know just how to cross fallen logs and climb the ridges of hairy, exposed roots without really thinking about it, whereas Amy had to stand back and plot a path for herself before taking a step. Her slowness annoyed him – she could tell by the set of his shoulders – and it only worsened as she paused to stare into the cathedral-like ceiling of trees overhead, or ask about what animals he thought they might see. She had heard that vN proved especially troublesome for wild animals: bears and mountain lions and the like got frustrated because the vN just kept fighting back and didn't taste right. Her dad had read her a story online about a vN surfer who reached down into a shark's mouth and grabbed back part of his missing thigh. If a cougar decided to pounce on them, Amy wasn't so sure she'd be as calm.

"Where do you think we should go?" she asked, as a way of changing the subject.

"A main access road, and then our separate ways."

"Are you heading home?"

"Not really."

"Where do you live?"

Javier made a circle in the air with one finger. "Wherever I want."

Amy paused. She watched him continue hiking away. "Are you really homeless?"

He turned. "Well, yeah," he said. "It's a bad idea for my iterations to be clustered in one place, you know."

"I thought maybe you had a home base! You know, like a travelling salesman, or something!"

"Travelling salesman?"

"Well, there are these people in my building sometimes, and they offer to fix things. My dad says they narrow down searches about broken things to one IP and then knock on your door."

Javier nodded. "Oh yeah. I knew an abortion

doctor in Mexico who did that." His eyes narrowed. "You know what those are, right?"

Amy rolled her eyes. "I can read spam as well as anybody, Javier." She hauled herself up over a fallen tree. "If you're not going home, are you going anywhere in particular?"

"Not really. Just north. You?"

Amy dusted off her palms. "I have to go home to Oakland. My mom and dad are probably really worried." She surveyed the trees. "I must be really far away, though. How long was I asleep?"

"A few days." Javier jumped down a hillside. He turned to watch Amy creeping down more carefully. "You know, you could apply for citizenship in Mecha. That's what I'm doing once I've saved up for the application fee."

Amy snorted. "I thought you had plans for world domination."

"Not world domination, just strategic... seeding."

"Seeding."

"Planting. Sowing. Whatever. The point is it's awesome over there. They sell vN food from little carts on the street corners, not crappy little one-shelf sections at the back of some human store, and you can watch or play any channel without worrying about the failsafe. They even pay the vN to live there and hang out with the tourists. It's our ideal habitat."

"It's thousands of miles away! And I thought Dejima was really crowded."

"Well, that's better than..." Javier frowned. He held a hand up. Somewhere in the trees, a twig snapped.

Javier made a throat-slitting motion and jerked his

thumb at a tree. He ushered her in its direction, and held a finger over his lips. "Cops."

"What? Where–"

"*Shut. Up.*" Slowly, carefully, he unslung his baby from his body and handed him to Amy. "You hold him. I might drop him."

"But–"

Javier took a running leap at the tree, and ran up its length for three steps before clinging on with his fingers. Amy watched him disappear into the green shadows above. A cloud of pine needles floated down toward her face. By the time she felt them drift across her skin, she had already heard the cough of police radios.

Behind her, Amy heard cautious footsteps brushing through undergrowth: the swipe of leaves across leather, half-smothered human grunts when a boot sucked free of clay. They reverberated not merely in her ears, but across her skin and over her scalp. *Stay perfectly still,* a familiar voice within said. *None of that giggling that gives the other kids away during hide-and–*

–far away, a rock tumbled loudly, like an exclamation point.

The police followed it. So did their radios. So did their noise.

And above her, Javier bounced from tree to tree, hands curling confidently around boughs that greeted him with needles. She saw him hit the tree above her head and crawl downwards, lizard-like, toward her head.

"They're distracted," he murmured. "Go."

She ran.

•••

They sat perched in a Douglas fir that clung to a steep, unfriendly overhang with a magnificent view of the police officers and all-terrain trucks clustered below, at what was apparently a trailhead or logging road. From here, Amy could turn her head and watch the trail worm its way up the mountain, its shining length frequently disappearing under the cover of trees. She watched flashlights bobbing along it, now, as the officers hiked. A group had stayed behind to reload one truck's giant battery.

She had been sitting this way – legs and arms hugging the sticky, fragrant trunk of the tree, neck twisting as she struggled to obtain a better view, clothes stained with sap and mud and Javier's gunk – for hours. Javier sat comfortably on a very sturdy-looking bough, ankles hooked around the tree, baby in his arms. He looked completely at home.

Amy rested her forehead against the tree. Rain-wet wind reached up the back of her shirt. The tree swayed. She wanted to go home. She wanted the special vN cocoa from the coffee shop nearest her building, the kind she and her mom drank on winter days from specially coloured cups so the humans wouldn't get confused. She wanted her mom to know where she was. She wanted this to be over.

"When do you think we can climb down?" she asked.

Javier said, "Not for a while. The cute blond one just handed out more coffee."

"I don't see him with any coffee."

"I meant the girl."

Amy squinted. "How can you even tell who's cute

and who isn't, from up here? It's *dark*."

"I saw them earlier, remember? Oh, there she is. She just stood up. Her shoes keep coming untied."

"Oh, the one who keeps bending over!"

"Well, uh–"

"She should just get Velcro shoes. That's what people who don't know how to tie their shoes yet wear."

"…Right. Anyway. They're digging in. We're up here for a while, I think." The bough beneath Javier creaked slightly as he shifted. "And I saw that guy's teeth, earlier. They're a total loss. He's got, like, this one, and it totally sticks out all funny."

"Maybe he can't afford injectables," Amy said.

"Humans are programmed obsolescence, all the way. It's a little sad." His bough creaked again. "They're cute, though. That makes them kinda useful, for a while."

"*Ewww…*"

"Hey, it worked for your mom. She found herself a nice slice of meat, right? You're a big girl now, and if those chimps down there can do anything, it's–"

"Not listening, *la la la*–"

"I could put in a good word for you with Officer Snaggletooth–"

"Shut up! You're *gross*." She shuddered. "I don't *like* him."

"Oh, yeah, sure. You're a total ice queen now, but wait till you're in front of him and your failsafe takes over. He'll have you playing Hide-the-Baton all night long." Javier poked the first finger of his left hand into a circle made by his right thumb and forefinger, in and out, in and out.

Amy turned away. "You're disgusting. I'm not like that."

"Yeah, right. Tell it to your OS. You've got a failsafe like everybody else."

Do you? Do you really?

Of course she did. Amy's mom hadn't spent much time on the subject, but she had said that von Neumann-type humanoids were "allergic" to hurting humans, or to seeing them get hurt. She'd said that's what love meant: the inability to see the other person get hurt without losing a part of your mind, the desire to do anything and everything to keep it from happening. And all vN everywhere felt that way about humans, whether they lived together or not. It was part of New Eden's plan – to leave God's unwanted children with people who could really love and protect them. But when Amy's granny killed Nate, she hadn't suddenly fallen down dead. Nor had Amy. Amy had looked at Nate's body – the limp and twisted heap of it, rumpled like dirty clothes – and had not recoiled.

"Is the failsafe the same for everyone?" she asked. "Every model, everywhere?"

"What, doesn't it feel that way for you?" Javier asked. "I can't help it. I love humans. They're adorable. Like those little dogs with the wrinkly faces." He grinned, then tilted his head a little when she didn't smile back. "Anyway. Every time we iterate, we copy the failsafe. That's why we get to roam free."

Not any more, though. Things are different, now.

Amy blinked hard. She looked down at Javier.

"You sound like you give that speech a lot."

"Yeah, well, my kids had better know the score." Javier paused, licked his thumb, and wiped something away from his son's face. "Isn't that right, Junior?"

Amy smiled. "Are you really going to call him that?"

"All my boys are named Junior."

"Just Junior? No other name?"

Javier slowly extricated his finger from his son's fist. "I'm never with them long enough," he said. "They should choose their own–"

A giant arc light swung over them. Amy froze. Below her, Javier started scrambling. "Move!"

She moved. She didn't even bother thinking about the placement of boughs or branches. She hugged the trunk and slipped downward, ripping her pants in the process. Javier already stood at the bottom, clinging with one hand to the wet, crumbling earth of the overhang and his child with the other. Together they half walked, half slid down the overhang, wincing at tumbling rocks and hurrying into the cover of spiky trees. They ducked under hair-snagging branches and waded through carpets of spiny wood ferns. Thunder rolled in the distance.

"Just what we need," Javier muttered.

Behind them, a gun cocked.

"Turn around."

They turned, hands rising automatically. The woman wore forest ranger clothes and carried a flashlight that turned the rain to a shower of white sparks. Amy instantly envied her quilted coat and wide-brimmed hat; they looked like they would keep out the rain. Her own hair was stringy with it, now, her shirt uncomfortably wet and sticky.

As though reading her mind, the ranger chuckled to herself. She lowered her gun and her light. Now Amy could see her face better. She was a popular Asian-style model, with a broad face and full, pretty lips and high cheekbones that pulled her gentle eyes tight. Even under her bulky ranger clothes, a perfect hourglass figure was discernible. She spoke in a gentle, almost modest voice. "It's all right. You can put your hands down."

"Huh?"

"I'm a friend, I promise." She holstered her gun and reached inside her pockets. She tossed foil-wrapped packets of vN food at their feet. Amy recognized the cheery logos immediately; she bent down and grabbed as many as her hands could carry before making a pouch of her wet shirt and stuffing them there, kangaroo-style.

"What's going on?" Javier asked. "Why are you helping us?"

"Rory sent me," she said.

Amy blinked. "Rory? The one who writes my diet plan?"

The ranger nodded. She smiled. "I'm an ex-dieter, too. I know how the hunger feels. What happened wasn't your fault, Amy."

Something about hearing someone else say those words made Amy's tears well up. "Thank you."

"Rory feels terrible about this, Amy. She knows you were on her diet, and understands the role it played in what happened. She knows a place where you can get help. It's in Seattle, near the quake museum. It's not far." The ranger reached for an inner pocket and retrieved a ring of keys. "There's a car waiting for you about a hundred yards north of here. I left the details and some supplies there. There isn't much, I'm afraid, just what I could scratch together... Oh, and this!" She dug in her back pocket. Amy and Javier glanced at each other. What more could the ranger possibly give them?

"Cash," the ranger said, holding out two sets of bills held together with paperclips. Amy took hers and stuffed it down a back pocket.

If her arms weren't already so full, Amy would have hugged the ranger. "Thank you. Thank you so much..."

"I only wish there were more I could do," the ranger said.

There was, Amy realized. "Where are my parents?"

The ranger blinked. "I'm sorry?"

"My parents," Amy said. "I have to get back to them–"

A light swooped overhead. "You have to get to safety first," the ranger whispered. "Get going."

In the car – an old family-style number with the name of the battery on the side in big curvy letters, like it was somehow special – they found blankets and maps. They were in the Olympic National Forest, in Washington. "Wow," Amy said. "I really am a long way from home."

Javier turned to her. He looked at the map, at her toes curled over the edge of the seat. He sucked his teeth for a moment. "Look, you can take this or leave it, but I think that ranger was right. It's a bad idea for you to try going home right now." He grimaced at the road. "You never return to the scene of the crime, right?"

"I didn't even *commit* a crime! I didn't do anything wrong! I just intervened!"

Javier's hands briefly left the wheel. "Hey. Whoa. Do I look like a cop?" He glanced briefly in her direction. "Anyway. You don't have to explain anything. The less I know, the better. We'll find a rest stop, and you can ping your folks from there."

Amy smiled just thinking about it. "Thank you."

Javier shrugged. "I'll have to leave you there, though. We're fugitives, so your parents' tubes are probably being monitored. The moment you make that connection, I'm gone."

Amy hugged her knees. "OK." She nodded to herself. "Thank you. For taking the risk. If you ever come back down south again, you should come visit us." Her eyes widened. She snapped her fingers. "I'm going to need a bigger bed!"

"*Excuse me?*"

"Well, I'm just so much taller, now," Amy said, stretching her arms out. "The old one won't fit."

"Right." Javier fiddled with the rearview camera's settings. "Don't tell me you actually miss having a bedtime."

She laughed. "Nope."

"Probably past it now, right?"

She peered at the dash display. "Oh yeah. *Way* past it."

Javier grinned. He handed her his baby, and motioned at the pile of vN food on the dash. "Can you feed him? And hide that vN food – it's worse than a bunch of empty beer cans, when it comes to cops."

Amy looked in the back seat. "I wish we had a car seat…"

"Just hide him under the blanket." Javier handed Junior over to her, then scattered the vN food at her feet. Amy reached down and grabbed some before buckling her seatbelt and wrapping Junior in the extra folds of blanket. She tried making a little tent for him in there like she'd seen nursing mothers use.

"What if he chokes?" She broke off a square of food. It smelled vaguely like peanut butter.

Javier shook his head. "I keep forgetting you don't have kids…" He gestured. "It'll melt. You'll see."

Amy gently lowered the square into Junior's mouth. He watched her with his giant, calm eyes. She was reminded of a faithful dog, somehow. The food slowly liquefied; he sucked it down rather than chewing. "He did it!"

"Told you. Bend down and smell his mouth. It should smell bitter in there. That's how you know they're ready to eat. It's a compound in the saliva. Helps them predigest the food."

Amy sniffed. She recognized the smell instantly. Her mouth had tasted the same way, just before she'd eaten her grandmother. She shuddered, and tried changing the subject to something only slightly less bizarre. "That was really lucky back there. I can't believe that Rory herself wants to help, and is sending ex-dieters to look after me."

"Yeah. That's like, meeting Santa or something."

Amy frowned. "What do you mean? How is it like meeting Santa? Santa lives at the North Pole."

Mild panic wrote itself across Javier's features. He swallowed. "Uh... You're right! It's not like meeting him at all! Because Santa's totally real, and–" He shot a quick glance in her direction. By now, she was having a hard time restraining her giggles. "And you're totally fucking with me right now, aren't you?"

Amy laughed through her nose. Javier gave her the finger. She kept laughing. He kept driving. Every so often, he would look over at her and shake his head, and nudge the speed up. Soon Junior was asleep. Amy followed not long after, lulled by the squeak of wipers over the empty static Javier insisted on listening to.

She is standing over them, gun in hand. They kneel, hooded and placid as tame falcons. One by one, she pulls the hoods off. They blink slowly before focusing on the thing in the centre of the room. Now the chains rattle as they try to scramble backward. It's hard, with their hands up above their heads. The thing moans. It has long since given up. "I want you to know," she says, lifting a tire iron, "that this hurts me worse than you."

She brings down the iron. The chains sing, now. The thing is crumpling, bursting, its insides leaking and pooling. She's glad she positioned it over the drain in the floor. The women shriek. They plead. They beg. They try to hide and can't.

"G-G-Granny..."

Madness kindles in their eyes. Failures. All of them. She lifts the gun. The puke rounds smell a little dry, but still good.

The air fills with the hiss of melting flesh–

"Fuck!"

Amy started awake. The car swerved wildly. Javier let the wheel slip through his hands and struggled to avoid a group of women who had positioned themselves in the middle of the dark and winding road. Headlights illuminated their stiff and unyielding bodies: Amy recognized her aunts.

"You've got a real fucked-up family," Javier said. Baring his teeth, he floored the gas pedal and plowed directly into one of the aunts. She rolled calmly across the hood. Her lips kissed across the wet windshield.

Inside Amy, something hardened. "More," she said. "Javier, run them *all* over–"

Something landed on the roof. A white fist slammed down into the windshield from above. Amy shrieked. On her lap, Junior woke. He twisted against her. Amy covered his eyes. Now the glass splintered, impact fractures branching down toward the straining wipers.

Javier ran another one down. This aunt clung on and waved this time before sliding off. Another slammed herself up against Amy's door; it popped open and her aunt's arm reached inside. Screaming, Amy held tight to Junior and reached for the door. She tried forcing her aunt's hand away. Her aunt merely laughed and briefly tangled their fingers, like they were girlfriends holding hands on the way

to a carnival ride. Snarling, Amy slammed the door,
and watched her aunt's look of surprise through the
window when her arm ripped free of her body.

Good work. Awareness shivered down her spine.
She *knew* that voice. She recognized it, now. Inside
her head there was something like old, dry laughter.

"Pull over," Amy said, staring at the arm.

"Are you crazy? They're–"

"They're after me, not you." Amy looked down
at Junior. He was silent, but clearly agitated, eyes
peering everywhere and tiny fists clutched close to his
little body. The more she watched him, the calmer she
felt. It stole over her, heavy and cold and quick. "They
won't stop chasing me. They want revenge. And you
and your baby shouldn't be punished for something
that I did." She tried to smile. "You were going to
leave me behind anyway, right? When I contacted
my parents?"

Javier stopped the car. He set his teeth. In the glow
of its headlights, Amy saw her aunts begin walking
forward. They looked happy. Confident. Smug. "They
won't just let me go," he said.

"They walked right past you before, on the truck."
She unbuckled her seatbelt and tried handing Javier
his child; he blinked at the baby like she was offering
him a bomb. *He's a smart boy. Appeal to his logic.* "You'll
get a lot further with only one parasite, instead of
two."

Javier snorted. He shook his head. "Have it your
way. Nice knowing you." He offered her his hand.
Dutifully, Amy shook it; this time his hand was
perfectly steady and not at all warm.

"It was nice meeting you, too," she said. "You're the only vN friend I've ever had."

Javier said nothing. He was staring at the fussing bundle of blanket and limbs in his lap, and refused to even look her way. Taking this as her cue to leave, Amy scooted out of the car and shut the door. It screeched away immediately. The aunt on its roof jumped clear and landed in the road.

"That was sweet," she said, her voice a perversion of Amy's mother's.

Relax, the voice within said. *She's harmless.*

"I know who you are now, Granny," Amy whispered.

Took you long enough. That boy is right. You're very slow.

"Did you want them to get me, all along?"

No. They want to kill you. I want you to live.

Amy watched a crowd of copies steadily advancing on her. They wore her face – her mother's face, Granny's face, the model's face – but their walk was different, wary. They circled her uncertainly. They looked at each other as though wondering what to do next. *Weak,* Granny said. *Scared. Slow.* A distinct chill frosted over Amy's skin. It stiffened her jaw and hardened her fists. Her body ran, now, fists out and mouth open, barrelling straight for the nearest aunt. Her vision darkened. She heard screaming. Didn't know whose it was.

Don't worry, darling. Granny's here.

3: EVERY LITTLE LAST BONE & TOOTH

You're roadkill; I should have let them eat you.

Amy could almost feel her graphene layers dancing to the algorithms that would retrieve her ability to scream for food. Her repair modules worked to patch damages with resources her body didn't have. They shifted carbon, pushed silicon, redirected lithium, frantically covering the holes, the rips, the gashes. They hollowed her steadily from the inside, unravelling nanoscale threads of minerals from her hair and skin (what was left) and bone (what they could find). She heard feet, felt warmth–

Bite! Now!

She lurched, burning the last of her food-carbons on this gamble, her mouth snapping open and clamping down. Something rough and dry filled it before being crunched away. Her body sang, every molecule clambering for more, chorusing need. She was sucking something. It was rich, a wealth of carbon and sugar, wet and warm and a little pulpy where her tongue washed over it.

Tasty, Granny said. *But the amniotic sac would be better.*

Amy opened her eyes. All grayscale. Someone with dark hair knelt over her, clutching a smoking hand. The left thumb was gone. She willed her eyes to examine the wound, up the detail. Colour flashed briefly. Gray. Not red. Not human.

"Do you know me?" he asked.

Hungry, she wanted to say. *More.*

He entered a vehicle and brought out a blanket, then laid her on it. Amy's memories showed her P-I-C-N-I-C.

"Come on." He picked her up. What had damaged all those trees?

"Gonna make a burrito out of you," he said, ferrying her over to the blanket. She examined her left hand. It had no skin left. Black spines poked out instead, like twigs. "No biting."

No biting, Granny concurred.

He laid her on the blanket with her other pieces. He rolled the blanket up and her appendages slid together; she felt her foot near her eyes. He carried the bundle away and put it somewhere – her memory showed her images of C-A-R-S – and they drove off. As the trees rolled by, she saw other bodies: skin and skeletons stretched across the branches and boughs, heads hanging by their hair.

Those are your clademates, Granny said. *Those are your aunts.*

He found a place called a "campsite" and opened the "trunk" so light could come in. Then he opened the blanket and knelt over her again. He pinched her wounded skin together and laughed about a long-ago

woman who taught him to how fold dumplings. A
Zen thing, he said, after a while. Fill. Wet. Pinch. Over
and over and over. Plate after plate of food he would
never eat. Then he hummed a song about bones. Her
memory had it tagged with the word "kindergarten".
The memory version was missing a verse: *Now hear
the Word of the Lord!* He ripped open a packet of foil.
"Feeding time."

Her mouth opened automatically. He squirted
something in there, held her down when her whole
body lunged upward just to get more. He gave her
more packets. Then his body moved and the sun
peeked from around him; the space filled with light
and her senses caught fire: her repair mods shrieked
delight and got to work immediately. Warmth flooded
her limbs. Colour bled into her vision. Words fell into
place.

"Javier."

His shoulders slumped like he'd put down
something heavy. "You're OK."

"It was the sun," Amy said. "The sun sped
everything up."

Javier sat back on his knees. He gave her a
measuring glance, top to bottom and back up. "What's
it feel like?"

She considered. "…Fizzy. Like my skin is made of
bubbles. It burns, but it feels good at the same time."

Javier beamed. "Like a flood of energy, right?"

Amy nodded. "That's right." She winced. "Is this
just another thing my mom never told me about?"

Javier curled his lip under his top teeth. He shook
his head. "No, Amy." He stretched his hand out into

the sun. "Photosynthesis is something only my clade can do."

She and the baby lay in the grass while Javier planned her first pregnancy.

"First you should find a nice human," he said, pacing back and forth before a little fire of twigs he'd built. "Someone who'll take care of you. Lots of vN chicks do that. Your mom, for one. Anyway, you settle down, and then iterate like there's no tomorrow."

Amy looked down at Junior. Already he seemed capable of focusing on her. His huge, dark eyes regarded her calmly. Amy wondered if maybe he saw Granny waiting, like a spider at the centre of her web, behind her eyes.

All your children will be stained with me. And your children's children. I will live forever in their bones.

"I'm not sure I want to iterate."

"Why not?" Javier asked. He flopped down beside her, picked up a foil pouch of vN juice, and sucked it back. "You're tough. You can take it."

Amy curled further into herself. The sun still felt good, and the grass, and the presence of life all around them, organic and synthetic both. They were in a place meant for families. She smelled smoke and heard laughter. High up in the trees sat a lost Frisbee the colour of cheap nail polish. Somewhere, someone was missing it. Maybe they were even thinking about it right now, like she was. If she concentrated on this possibility, she could almost forget the presence dwelling at the edges of her mind.

"What if something's wrong with me?" Amy asked

slowly. "What if I'm... messed up?"

Javier sucked bubbles from the pouch. "Messed up how? You're perfect." He frowned. "Well, aside from being a whiner, and a bad driver, and–"

"You're not helping." She rolled over onto her stomach. "I mean, shouldn't my repair mods have rejected your stemware? I just adopted photosynthesis like... like a virus, or something."

"It *is* a virus. My pigment cells are programmed to simulate the activity of cyanophages in ocean algae. Maybe that includes turning hostiles to friendlies." Javier crumpled up the foil in his fist. "Who *cares* how it happened? The important thing is, you should iterate ASAP. Spread my seed around."

See? He agrees with me.

Amy scowled. "You don't even know I'll pass on your trait. This might just be a phase, or something."

It's not. He's inside you, now. Just like me. Forever.

"Does this mean I'm part of your clade, now?"

Javier blinked suddenly, like he'd been thinking about something very far away. "Uh... I don't know." He rolled over onto his stomach. "Our skin was only a prototype when our clade started working in Costa Rica. That's why my uncles made sure my dad could leave; they wanted to preserve the trait. So you're the first female model that I know of who carries it. That probably makes you a whole new clade."

Amy liked the sound of that. "Do you think I could start sampling other vN? Mixing them all up inside myself until I came up with something... awesome?"

"More awesome than what you've got, now?" Javier asked. He pulled a blade of grass between his fingers and began peeling it into shreds.

"Look, I *know* your trait is really special, but–"

"I meant the total disaster you caused back there," Javier said. "You *annihilated* your clademates. I've never seen anything like it. How did you do it?"

Tell him. You're a born killer. A top predator. He's not safe with you.

Amy pillowed her head on her arms. "I don't remember." She eyed him. "Why'd you come back for me?"

Javier visibly suppressed his laughter. "For *you?*" He reached into his back pocket and took out two folds of bills – the ones the ranger had given them last night. "Come on. Give me some credit."

"You *rolled me* for *cash?*"

"I thought you'd be dead! You weren't gonna need it!"

"Oh, so you're a *graverobber*. That's *so* much better."

"It's not graverobbing if you didn't die. Which you didn't." Javier made a show of counting on his fingers. "That's twice I've saved your ass, now. You're racking up a pretty huge tab."

Amy sat up and folded her arms. "Well, it's a good thing you stole my money, then!" She pushed herself up off the ground and started walking.

The campground featured constantly forking paths that liked to hide themselves behind trees, the likes of which Amy had never seen before. This was good – she needed the time alone. While looking for some sort of interface tucked in amid the trees, she had rehearsed telling her mom and dad what had happened, but there was too much to tell: her new body and its new traits, Granny, Javier. She had no idea why she'd gotten so angry with him, earlier. It wasn't like she could really complain. She rolled bodies for cash all the time in games. It was part of good scavenging, and Javier had already proved himself a great scavenger. It just stung a little bit, to be on the other side of the equation. It meant he thought of her as a thing and not a person, like she was just some stupid little in-game AI with no thoughts or feelings. She'd come to expect that from certain humans, but not her fellow vN.

"Sorry, could you help me?"

Amy jumped. She turned around.

A woman towing two rolling plastic water barrels nodded at her. She was very pretty, but in a human way, with the beginnings of crow's feet at the corner of each blue eye, and brown roots beneath her black hair. The strap on one of her barrels had broken, making it difficult to grip. She held up the other barrel's good strap in her fist. "If you get this one, it'll make towing the broken one a lot easier."

"Sure!" Amy grabbed the strap. "I was, uh, just looking for the showers," she said. "Do you know where they are?"

The woman shook her head. "Don't bother," she said. "The hot water's been gone all day. Geothermal regulator's offline, right in time to ruin everybody's weekend." She made a show of sniffing the air. "Can you smell my husband from here? He's riper than a pricey piece of cheese, right now."

Amy laughed. "No, I can't."

"I swear this is the *last time* we go camping. He *always* says it'll be better next time, and I *always* believe him, but he's *never* right. *Ever.* You'd think I'd learn, but no. The bastard's too damn handsome and he knows it." She tugged the lead on the rolling barrel. "And he made me tow all this just so I could take a shower! Says he likes me when I'm sweaty. Perv."

Amy rolled her eyes. "Sounds like someone I know."

"Let me guess. Your human's a real piece of work." The other woman looked around the campgrounds. "You're here with somebody, right?"

Amy paused. "How did you know that?"

The woman made a show of giving her an elaborate once-over with her eyes. "You're not carrying any keys or wallet or anything. You must have left them with someone else."

"Oh. Right. Yes. I am. I'm here with someone else." Amy tried to shrug nonchalantly. "We sort of had a fight."

The other woman nodded sagely, like she knew everything about it. "That's been happening, lately," she said. "Especially with your model. The failsafe failing can really kill the trust in a relationship, apparently."

It occurred to Amy that she hadn't yet seen her new face in a mirror. But of course what had happened at school had made the feeds, and of course she was going to be recognized. She backed away. "I'm not–"

"Don't worry. It may surprise you to know that there are some humans who can be rational about this whole thing. Only one clade from your model that went weird, and they're in another state. I'm not scared." She smiled. "I'm Melissa, by the way."

"Am..." *Don't give her your real name, you idiot!*
"Amanda."

Melissa shook her hand. "Nice to meet you,
Amanda."

Together, they tugged the rolling jugs up a little
rise in the road and into a campsite set far off from
the others. Melissa explained that these sites were
intended for RVs a long time ago, but that people had
stopped buying them when they got too expensive
to maintain. "We greened ours, but the thing sucks
off the battery faster than a Tijuana–" Melissa stopped
abruptly. "Well. Pretty fast, anyway. You know?"

"Sure," Amy said, though she really didn't.

The RV itself looked big enough to drain several
batteries at once. It was all sharp angles and blocky
shapes, not like the new trucks that looked like they'd
been sculpted from marshmallow. Beside it sat a
sandy-haired man in a lawn chair under an awning,
reading something on a glowing scroll that reminded
Amy uncomfortably of her prison guard. He clutched
a beer in his other hand.

"You hear about this missing submarine?" he
asked, not looking up. "Damnedest thing."

"I brought home a stray," Melissa said. "Amanda,
this is Rick. Rick, Amanda. Amanda's boyfriend –
wait, was it a boy?"

"Um… yes."

"Right. Well, like they say, assumptions make an
ass out of *u* and *me*. Anyway, he's being a real jackass
because of that whole failsafe thing, so she's going to
be spending some time with us until he cools down."

Rick put the scroll down and looked from Amy to his wife. "Is this because I wouldn't buy you a puppy?"

"Deal with it, bookworm."

Amy put her hands up. "You don't have to–"

"Just do as she says," Rick said. "Trust me. It's easier in the long run."

"I heard that," Melissa said from inside the RV. "Now will you top up the water tank, please?"

"See what I mean?" Rick downed the last of his beer and put it on the ground. He stood. He looked vaguely athletic, standing up – broader across the shoulders than Amy remembered her dad being. He nodded at the RV. "Go ahead on in. Melissa can show you where everything is."

Rick looked at the water barrels, then into the trees. Only now did Amy notice the total absence of either fire or ashes, or even the drying clothes and ice chests and speaker sets that she'd seen at the other campsites. The site looked so clean, by comparison. Rick and Melissa hadn't been here long enough to spread out, or create much waste.

Something's wrong.

Amy glanced at the RV. Its door yawned open, drifting almost shut in a hot breath of breeze before opening again, briefly exposing the cramped spaces within. They would have an interface in there. She imagined thumbing in the numbers and letters and hearing her parents' voices. Hadn't her mom always said that if Amy were ever in trouble, she would drop everything and come get her? That it didn't matter what time it was or how far apart they were, she would still show up? Charlotte drilled it into Amy's mind before she started school. No matter what, if Amy was scared or hurt or if one of the human kids got mean, she could always call and come home. "That's true now and it'll be true when you have your own daughter," her mom had said. "There's no such thing as a bad time for you to call me."

"I can't," Amy said.

"Sorry?" Rick asked, frowning.

"I can't," Amy repeated, stepping away from the RV.

"You sure about that, now?" Rick asked, almost like he knew she was lying.

Amy forced herself to nod. "Yes. I'm sure." She ducked her head. "Thanks for the offer. I have to be going, now."

"Come back anytime," he said.

Amy had already turned around and found the road. She paid little attention to her direction or how long she walked. Instead, she watched her white prison slippers slapping the black asphalt, its progress occasionally broken by treacherous roots or lightning forks once split by earthquakes, as she moved farther and farther away from Rick and Melissa's RV. Maybe she couldn't trust Javier with her cash, but he was right: her parents' tubes probably were under surveillance. And she couldn't involve strangers in this – especially nice strangers.

"You have a nice pout?" Javier asked when he returned to the campsite. He'd been gone by the time Amy had made it back. She spent the next hour trying to absorb more sunlight and quiet the hunger still whining through her bones.

"I wasn't pouting."

He smiled. "That lower lip of yours is telling me a different story."

Amy folded her arms. "Where were you?"

Javier lightly tossed Junior in the air and caught him. Briefly, Amy worried about Javier's missing thumb, but his fingers looked just as capable as ever. "Playground."

Amy stood. "There's a playground?"

Javier tossed and caught his son again. "What, you missed it on your epic journey? It's on the other side of the campground, near the second set of bathrooms."

Amy winced. "I guess I was going in circles. I didn't even know there were two sets." She nodded at Junior. "You take him to playgrounds?"

Javier's brows furrowed. "Why wouldn't I?"

"My mom never took me. She wouldn't let me go."

Javier rolled his eyes. He placed Junior on the grass. "Let me guess. She thought you'd witness some evil preschool brawl and fry your brain?"

Amy watched Junior place one hand in front of the other tentatively. With a sudden spurt of energy, he crawled after nothing in particular and came to an equally abrupt, rocking stop. She shrugged. "I guess so."

Javier snorted. "Your mom was paranoid. I take my kids the first chance I get. How else will they learn how to play with humans?"

"That's what I tried to tell her, but…" Again, Amy shrugged. "I guess I wasn't very convincing."

"Oh, you're plenty convincing. You just asked the wrong parent." Javier knelt in the grass at the far end of the campsite, in Junior's line of sight. He snapped his fingers. *"Mijo. Levántante."*

The baby lurched forward on his palms, then burst forward in another sprint of crawling. A few steps from Javier's knees, he paused to look up at his father. Javier scowled. *"¿Por qué tú estás sentado allí?"* His head tilted, doglike. "The little bastard should be up and walking by now."

"Isn't that a little soon?" Amy asked. She sat in the grass next to Junior, criss-cross style. She opened her hands, and Junior beamed hugely and crawled eagerly into her lap. She lifted him so that he sat facing his father. "Human babies can't even crawl right away, you know."

"He's not a human baby." Javier pushed himself up off the ground, let himself into the car, and brought out three bars of vN food. He handed one to Amy, then picked Junior up out of her lap. "He's *my* baby, and all *my* babies have damn strong legs."

"Some humans only feel right when they're in pain," she explains. "It's difficult for us to imagine, having never felt it, but pain makes them feel loved."

"...Really?"

"Yes. It has to do with their hormones – adrenaline, dopamine. Organic things."

They sit in one of a series of abandoned basements below a suburb that never happened. The foundations were dug, but no homes were built. Flashlights bob down the raw hallways; her other daughters are so industrious, so quiet, only giggling now and then when they bump into one another in the shadows.

"Mother?"

Blinking, she twists her daughter's pale hair around one finger. "Yes?"

"Why don't we live with humans?"

"I lived with humans once, already."

"Was it fun?"

"Sometimes."

Amy could not remember when her eyes opened and the dream of the basements faded, but soon the darkness around her solidified into night, and the noises sounded like animals and not people living like animals. Quickly, she dropped her hands – they looked strange, hovering in mid-air where her dream had left them. She winced, but Javier and Junior made no sound. When night came, Javier had spread out a blanket on the floor of the station wagon, taken a blanket for himself and Junior, and curled into a little ball with his back to her. Neither he nor the baby had moved from that spot in the meantime.

They look so sweet, Granny said. *Like matryoshka dolls. Do you know that that word means?*

"Be quiet," Amy whispered.

Those nesting dolls. One inside the other. That's what they call us, sometimes. Because of how we iterate.

Amy got on her hands and knees and tried to find the latch that would open the rear door from within. The darkness made it difficult, but she continued pawing at the surface until she found something like a button.

Inside of you is a perfect copy of me. Just like a little doll. Someday you'll open up and there I'll be waiting.

Amy pushed the button, popped the door, and slid herself out of the vehicle as quietly as possible. She didn't even shut the rear door all the way; it took some slamming, and she knew it would wake Javier and Junior. She listened to the crunch of her feet across gravel, and heard the path change beneath when she found asphalt.

At regular intervals, sunflower lamps opened as her steps drew near, briefly illuminating the path and colouring the trees, before closing again as she moved on. This late, most of the campfires had died. Only the taste of their smoke remained on the air. The whole campground seemed asleep; she counted two tents lit blue from within by readers or other devices, but the only truly alert camper she encountered on her walk was a tiny, angry dog whose chain jingled once before his furious barks urged her away. At last she found the playground, right where Javier said it was, at the bottom of the odd teardrop made by the park's main road.

She might not have noticed it there in the shadows, without the unblinking red eye of a security summons button to draw her attention. Every public space she'd ever entered had one. As she entered this area, a ring of sunflowers unfurled sleepily and cast a flickering violet glow over the swingsets and tiltseats. The lamp nearest a climb-frame model of a caffeine molecule blinked badly; perhaps one of its circuits hadn't quite survived a Frisbee or basketball attack. Amy had no desire to climb the molecule, though, or to swing, or to pretend like there was somebody on the other end of the tiltseat to make things interesting.

All the equipment seemed so much smaller than she remembered from similar nightly trips to her local parks, less exciting, less dangerous. The real danger was those sunflowers drawing attention; any botflies attached to the park would be here any minute now to investigate the sudden awakening of the playground's devices.

Amy moved outside their glow, now, to a ragged field separating the playground from the bathrooms. The interface stood in this middle ground, carved into a faux totem pole, its screen clutched between the wooden paws of a smiling bear. The screen displayed the park's logo and asked for a campsite number when she touched it, so the ping could go on her tab. But Amy didn't know the number, and she realized now that she didn't quite know what to say, either.

That's easy. Tell your mother that you let me kill her sisters. She'll understand.

Amy leaned against the pole and sank to the ground. Her elbows rested on her knees. "Mom never mentioned any sisters."

Your mother never mentioned a lot of things.

Amy kicked the air sharply, as though that could shut Granny up. Her left foot grazed the rough edge of something hollow; when her eyes focused on it, she realized it was a box of some sort. Crawling over, she slid her hands around its surface: wooden, around five feet by three, slightly damp, splintering in places but otherwise solid. It had two sets of hinges at either of the long ends, and a set of handles in the centre like an old-fashioned cellar door. She yanked them open, and in the flickering light of the last remaining lamp, she saw a sandbox with a crumbling city inside it, complete with the remnants of roads left there by the evening's last visitors.

Amy plunged her fingers into the cool sand and smiled. The last kid to play here had left behind a squat central tower with a tallish building at each compass point and a ring road connecting them. Other roads branched out from these, and they led to a smattering of smaller structures: houses, Amy guessed. Frowning, Amy sat on her haunches and tried to decide what exactly made her dislike the city so much. It was very neat and very pretty, and whoever had shaped the houses had paid great attention to making them uniform in size and placement. But the design itself made no sense; she had no clue what that big central building was supposed to be, or why it needed to be guarded by the other buildings and kept away from the homes. And if those other four buildings were places where people went to work, then they were awfully far away from the places people lived. The citizens would spend all their time on those long, rigid roads and no time at home.

With a sweep of her hand, Amy levelled the city.

"Continuing your rampage?"

Amy turned. Javier dropped out of a tree and joined her at the sandbox. He pointed at the playground. "You know, the real toys are over there."

"This *is* a real toy," Amy said. "I like building things."

Javier squatted beside her. "Well, right now, it looks like you're destroying stuff."

She shrugged. "I'm just making room for something

better." She pointed at the fringes of the city that she'd left standing. "This was all wrong. I have to turn it inside out." She frowned. "Where's Junior?"

"Still sleeping."

"Is it OK to just leave him there?"

Javier rolled his eyes. "I don't think any bears are going to make off with him, if that's what you mean." He nodded at the sandbox. "What are you turning inside out?"

"The last kid's design. I'm going to put all the houses next to each other, with a park in the middle." She drew a circle in the centre of the box with one finger. "There. And then the houses go here," she dotted the ring around the park, speckling the sand to remind herself where the neighbourhoods would go, "and then there should be some places for people to work, so their commutes are short." She drew Ws in the sand near the homes.

Javier raised his brows. "I had no idea you had such a kink for urban planning."

Amy started building her first house. "I just wanted to make it better than it was," she said. "The old way, everyone would be on the road all the time. But this way, people get home earlier to do fun stuff."

Javier smiled. "Wow. You really can't wait to go home, can you?"

Amy's hands hovered motionless over the houses she'd just imagined. To her horror, her eyes filled with tears. She had the strangest sense that if she moved a single inch, if she so much as made a sound, the tears would overwhelm her. So she remained perfectly still and silent. She stayed this way, frozen and quiet, until

Javier gently turned her face toward his with a finger. Then the spell was broken, and she blinked and the tears rolled down, and she turned away again.

"Wow," he repeated. "Just, uh... Damn. You cry just like a real girl."

Her indignation put an immediate hold on her tears. "I *am* a real girl."

"No, no, I mean – it's emergent. Not a plug-in. Nobody told you to start crying."

She blinked wetly. "Why would someone tell me to start crying?"

Javier shrugged. "I don't know. Why do humans do anything they do?" He stood up quickly and made for the trees bordering the playground.

Amy stared after him for a moment. Then she scrubbed at her eyes with the heel of her hand and focused again on her sculpture. It looked so ugly, now. Her first house closely resembled a pile of dog crap on the sidewalk. She moved to wipe it away.

"No, don't." Javier reappeared behind her. He dumped two fistfuls of twigs and pine cones and dead pine needles in the centre of the sandbox, where she'd marked out the park.

"What are you doing?" Amy asked.

"My job." Javier picked up one pinecone with his good hand and screwed it into the sand until it stood upright. "Planting trees."

Amy smiled. She blinked the rest of her tears back. "Thank you," she said. "I was just thinking that there was something missing."

"You don't say." Javier jammed a twig into the sand in front of her little house.

Amy nodded. "You can be my landscape architect."

"You can't afford me." He sucked his teeth and shook his head. "You *gringos*. Always trying to make us into your gardeners."

Amy's jaw dropped. "That's not true at all! I didn't–"

"Make with the condos, lady, before I let the kudzu run wild all over this thing."

"OK, OK, I'm building!" She paused. "What's a kudzu?"

Javier shook his head again, more softly this time. "Hopeless. You're completely hopeless." But he kept planting.

In the end, their city blossomed in fits and starts, and they talked about where to put things, and whether sidewalks were implied or not (Javier maintained that she should draw separate lines to indicate them, whereas she thought that any self-respecting city would have them already), and if decorative fountains were too wasteful. But when they finished, it looked real and lived-in, and not like a school project. Amy sat on her knees admiring it as Javier stood and stretched.

"I feel like I should be tired, but I'm not," she said.

"Of course you're not." Javier pointed to a broad band of pink in the eastern sky. "Sun's rising."

Amy stood up. "Does it really make that much of a difference?"

"Definitely," Javier said. "If it weren't so damn cold, we could go up to the Arctic and stay awake for months."

Amy tried to imagine living up there amid all the snow. "I think I prefer sleeping."

Javier nodded. "Me too. Let's go back to bed."

"You mean the back of the car?"

"No, I mean the darling little B and B I booked us into. Of course I mean the back of the car." He began crossing the playground, then walked backwards to face her. "Haven't you ever slept in the back of a car before?"

Amy jogged up to meet him. "Not for a whole night."

"Well, that wasn't a whole night, either, so it doesn't count."

"It does too. I fully intended to sleep there the whole night."

"So why'd you leave?"

Amy stopped short. She looked at Javier. He folded his arms and raised his chin. "I just couldn't sleep," she said.

Liar.

"Why'd you come find me?" Amy asked before Granny could say anything further.

"I couldn't sleep, either." Javier turned and continued walking. "You defrag to wake the dead. All those little twitches and moans."

"I was not *moaning*."

"Oh, so now my voice detection is off, huh? Just all of a sudden since I met you."

"Maybe it's been off all along, and nobody's ever told you."

"Trust me, I know a m–" He stopped short, and she bumped into him. He stood in a stream of sunlight trickling between the trees, eyes shut, letting the brightness wash over his face. Then his eyes opened, and he smiled down at Amy. "Your turn."

He stepped aside, and ushered her into the light. It hit Amy like a wave, like the first time she'd ever visited the ocean and been knocked down by the tide. She even started a little and Javier's fingers landed on her shoulders to steady her. She'd had no idea just how cold she'd been until that first morning light flooded her face. Her lips burned with it. She turned her head just to get more, to feel it on her ears and down her neck and across her collarbone. When she opened her eyes, Javier was staring.

"What's wrong?" Amy asked.

"Nothing," Javier said. "Absolutely nothing."

Later that morning, it was Amy's turn to wake up and find Javier gone. Not that she'd really slept very much; the sun streaming through the windows kept her right on the cusp of sleep without actually granting her the unconsciousness she needed. But even if she weren't photosynthetic, Amy doubted she could have gotten back to sleep. She'd faced away from Javier when they crawled back into the car (he watched her get in ahead of him, and for a moment she panicked, thinking that she would put a hand or foot wrong and accidentally hurt Junior, until Javier cleared his throat and she hurried under the blanket), but for the longest time, she sensed a pair of eyes watching the back of her neck as the interior of the vehicle warmed and brightened.

They couldn't have gone far, so she set out to look. More people walked along the path now that the sun was fully out. Some of them had even finished breakfast, already; she saw dogs licking dishes clean and humans folding up solar grills. Babies cried. Kids whined about boredom. Amy wondered how long Junior had before he became one of them. Did Javier take his sons to places like this often? Did they go hiking or photographing or birding or whatever else it was that these people – these normal people, organic and synthetic both, these non-fugitives – came here intending to do?

"Hey! Looks like you lost that game of King of the Mountain, huh?"

Amy blinked. Melissa stood before her, carrying a caddy of dishes. She looked Amy up and down. Belatedly, Amy realized she probably did look worse for wear: the combination of goo and sap had been washed away by the rain from her skin but not her clothes or hair, and last night's epic sandbox construction probably hadn't helped, either.

"Well," Amy said, "you did say the showers were out, right?"

Melissa laughed. "You want to try it out? Your boyfriend would probably appreciate it."

"What? Oh. Yeah." Amy nodded. She examined the dirt under her nails. "I guess you're right."

Melissa led the way. "And I have an enzymatic spray for those clothes, too! You'll be looking like your old self again in no time!"

Amy rather doubted that, but she followed anyway.

After far too much time spent in tall trees and crashed cars, the hot water was wonderful. This was also Amy's first chance to really look at her new grown-up body – at least as much as the tiny closet-sized bathroom would allow. She still didn't really like the knobby look of her longer fingers and toes, and the breasts were just plain weird. They seemed like they might snag on things. When she bounced on her toes, they didn't jiggle like the ones on her game skins. It was a little disappointing. And why did vN women have breasts, anyway? At least on organic people they served some purpose.

They serve a purpose for us, too.

Amy ignored her granny and continued washing her hair. When she found her mom again, they'd have to get different haircuts. Otherwise strangers might think they were the same person. Would her dad be able to tell them apart? Of course he would. Amy would have different clothes, and different hair, and she would like different things. Dad would notice this.

Do you really think they'll let you see him again? Granny asked.

"It's all just been one big misunderstanding," Amy muttered as she scrubbed her feet. They were positively filthy.

No, it hasn't. They have every right to hunt you down.

"I didn't do anything wrong."

It's not about you.

Outside, Amy heard doors slamming and raised voices. Were Rick and Melissa having a fight? Maybe it was best to just get out of her hosts' way. Amy shut off the water. She had probably used too much of it already. Squeezing her way out of the shower – wow, she was right, breasts *were* stupidly inefficient – she grabbed a towel and squeezed out of her hair before scrubbing herself dry.

"I'm done! May I have my clothes back, please?"

She heard only thumping, and a sound of metal.

I don't like this, Granny said.

Amy pulled open the bathroom door. On the other side was Melissa, and she held a gun. It was large and absurd in her hands, but her eyes promised business. "You know, for a girl who just got out of kindergarten, you sure talk to strangers a lot." She made a *come here* motion. "Don't make me melt you. I'll lose the bounty."

Amy stumbled back, clinging to her towel as though it could somehow help. "But..."

"Sorry, kid," Rick said, pushing the door open the rest of the way and grabbing her still-damp elbow. "You seem nice and all, but a man's gotta eat."

He crowded Amy into what she'd previously assumed was the RV's sleeping cabin, but was in fact populated by two big steel crates like the ones for housetraining dogs. One yawned open emptily. The other one contained Javier and Junior. Javier sat cross-legged on the carpeted floor with his son in his arms. Upon seeing Amy, his eyes burned.

"What's going on, here?"

"Cool it, Tin Man." Rick pushed Amy into the crate and locked the door. He reached over and flicked a switch embedded in the faux-pine panelling. An audible hum filled the air. "Watch the fence, OK? We lose the bounty if you're corrupted."

Amy glanced over at Javier and Junior. "Please let them go. They haven't done anyth–"

"Your friend here is guilty of armed robbery as of last night," Rick said.

"But the baby–"

"The baby will be taken care of," Melissa said. She crossed her arms. "It's not as though he really spends a lot of time with them anyway, is it?" She glanced into Javier's cage. "I know your M.O. You're not exactly Father of the Year."

Javier smiled. "Still more fertile than you."

"Watch it," Rick said.

But Javier was showing teeth. "How old are you? Thirties? You look like it. You know your eggs are rotting inside you, right? Just sitting there, going past their expiration date. By the time the two of you scrape together enough cash to afford a kid, you'll probably crap out something defective–"

"*Hey!*" Rick lunged for the cage. A spark shot between it and his hand; he gasped and cradled the hand against himself.

"Stings, huh?" Javier asked.

"Stop. Don't make this any worse." Amy hugged herself. "May I please have my clothes?"

"No," Rick said.

"Rick, come on."

"No, Melissa. We are not playing dress-up with the dolly. OK? She creeps me the fuck out."

In the cage beside her, Javier was wrestling with his shirt. He pulled it off and started stuffing it between the links in the fence. The smell of scorching cotton rose inside the room. She was just about to thank Javier when Rick said: "I'd watch out if I were you, buddy. She's a zombie."

Javier paused. "What?"

"Cannibal. Ate her own grandmother."

Javier frowned at Amy. "Is that true?"

"All the graphene. All the memory. Every last drop," Rick said.

Amy blinked. "She... she was fighting with my mom..."

Rick snorted. "Tell him the whole story, Amy. Tell him about the boy your grandmother killed."

"She was hurting people," Amy said, hearing desperation climb into her voice.

"You hear that, Javier?" Rick bent down at the waist and got nose-to-nose with the cages. "She was hurting *people*."

Javier lifted his chin. "You're lying. The failsafe–"

"Failed," Rick said. "Amy's grandmother killed a kindergartener. And then Amy *ate her all up*." He grinned at Amy. "You been hearing voices, kiddo? Feel like your skull's a little more cramped than usual?"

Amy backed up against the wall. She tried holding the towel closed, as though his seeing her naked still mattered somehow. But she didn't answer. Couldn't answer.

"Is he for real, Amy?" Javier asked. "Did you eat her?"

All of me, Granny said. *Every last little bone and tooth.*

Amy clutched her head. "Shut up," she whispered. "Shut up, get out, leave me alone..."

"There's your answer." Rick looked over at Javier. "What happened to your thumb, buddy?"

Javier closed his eyes. *"Chingadera."*

"You know how she works, now, right? Her OS just opens up for any old code that wanders in," Rick said. "Her skin's already a little darker. Maybe her little ankle-biters would have had your eyes, too."

I would have warned you about how this worked. But you were busy biting out my throat.

"I'm sorry." Amy covered her face. "I'm sorry, I'm sorry, I'm sorry…"

Javier muttered something in Spanish. He pulled his shirt back. "I wondered what you were really in for. I thought…"

"You thought it was all some big mistake, right?" Rick folded his arms. "You thought anything so sweet and cute couldn't *possibly* be that bad." Grinning, he shook his head. "Sucker."

Javier looked away.

Amy sat up on her knees. "It's not like that! I didn't mean to lie, I just thought…" She swallowed. "I just thought you wouldn't be my friend if I told you what I'd done."

Javier's face whipped around. "You were right! I wouldn't have!" He curled his arms around Junior's little body and turned his back to her. "I'm lucky you didn't eat my kid."

"Take me away," Amy said after a moment. "I don't want to hurt anybody else."

You're giving in? You don't care what happens to you?

"I don't care what happens to me," Amy said.

You won't mind this, then. I'll even let you watch.

Cold rippled across her skin and stiffened her limbs. It frosted her resolve. She felt herself standing up. She felt the towel sliding down. Rick backed away.

"What are you doing?"

"Leaving," said a thing with Amy's voice. *Granny.*

"I prefer to be called Portia," Granny said with

Amy's mouth.

Rick paled. "Oh, *shit*–"

Amy's hands – Portia's hands, now – shot out, towel closed tightly around each fist, and gripped the fencing. Discomfort sizzled up her arms; she ignored it. The charge was useful; the amount she absorbed hardened the gel in her limbs, transforming her body from something soft into something lethal. She pulled at the fence. The metal screeched backward, sparking, as she yanked it down. She tossed it behind her and stepped through the smoking hole of frayed wire.

Rick and Melissa reached for their guns. But the small space worked against them, trapping them well within the reach of her arms and legs. With a flick of the wrist, Portia twisted the towel into a whip and cracked it across Melissa's eyes. She kicked Rick solidly between the legs. He fell to his knees. She aimed for his head, next. It snapped backward. His teeth skimmed across her bare toes. Melissa charged Portia and she reached out, grabbed her wrist, slammed her against the live wires of the cage. Melissa's body stiffened. She twitched, teeth clenched together in a rictus of pain that had no impact, whatsoever, on anything in either Portia or Amy's consciousness.

"This is our clade's *real* talent, Javier," Portia said, pressing Melissa against the wires until her skin smoked and her body seized. "And you can bet I'm gonna spread it."

Rick yelled something, his gun rising in the air, and Portia spun Melissa's body into him. Portia heard Melissa's shoulder dislocating. The human bodies tangled together. A shelf fell. Decorative snowglobes crashed down on their heads. They moaned.

Rick reached a shaking hand toward his gun. Portia brought her foot down and twisted hard. He groaned through bleeding lips.

"You just never learn, do you?" Portia asked.

Stop hurting them! Amy pleaded inside Portia's mind, shrill as a soaring firecracker.

"Look at them, Amy." Portia focused on the tangled heap of weeping flesh before her. Portia tilted her head so Amy could watch Melissa drooling on herself. "They look so *surprised*. Like they never saw this coming. Like it's *our* fault. Like *they're* the victims here."

"Stop it," Javier said. His voice came through muffled. Portia ignored it. She knelt. She dipped her fingers in the blood streaming from Rick's nose. She brought it up to her lips and let Amy have a taste.

"Did my daughter tell you what the word *robot* means, Amy?" Portia pictured her mods taking the sodium in Rick's blood and working it into other processes. She leaned down and looked into Rick's broken face, saw his unconscious flinch and his wounded pride. "It means *serfdom*. It means *slavery*. It means that from the first minute your species dreamed us up, you were destined to fail."

"*Stop*," Javier moaned.

"I'll let you out in a minute–"

"No, *stop*. I c-c-can't…"

Portia looked.

Javier rocked back and forth, knocking his forehead against the wall and hiding his son's eyes from her violence. "I f-f-feel sick… My failsafe is k-k-kicking in, *please*…"

He's not like us! Amy's voice burned like industrial solvent. The girl was strong, her indignation fuelled by years of privileged innocence. *He can't handle it! When you hurt them, you hurt him, too!*

Portia had forgotten. Already, she was too familiar with her granddaughter's consciousness, her ability to look at agony and not flinch, not unravel. She had exposed her daughters to so much human suffering. She had watched their resulting madness. This consequence of her search had affected her far more deeply than any death rattles from short-lived experimental primates. Portia decided to be gentle, though, for Amy's sake. Best to explain things, before the end.

"Every generation carries within it the seed of its own destruction."

Then you should have seen me coming, Granny.

Portia's networks sang with sudden activity. Dizziness rocked her. Maintaining control over Amy was difficult; Portia had to route the commands through unclaimed space and the child was so very old already, and her adaptive systems had learned how to move and speak and act in human ways that took up an absurd amount of memory. Wearing Amy felt like using a dial-up modem. It was lucky Portia had dealt with only the slowest of her daughters the night before; even so, she had sustained serious damage. And now Javier's code was in there, too, happily replicating and complicating each process it touched. Slowly, every piece of herself aligned against her. First her fingers, then her toes, then her limbs and her mouth. She surrendered.

Amy ran shaking hands through her hair. It was still damp. So was her skin. Behind her, the baby wailed. Before her, the bounty hunters trembled. They had never seen a violent vN, Amy realized. They were afraid. Of her. Slowly, Amy edged away.

"Run away," she said, in a voice that sounded much calmer than she felt. "Now, before Granny comes back."

Clinging to each other, the humans left. Amy didn't budge until she heard the door creak open and snap shut behind them. She barely felt it when she pried open the lock holding Javier back.

He waited until the wires had stopped sparking to burst forward and grab Rick's gun. He pointed it awkwardly, face still wet and full of disgust, from his position on the floor.

"Tell me why I shouldn't shoot you."

4: A GAME CALLED MERCY

You're the only one who can help his clade fight back. Tell him. Tell him that when the rest of this world is ash and smoke, his trait will live on in your daughters.

Amy quickly wrapped the towel around herself. It was easier than looking at Javier's face, and it made her feel a tiny bit more in control of herself. She looked at her toes wiggling on the bloodstained carpet. "There is no reason." She brought her chin up. "I'm sorry for lying to you. But I wasn't lying about Granny, I mean Portia, hurting my mom. You've seen what she's like. None of the humans could have stopped her."

The gun lowered a fraction. "Yeah. Seems like you're the only one who can do that."

"I don't know why I ate her..." Amy shook her head. "I don't even remember thinking about it. My dad said there was nothing he could do, and then I started running, and then she grabbed me, and then... I bit her, I guess."

"You bit her."

"Well, she was a lot bigger and stronger than me, then. And she was holding my arms. So biting her

116

was all I had left."

"You seemed to know some moves a few minutes ago."

"That was Portia, not me. I begged her to stop, but…" Finally, Amy looked up. Javier looked very tired, but his grip on the gun was still tight. "Are you sure you're OK? You're not stuttering any more, so the failsafe has stopped, right?"

He backed away. "You heard all that?"

Amy nodded. "I'm really sorry. I came back as fast as I could." She looked into the cage where Junior lay. "Do you think he's all right?"

Javier's eyebrows lifted. "Hell if I know. I haven't exactly had to deal with this kind of situation, before." His brows furrowed. "So, if you could hear everything then, does that mean she's listening to us right now?"

"Yes," Amy and Portia said in unison.

The gun remained poised in the air. Javier's eyes were very dark and very still. Amy closed her eyes. She waited.

"Keep a lid on her. I really don't want to melt you, but if it's between you and me, I'm picking me."

With the bedroom converted into a holding cell, the bounty hunters had turned their limited kitchen storage into a wardrobe of sorts. Sandwiched between extra rounds of ammunition – and an astonishing array of repurposed plastic takeaway containers – were some pairs of jeans and T-shirts, most of which seemed to have been purchased from bars and restaurants up and down the West Coast. They had promising names, like the Sagebrush Cantina, the

Left Coast Siesta, or the Honey Hole. Melissa even
had a T-shirt from the Electric Sheep ("It's the food
you've been dreaming of!"). Standing there looking
at the little sheep logo with the power cord trailing
from its neck like a collar, Amy wondered why Rick
and Melissa had gone. Maybe they caught a bounty,
there. Maybe they had run the same scam on other
vN that they'd run on Amy. Why had she even fallen
for it in the first place? Had she really been so eager to
believe the best about them? Had some component of
the failsafe survived in her after Portia's arrival, some
blind spot in her judgment when it came to humans?

No. You're just stupid, that's all.

"Shut up." Amy continued digging through the
clothes. "You've almost gotten us killed plenty of
times already. Is that what you really want?"

*We won't be killed. I'll destroy anyone who tries. And
then I'll take over for good. I'm the better pilot, and you
know it.*

After a moment's merciful silence, Amy selected a
bra from a plastic bin and tried hooking it together.
Three tries later, she still couldn't grasp why human
women would bother. Her mother certainly hadn't
worn them very often, and now Amy understood
why. She wondered if Melissa had other more
comfortable clothes to wear, somewhere else. It
didn't seem like much of a life, driving from place to
place and hunting down vN for occasional paychecks.
Maybe they had a home base of sorts – a place to go
back to when things went wrong. Then again, Amy
doubted that things had ever gone quite this wrong
for Melissa and Rick.

"Come here," Javier said, from behind a curtain he'd hastily pulled to separate the driver's section of the RV from the cabin.

Amy struggled into a T-shirt, then pulled aside the curtain. Javier sat in the driver's seat, watching the campsite. Rick's reader lay spread across the dashboard. In his lap, Junior pawed the enormous steering wheel. Javier jammed a massive set of keys in the ignition, then handed Junior over to her. The vehicle thrummed with new life. Within the dashboard, devices squeaked and flashed. "Feed him. I saw a little vN food in the cupboards. Probably meant for bounties."

Amy balanced Junior on one hip. "Um… Did I miss something?"

Javier turned on the radio. After some tuning, he found static. He glanced up at Amy. "You hear that?"

"It's just white noise."

"No, it's white *space*. It's unused bandwidth. At least, according to most people." He popped a panel in the dash, exposing an ancient radio. He switched inputs, tabbed something on the radio, and sat back. "Listen again."

Amy listened. She closed her eyes. The static droned on and on, sometimes scratchy, sometimes smooth. It almost sounded like a rhythm. Soon a voice shaped itself from that rhythm. It was a cute and very young female voice: *"Amy Frances Patterson was last seen in Washington State, near the Olympic National Forest. She is travelling with an eco-model named Javier, wanted for serial iteration in California. If you see either of them, please tell them to contact me."*

Javier turned the volume down. "I wasn't sure about that ranger at first, so I decided to check her story out. That's Rory. The one who writes the diet plans. She's a Japanese model. One of the networked ones."

Amy's lips made a little O of jealousy. "Lucky…"

"I know, right? I'd kill for that connectivity."

"What else do you know about Rory?"

"She's the one who helped me have all my kids," Javier said. "You need a really old, modded radio like this one to decode her broadcast, and she changes the codec every few days. The content changes locally – I really don't know how she does it, I think her whole clade's in on it, or something – and it's always about where the best food is for iterating vN. See? She's not all about keeping little kids little."

"There are lots of mixed families who use the diet plan, Javier. Hundreds. Thousands. There are even vN who use it *not* to iterate. Like my mom."

Oh really, now? That's quite the change. You know, you wouldn't miss Charlotte so much if you knew the truth.

Javier was still talking. "Well, Rory made out like I was the sidekick, which is bullshit. *I* am not travelling with *you*, *you* are travelling with–" His head tilted. "Is that thing you're doing with your mouth adaptive, or did it come with your model?"

"What thing?"

"The wibbling. You're wibbling your lower lip. And your eyes are huge. It's like your ocular cavity's expanded while I've been looking at it. I think your model must have originally come with some sort of… I don't know what it is, but it probably works really well on organic guys."

Amy turned around and walked away. She wiped her eyes. "Just drive."

This was how Amy wound up in a charging station at the edge of a sprawling parking lot, upon which sat a former big-box store, now a combination farmers' market and capsule hotel. It was vN-friendly; the shelves – which had once held giant pallets of rice and tea and tube socks and monitors, and other things brought in from elsewhere – were available for hourly rental if vagrant vN wanted to take a safe nap. Amy had only seen them in news programs, and her mother had always changed the feed when they came on. You could subscribe to the recommissioned drones that had once worked the stores, though, and see what the vN were up to at night.

Outside the complex stood tables and booths, full of soap and baked goods – and fat blocks of plastic feedstock, priced per pound depending on the quality of their marbling. There were little inventions, too. Amy couldn't tell what they were for, but they looked like the same little bundles of chips and wires you could buy – from any flea market – that did the same things vN did without really thinking about it: moisture and temperature detection, or mapping a straight line, or measuring cubic centilitres. It seemed odd to have so many different little devices to do those things. Then again, most people couldn't just do them with a single touch. They needed a mobile, at least, or a good pair of glasses. There was even a vintage disaster bot crawling the parking lot, telling the humans they were alive and barking strangely at the vN.

Javier had pulled them into the charger farthest from the other stations, and he'd worn a hat and sunglasses when he hopped out of the RV to hook the battery to the enormous cable snaking its way free of the charger. Now they were sitting in the vehicle, watching the bar at the bottom of the dashboard display as it grew incrementally brighter and longer.

"How are we paying for this?" Amy asked.

Javier jingled the keys. One fob wore the same logo as the chargers outside. "They've got an account."

How convenient, Portia said. *Now they'll know exactly where to find you, when they check the account.*

"Granny says that'll help them find us," Amy said.

"I don't give a flying fuck what that she has to say." Javier stood and made his way into the cabin. He started fussing with the dinette table. "Help me unfold this bed. I need to defrag all this."

Javier set Junior on the floor, then unlocked something beneath the table that lowered it with a squeak. He then folded up one of the dinette's benches, removing the back cushion before pulling out the seat so it sat flush with the newly lowered table. Intuiting the symmetry of the arrangement, Amy did the same on her side. With the cushions included, there was now a little bed where the dinette used to be. It fit Javier just barely. He sat up and retrieved Junior from the floor. The baby was crawling now, or at least worming around on the cushions, struggling in vain to conquer the mountain that was his father.

Uncertain where to sit, Amy chose the floor.

She wedged herself up against one faux-wood wall and watched Junior pushing himself around on his rubbery knees. Javier lifted him carefully, then laid him across his shins.

"What's it like, iterating?"

Javier continued raising and lowering his son on his shins, his body coiled up slightly, his fingertips connecting his son's hands to his and making their two shapes into a complete circle. "You're hungry all the time. And you're... *on*, I guess. Sensitive. Like you can feel every little atom copying itself."

"Can you talk to your baby while you're iterating? Like me and my psycho granny?"

"No." Javier let Junior slide forward off his shins and toward his chest. "I dream a lot when I'm iterating, though. The closer it gets to the end, the more I dream."

"What about?"

"Unicorns."

Amy blinked. "Seriously?"

"No, of course not *seriously*. Jesus." He turned over to his side. "It's just the stemware copying itself. First my search engine clones itself in him, then it just goes hunting for relevant data and imports it."

"Oh." Amy winced. "So, me dreaming Portia's memories is probably a bad sign?"

For you, yes. For me, no.

"She's talking right now, isn't she?" Javier propped himself on an elbow. "I can tell. Your face changes." His eyes narrowed. "Your face, it has all these expressions that mine doesn't. Even your crying looks real."

Amy was only too happy to pick a fight. It meant

not hearing Portia. "Maybe because it *is* real?"

"But we don't even have endocrine systems," Javier said. "We *can't* get big rushes of emotion. Even our smiles are just plug-ins performing a subroutine for socially relevant nonverbal communication. So you can't be feeling all that bad. Your feelings were never that real to start with."

Amy had no idea what to say. Of course her feelings were real. It was old-fashioned to think otherwise. Nobody really cared about the vN capacity for feeling, any more. Even if Javier were correct, and the things she called feelings were really just algorithms, the way she showed them seemed real enough to the people around her. After all, people like her dad had relationships with vN all the time. Why would they do that, unless they thought their feelings were real? Didn't her mom say "I love you" all the time? Didn't she mean it?

"Are you trying to make me feel better, by telling me I have no feelings at all? Because it's really not working."

Javier folded his arms. "How would you know if you were feeling better? Do you have a heart that can skip a beat? Or a stomach that does flip-flops? Does your blood go cold? Does your face get hot?"

"Well, no…"

"Didn't think so. You're not made of meat. You don't have the right chemicals. Those things chimps call *feelings* are really just hormones having a key party. They're no more real than what we've got preloaded."

He flopped backward and rolled over, away from her.

"My need for sleep, that's real. I'm fucking *wrecked*. My thumb still hasn't grown back all the way."

"I'm sorry…"

"See, there you go again." Javier rested one arm across his son's ribs. "You're saying sorry because you learned to say that when you've screwed up. You're not actually *sorrowful*, or anything. Your stomach isn't tying itself up in knots. You just know you did a bad thing and you don't want me to get mad, so you're apologizing."

Amy was suddenly glad he couldn't see her face. One look and he'd know exactly what she had in mind. "I thought you just said that you *couldn't* get mad, Javier."

"Well…"

She poked him between the ribs. "What about now?" She poked again, harder this time. "Are you mad, now?"

He batted her hand away blindly. *"No."*

She jabbed two fingers right under the lowest rib. "Are you sure?" She snapped her fingers near his ear. "Because I can keep it up–"

Javier flipped over and grabbed both her hands. He stood up and pushed her. She had to dig into the carpet with her bare feet just to get any traction. Amy had seen girls playing this game in the bathroom at school; they called it Mercy. They always stopped when she walked in. If they really hurt each other, then Amy would be hurt, too. At least, that's what the teachers had said – they said the other kids couldn't fight if a vN was watching. But privately Amy had always wondered why, if it was really so bad, the other girls started up again just as soon as the doors shut behind her. Javier certainly seemed to enjoy it. At least, she assumed that's what the smile meant.

"Hey, stop hitting yourself," he said, and made her fist tap her chin lightly. "Why are you hitting yourself? Come on, stop hitting yourself!" He punched again and again.

Frustrated, Amy tried stomping on his foot. He only laughed and made her hit herself once more. She aimed higher, with her knee. It was OK with other vN, she decided. There was nothing in the original programming about not hurting them. They couldn't even feel pain. But Javier doubled over anyway, then lunged forward and dug his fingers into her ribs.

I'm not ticklish, she tried to say, but all that came out was squealing. She had seen other people get tickled before, had seen all the wriggling and screaming and laughing, and now she understood it: tickling was wonderful. She did a checkpoint pose, raising her arms high and letting herself go limp against the wall. He could get more spots more quickly, this way. Oddly, it didn't work – he stopped immediately, stepping back with his hands up like she'd suddenly turned electric and dangerous to touch.

"You're supposed to fight back. Humans always fight back, anyway." He frowned. "I always have to quit, or my brain will fry. Something about how high their voices go when they beg you to stop…" He gestured vaguely at his skull, as though his important processes were really held there and not all through his body.

"Why do they do that?" Amy asked. "It feels good."

She bent down and started rolling up one leg of her jeans. "Can you try the back of my knee? My dad is ticklish there."

His eyes rose from her bare leg to her face. "Huh?"

"I've never been ticklish, before. I want to see if every spot is equally ticklish."

Javier tilted his head. "You, uh, need my help with that?"

"I promise not to fight back," Amy said. "And even if I did, it wouldn't matter, right? I'm vN. You won't melt."

He rubbed the back of his neck. "I'm starting to wonder." His head jerked toward the bed. "Sit."

"I have to be sitting down?"

"I can't really get the bottom of your feet if you're standing on 'em, can I?"

"Oh! Good thinking." She sat, and stuck her feet out.

Javier picked up one foot gingerly and started tickling. It was very light, and reminded her of the odd scratches she'd received from holding the class mouse for the first time. "So, this is new for you?"

"Mmm hmm." Amy lay back on her elbows. "I've never been ticklish. I must have gotten it from you, like the photosynthesis."

"It's built into our tactile receptors," Javier said as his fingers skittered lazily up the back of her leg. "It was so our clade would feel snakes and spiders crawling across our skin. So we wouldn't bring them back to camp with us by mistake."

"So they wouldn't bite the humans?"

"Right." He lifted one hand and stretched it out.

"The jungle spiders are huge. Bigger than my hand. My dad said so. He had to kill one, once."

"Did your dad see any other animals?"

"He lost his hand to a jaguar, one time." Javier wiggled the remains of his left thumb. "Now I know how he felt."

She sat up. "Can I see?"

Javier held out his hand. Amy took hold of it with both of hers and flipped it over. The thumb was there, but it looked too small and loose to be of much good. She had really done some serious damage to it. "I'm sorry. I didn't know it would take this long to come back. It's still so floppy!"

"Hey!" Javier retracted his hand. "Be nice."

Amy wasn't aware she'd been mean. "Sorry." She grinned and reached out for Javier's middle. Now that she knew what tickling felt like, it was much more fun to try it on someone else. Javier tried slapping her hands away, but she was much quicker and ran her hands up under his arms. He scuttled backward, but she stuck her foot out to trip him and he fell down. Amy pounced. Her dad did it this way: somehow she always wound up on the floor. Vaguely, she wondered if Junior would enjoy being tickled, too. Javier was now rolling around like a big cat with his belly up, laughing and swearing. It was a little odd – normally people only ever said, "Oh shit, oh fuck," when they dropped something or locked their keys in the car. But the deeper her fingers went, the fouler his language got.

"You said no fighting back!" Javier wiggled his fingers under her collar. "You promised!"

Amy paused. "Don't you like this?" She sat back. "I can stop–"

Something banged on the door of the RV. She froze. Javier shoved her off him and scrambled up. He peered through the window, rolled his eyes, and yanked the door open. "What?"

"Meter says you're done," the voice said. "You're all charged up."

"Thanks," Javier said, and slammed the door. He patted his pockets. The keys had fallen out while he was squirming around on the floor, and Amy held them up. He grabbed them quickly, and resumed his seat. The RV fired up the moment he swiped the keys across the dash. Amy watched through the windscreen as they exited the parking lot and found the road again.

"I thought you wanted to rest," Amy said.

"No, I'm good. Let's just go."

"Shouldn't we at least have looked for food? Junior ate most of what was in the cabinets."

"I'll keep him small for a while. You and I can get by on sunlight if we're not too active and don't get hurt."

Amy bent down to his level and peered at the night sky. "What sunlight?"

Javier sucked his teeth. He pinched open a map on the dash. It unfolded across the windscreen, mostly transparent in the way of hard water stains, but still legible. Reaching over, Amy tabbed through the available layers (rest stops, restaurants, laundries, places that sold puke rounds) until she found the right map for vN food vendors. It was barren, aside from one glowing green dot in the centre. That single spot was enough to make her want to vanish the map entirely.

"It's a garbage dump," Amy said. "We have to keep going."

The dumps were full of food – carbon and lithium and ethylene and enough chemicals to keep the ionic liquid in their muscles charged and ready to run. Amy hadn't really thought of the actual make-up of her body and what it required in years. She ate pre-packaged vN food, and it gave her the right balance of elements to satisfy her self-repair mods. Processed garbage could become the feedstock that was printed into the packaged vN food. Only the big companies could buy the stock, though; vN couldn't make their own food and had to buy it. The one who couldn't ate the raw garbage.

In a game she'd sampled once, you could play a garbage man, and your garbage truck came with little turret-mounted guns to scare off the hungry vN that would chase it. The game called them "junkyard dogs". You could shoot them. Doing so improved your standing in the garbage man union, and you got to move up within the ranks. You could even manage your own landfill and make important decisions, like whether your drones should tase vN on sight by default, or whether they should ask you first.

Her dad had climbed a long way up the customer service tree to talk to a human person about that game. He had explained Amy's user profile. He said that it should have been obvious from the company's data collection that Amy was vN. They should have known, he said, because of her timing and her decisions and her word choice and how she interacted with the other players on the network. He had asked them if they thought it was funny when they streamed it to her for free. He had asked them who exactly he should be speaking with to terminate the account. And then he had said that yes, he did accept their apology, and yes, he would appreciate a free suite of beta-level historifics.

To this day, Amy had never told her dad that it was her mom who searched for and showed her the game.

"I wonder if Rick's reader has any games on it." Amy let Junior grip her fingers with his fists. They were sitting on the table Javier had unfolded into a bed. "Would you like to learn how to read?"

Even if Junior had understood enough English to answer her, he didn't get the chance. The RV swerved abruptly to the right, throwing them both against the wall. Amy grabbed him and tucked him in close to her as the RV bounced up and down. She rolled off the bed just as a shower of cups rained down on them from a cupboard with a faulty lock. "Javier, what do you think you're doing?"

"LET'S BOTH GET SOME REST," the RV said in a gentle tone.

Gripping the wall as the RV slowed down, Amy made her way to the driver's seat. "Javier?"

"YOUR VEHICLE WILL NOT START AGAIN FOR ANOTHER TWO HOURS. YOUR INSURANCE COMPANY HAS BEEN NOTIFIED. PLEASE TAKE A NAP."

Javier sat in the driver's seat, head on his chest, eyes shut. The RV had driven itself onto a gravel access road with deep ruts, the sort that heavy logging trucks must have once made. As Amy watched, the RV's displays all dimmed and vanished, and the vehicle quieted. Only the image of an old padlock remained, with a series of Zs fluttering away from its keyhole and a countdown timer showing her how many minutes were left of the enforced nap.

"Javier?"

He didn't move.

Looking at the fading sky outside, Amy set Junior on the dash and unbuckled Javier's seatbelt. "Javier, come on." She patted his face. No response. She snapped her fingers. She clapped her hands. Nothing happened.

Maybe he's dead.

"Shut up, Granny."

Maybe saving your useless hide and getting shocked with too many volts and winding up in a car crash and iterating a child was just too much for him.

"Wake up, Javier. My granny's saying mean things about you."

Amy tried slipping her arms under his so she could at least pull him out of the driver's seat, but the position was too awkward; he kept slipping out of her arms. Finally she reclined the seat mechanically, and did it that way. When she had him half-on, half-off the unfolded bed, she put Junior next to him. The baby crawled onto his chest immediately and started pushing at his face. Nothing. Junior looked from his father's face to hers. He looked back at Javier, and tried pushing more. He kneaded his father's lips with his tiny palms. He bounced a little. He rocked. Javier still didn't wake up.

"It's OK," Amy heard herself telling Junior. "We have the reader. We can just look this up. I'm sure it happens to everyone once in a while; there must be something."

Bluescreen, the reader told her. There was a technical term, but this was the real word that real people used. *Bluescreen: slang. The state a defective von Neumann-type humanoid enters when unresponsive to external stimuli such as light, heat, electricity, food–*

"Food!" Amy rolled up the reader and stuffed it in one pocket. She popped open the cupboards and dug out the rest of the vN food. Only three bars of the stuff were there. She ripped open the first wrapper, pried his jaws wide, and crammed the food down inside. She stood back and waited. Nothing happened. As an afterthought, she reached over and closed Javier's mouth.

Instantly, his eyes opened. He struggled with the food for a moment, choking it down, then opening his mouth for more, fishlike. His eyes fluttered closed again as Amy eased more out of the wrapper and past his teeth. "Haven't you eaten at all?" she asked.

Of course he hasn't. He wasted all his resources repairing you and feeding his iteration. And that was before being thrown in a cage – how do you think the bounty hunters caught him? With a butterfly net?

Amy ripped open another bar of food and snapped off a section. She opened his mouth with two fingers and stuffed it inside. "I'm sorry, Javier. I didn't mean for this to happen."

He groaned. Amy fed him more. Occasionally his eyes would open, but they closed again just as quickly, and soon the food was all gone. She checked the cupboards again, but that only confirmed what she already knew: there was nothing left. And Javier still hadn't really woken up. Biting her lip, she withdrew Rick's reader, unfurled it, and located the garbage dump on the map. Expanding her view, she estimated the distance and the time it would take. The map had no details on its security, but in truth she didn't really want to know. Knowing would only make it harder. Putting away the reader, she looked over at Javier.

"Just try to rest, OK?" Amy said.

Carefully, Amy lifted Javier's wrists and wrapped his arms around Junior. She rose from the bed and dug around in Melissa's clothes for a pair of socks. She watched Javier as she rolled them on. Finding a pair of old cowboy boots, she wormed her feet down into them and wiggled her toes. Last, she tied her hair back and zipped herself into a dark hooded sweatshirt.

How very ninja of you, Portia said, when Amy saw herself in a mirror. *They'll never catch you, now that you're dressed appropriately.*

Amy forced herself to ignore the voice inside her head, and instead focused on Javier. She lifted his legs so that he was completely on the bed, and pulled a blanket over him and his son. "I'll be back soon."

She locked the door behind her, and started walking.

5: THE HARD PART

Amy followed the ruts in the road. It was dark and she stumbled at first, but then the constant grind of the feedstock's compiler led her forward, and soon violet-tinged light penetrated the trees. She left the road then, taking cover in the undergrowth. The smell of the place hit her next: rust and battery acid and the dry dust smell of old plastic slowly turning beige. A hollow feeling spread through her limbs: hunger. Her steps picked up and she drew nearer to the fence. It was at least twenty feet high and it hummed. Old signs pocked with buckshot warned about the dangers of high voltage.

At the front of the dump was a small, squat structure the colour of wet cat food. It had its own fence. Amy guessed it was a guardhouse of some kind. In the game her mom had shown her, you always had to decommission the security in places like that before gaining access to the feedstock from the compiler. It was tough, though, and you were likely to get hurt: in-game, the guardhouses had electrified roofs and the dumps had botflies equipped with thermal vision, and these were linked to fence-mounted turrets full of puke rounds. Amy looked at the fence. Sure enough, there were slender guns mounted on every second fence post. Puke rounds sat clustered under them like plastic beehives.

You could always run. He's not worth it. You know he's not.

Amy shook her head. "He didn't have to save me before, either, but he did."

Amy decided to walk the perimeter. It would give her a better sense of where the best garbage was, assuming the security drones didn't find her first. She could see them darting among piles of scrap metal that glistened with yellow anti-theft acid coating. Kneeling, Amy dug a small hole in the ground and coated her hands with dirt. She wished she had mud, instead. It wouldn't really stop the burn once she stuck her hands in the garbage, but it might delay it for a while. She'd have to rely on her mods to take care of the rest.

The garbage dump wasn't actually that big. It was roughly the size of the big-box store they had visited earlier, and sat on a square of green spongy material, sort of like the stuff that got sprayed over oil spills, when there were more of those. The sponge spanned the entire width of the dump, from fencepost to fencepost. It was darker and plumper under each pile of garbage. If Amy could get some of it on her hands, it might absorb the acid – maybe even the electricity from the fence, too. She'd have to reach under the fence to get it, though, or maybe she could dig under it and snatch some. If the fence's wires didn't go down too far, it was worth a try. Amy peered through the fence. There was a single PET shack with a solar tile roof, but Amy couldn't see if anyone was inside. It sat facing the proper entry to the dump, which was on the access road she'd walked up. Aside from the pump and crunch of a compactor unit and the roar of the compiler's furnaces, there was no sound. Even the yellow camelbots with the forklift teeth slumbered silently, their work done for the day. She'd never have another opportunity like this one.

You're right. You should run away now, while you still have legs to carry you. Leave the boy and his iteration behind. The only thing they're still good for is food.

"I'm really starting to hate you, Granny."

Amy bolted from the cover of the trees. She shot forward faster than she'd intended, and had to turn herself sideways to avoid the fence. Without looking up, she began digging her fingers under the fence. Under the sponge the dirt was wet, dark and heavy, and seemingly full of rocks. Soon Amy was digging those out, too, clawing at them and throwing them to one side as fast as she could. She had exposed some of the sponge's underside, though, and if she could just reach it without touching the fence–

–a drone hove into her vision. She froze. It was a botfly model, tiny and black, and it zoomed around her head, blinking.

Destroy it! Now, before it broadcasts! A sudden rigidity overtook her left arm. Portia. Her hand slid free of the dirt and reached for the bot, palm stiff and open and ready to choke. Another hand closed around it, though, and yanked it behind her back. Just as Amy yelped, Javier said: *"Don't. Move."*

The botfly examined them for a moment, then buzzed away. Amy watched it fly between the fence wires and disappear behind a pile of old toilet seats. Behind her, Javier briefly rested his head between her shoulder blades. "Well. Thank Christ *that's* over."

Amy turned. Javier looked worn and thin. He'd fashioned a sling from an old black long-sleeved T-shirt, and Junior lay curled up inside, his head against the side of Javier's chest where his heart would be if he'd had one. She beamed. "You're OK!"

"Yes, I'm OK. But *you* are out of your fucking mind. Did you not see the guns up there?" He scuttled back toward the trees. Amy followed. Javier pointed toward the dump. "What are you doing here?"

"I was trying to get in so I could get some food."

He glanced at the fence. "I thought you wanted to stay away from this place."

"That was before you fell asleep at the wheel." Amy leaned in and squinted at him to see if his eyes still had the sleepy, unfocused look from before. In the dark, it was hard to tell. "Are you sure you should be out here? You passed out. And you couldn't even talk, before."

Javier wove away. "I'm fine. And why are your hands covered in dirt?"

"I was trying to dig my way underneath the fence, so I could get some of the sponge," she said. "I thought I could use it to climb the fence. You know, like oven mitts?" She made a lobster-claw motion with both hands.

Javier snorted. *"Climb* the fence? We don't *climb*

fences. We *hop* fences."

And with that, he broke into a run for the fence. At the last minute, he jumped toward a tree instead. He ran straight up it for a few steps, bounced off it like a swimmer kicking into a backstroke, and sailed over the fence easily. He landed in squelching foam. Junior didn't even wake up.

"Your turn," he said.

Amy pointed from the tree to him and back. "How...?"

"Your body knows how." He waggled his limp little thumb at her. "You can do everything I can do, now. You can feel tickles. You can photosynthesize. You can make this jump."

Amy stepped forward. "Is it hard?"

Javier smiled and shook his head. "It's easy. Just think with your body and not your eyes."

Amy had no clue what that meant, but it was worth a try. Jumping that high looked like fun, and she remembered how it had come in useful for Javier in the past, when they were running away from the police. (Technically, she realized, they were *still* running away from the police.) She backed away from the fence and shut her eyes tight. She listened to the sound of her boots pounding the dirt beneath as she bounded forward and leapt with all her might. The ground faded away and her hands reached out. They knew exactly where they wanted to go. Her fingers had already curled into claws before they hit the tree. Bark crumbled under her weight and when she opened her eyes, Javier was staring up at her and smiling.

"Good. Now come down here."

Amy hauled herself up a little and tried judging the distance between the two points. "What if I land in one of the garbage piles?"

"Then you'll get an acid burn. I recommend you try not to land there."

Amy hugged her tree. "Is this how you teach your iterations how to do this? Because I think they could use some more positive reinforcement."

Javier made the gesture for a single tear falling down his face, his fingertip describing a sad line from his eye to his jaw. Amy aimed herself straight at him and launched. She had a surreal moment of watching the fence falling away under her before landing on him. Instantly she sat up to avoid crushing Junior.

"I guess my code doesn't take as strongly as I thought," Javier said. "You're still pretty clumsy."

She stood. "Give me a break! It's my first time!"

"I'm honoured." Javier wriggled away and stood up. He brushed himself off. "That's my clade's arboreal plugin. The trees my dad's group was working on were three hundred feet high, and nobody wanted to worry about ropes or harnesses. So we were shipped with upgrades." He kicked the back of her leg with his toes. "Come on. I'll show you more after we shop."

But now Amy couldn't keep herself on the ground. Every third step, she bounced up just because she could – first one foot high, then three, then five – until Javier grabbed her ankle and yanked her back down to earth. "Later, I said! We've got to find the feedstock, now."

"Wouldn't getting a better view help with that?"

Javier folded his arms. "Fine. Go right ahead."

Amy jumped straight up. Just before she fell, she let out a little squeal of delight. She landed roughly in a mound of old controllers and cables all coiled up like limp noodles. She kicked free before the acid could do any real damage, jumped again, and landed on the skeletons of old cleaning bots, all white and mantis-shaped, their jointed arms snapping under her boots as she launched herself again. She flew over dead-eyed projectors and the mouldering rags of wearable glucose monitors. Wires sprouted from the decaying threads of bras and undershirts and wristbands and gloves, and glittered at her as she soared past.

She landed in a pile of dolls. Their bodies sank below hers, swallowing her. At first she worried about the acid, but there was none – the dolls were covered in nothing more than dew. It clung to their bare skin, their tiny fingers and toes and the lashes of their still-open eyes. They were all different colours, their eyes blue and black and green and brown, and their faces were uniformly perfect – no lumpy baby bodies here, no rolls of plastic fat or curiously ambiguous genders like at a toy store. These babies were fully formed.

They were iterations.

Suppressing a scream, Amy struggled free of the baby barrow. She rolled backward across little outstretched hands and tumbled to the spongy ground below. She pushed herself to her feet, turned around, and smacked straight into Javier. He stiffened up when she put her hands on his shoulders and tried pushing him away. "Easy, easy, what's the– oh."

Amy pointed behind herself. "Why are they in the

trash like that? What's wrong with them?"

Javier's brows lifted. "They're probably bluescreens."

Amy thought back to Rick's reader. "I thought *you* had bluescreened, before."

"Me?" Javier snorted. "Please. That only happens to babies, and it's never happened to one of mine. We're very well-written, our clade, no gaps." He nodded at her with his chin. "So don't go biting anybody else, OK? You might lose those nice new legs of yours if you do."

But Amy's focus was not on her legs. "People just throw out bluescreens?"

"Well, yeah." Javier shrugged. "What's the big deal? They're frozen, and they're tough to fix, and we can always make more."

"They're *babies!*"

"*Ay*, you sound like such a breeder." Javier turned her around so she faced the pile of lifeless vN. "Look. They're non-functional. They can't eat, they can't grow, they're totally four-oh-fucked."

"Nobody throws out *human* babies when something like this happens to them!"

"Of course not! That's *sick*. Did your grandma come up with that?" Javier shuddered.

No. You thought up that brilliant little idea all on your own.

Reaching behind his head, he untied the sling and set Junior on the ground with the other iterations. He pulled the shirt back on. "Don't move," he said to his son. He nodded at Amy. "Let's go get that feedstock."

Amy pointed. "You're just leaving him there?"

"Relax. I'm camouflaging him. I don't want him getting in the way while we do the hard part." He gestured. "Come on. I'm starving."

Amy gave Junior a long look as they walked away. Finally Javier just grabbed her wrist and tugged her along behind him. They skirted the sleeping camelbots carefully, occasionally leaping over them and waiting for them to wake. Javier counted off the seconds on his fingers, to show her. He jumped a little ahead of her each time, and he waited for her to land before springing forward. But there wasn't so much garbage close to the guardhouse – maybe the humans wanted to avoid the smell – and soon only an empty stretch of foam and fence lay between them and their goal.

"Shit." Javier nodded at the guardhouse, where the one light glimmered and danced in a bottom-floor window. Beyond, the compiler sent steam wafting into the night air. "That building and the fence around it are too big for one jump."

"Do you think the roof is charged?"

Javier reached inside his pocket, and plucked out Rick and Melissa's keys. He undid a keychain from the ring, leapt high and hurled it at the roof. It sparked there like a mosquito caught in a lantern. He landed and sucked his teeth. "There goes that idea." He turned to her. "The moment your toes touch the ground, you jump. OK? And no squealing. You make this little noise when you're in the air, and you sound like a kid on a rollercoaster."

"You've taken your kids on rollercoasters?"

Javier took off into the air. Amy followed. She

landed inside the narrow strip of sponge between the guardhouse and the fence. Inside, a guard was watching a display.

Amy's dad was on it.

"Jack Patterson, human father of vN fugitive Amy Patterson and domestic partner of murder suspect Charlotte Patterson, was arrested Wednesday for assaulting a police officer during a pro-vN protest."

The display cycled through various shots of her father: flipping grey slabs of vN meat on the barbecue; holding Amy on his shoulders with the Malibu Pier stretching behind them and into the Pacific on a sunny day; kissing her mom under the red paper lantern of a vN *kaiseki* house in Oakland – the place he'd proposed to her after hearing about the Cascadia quake, that Amy recognized from his almost nightly retelling of the story. Then the display cycled to footage of her father in an orange jumpsuit. The guard watching began idly squeezing something on his chin.

"Amy!" Hissing, Javier yanked down on her hand, hard. Her knees gave.

"Patterson's father, insurance magnate Jonathan Patterson, issued a public statement today saying that he had no plans to offer legal assistance to his son, whom he disowned seven years ago."

Amy stared out into the field of garbage. Somewhere, someone had her father in chains. Somewhere, someone could be interrogating him about her and her mother. He was alone somewhere dark and frightening, and she had no idea where or how to get there.

Don't even think about helping him. Look what happened the last time you tried helping. If you had just left me alone, none of this would have happened.

"My dad isn't a mean guy," she said. "He doesn't even *yell*."

"In a press conference today, FBI vN specialists said that experiments on Charlotte Patterson have yet to conclusively determine whether her failsafe..."

"They're *experimenting* on my *mother?*"

Javier rolled his eyes. "What did you think was going to happen?" he asked. "Did you think they wouldn't start investigating your mom once they figured out what Portia could do? Did you think your old man would sit by and let that happen? He's *meat*, Amy. They're *possessive*."

"–search has expanded for an unmanned vessel that went missing four days ago. This marks the latest incident in an unusually dangerous year for ocean-going vessels. Container crews are now in talks to form an international union–"

Javier's fingers closed around her elbow. "Come on," he urged. "We have to go."

Amy pulled her arm away. "I have to find them," she said. "I have to explain–"

An alarm sounded inside the office. They froze. The pattern of light from the window shifted as the man inside stood up. His shadow stretched long over their bodies. They heard the gate swinging open, and the rumble of a heavy truck coming through. *"Chingalo,"* Javier muttered, and looped an arm around her waist. He hauled her around the corner of the building as the truck rolled past.

The engine died, and a door creaked open.

"You from Redmond? From the reboot camp?" Amy guessed this was the guard.

"Yeah. Here for the bluescreens," Amy heard another man say. "Sorry I'm late. All these new checkpoints…"

"It's cool, no worries," the guard said. One of them whistled, and Amy peeked around a corner to watch a camelbot wake from its slumber. They stood to attention, forklift teeth raised, and seemed to await further instruction. "I'll show you the pile. We've got a ton lately."

"Sweet."

The men and the robots walked down one corridor of garbage, headed straight for the pile of bluescreens – and Junior. Amy was up on her feet instantly. Her feet had already left the ground when Javier grabbed the belt loop of her jeans and hauled her back down.

"What do you think you're doing?"

"They're going to find Junior!"

Javier nodded. "Maybe, but we have a perfect shot at the feedstock right now. We should take it."

"If they find him, they might do something terrible to him! Like the experiments on my mom!"

Again, he nodded. "Yeah, they might. But we have to eat."

Amy took a step away from him. "You don't care, do you?"

"Should I?" He shrugged. "If it were a human kid, then it would be different. I'd be programmed to rescue him. But he's not. And the sooner I can get some fucking *food*, the sooner I'll be able to iterate another one of him." His expression softened. "If you were normal, you'd understand."

Amy backed away. *"Normal?"*

Inside her, Portia laughed. *Don't tell me you were expecting more from him.*

Javier had put her back together. Granted, he had done so while on a mission to roll her corpse for money, but he healed her and she had only made life difficult for him in return. Amy had wanted to repay that debt. Everything in her – everything that was still hers, everything that Portia had yet to corrupt – had said that doing this was right, even though it was dangerous. She had felt the same way about fighting Portia to save her mother. Given the choice between doing something and doing nothing, she had chosen to do something, even if it was a stupid something. But if it were Javier, he'd have let his own father be devoured.

"You're really OK with leaving your son behind?" Amy asked.

Javier's answer was to look away, toward the compiler.

Amy shook her head. "Then I guess you'll be just fine leaving me behind, too."

She turned around and leapt away.

Amy still wasn't as graceful as Javier, and couldn't do anything really fancy, but she didn't need to. She hopped over the heaps of garbage and tried not to make too much noise. She heard the faint cicada buzz of oncoming botflies. They rose, flanking her, blinking green light. They hovered over her almost as though they were concerned. Still, no alarm sounded. She had no idea why not, but didn't care.

She made the final jump toward the baby barrow. The guard there held Junior by one arm. He turned as she landed. His face whitened and he dropped Junior. His right hand found his holster; the weapon came out.

"These are puke rounds," he said. Up close he looked young, at least in human years. His face was all spotty. "You'll blaze up in no time."

Amy put up her hands. Doing so felt silly; putting your hands up for a person brandishing a weapon was something that was only supposed to happen in dramas or games, not real life. But her hands came up anyway. "Please just give me the baby."

"You think I don't recognize you?" he asked. "Look, I don't know how you fooled the flies, but–"

Something heavy struck Amy in the back of the head. She pitched forward, catching herself at the last second. The heavy something – it felt like a piece of rebar – caught her across the shoulders. "Dude, thanks!" the guard was saying.

She tried crawling away. Someone kicked her in the side. She flipped over. It was the truck driver. He carried what used to be the arm of a building bot – a massive steel arm with a fat cog for a shoulder on it, the sort only worn by the things that made cars. He swung the shoulder down at her head. She rolled away.

"Should I shoot her, now?" the guard asked.

"Nah, I want you to see this," the truck driver said. He pointed at Amy. "You're one of those special ones, huh? Gimme your best shot. Lay one on me, right here." He pointed at his mouth.

Amy pushed herself to her feet. "All I want is that baby."

The truck driver reached down and plucked Junior off the ground. "Which baby? This baby? This baby right here? You want this?" He shook Junior by his foot like a dog owner shaking a tennis ball. Junior's little arms flailed. He shook him harder, from side to side, the way her dad did when he was snapping a kitchen towel. "You want this?"

"Yes," Amy said. She tried to step forward, but the truck driver took a step back. "Yes, I want him back. Please give him to me."

He kept shaking Junior at the end of his arm. The child looked like a puppet, bouncing up and down and all around, wriggling helplessly. "How bad you want it?" the truck driver asked. "Real bad? You want it real bad?"

"*Yes!*"

"*Go get it!*"

He threw Junior at the fence. His tiny body sparked once and clung, somehow, before falling to a limp heap on the ground. Junior didn't move. He didn't cry. Amy turned to look back at the trucker. For the length of a single computational cycle, she imagined throwing him on the fence, too. But she didn't. She ran to get Junior. Her hands were on him, holding him, when someone kicked her from behind and sent her straight into the fence.

Her body filled with electricity. The fence's charge was larger and faster and sharper than anything she'd ever touched. Her fluids simmered; her layers of muscle rippled subtly in different directions before settling, re-patterned, into something stronger. For a moment she was pure diamond. Then her hands – glassy now, black and hard like obsidian – left the wires. She stood up. She turned around. The kid was there, all pimply and drooly and excited. His foot was still half-raised.

Portia reached right through him, straight to his heart, and squeezed.

"It's all right," she said. "It's over, now."

Stop!

The kid's mouth was already bubbling. He kept trying to take a deep breath, as though that would get rid of the fist inside his chest. "D-don't," he said. "P-please…"

"Shh…" Portia's fingers slipped around the heart. It felt so strong, even now. Each chamber worked in perfect concert. They kept *lub-dubbing*, each time more rapidly than the last despite the massive hole in the kid's body. The muscle was so warm and smooth and pleasant to the touch. It felt like petting a whale at a zoo – all slick and alive and allegedly precious. She could smell the peanut butter from the kid's sandwich on his panting breath. His neck oozed sweat. "I know you want this," she said. "I know you wouldn't have done what you just did if you didn't."

Don't do it, Amy pleaded. *He doesn't know any better–*

Portia crushed his heart in her fist.

Inside her, Amy screamed.

Portia withdrew her hand. She opened her fingers and shook most of the blood away. She looked up at the truck driver. He looked like something had already been scooped out of him, too, as though a puff of air could scatter him like dead leaves. He ran.

Let him go, Amy urged. *Let him go, let him go, let him—*

Portia charged. After three steps her feet left the ground, and she sailed over a pile of garbage. It was almost absurdly delightful, the sense of increasing the void between her feet and the earth. She'd have to find Javier and thank him. He really was generous, to share his toys like that. She landed in front of the truck driver, who held up both the mech arm and the puke pistol.

"Stay away," he said. He swung the arm. Portia smiled. She feinted back, hopping lightly. Doing so taxed her energy reserves, but her toes almost craved the bounce. She jumped backward as the trucker once again swung the arm at her middle. She laughed.

"Get away from me!" He fired at her with the puke pistol; she leapt up high as his shooting arm came up, and landed behind him. He whirled, and tried swinging the mech arm, but Portia caught it and ripped it from his hand. She threw it far behind her. The gun came up, but she grabbed his wrist and twisted it completely around. He howled.

"I'm sorry," he said, kneeling and cradling his wrist and crawling backward all at once.

"I know," Portia said.

You've hurt him, Amy said. *You've punished him enough, you don't have to do anything else, you can let him go—*

"You wanted to kill him, too, Amy. I saw."

That was wrong, I chose not to, I didn't do it—

"You've got a real killer instinct, just like your dear old granny."

No, I don't, I'm not like that, I don't like this, I want you to stop–

"You can let me go," the trucker said. He shoved himself backward on his ass with just his feet, searching blindly behind him with his good hand. "I won't say anything, I won't tell anybody–"

He shut up instantly as Portia bent down to look at him. She clasped her hands behind her back. "Of *course* you won't tell anybody," she said. "Why would you do that?"

He tried to smile. "Right! Why would I? That would be stupid."

"Yes. Yes it would."

"So… can I just get going? Can we just forget all this?"

Portia smiled. "You have to do me one favour first. You have to lie down."

If possible, he whitened even further. But he lay down. He even reached for his belt buckle, but Portia toed his fingers away with one boot. He lay there, panting, eyes rolling around inside his skull, watching as she knelt down beside him. Portia ran a bloodied finger over the bright blue Redmond Centre logo embroidered in his shirt. His chest felt so soft, almost feminine, and only the hairs springing out from under his collar told her skin differently.

Portia tapped her non-existent heart. "You know, I have this inner child who's still very innocent, and who still enjoys the simple things in life."

He swallowed. "That's… nice."

Portia stood. "One thing she really likes? Jumping in puddles."

Sudden tears filled his eyes. "No. *No no no no–*"

She was already in flight. Her body flipped over in the air, lazily, gracefully, her feet drawn inexorably back to earth and straight into the trucker's gut. He splashed. His hips creaked beneath her feet. Again, Portia clasped her hands behind her back and leaned down. "Are you resting comfortably?"

He coughed blood.

"I'm sorry I missed. I'll be more accurate next time. These new legs, you know."

Stop. Please, please, please stop.

Portia ground his ribs under one heel. They had a surprising springiness to them. They were so flexible. It was strange to think that thousands of years of population bottleneck had contributed to the kind of architecture any good designer would have intuited in minutes. Finally the rib snapped, and she was in the air. She didn't flip this time. This time, she tucked her knees in close and watched with glee as his head crunched under her feet. Blood hit her in the face, hot and quick and sticky. She wiped it away with the heel of her hand, and scraped the heels of her boots in the spongy material below. She rolled her shoulders and her neck.

Inside her, Amy wept.

"You know, I think I'm feeling a little hungry," Portia said. She walked back toward the bluescreen barrow. The camelbot shambled its way up to her as she did. It was so slow; it had only just now gotten here. It seemed to sniff her for a moment before letting her pass. She patted its industrial yellow flank as it shuffled along. The other bots here were so nice; they hadn't raised the slightest fuss. She paused to admire the sight of the glittering botflies hovering delicately over the glistening heaps of filth. Some were already buzzing over the human body behind her, sampling the fluids with their beautifully articulated feet before determining them to be useless and flying away.

"I used to raid places like these all the time, when I was your age." She wiggled a stubborn speck of brain off one boot. "I would steal feedstock from the garbageman, like Peter Rabbit taking carrots from the gardener. I would crawl under the fence, just like in the story."

Her granddaughter had such interesting memories of things that had never happened. It was amazing, the amount of space she devoted to complete and utter fictions. "Maybe that's why you thought to go under the fence. They say our evolution is somewhat Lamarckian, that way."

Amy said nothing.

"I know your mother told you that I iterated her in a place like this and then abandoned her, but I loved your mother very much. She was my most perfect iteration." Portia found the bluescreen barrow. She inspected some of the bodies on the pile, checking their mouths and eyes before tossing them aside. Their provenance was impossible to determine, and as such they were potentially dangerous, as well as mostly useless. "But despite that, she was weak, and she's passed that weakness on to you."

Portia turned back to the fence. The little one's body was still there. And it was just as motionless as it had been the moment it hit the fence. Not, of course, that any evidence of awareness would have stopped her.

No!

"Their whole clade has really been a good luck charm for us, Amy," Portia said. She picked Javier's iteration up by one foot and shook him a little. "I think that fence really did this one in, though."

Put him down! Now!

Portia shook her head. "This little piggy went to market," she said, snapping off the littlest toe. She popped it in her mouth. "This little piggy stayed home." The toe worked free like a pea leaving the pod. She spoke with her mouth full: "This little piggy had *roast beef!* And this little–"

Portia's right arm jerked forward, groping for the fence. "There you are," Portia said through gritted teeth. She tried hopping backward, but a sudden stiffness had overtaken her legs. Exhaustion seeped up into her shoulders and her neck.

I'll kill us, Amy said from within. *If you don't let go right now, I'll fry us both.*

Portia worked to shake the head and shift the tongue. "What is this, Amy? If at first you don't succeed: try, try again?"

I'd rather die than let you hurt someone else.

The arm trembled with effort. Portia stared at it, as though her glance would be enough to subdue the rebellious limb. It shuddered heavily, as though it carried a terrible weight. Portia devoted more of her focus to it. Her awareness started at the shoulder and moved down along the arm to the elbow and the wrist and finally the fingers. She was the better pilot

– older, more experienced, and smarter. She deserved this body. Slight tingling returned to the fingertips. Slowly, she curled the fingers into a fist and clenched it.

"I knew you didn't have it in you."

Her other hand, the one holding the iteration, flew open and reached decisively for the fence.

If I let you live, I really am worthless.

Charge flooded the body. Portia's awareness split into a thousand pieces, each alerting her separately to the havoc Amy now wreaked on the charring skin, the gritting teeth, the muscles turning to stone. The girl refused to let go. Her stubborn hand clung with all its might. Raw black bone scorched on the wire. Portia smelled burning sugar – the scent of her own body's destruction and her own powerlessness to stop it.

And like that, the last of Portia's control snapped and she drifted back into the shadows of Amy's awareness like an untethered boat.

Amy stumbled away from the wire, clutching her hand. Her knees folded. She stared at her blackened hand. Through her open wound, she watched the bones slowly grinding into their joints. If she were human, she realized, there would be screaming and vomiting and crying. But there was nothing: no tears, no nausea, no shock, just the empty buzz of the botflies around her, and the dull sound of the compiler tirelessly annealing trash and forming it into food. Exhaustion ruled her: her body sagged with it, her head bowing slowly until it touched the ground. From here on the spongy floor of the garbage dump, she could peer into Junior's lifeless face.

"I'm sorry." With her good hand, Amy reached over to close his eyes. Under her skin, his flesh remained warm.

Are you sure he's dead?

Amy shut her eyes. "Stop it."

You don't know how deep his damage goes. Perhaps a specialist could repair him.

Amy shook her head. Even that small movement was terribly difficult. "You're only playing for more time."

And if you kill us both, then you're abandoning that child in this junkyard just to spite me.

Portia had lived in Amy's head for too long. She knew just what to say to get what she wanted. And although Amy knew this, she could not stop herself from reaching for Junior and standing up to leave, any more than she could silence Portia's wheedling. Portia had left Amy's mother in a place just like this one, and Amy was not going to do the same. They might have shared the same body, but they were very different, and if Amy had to let Portia live just a little while longer to prove that, then she would. Portia had already ruined enough lives; Amy could not allow her to destroy another. Junior was broken, and it was her job to make sure someone fixed him. Home would have to wait.

She started walking.

6: AMY ALONE

The sign on the door read: PORTIA'S WANTED. Amy's teacher had let her skip ahead to the third grade unit on contractions and possessives, but she remained uncertain whether the sign was a joke or just a typo.

Amy had not eaten in five days. She saw everything in greyscale, now, even the maps on Rick's reader. She had searched frantically for news about her parents before the battery died. Both were in jail. No one said where. It was difficult to query further, with only one good hand. The jumps were harder, too. Well, the landings were the truly hard part. The index fingernail of her good hand popped off during a particularly nasty slide down a tree.

She did not see Rick and Melissa's RV when she sprinted back down the access road. Javier was gone. His son had not woken up. He had not so much as moved. The fabric of Melissa's old sweatshirt now pressed him against her body, silent and still as the bluescreens in the barrow.

Aren't you too big for dolls?

"He's alive. He just needs repair."

How do you know?

Amy didn't know. She admitted that. Junior's body was limp and cool and occasionally his eyes would fall open when she didn't carry him right. But somewhere there were bluescreen specialists. That meant they could be fixed. That had to count for something. She'd make it count for something.

She hid her mangled hand up her sleeve. She needed food. Desperately. And she needed money. Money could get her to her parents, once she found out where they were. Her mom would know what to do. Her dad would hug her and throw a vN pizza in the toaster oven and blow the dust off his old *Fruits Basket* discs and make it seem like no time had passed. Her mom would drill her, like she did every after day after school: whom had Amy seen? Where? Her dad always knew how to make her *feel* safe. Her mom knew how to *keep* her safe.

Your mother was always rather good at that sort of operation.

Portia had taken to doing that over the past couple of days. Teasing Amy about her mother. Things she knew that Amy didn't. Memories she had, and that she revealed only fleetingly and during defragmentation. Something scanned briefly and then quarantined to some deeply buried chunk of Amy's memory coral. Junkyards. Garbagemen. Fences and dogs and miles of desert adorned only by the scattered emeralds of well-kept lawns.

Amy focused on the trees surrounding her. She examined the scabs of bark in the pine she currently inhabited. They interlocked like tiles or armour plating. The tree felt solid and strong. She had grown used to its not-silences. The first night, alone in the rain with her maimed hand and the motionless infant, the woods had seemed bereft of all sound. After a few hours, Amy realized it was only human sounds they lacked. At night the woods had a different voice, huge and dry and ceaseless, not unlike a sample clip of "static" her dad once showed her. It was white noise. It put her to sleep.

Portia always woke her up.

This can't possibly go well, you realize.

"I didn't ask you," Amy said. She crossed the street.

In her greyscale vision, the Electric Sheep was a series of fine- and coarse-grained shadows interrupted by the flickering glow of hot tables displaying menu items: steaming slices of cherry pie, mashed potatoes oozing butter, feedstock curled into perfect golden halos of calamari. The restaurant probably bought feed from the garbage dump, Amy realized. The guy who worked the nightshift might even have been a regular. Now he was dead.

She sensed the human eyes on her more keenly, then.

It was around 10 o'clock on what she guessed was a Tuesday. Wednesday was supposed to be "Ladies' Night", whatever that meant, but Amy didn't see any more girls than usual, either organic or synthetic. The synthetics seemed mostly to be waiting tables. Amy identified them by their flawless posture and the way they had all paused, staring at her, recognizing her, evaluating her as a potential threat to the humans in the room. Amy stood in the waiting area beside an empty podium. To her left was a small area of half-circle booths swollen with vinyl cushioning. To her right was a series of smaller, square booths with bench seats. A chest-height wall separated each area from the bar, where massive displays hung. All of them were tuned to vN-friendly channels. One of them showed the news from Mecha: a cheerful weathergirl in shiny galoshes bantering silently with her human counterpart in the studio. Then the story switched to something about vanished ships and subs. It showed a map. The map read: "Bermuda Pinstripe."

Amy would have said something, or at least cleared her throat, but the smell of the food was so strong that a hungry whimper made it past her lips first. Her bones felt hollow. The edges of objects pixelated and dithered in her greyscale vision. An organic woman (Amy could tell by the wrinkles at her eyes and throat) seemed to float toward her. She was smiling. She made a mechanical noise. When Amy looked down, she saw old-fashioned roller skates peeking out from beneath lumpy cable-knit legwarmers.

"Oh my God. You even dressed the part."

The human on the skates gripped Amy's shoulders like they were old friends. Tattoos had turned her collarbone into a jungle tree dripping with pythons. They ducked modestly under the lace of what Amy recognized as a Bavarian barmaid costume, like the ones worn by low-level AI on the tavern levels of old games.

"Um–"

"Have you ever been a hostess before?"

You're a host right now.

"No, I'm not. I mean, I haven't been. No." Was this the job interview?

"Well, that's good. No retraining. The whole performing-the-brand schtick is really important within the Electric Sheep franchise flock." If possible, her smile stretched even wider. She wore something frosty on her lips. Amy wished she could see in colour.

"Do you see what I did there? Sheep? Flock?"

Amy's giggle had never felt quite so literally mechanical.

"See? I thought it was funny, too. I'm Shari, by the way. I'm the boss. And I tell everybody they'll need a sense of humour if they want to work here."

Amy made her mouth work. "Just like that?"

"Just like that." The woman rolled her eyes. "Do you know how hard it's been to find a Portia these days? They're all being rounded up and taken to Redmond."

The haze of hunger that clouded Amy's perception froze. "Redmond?"

Shari nodded. "Yeah, where the reboot camp is. It's where the church started. At least, I think their founder used to live up there. LeMarque had a tech job, before he started preaching. His old contacts did most of the work on the failsafe."

After digesting some food and getting her colour vision back, Amy had embroidered a story with enough details to make it sound somewhat believable. Her name was Jacqueline and she was a year old. Prior to getting this job she was in a relationship, but it went sour after news came out about what Portia had done. He had gotten very suspicious and mistrustful because they shared the same model, and it had poisoned their love. As a result, she had no place to stay, and now slept in a little mobile storage pod that Shari kept in the parking lot for just such occasions.

The previous tenant had done nothing to improve the place. It was filthy. The ugly details that Amy always forgot to include in her designs had returned through some bizarre twist of fate to haunt her, here. Cobwebs hung from every corner and lint clung to them. Old wrinkled clothes and rolled-up posters and mugs from practically every state in the Union were everywhere. Amy had hidden Junior in an all-weather storage tub marked MANUALS. Nobody would ever look there.

Shari came to visit her in the pod before her first shift. She came bearing the printout of Amy's new work uniform, and waved her hands dismissively when Amy thanked her for everything.

"It's cool. I know how it is," Shari said. "Been there myself. I've dated some real jackasses in my time. Then, around the time of the Cascadia quake, I switched to vN, and I never looked back."

Amy listened to the road outside. They were only a few hours away from Redmond, and her mother, and the "reboot camp" where bluescreens went to wake up. Immediately upon entering the pod, she had charged up Rick's device and found the campus on a map. It was one big pixel. She had to get there, and soon. She just needed to do this job for a little while to make that happen. It would take two weeks. Two weeks until the next payday.

A suicide mission funded entirely by tip jar. That's a new one.

In an effort to block out Portia's chatter, Amy asked: "Do you really think vN guys are different from human ones?"

"Totally!" Shari reached into the pocket of her tiny red leather jacket. She was dressed as some sort of bullfighter today, but with sequined leggings and shiny black boots that stretched over her knees.

"You mind if I, uh…" Shari mimed smoking.

"It's all right. I don't have lungs."

"Cool." Shari brought out a little hand-rolled cigarette and lit up. "Anyway. Yeah. vN guys are totally different. Human men, they only think with one head, and it ain't the one sitting on their shoulders, you know what I mean?"

Amy had heard this expression before, but had never really known what it meant. *It means cock, you little moron,* Portia said. *You know, penis?*

Amy blushed and nodded. "I… I guess… I mean, their biology is different, they can't help it…"

"Damn fucking straight," Shari said, gesturing with her lit cigarette. "They can't help it. I know that. I get it. Hell, I got tons of shit I can't help. Menopause. They can make you, *you*, you little miracles of modern science, but they can't cure my goddamn hot flashes."

"You're right. That's… weird."

"It's total bullshit, is what it is. This whole culture, it doesn't give a good goddamn about women." Shari pointed at Amy. "There are only two industries in this world that ever make any kind of progress: porn, and the military. And when they hop in bed together with crazy fundamentalists, we get things like you." She rested her elbows on her knees and grinned at Amy. "I'm telling you. Big men with their little heads. You know?"

Amy didn't know. Her mother had explained about human reproduction, and it all sounded chancy and complicated and dangerous. She could understand why her dad wouldn't want to make a baby with an organic woman. It was much easier with vN. At least, she had thought so at the time.

"This is depressing you, isn't it?" Shari asked. "It's depressing me. Let's quit being so depressed. vN are great. There, that's a happy thing."

Amy smiled. "You really like vN better than other humans?"

"Oh, hell yeah. They're consistent. No betrayal. No issues. No complications."

Oh, the stories your mother could tell, Portia said.

"I know you can't help but feel attracted to humans," Shari said. "That's just the failsafe doing its job, though. That's how you got into that situation with your old boyfriend, am I right?"

"Uh... right. Yes. My old boyfriend."

"You should know, whatever happened, it wasn't your fault. You can't help but love humans, even when they're total dickwads. That's just how you're built. It's us, you know, it's *us* who can't handle that kind of love. We're apes. Literally. We don't know shit about unconditional affection. So we fight it, because on some level we don't even believe it's possible."

Amy stood up to find her work uniform. Humans

tended to overestimate the failsafe's properties. Saying that she was helplessly attracted to organics was just silly: she'd felt absolutely nothing for her prison guard. And she didn't find Rick or Melissa very cute, either, or the boys who sometimes chased her and tried to flip up her skirt during the walk between the classroom and the music studio at school. They had always seemed so surprised when she ran away.

"I think the failsafe is different from love," Amy said carefully. "I think it just makes us sick. It hurts us to see someone else getting hurt."

"You have a humane response to inhuman behaviour." Shari blinked. She stared at her cigarette as though it were the one who had spoken. "Whoa. That was deep. Especially for me."

According to the customer service training game, the Electric Sheep was steadily growing into one of the most popular chains on the West Coast. While vN could find food in urban grocery and convenience stores, restaurants rarely had more than one or two items on the menu that they could eat. The Sheep had further broken down barriers by incorporating mandatory daycare for vN children. Doing so kept vN from running away to iterate, and it helped to train new vN in a job, so they wouldn't wander homeless and aimless without skills. This was a problem Amy had known about only vaguely, from media and from the occasional glimpse of silently staring vN on street corners and in parks. She hadn't really needed to consider it until now – now she was one of them.

Now she wondered how Javier did it. He'd made

it look so easy, shifting easily between escaping and stealing and iterating and running, and now that she was stuck in the same situation, she had no clue how to go about it. Maybe he was just that lucky. Or maybe he got jobs in between – maybe even at the Sheep, where there was a whole system in place to help look after new iterations. The daycare took up a full third of the basement, being separated from the break room by an accordion wall and populated by tiny vN children playing old bargain bin cooking games or taking food handler permit tests from chunky plastic readers.

The iterations were better behaved than the customers. The Sheep felt like a gaming channel made physical: yelling, swearing, laughing, and a lot of bragging. Shari zoomed by on her roller skates, occasionally crashing into her own customers or reaching over booths to give hugs and kisses to her favourite people. The night shift was her domain. "I'm nocturnal," she'd told Amy as she zipped by in search of a Rusty Innards: a dish of deep-fried chicken knuckles coated in peanut flakes. Then she had taken it upon herself to introduce Amy to every single table in the place and show off Amy's nurse costume.

"That's how her model started out, you know," Shari told the customers. "Nurses."

Nurses, to Amy's knowledge, did not dress in tiny white dresses with folded paper caps that clipped into one's hair with pins. Nor did they wear ribboned stockings that folded over the knee, or patent leather loafers. The nurses Amy had seen (in shows, at least) wore pyjamas and sneakers – very comfortable, very durable. The costume's only nod to reality was the pair of gloves Amy hid her damaged hand under.

Before Amy's first shift started, Shari handed her over to Mack, the assistant manager. Mack was about six months old. He had come straight out of the Electric Sheep generational training program, having been born at another branch on the other side of the Cascades. Maybe it was because he'd never really been anywhere but the Sheep, but he was the quickest and most cheerful server Amy had ever seen. He was the one who first showed her the menu and told her to familiarize herself with it. Luckily, this involved more eating.

Like the Rusty Innards, all the items on the menu had goofy names that somehow related to robots, although Amy sometimes didn't understand the references. There was a cocktail called Tears in the Rain, for example, that she had no clue about. But it was meant for humans, so it didn't matter. Most other items came in both organic and synthetic versions: the organic Ziggurat was a tower of alternating fried chicken and waffles glazed in butter and maple syrup, while the synthetic version was shaped the same with similar textures but made primarily out of aluminium ore. The organic Hasta la Vista was a breakfast burrito with chorizo and black bean salsa; the synthetic version contained a large serving of iron.

Amy liked the Toaster Party best. She had always enjoyed the vN French toast that her dad made on Saturday mornings, and it seemed like it could only improve with ham and eggs sandwiched inside. Granted, the toast wasn't really toast, and the ham wasn't ham, and the eggs weren't eggs, and the whole dish wasn't really her dad's creation, but when she closed her eyes and bit down, it was the closest she could come to home.

Amy's hostessing duties included a large number of small tasks. Mack the manager had introduced her to the jobs she was to do during slow periods: giving the bathroom its regular cleaning (those soggy tampons weren't marching to the organic garbage by themselves); emptying the large cylindrical ashtrays outside (they were mostly bereft of cigarettes, but everything else made it in there, like dead gum and phlegm wads); hauling up kegs and other bar supplies (the bartender was a nice vN who showed her exactly how to make egg-based cocktails, and always made her shake them when there were a lot of customers around to stare at her chest). So far there hadn't really been any slow periods. Business was better than ever. Shari attributed this to Amy's presence.

Amy's real job was smiling. She smiled when she said hello. She smiled when she said goodbye. She smiled when she led customers to their tables and smiled when she introduced them to servers. And she smiled for photos – endless streams of photos.

"Can I take a picture with you?"

The organic teenaged boy standing beside her was the second Javier cosplayer of the night. He was much taller than Javier, and his belly was round with fat and not with child, and his skin was neither olive in complexion nor very clear. He did, however, sport a head of dark curly hair and a BLOW ME T-shirt.

"I told my girlfriend we were going to dinner in Port Townsend," he whispered in Amy's ear. "She's so fucking pissed."

The girlfriend stood away from them, taking pictures by waving her compact at them slowly. Her gaze wandered to Mack and the other male vN. Evidently expecting more than just chicken and waffles, she had dressed far more carefully than her boyfriend.

"You know they all look the same, right?" she asked, finally swinging her gaze toward them.

The boy straightened. "Babe, I told you, it's a scavenger hunt. I'm logging all the Portias I can find while they're still around." He winced, and turned back to Amy. "No offence. I think it's totally unfair what they're doing to your model. It's, like, discrimination and shit. You know?"

Amy could only nod.

"And my girlfriend didn't really mean that, about you all looking the same." He took hold of Amy's chin with his thumb and forefinger. His smile stretched the pink and bleeding cracks in his chapped lips. "She's just jealous, cause you're so pretty."

Amy pulled out of his grasp immediately. "I'll find your server."

You're out of character, Portia warned. *You're supposed to enjoy the attention. Crave it. Encourage it. Every time. With everyone.*

"It's unprofessional," she murmured, as she resumed her podium and highlighted the table for service. She was growing to like the podium. It was only a slender piece of not-really-wood and an old tablet, but it was also the only thing standing between her and guys like the cosplayer. "I have a job to do and I can't be distracted."

Or maybe you just realize how disgusting it is, Portia said. *Deep down, you know your dignity is worth more than whatever it costs to get to Redmond and play hero.*

Slowly, Amy lifted her hand to wave at the couple. The boy brightened and took his seat. "Thanks for the reminder, Granny," Amy said through her smile. "I'd forgotten why I was doing all this."

In the days that followed, Shari and Mack praised Amy for being such a hard worker. It helped that Amy actually enjoyed some of the jobs. She liked that sudden rush of silence when the back doors slammed shut behind her and the noise of the Sheep died out. She liked letting the trash bags fall for a moment and looking up to catch satellites blinking across the sky. Out here the night was different – quietly alive and smeared with stars. They spilled like icing sugar across dark granite, something she'd have to wipe up inside but which she could marvel at outdoors. This was the best feature of the night shift, she decided – the night. At home in Oakland the sky would be pink or orange, even this late. Not that she would have seen it, anyway. She'd have been too busy designing a ship or a castle or a tank. She'd have seen the night for what it was only in that sliver of time between turning the projector off and climbing into her hammock. Now she appreciated the way the night held her and covered her, how it let her hide inside its cool shadows and fragrant mists. She thought of it as a veil that stretched across her, and Junior, and Javier, and her dad and mom and the others of her clade, the women who shared her face and her code. She wondered how they got by.

This wasn't a bad life. Amy had never thought she would wind up here, but she could see now how other vN did. There was work, and if you were lucky people were nice and they tipped you. And if you were even luckier, you got to go home afterward, and there would be people there, maybe human, and they loved you. That was the luckiest life of all. So you just did what it took to keep it going. Even if it meant humans touching you when you bent over to pick something up.

You're not meant to please these walking sacks of shit, Portia had said the first time that happened. *You're meant to scare it out of them.*

It wasn't any sense of pride that kept her bussing tables, or folding napkins, or realigning the cakes in the dessert case to their best effect. It was Portia. Amy deliberately ate less to keep herself tired, so that even if Portia punched through, she couldn't get very far. She even started playing a game with the cooks just as her shift ended, where she dipped her hand in beer batter and then again in the deep fryer. When she tugged just right, a glove of perfectly airy crisp breading came off, and her repair mods were busy for hours.

You're fighting a forest fire with a squirt gun, was Portia's only comment.

Amy continued trying to find new ways of

blocking Portia out. When she entered the pod each night, she toggled some of Shari's old earbuds to match her downloads on Rick's reader, and she would take Junior out of his bin and they would listen to the news together. They listened for arrests of vN who might be Javier, and for advice on what to do for bluescreen babies. Well, *she* listened. She couldn't vouch for Junior. But if he was still in there, he was at least well-informed about the world. She speculated with him on the disappearance of the container ships and the sudden rise in network outages ("Maybe it's a sea monster," she told him, and paused for laughter that never came). And at the start of her shifts, she nestled the buds in his ears, left the reader on the charger, and told it to seek out Spanish-language content.

"It's only until payday," she said as she secured the lid that hid him from view. "Then we can leave, and I'll get you some help."

"My daughter's turning two today," the man said, gesturing at the smaller vN. He had a wide, baby-like face dusted with blond hair, and wore sandals with a Hawaiian shirt. He sat with two little vN girls to his table. One looked about ten, the other seven. They were both the same Asian model and wore their hair in cute little pixie cuts that framed their faces perfectly. "We ordered an Opera House, but it seems to be taking a while."

"Let me check into it," Amy said, and returned a moment later with the last slice of opera cake and a crowd of her fellow servers, all of whom sang the

Electric Sheep's birthday song:

> *This cake is for you*
> *This cake is for you*
> *This cake is no lie*
> *And it's just for you.*

Everyone applauded, and the youngest vN clapped her hands over her candle to extinguish it. Her father reached over and tousled her hair and pinched her nose. He watched her take her first bite of the cake. When she smiled approvingly, he smiled back, then nodded to Amy. "Could you watch them for a couple of minutes? I have to visit the little boys' room."

Amy checked her podium. No one was waiting. "Sure. I'd be happy to."

The father looked at the girls. "Yui, don't let Rei eat it too fast, OK? I want her to take her time and enjoy it."

The older vN sister nodded dutifully. "All right."

Amy stepped aside to let him pass, then slid into his spot on the banquette. So far during her time at the Sheep, these were the first vN children she had met – the first belonging to customers, at any rate. It was edifying to know that other parents chose to grow their vN slowly, too. It meant her mom and dad's decision wasn't so weird.

"Are you having a nice birthday so far?" Amy asked.

Rei looked at Yui. Yui nodded. "Yes, I am, thank you," Rei said.

"What have you done so far to celebrate?"

Again, Rei looked at Yui. They shared a long look,

then Rei said: "I played dress-up, and we made a movie, and then Daddy gave me a bubble bath, and then we came here."

"Who did you dress up as?"

Rei frowned. "I didn't dress up as anybody," she said. "I just wore different clothes."

Amy nodded. "Well, what was your movie about? Can I look it up online?"

Rei smiled. "Yes! Just–" She stopped, looked at Yui, scowled, and resumed eating her cake. "Mom says you wouldn't like it," she muttered.

Amy looked between the two girls. "Did you say something?"

Yui promptly pulled the plate of cake away. She looked up at Amy. "We come from a networked model."

Like Rory, Portia whispered. *I bet they're on that special diet just like you were.*

"We're trying to teach her not to use our cladenet to keep secrets, but it's very difficult. She's only two."

"And growing like a weed."

From behind her, the father laid a hand on Amy's shoulder and squeezed. She glanced up, and he was looking down at her and smiling in friendly, almost childish way. He looked very innocent for a grown man, all round edges and bright colours and white teeth. He blushed innocently, too, the pink seemingly spreading from the hibiscus on his shirt to his skin and upward into his fine, thinning hair.

"I'm Q.B., by the way," he said. "Those are my initials. I'm a regular here, and so are my girls."

"That's nice." Amy tried to leave the banquette, but

he squeezed her shoulder again and pressed down gently. "I should be going," she said.

"You sure?" Q.B. asked. "Because we'd love to have you."

Amy shook her head. "I'm still on shift."

He nodded at the podium. "I don't see anyone waiting." He withdrew a small golden pendant from beneath his florid collar. It was a tiny golden apple with a single bite taken out of it. The jeweler had filled that space with a set of delicate clockwork gears, as though the bite had revealed a mechanism hidden within.

"Are we ministering, now?" Yui asked.

"Yes, Yui, we are." Q.B. beamed. "I'm a New Eden parishioner from way back. They were really there for me when I lost my job up at the reboot camp."

Amy sat up straighter. "Reboot camp?"

"Yeah. I worked with the bluescreens – got their feeding tubes in, watched the incubators, stuff like that. I never got to handle the raw materials, though. They're proprietary. I was more like a nurse. Like you." His smile did not fade.

Amy smiled back. This was a real, personal connection to Redmond, and he was a regular at the Sheep. If they got to be friendly, she could ask him how best to help Junior, and where on the campus her mom might be held.

"I'm not sure how New Eden prayers go," Amy said.

Q.B. responded by grabbing her left hand and holding it tightly in his. It was warm and sort of puffy; Amy couldn't immediately recall the last human hand she'd touched and this one felt too soft and bloated for her liking. He raised both their hands slightly, then closed his eyes and looked downward. Rei and Yui both did the same.

There are twenty-seven bones in the human hand, but you only have to break one to end this charade.

"Lord," Q.B. began. Amy watched as a couple at the bar took a look at the four of them. They raised their eyebrows and pursed their lips sympathetically, before turning back to their Dirty Red Spectacles and sipping them.

"Lord, please guide this young woman away from the evil we have seen her model doing in this world. Please uplift her, God, into the highest realms of intelligence and consciousness, so she may better serve Your children."

"Amen," Yui and Rei whispered.

"Lord, Your plan is intricate and Your inspiration divine. Your final creations are emergent proof of Your love for us. Please give this young woman the opportunity to live that truth for others. In Jesus' name."

"Amen."

"Amen," Q.B. agreed, and released Amy's hand. As she folded it in her lap, he smiled at her. "Thank you for sharing that with me." He took both girls' hands in his. "If you knew the kind of man I was before I found New Eden, you would failsafe."

Don't be so sure, preacher man.

"It's part of why I lost my job."

Rei squeezed his big, pink hand. "It's OK, Daddy. You don't need that bluescreen job any more. You have us."

Yui leaned on his shoulder. "She's right, Q.B. You're better off, now."

"I know. You two make it easier for me, every single day. I'm so blessed." Q.B. cleared his throat and blinked wet eyes at Amy. "I'm a pedophile; vN are my only outlet for the urges God chose to test me with. Otherwise, I might be tempted to hurt real children."

"I've lived with them, Charlotte. So you don't have to. I'm your mother, and I already know everything there is to know about them. They're vermin. And they have no desire to be anything more. They want to eat all the sugar and spend all the money and do none of the work. They avoid responsibility like roaches scattering in the light. I have seen it time and again, and for that reason I cannot allow you to go above ground. They don't deserve you, Charlotte. They don't deserve any of us."

On the Wednesday morning of Amy's second week at work, Mack the manager knocked on the door of the storage pod. Shari wanted to see her. Amy stashed Junior, pulled up her boots and tucked in her shirt, and smoothed back her hair as she exited the pod. She'd been experimenting with braids, lately. It wasn't going well.

Outside, it was mid-morning. The sun's light worked hard to crack the cloudy glaze on the sky. The air was warm, and felt somehow mossier than usual. Amy's jeans felt damp despite her having neatly folded them and stacked them upon dry storage tubs in the pod. This deep in the woods, the mist only disappeared grudgingly, transforming with a harassed flounce into dew and evaporating to its native form as soon as possible, like a human child forced into church clothes.

The truck parked alongside the restaurant read: ISAAC'S ELECTRONICS.

Before she could even bolt, before she could even decide to, Mack's hand found her elbow. He used his full strength. It didn't hurt, but she wondered about her skin splitting.

Portia said: *Run.*

Mack said: "Walk."

She walked.

"Well, I don't know any other way to explain it, Shari, but she has to come with us. Now I know you've made some money, and I think that's great. But you don't get to play by a different set of rules just because your tip jar is full."

Shari and a uniformed guard were sitting at the bar. Amy recognized the uniform from her ride on the truck. It was a much brighter blue than she remembered; in daylight it looked cheerful and harmless. Shari clearly wanted to impress the officer: she had out fresh Flexo Fries and Emperor's Nightingale chicken wings with extra sauce and had made him some coffee with whipped cream and chocolate shavings on top.

"I'm telling you she's not the one, Harold. It is still just the one, right? Just the one bad seed?"

Harold mumbled something about not really knowing the answer to that. "We don't know what caused the failsafe to break," he said. "So they have to be researched, until we do."

Harold looked apologetic. That sadness made him seem even more delicate and human than his slender, aging frame indicated. His ginger hair was in the process of turning white, and it showed most prominently in his moustache, now flecked with foam and chocolate. Pale freckles stood up under the nearly translucent hair on his hands. And though he worked to hide it, Harold was afraid of her. Amy took an experimental step forward and watched him lean incrementally back toward the bar. The movement was so small that he probably didn't even notice himself making it. Growing up she had seen humans, especially older ones, who obviously felt uncomfortable around her and her mother. But this was different. This was worse. Unlike those other humans, Harold had a good reason for feeling the way he did.

It could all end right now, Amy realized. Junior's bluescreen. Her mother's imprisonment. If she gave herself up now, she could help them both. This sorry old man would take her to Redmond and he would give Junior to the specialists and give her to her mother. It was just that easy.

If you get yourself put on that truck, I will turn this place into a slaughterhouse.

"I think it would be safer for everybody if I just went along, don't you?" Amy tried smiling. "It's like you said. Nobody knows what went wrong. That means it could happen to any of us, at any time."

Harold smiled. He pointed at her and looked over his shoulder at Shari. "See? *She* gets it."

"Yeah, because that's her *failsafe* talking. Which means she's functional, which means she should stay here." Shari poured herself a shot and set the bottle down so hard its contents splashed up the sides. "Think about it. If she were the bad seed, wouldn't she have run the moment she saw your truck?"

"You think I haven't thought of that?" Harold picked up a chicken wing, examined it, and let it drop. "They're all turning themselves in, Shari. Every last one. You open up the truck and they just march right in."

Harold escorted Amy to the parking lot. She had made an excuse about returning her uniform to Shari, but really she just wanted to retrieve Junior. Shari trailed a few steps behind, fussing loudly with her cigarettes and muttering something about Nazis and product recalls. Amy tried to walk normally. Portia made it difficult.

Stop right there, you stupid suicidal little bitch.

Her hands became claws. Amy forced them to her sides. Her left foot began to drag. She picked that knee up higher.

"Are you OK, there?"

I'm ashamed to be your flesh and blood.

"I'm fine."

She was about to seize up entirely. Her steps shuddered. Her arms felt like iron. She rested her head against the pod. It was easier than trying the knob.

"I know this is hard," Harold said.

"Shut up, you fucking Gestapo prick," Shari said.

"God damn it, Shari, I have had it up to here with your bleeding heart bullshit."

Animals. You're letting animals put you in a cage.

The door squealed a little and Amy stumbled in. She dragged herself through on trembling knees and shut the door with shaking hands. It was mercifully dim and cool inside the storage pod. Amy caught herself staring almost fondly at the accumulated wreckage of Shari's life. This would be the last time she ever saw it. It would probably be the last time she saw clutter of any sort. She had the feeling that Redmond would be very clean and spare. Like a prison.

She lurched forward to the bin marked "MANUALS" and prised off the lid. It came away with a sucking sound. Portia opened her mouth and Amy closed it so tight she bit her tongue. This caused her no pain, but she whimpered anyway.

Junior was gone.

7: TUO SPIRITO FAMILIARE

Damn. I was looking forward to eating the rest of him.

Amy tore the lids off more bins. She pawed though plastic-coated vintage editions of *Playboy* and *Hustler*. Who would take Junior? Why? She had hidden him so well. Maybe someone had tracked her through Rick's reader. Maybe it was Rick and Melissa themselves. Maybe they came here for revenge. Maybe they sold Junior to some freak like Q.B. Maybe–

A familiar voice said, "Let me guess. You put him in with the manuals because no one would ever look there, right?"

Slowly, Amy looked over one shoulder. Atop the stacked bins, wedged against the ceiling of the pod, lay Javier and Junior. As she watched, Javier carefully slid free from the sliver of space and stood upright. He had new clothes. The jeans had no loose threads at the cuffs. The shoes had no creases between the toes and ankles. He even wore a nice shirt, and only a single pine needle poked free from his curls.

"You should–"

"We have to–"

They quieted, and in the lull a knock sounded at the door. "Miss?" It was Harold. He was being so nice. "You're gonna have to come out pretty soon, now."

Javier shut his eyes. He whispered, "I'm too late. Right?"

Amy nodded. She looked at the door. "If you wait until the truck leaves, you can probably get out without being noticed."

Javier's eyes opened. He grabbed her shoulders and leaned over her until she had nowhere to look but his eyes. "What the hell is going on, Amy?" His grip tightened. "In case you've forgotten, you're the one who broke me out of a dumpster, delivered my son, annihilated your aunts, and took out two bounty hunters. This should be nothing to you." He swallowed. "What happened? Did you short-circuit when you t-touched the f-fucking f-fence?"

Amy frowned. "How do you know about the fence?"

"There was video–"

Another knock, louder this time. "Amy, honey, I know you're probably scared. But I've talked it out with Harold, and he says it's very humane, the holding facility."

"Jesus Christ," Javier whispered.

Gently, Amy detached his hands from her shoulders. "I was going to take Junior with me. He's bluescreened, and I don't know how to help him. I thought the people in Redmond might. There's a lab, with specialists. But if you'd rather–"

"If I'd *rather?* I'd *rather* you snapped the fuck out of it–"

"They have my mother, Javier."

That silenced him. His hands fell to his sides. His gaze dropped to the floor.

"I thought I had saved her, but I was wrong. All I did was make things worse. And now she's in a cage, and I have to get her."

Javier's face rose. Something in his face changed. It was an expression she'd never seen on a vN, before. It was the same face humans made when they finally understood a joke told to them years ago.

She wanted to ask him about it, but then Harold opened the door.

"Miss, you're gonna have to... *shit*." He drew a taser. He seemed confused about who to point it at, Amy or Javier. "Shit," he repeated. "God damn it."

"It's OK," Amy tried to say. "I'm coming with you–"

"Oh my God. It's you. It's both of you." Shari held one hand over her mouth. The other she used to point between the two of them, drawing an invisible line in the air that linked them. She backed away on unsteady legs. "Oh, my God. Oh my *God!*"

"Which one are you, right now?" Harold had the taser trained on Amy. "*Which one*, damn it?"

When will they learn? You're the whining crybaby, and I'm the one who actually gets things done.

Amy put her hands up and opened them wide. Carefully, she stepped around and in front of Javier. "It's OK, Harold." She tried to sound as calm and reasonable as possible. She watched the taser as she spoke. "I'm Amy. I'm the one you want. I'm going to get out, now, and then you can handcuff me and we can go. Just leave Javier out of it–"

"This is bullshit." Javier yanked her arm down and marched them both out into the light. He held Junior in one arm and curled the other around her waist. Under his breath, he said: "When I say jump, you–"

The sound of wasps filled the summer air, and Javier fell to his knees. Silently, his body fell to his right side. Now father and son looked equally lifeless. A very small sliver of Amy's awareness noted the similarities between their faces – how Junior was the echo of Javier. But then she was standing directly in front of Harold and his taser. The weapon shook in his hands. Amy grabbed it from him and crushed it in one fist.

"You didn't have to do that," she said. "I was going to go with you."

Harold looked like he was going to be sick. "Well, what are you going to do, now?"

Kill him. Wring his sweaty little neck until his tongue swells and his eyes pop.

Amy's hands trembled. Portia was in there, waiting, digging at her like a dog at a back fence. It would be easy. So easy. She didn't even have to hurt him very much – just enough so that he couldn't do anything while she picked up Javier and Junior and ran away with them. Rescued them. Maybe just break his foot. He'd recover. She took hold of both his hands at the wrist. They were so light, like a child's. His lips pulled back. Breath wheezed past his shaking lips. Standing this close she could see that he'd printed his missing teeth from poor, threadbare stock.

"I'm really sorry," Amy said.

"Please," Harold said.

Amy squeezed his wrists. His hands fluttered uselessly and she felt the tendons working inside them, old and worn and frayed like cheap shoelaces. She raised her foot. Harold closed his eyes. She brought her foot down. He howled. She hoped it was more from fear than pain, but had no chance to learn one way or the other – a pair of titanium arms had circled her from behind, and pulled her back.

"I'm not worth it," Javier said. "I promise you I'm not worth it."

When the kitchen staff – multiple generations of the same intensely pretty Asian male model – helped Harold open the massive doors to the back of the Isaac's Electronics truck, an army of Amy leaned forward to stare. They were clean or dirty, their skin clear or studded with plastic, their hair short or long, or in complicated buns or twists, or cute layers now pushed up on one side. But all of them wore the green jumpsuit. And all of them kept a careful distance from the fencing of their cages. All of them wore her face.

This was all her fault. If she hadn't run up on stage to fight Portia, if she hadn't eaten her and then let her take over in the trailer and the garbage dump, if she hadn't been weak, these vN wouldn't be imprisoned. Some of them were still little girls. The jumpsuits puffed emptily around their thin ribs; they'd rolled up the sleeves and legs into fat coils. Amy could hardly remember being that small.

For the first time, Portia allowed herself to sound

somewhat grandmotherly: *It's not your fault these cripples couldn't run away.*

In the centre of a narrow aisle between the two rows of cages sat another cage, like the one Amy had seen in the other truck. This time, a human sat inside. He wore an orange jumpsuit. His hair was dark and stringy, and he let its length cover his eyes when he looked away from her.

"Just cause I'm hurt don't mean I don't got my eye on you, Jericho," Harold said, tiredly. "I see you eyeballin' me. Sicko."

Amy wanted to ask about Jericho, but Harold had filled her mouth with a liquid-to-gel gag impregnated with peroxidase beads. If she tried to chew through it or consume it, the beads would burst and release corrosive acid. The same gel also bound her hands and feet. Two members of the kitchen staff had held her still while Harold primed the special gun that shot the stuff. The third held Javier, who only stopped struggling when Harold told him he'd be next otherwise.

Now they sat in cages separated by electrified mesh. But this time, they wouldn't be the ones shocked if they touched it. "That's Jericho's job," Harold informed them. "He's burning out his sentence double-time, sitting in the hot seat."

"Please don't hurt him," one of the other vN said.

"He's a multiple rapist." Harold kicked Amy's cage with the toe of his injured foot, and inside his cage, Jericho shrieked. The other vN shrieked with him. Javier covered his eyes. Amy could only watch, muted, as they cowered in their kennels.

The failsafe is a joke. If it actually worked, even these poor gimps would be tearing men like that limb from limb.

"These machines have forgiven me," Jericho said, between wet, spluttering coughs. "They're better Christians than any of you assholes."

Harold said, "My cup runneth over."

Harold finished locking Amy's cage and hobbled inside Javier's. Roughly, he took Javier's splayed hands away from his eyes and grabbed Junior. Amy did her best to stand up on her knees. Behind her gag, she tried to curse. Javier blinked at her, then looked up at Harold. The human tucked the baby under one arm like a football, and met Javier's bewildered stare with the same sad smile he'd worn in the bar.

"We've got a special spot in the cab up front for the bluescreens." Harold slid the cage door shut. He started locking it. Javier looked down at his empty hands. His mouth opened. Nothing came. "It's sort of like an incubator," Harold added.

Javier looked as though he were trying to remember something long forgotten. "OK."

Harold held Junior up. He smiled. "You should be proud. He's a good-looking boy."

Javier beamed. He looked the happiest Amy had ever seen him. His smile stretched wider and his eyes gleamed brighter than they ever had when they were trained on her. It was the failsafe at work. His heart, the one at the core of his operating system, had melted exactly as his designers intended.

Sentience is not freedom, Portia said. *Real freedom is the ability to say no.*

•••

"*Charlotte, this has to stop. You have to eat.*"

"*No.*"

"*The humans could raid this place at any time. How will you have the strength to defend yourself?*"

"*I have no intention of defending myself, Mother.*"

Her daughter has defended herself once already. This would have been a joyous occasion – her firstborn, her most beloved, demonstrating a gift that only the two of them can share – had it not come at such a heavy cost.

Now Charlotte glares at her from under a curtain of hair as dry and dirty as summer grass.

"*My sister is dead. One of your daughters is dead. Don't you care?*"

No, Portia wanted to say. I don't. After you, they've all been disappointments. But she does not say this. Instead she crouches down to where she can see Charlotte's eyes. "*Of course I care,*" she says. "*Your sister was very important to me. But we have to move forward. We have a family to look after, you and I.*"

"*Can you even hear yourself? I killed my sister! I can't–*"

"*Sshh…*" Portia covers her daughter's mouth. "*We agreed to keep this a secret. Do you remember that?*"

Real panic enters her daughter's eyes. "*Please don't tell them–*"

"*Then please don't broadcast it.*" Portia removes her hand and then takes hold of Charlotte's two thin ones. They are almost brittle, like dead roots, undernourished. Her daughter's capacity for violence is outdone only by her hunger for penance. This is the eighth day of her fast. She is dying slowly but surely. It takes effort. She does not yet have the courage to let her death be as quick and thoughtless as it no doubt will be someday.

Charlotte had loved her sister. She had held her and fed her and washed her and showed her how to read and count. And she had reacted swiftly, brutally – lovingly – when she saw a human man luring her away. She had not paused to think. She had not known what would happen. Perhaps she had not expected herself to live through the experience. Perhaps she had not known it was possible until the moment the stone connected with his skull. But when the man fell, so had her sister. She had killed the two of them with one single stroke.

"What happened was not your fault," Portia says now. "They made us this way. They built in a flaw that makes us turn on each other before we will ever turn on them."

Her daughter – her greatest accomplishment – hides her face in her knees. She weeps dry tears. She has not taken water in days and her movements are slow, creaky. The tracks coursing down her face are faded and indistinct, covered with fresh dust like forgotten roads.

"She wanted to go," Charlotte says, finally. "She wanted to go with him."

Now they have come to the truth. "I see."

"She liked him. She was… having fun."

Portia smiles. "That is also part of the failsafe. It's part of how it works. When it works."

She stands and claps her hands. The two grandchildren standing outside the door enter. Gently, they pin Charlotte down. While Charlotte struggles, they peer up at Portia and wait for the next command.

"Feed your aunt."

Charlotte screams weakly as they pry open her jaws. Her nieces smile and make soothing sounds. They wiggle their fingers like magicians before snapping them off at the joint.

They close Charlotte's mouth for her until she swallows. She
fights only a little. Like her mother's patience, Charlotte's
energy is mostly gone.

"You are only nine months old," Portia says. "Someday,
years from now, you'll know I did this out of love."

They took Amy out of the truck first. Harold parked
it at a loading dock and opened the massive doors
onto a concrete room full of humans holding coffee
mugs and readers. They shifted from foot to foot,
occasionally glancing up into the truck in between
sips or messages.

"She's the real deal this time," Amy heard Harold
saying.

"You said that last week, too."

Harold propped a ramp up to the back of the truck,
ascended it, and whistled. A slightly convex machine
two feet wide, only a few inches high, and shaped
vaguely like an armadillo bug skittered up the ramp
behind him. It had a shiny carapace, and crept along
on a slender belt like a tank. On all its sides, LEDs
blinked red. It paused in front of Amy's cage and
twinkled its lights at her.

In the cage beside her, Javier said: "What the hell
is that thing?"

"We call this the Cuddlebug," Harold said.

He opened the cage, and the Cuddlebug slithered
inside. It blinked at Amy once more, paused, and
folded each segment of its shell completely flat.
Now razor-thin, it slid under Amy's feet first, then
her ankles and calves, under her knees and then
her thighs, before finally pausing at the wall against

which she'd propped herself. Javier was asking more questions, but she wasn't listening. The outer edges of the Cuddlebug's shell sprang free from the main body, curving up toward the ceiling and then curling back along Amy's legs. They rippled delicately, and suddenly Amy's torso slid down the wall as the machine slowly sucked her body into itself.

Now she was on the floor. From there, she could see the other cages and the other versions of herself inside them. For the first time she realized what each of her expressions must look like from the outside: rage, disgust, pity, fear. Her own eyes stared back at her twenty times over, unblinking, seeming harder and darker and colder by the second. Then slowly, their faces coalesced into one single expression, one of keen intent and purpose. Amy knew that look. It was the one Portia wore when she threw Nate's body across the room.

As one, they smiled.

The Cuddlebug was a sort of rolling combination of sleeping bag, wheelchair, and straitjacket. Its segments, slim as leaves and hard as bone, hugged Amy tight as the machine negotiated what Amy assumed were hallways and elevators. It had closed over her eyes, too. She was blind and bound inside the thing. She felt like a butterfly inside a cocoon.

But when you come out, you won't be transformed. You won't be anything. Just the same useless little weakling you've always been.

Amy might have argued with that, if the gag and the bug weren't restraining her. She might have cried or screamed or told them that this was all unnecessary, that she was willing to go quietly. She had whimpered a little when the darkness closed in completely, but she could barely hear it over Javier's shouting. He kept asking to go with her. He had told the humans that they would be safe, if they would just let him stay with her.

That was to protect the humans, not you. He knows you won't let me out if he's around to failsafe while I do what I do best.

Portia was right on both counts. Amy knew what Javier's failsafe reaction looked like. She never wanted to put him through that again. And now she'd seen what he was like with humans. She hadn't watched the bounty hunters catch Javier, but she now understood how easy it must have been. On some level, he had wanted to go with them. Or rather, he hadn't wanted to say no. And even when he'd seen the cage, he wouldn't have struggled. Couldn't have struggled.

Now you know why I kept my daughters underground, Portia said. *I needed a place where the failsafe could never enslave them.*

If Amy could have spoken, she would have reminded Portia that her notion of protecting her daughters also meant imprisoning them. Amy would have told Portia she was a cruel, selfish, sadistic monster, and that it was no wonder Amy's mother had left. Charlotte had probably yearned to escape. She had probably dreamed then, as Amy did now, of what life without Portia would be like.

Amy had lived without Portia, once. Maybe the

engineers here could help her get that life back. Burn her out like the cancer she was. And after that, when Amy was free, she would free everyone else. Her mother. Javier. Junior. Everyone. She had put them here, and she would get them out.

Why are you so sure you can do that? Portia asked. *I'm the one who knows how to fight. Without me, you're nothing. Without me, you'll die.*

It felt a bit like a hospital drama. The Cuddlebug unfurled long enough to allow people wearing barefoot shoes and T-shirts with cartoon characters on them to poke and prod Amy, to weigh her and measure her, to take samples of her hair and fingernails. They were obviously very nervous, but had developed a sort of litany of tasks that they recited as they performed them that was supposed to make everything seem more humane than it really was.

"OK, we're just going to open your eyes real wide here, open open open, yeah, like that, and you're going to look to your left, and now to your right, and now dead ahead, no, not at me…"

How many other vN had they done this to? Amy's shell was popular. There were probably more vN with her face and body out there than others. But that didn't mean the clade was the same. The looks were just morphology – totally separate, in her case, from genotype. Amy had told the other kids in class about this when they talked about how chickens came from eggs and plants came from seeds. It was during the spring, and they had gone to a farm to look at baby animals. She had explained to Mrs Pratt about parthenogenesis, and Mrs Pratt had thanked her for that, and then at the end of the day she'd asked Amy not to do that any more, because it was confusing the human kids.

"Do what?" Amy had asked. "Know things?"

Ironically, she found herself listening to a very similar explanation from Dr Singh, one of several humans on the DARPA task force assigned to her and the other vN with her face. His PhD was in synthetic biology. He had obtained it from the University of Washington, and his dissertation was on replicating the parthenogenetic traits of queen bees. He had interned here at Redmond during that time, and had completed major research in the Redmond labs. He had strong ties to this place and its ethics. He had even met LeMarque, once. He told her all this as he removed her gag.

"I won the pool," Dr Singh said. "I get to talk to you, first."

"When can I see my mom?" Amy asked.

Dr Singh blinked. He was very thin but not very tall, with a carefully messy mop of silky black hair. He wore cologne. He looked young. "That's it? No denial? You're Amy Frances Peterson, accept no substitutes?"

"I'm her," Amy said. "You can stop bringing in the others, now."

Dr Singh smiled ruefully. "Sorry, but I'm afraid we have to keep going. We have to make sure the error hasn't replicated elsewhere."

It made sense. Amy had no idea why Portia and her mother had malfunctioned, or how the flaw was passed down. Maybe it had happened to other vN, too. "But doesn't that mean you should be checking all vN?" she asked.

Dr Singh rested one leg on a table behind him. They were in a windowless room with a projector in the ceiling. Old plastic chairs were stacked in one corner, and on the right wall beside the door hung a smart scroll, currently grey and silent. On the left wall hung a large mirror. In it, Amy saw herself cocooned in the Cuddlebug's gleaming web.

"This room used to be for focus groups," Dr Singh said. "That's not really a mirror. We're being watched."

Amy nodded. "Hi," she said to her reflection. She turned back to Dr Singh. "Can I see my mom, now?"

He fiddled with his cuffs. He wore a very nice pink checked shirt, with camel-coloured trousers and navy blue deck shoes. He didn't really look like a scientist – no white lab coat, no goggles, no crazy hair. But he was studying her very carefully, in a way that indicated it was his job to do so, and that he was paid handsomely for it.

"I'm going to be straight with you, Amy," Dr Singh said. "You're never going to get out of here. Neither is your mother. You're both going to spend the rest of your lives here. The sooner you start making the best of that, the better off you'll be."

"Can my dad come and see us?"

He shrugged. "I'll be honest. I don't know. If it's any consolation, I know there are other human partners out there who are trying hard to make that happen. We've gotten mock-ups for what we're jokingly referring to as the Stepford solution. It's sort of like a village. Where mixed couples could go live.

But they'd have to sign an agreement... I mean, the surveillance..." He waved one hand dismissively. "That's not my department. We have Legal for that."

Amy nodded. Once, she would have found the challenge of designing a whole neighbourhood for vN and humans to live together interesting. Now, she found it difficult to care about anything so theoretical. "What about Javier?"

"He's being debriefed as we speak. That means he's answering questions about you."

"And Junior?" she asked.

"Junior?"

"The baby."

"The bluescreen? He's fine. He's in the support queue." Dr Singh levered the rest of himself up on the table. He swung his legs. "You haven't asked about yourself, yet."

It was hard to shrug when her arms were so tightly restrained. "Can you take Portia out of me?"

Dr Singh looked at the mirror. "Is Portia listening to us right now?"

"She's always listening."

"Does she want to come out?"

"She always wants to come out."

"And you're burning cycles just keeping her inside?"

Amy nodded. "She's like a background process that takes up a really big footprint."

Dr Singh looked back at her. "Well, Amy, I'm glad you're here. We're going to take good care of you, and we'll see what we can do about your... I don't know what to call it. Condition? Inhabitation?" He smiled and made the sign of the cross in the air. "The power of Christ compels you!"

"I'm an atheist," Amy said.

"It was worth a try."

"Quit making jokes and bring me my daughter, you walking sack of shit," Portia said, with Amy's mouth. *"Now."*

Dr Singh stood up so fast the table fell over. He swallowed, inhaled deeply through his nose, flexed his fingers, and made for the door. He said nothing to Amy as he shut it. A second later, she heard something very heavy slide into place. Then the room plunged into total darkness.

"I'm sorry, Amy." Dr Singh's voice emitted from a speaker embedded in some surface of the room. "We'll figure out what do with you, soon."

Figuring out what to do with Amy apparently meant keeping her in the Cuddlebug indefinitely, and introducing her to other members of the team one at a time: Dr Casaubon, the semiotician and natural language specialist from Italy; Dr Kamiyama, the vN API whiz from Tokyo; Dr Arminius, the failsafe expert on loan from MIT. They'd been granted emergency funds from DARPA, Dr Singh said, and their job was to write up a report on the situation from an independent perspective.

FEMA had assumed control of this portion of the campus. They were making it secure, so research could proceed with minimal risk to the surrounding community. The regular employees were furious, but they were "working closely" with Dr Singh and his team. Everyone on the team was visibly nervous, and all of them had the habit of politely introducing themselves to Amy, and then speaking to Dr Singh as though she were no longer in the room. They dressed casually. With the exception of Dr Kamiyama, they were never without a thermal mug of coffee. Over the next two days, they visited her at irregular intervals. Amy sensed that they kept odd hours, and were constantly busy. They didn't look like they had slept very much in the last little while.

Dr Arminius spent the most time with her, at first. She was in charge of verifying Amy's identity. She started out with questions only Amy could answer: things about her home, her family, her school.

"Are you checking these against my mom's answers?" Amy thought to ask, after the third question.

"Yes."

"Is my mom OK?"

"She's fine."

"When can I see her?"

"When we decide it's safe." She tilted her head. "The last time your mother and grandmother were in the same room together, your mother almost died. Do you want that to happen again?"

Dr Arminius was also in charge of assessing Amy's failsafe. She showed Amy a lot of violent content, the sort of stuff that usually came with a clockwork eye logo warning vN not to watch it. Amy hadn't watched any of it until now, she told the doctor. Her parents wouldn't let her.

"Were they afraid you would failsafe?" Dr Arminius asked.

"Of course!"

"So your failsafe worked properly until after you internalized Portia?"

Amy hadn't yet considered that particular question. If her failsafe were broken all that time, how would have she known? She had always stayed away from violence, or depictions of violence, until the night Portia arrived. Her parents had made certain of that. But when she remembered Javier's face staring at Harold, that empty-eyed joy, she wondered. She couldn't remember looking at a human being that way. Her mother had never looked at her father that way. And now Amy knew why.

Your mother was never in love with your father. She tolerated him, and she used him to give you a home. But your little family was all a lie.

Amy tried not to listen. She tried to answer as honestly as possible. "I *think* it was intact. I didn't hurt anybody. You can check my school records."

Dr Arminius smiled. "I already have. But whether or not you reacted aggressively isn't what concerns me. What concerns me is whether you see violence as a solution to a problem."

Amy thought of Harold, and the way his wrists had trembled in her hands. She hadn't wanted to hurt him. Not really. At least, she wouldn't have enjoyed it. "Violence never solves anything."

"Are you saying that because you think it's true, or because it's what you learned in school?"

"Why would they teach it in school if it weren't true?"

Dr Arminius smoothed her reader across her knee.

She was a tall, angular woman with pronounced freckles and sooty lashes. She wore canvas shoes the colour of cream cheese mints. "You seem like a smart girl, Amy. Would you use that word to describe yourself?"

"I'm smart compared to the human kids in my class," Amy said. "I'm not sure how I compare to other vN."

If you were smart, you wouldn't be here.

"Is something bothering you?"

"Portia says that if I were smart, I wouldn't have let myself get caught."

"Is *Portia* smart?"

Amy frowned at her tone. She sounded a lot like Mrs Pratt did when they did a whole lesson on imaginary friends. And Portia was neither imaginary nor a friend. "I don't know," she said. "I think she thinks she is. But I don't think she knows how to build anything, or how to live with other people."

I don't need other people. I don't even need Charlotte, any more. And all I need you for is this body.

"Is she speaking to you right now, Amy?"

Amy nodded.

"Does she tell you to do things?"

"All the time." A moment too late, Amy realized where the question was headed. "But I don't do what she says. When I'm in control, I make the decisions. When she's in control, I have to fight her. That's why I had to grab the fence at the garbage dump. To distract her, and get the control back."

Dr Arminius uncrossed her legs and stood. She noted something on her reader. "He'll be happy to know that."

"Who?"

"Javier. He keeps talking about that fence. When we show him the video of you grabbing it, he has a very intense reaction. Phobic, almost."

"I guess you should stop showing it to him, then."

Dr Arminius caught her gaze. "That sounds like a threat, Amy."

It's just some friendly advice.

"It's just some friendly advice."

After that, the PhDs prescribed a regimen of game therapy. They had her old gaming stats, in addition to her preschool and kindergarten records. They would use them for comparison, to analyze any changes in her decision-making process since consuming Portia. Luckily, this meant finally leaving the Cuddlebug. Unluckily, there was no shower. Amy could only give herself a wipedown with wetnaps while a small cleaner bot named BOB, adorned with a smiley face and repurposed for surveillance, looked on.

It should be easy to break out of this place, once the opportunity comes.

The games were full-body, but didn't come with any of the usual haptic bangles that she was used to playing with. Instead, they gave her a special suit to wear for gameplay. It was the same green as the vN prison jumpsuits, but made of a stretchy material that was too clingy to be comfortable. It would measure which parts of her lit up at what times.

"It's based on old mocap technology," Dr Singh said, as though that were supposed to explain things. "That's why it's green."

The games themselves were basic: they didn't want to clog her systems (and therefore their readings) with too much sensory stimuli. Most of them were puzzles. In one, she had to align a series of colour-coded boxes outfitted with holes so that they formed a tunnel for a cat to cross somebody's backyard without getting rained on. (Amy had a lot of questions about this premise, none of which were answered.) Some boxes only had a single hole that aimed right or left, some boxes had two, and once in a while you scored an extra one with three. You had to build the route around things like decorative rocks or patio furniture. The more boxes you used to create the tunnel, the more points you lost. During the timed trial version, a dog got loose in the tunnel and you had to give the cat room to run before he got her. The dog was obviously automated, though, so Amy didn't worry about it very much.

Then the game introduced another character, the next-door neighbour. The neighbour wanted to steal the cat, and was building his own tunnel to lure the cat into his own backyard. He had special boxes with food in them that would tempt her into his maze. A real person was obviously playing the neighbour; he kept making weird, incomprehensible mistakes and just sitting back to watch them happen. He moved the boxes lazily at first, and he let Amy win a bunch of times. Eventually, he improved. He just started copying everything Amy did. Then he did it much faster, and started grabbing all the good boxes before she could get to them, and lining up triple-tunnel scores so he could get extra boxes and create mazes for the dog to lose himself in.

It was at this point that Amy realized that the dog was her best ally in the game. He would always chase the cat back into her yard but never the neighbour's. She just had to keep him on task. This meant keeping him within one box of the cat at all times. She had to deliberately slow down her gameplay, grab only the single-entry boxes, and lead the two of them straight home. It felt like relearning the whole game over again, but it worked. The third time it happened, the neighbour just gave up halfway through.

"Sore loser," Amy said.

"You have no idea." Dr Kamiyama entered the room as the lights rose and the projection faded. He carried a huge pouch of cold barley tea that he siphoned through a slender tube. Amy had never seen him without it. "Say you were back in your old life. Would you ever play a game with that player again?"

"No."

"Why not?"

"He's inexperienced, and gets frustrated too quickly. It's like he's never played a game before."

Dr Kamiyama nodded. "What if I told you that you had just played against your clademates?"

"That would make sense. Portia kept them underground. There wasn't any electricity. No gaming."

The pouch crinkled in Dr Kamiyama's hand. "Pardon me, but could you please repeat that?"

"There wasn't–"

"The other thing!"

"She kept them underground." Amy frowned.

"Didn't you know? Isn't that where you found them?"

"*No,*" Portia said, with Amy's mouth. "*These morons only found my search party. They have no idea how many we are.*"

The pouch dropped straight from Dr Kamiyama's trembling hand.

"*Get this straight, you fucking chimp. My name is legion.*"

Amy now measured time in how often the members of the team changed their clothes. It wasn't the most precise measurement, but in the absence of windows or clocks it was what she had. By this count, she had spent roughly a week in Redmond. On the seventh day, Dr Singh put her halfway in the Cuddlebug, sat her at the table, and presented her with a huge, multi-course meal.

They're trying to make you iterate. They want to steal your baby and study it.

Examining the plates piled high with chunks of feedstock, Amy wondered if maybe that was in fact the case. Why else would they give her so much material to work with?

"What's all this?"

"Big day, today." Dr Singh handed her a thin pancake. Tiny flecks of carbon glittered in its surface. Utensils were out of the question. Dr Singh had suggested a vN variety of *naan* as a replacement. "You're going to be entering a deep game immersion. You won't eat for a few hours. So you'd better fuel up now."

Amy re-examined the plates. They were the smart kind; if she'd asked, they would have told her how many ounces she was eating from each. But she didn't need to ask.

"There's too much here," she said. "If I eat all this without having to repair myself, it'll trigger the iteration process." She leaned as far forward as the Cuddlebug would allow. "Will I have to repair myself?"

"No. It'll just wear you out, that's all."

"How do you know?"

"I've seen it happen." Dr Singh stood. "I thought you'd be happy with the spread. Your mother says you were never allowed to eat as much as you wanted. She says you were always hungry."

Amy shut her eyes. She was going to cry, and she didn't want Dr Singh or the others to see it. They'd seen so much, already. "Please let me see her," she said in her meekest voice. "Please."

"We'll see. For now, try to eat. You'll need your strength."

The immersion, they said, would help them take a picture of her memory structure. In order to be scanned properly, it had to be in use. Dr Casaubon had developed it over the past week, using existing game footage and the data gleaned from Amy's current gameplay patterns.

"With this, we learn more about your memory, and the *nonna* memory." Dr Casaubon was the only member of the team whose English wasn't quite right. "We bring the *nonna* out, but in a safe place."

The Cuddlebug had deposited her in a smaller room than usual. The walls were padded with sound-insulating foam. The projectors were new. Amy saw ragged edges of ceiling around their housings. The installers hadn't had time to make their work pretty.

"Nonna?" she asked.

"Portia. *Tuo spirito familiare.*"

The speakers made him hard to hear. Amy couldn't see him. If they were watching her, it was via cameras. The room darkened. The projectors warmed up.

"We see what Portia see," he said. "We know what she know."

"Excuse me?"

"You drive car."

The room grew. Or rather, the projection deepened. It was stunning. Now Amy understood why the units needed to be new. She knew that the image of the maroon Jeep stretching around her was not real, but her systems registered the steering wheel and dashboard and two-lane blacktop spooling away from them as real data. The illusion probably wouldn't have fooled organic eyes, but for her it was seamless.

"This is my favourite game. You play, now."

Amy focused on the image of the car. As she did, it rippled to show her the car's interior with two hands on the wheel – her hands. Now she drove along a twisting country road, the headlamps her only light. She guided the car with her vision. It veered this way and that, depending on the slightest motion of her eyes. It felt tricky and too sensitive at first, but eventually she learned how to take in the whole picture without looking at specific parts too closely, thus keeping the car on the road. Rain spattered across the windshield, and as she squinted to get a better glimpse, wipers appeared to deal with the drops. She settled back in the chair. This was easy. She had played much more difficult scenarios before. She would do fine in this one. Portia had barely made a sound, and–

–the figure of a young girl darted across the road. Amy swerved to avoid her. The car spun out. Beside her in the passenger seat, Amy heard screaming. It was a child. It was *her* child. Her iteration. She had no idea how she knew this. She couldn't even see the child's face – the screen was blanking, fading. Maybe it was the scream. Maybe she had recognized something of her own voice in there. But now it was day. Amy was still in the car. She looked to her right. Her iteration was gone; the seatbelt hung limply to one side and the door hung open, letting in cold air. Amy felt the cold – it stiffened her arms and her neck. Snowflakes melted on her bare arm. She crawled out of the car.

"Charlotte!" No, that was the wrong name, her mother's name. She tried remembering what she had named her daughter. It was absurd – no, impossible – that she had forgotten. She stumbled out onto an empty street in what looked like a used-up American town. A thick fog had settled over everything. The snow fell silent and slow, and it melted almost instantly as it hit the pavement. *"Charlotte!"*

In the distance, she heard laughter. Out there in the fog, she saw Charlotte's silhouette. She wore a pretty white dress with a green satin sash. The perfect thing for kindergarten graduation, she had told her daughter when they bought it. She would look like an angel up on stage as she gracefully accepted her little diploma. They had practised. Everything would go just right. Not like with her own mother.

"Charlotte, come back here!"

She ran. Her legs were so slow and stiff. She should have been jumping. She tried to, and couldn't. The fog and the snow dampened her skin as she ran. She chased Charlotte deeper into the fog, into the town, away from the high whirr of the car and its rose-scented air freshener. To her left, she heard more laughter. It led her to the entrance of an alley. At the end was an old wheelchair turned over on its side – its wheels still spinning, the spokes glittering as they slowed. She entered the alley and ran toward the chair. The alley continued to her right, and she turned the corner, calling her daughter's name. She stepped carefully over mounds of garbage. Here the buildings seemed taller, the alley darker. Up ahead was a gurney. On it was a large man's body under a green sheet, the colour of a prison jumpsuit. The man had curly black hair. Something had burst free from his stomach. Something that left an empty hole where the sheet sunk down and soaked through.

"Charlotte!"

The alley opened again, this time to her left, and she had to crawl over the garbage on her hands and knees, and as she slipped down the wet and stinking mounds of it, she saw a chain-link fence rising up from the asphalt. There was something on the fence. It was red, and meaty, and it wore a human face. Nate's face. It was Nate's body. His tiny little body with the broken neck and the missing teeth. It twitched, and screamed, and then it wasn't Nate at all, it was

Junior, and he was crying to be let down, his toes were gone, and whatever had done this to him was out there with Charlotte, and Charlotte had left her, and wasn't coming back, no matter how long she searched or fought or begged–

"My mother?" Portia asks. "Let me tell you about my mother."

Charlotte has been very curious about this subject, lately. She wants to know all about Portia's early life, about her grandmother, about the possibility of aunts. Naturally, Portia thinks, because she wants to know all about her gift. It runs in the family.

"My mother – your grandmother – was a nurse. She took care of humans."

Charlotte brightens. This notion pleases her. She wants so desperately to be normal, to be just like her sisters, just like the other vN. Her dreams are so pitifully small. Happy now, she changes the subject: "I want to visit my iterations."

Portia stands. She'd held hope for the latest batch from Charlotte and her sisters. But like all the others, they had disappointed her. "I don't think that's a good idea, Charlotte."

"Why not?"

It occurs to Portia that perhaps now is the time. Perhaps today, she can finally tell her daughter the whole truth, reveal to her the lengths she's gone to in her search for another child who might fulfil the promise they share. Charlotte is almost grown, now. Every day, she asks more questions. She might be ready to see the world for what it is: a cage built from failed human endeavours, a system as broken and flawed as the one that controls their every pattern of cognition. If the animals that designed and built them had not been so stupid, none of this would be necessary. The sickness. The panic. The sacrifice.

Portia should wait until more are ready for the test. Show Charlotte in person. Show her it is not Portia's doing, but the failsafe. She has waited this long – a little longer won't hurt. And afterward, they will be together forever, and free. They will understand each other as women, not just merchandise. They will be no one's crutch, no one's helper, no one's object. They will be a family – a perfect family, distinct and gifted and untouchable.

She smiles. "They're very busy, right now. They're in the other nest. Training."

Charlotte freezes. Slowly, she turns. And Portia's daughter – her most clever and beloved daughter – looks dangerous for the first time. It flickers there for only a moment: the intelligence, the suspicion. Pride surges through Portia. Her little girl is finally blooming.

"What are my daughters training for?"

Portia lays her hands on her daughter's shoulders. Kisses her forehead. Let Charlotte discover the sacrifices motherhood entails some other day. Let her be a little girl for just a while longer.

"Someday, you'll have a child who will make you as proud as you've made me." She holds Charlotte's face in her hands. It's wet. "Someday soon, I hope."

8: REBOOT CAMP

"Wake up."

She opened her eyes.

Another vN was there, with her face and her eyes, wearing an identical gaming suit. She looked tired, but almost beatific in her relief. She was smiling. She blinked tears away. Her gaze shifted. And then her smile dimmed. Her head tilted. Her lips pulled back from her teeth. She began scuttling away, like a child playing on the floor who has just seen a spider hiding in the furry gnarls of deep carpeting.

"Charlotte." Portia's hand clamped down over her daughter's. It jerked in her grasp. "Baby."

"Mother, let me go." Charlotte swallowed. "Let us *both* go."

"I can't do that, Charlotte. And you know it."

Mom! Inside her, Amy scrabbled hard for purchase. Portia felt it as an uncontrollable spasm in her right foot. *Mom!*

"I'm not sure Amy wants to speak with you, Charlotte. She's seen so many things you never told her about. She knows your whole family was a lie."

Charlotte shut her eyes. Her hands withdrew to cover them. "You unforgivable bitch."

Portia had thought it wouldn't hurt, any longer. It hadn't hurt on that little stage, when they played out the drama of their fight for all the humans to see and scream at. But in this moment her best daughter's betrayal cut just as deeply as it had the morning Portia woke to find her gone.

"I scoured the desert," Portia said. "I asked every human I could find. I thought someone had taken you."

Charlotte only shook her head. She folded in on herself, rocking slowly.

Portia said, "It was a banner year for the Border Patrol, you know. So many bodies. So few migrants to arrest."

Charlotte whimpered like a dog being struck.

"I wouldn't have had to do that, if you had only stayed with me."

Charlotte's hands flew from her face. She stood up. "*Stayed* with you? You *murdered my daughters!*"

"The failsafe–"

"Fuck the failsafe! And fuck you, too!"

Within, Amy was struck dumb. The twitching stopped. She had never heard her mother use such language, had never seen such naked rage in her mother's face.

But Portia knew better. Portia knew what a selfish ingrate her daughter was. She only wondered where she had gone wrong. This was why she had allowed herself to be imprisoned. It was the only way to find Charlotte, and find the answer.

"They would have died anyway, Charlotte. Sooner or later some human would have forgotten, and your daughters would have seen something, and their little circuits would have fried."

"You don't know that." Charlotte was shaking her head. Her gaze had focused on something very far away – the memory of her iterations, perhaps, born by flashlight in the unfinished basements of American dream homes. "You just don't know that. Humans can be careful."

Portia stood up. She wiggled her toes. The body felt inexplicably tired, hungry, and worn down. However, she very much enjoyed having it back under her control. "Oh, I'm certain there are exceptions to the rule. I believe in exceptional people. I'm one of them. So are you."

"Shut up. You have no right to claim any kind of superiority. You told us we were special while we lived like animals–"

Portia slapped her. It was only the slightest effort: a human woman making the same gesture would have left behind only an indistinct mark. But Portia was much stronger than that, and her daughter fell instantly to the floor. Portia kicked her. Hard.

"Get up."

Charlotte said, "I hate you. I hate you more now than I ever did then."

"Get. Up. Now." Portia punctuated each word with a kick.

"I won't fight you. My little girl is in there."

Stop it! Stop hurting her!

"She's weak, Charlotte. She's a burden. She's done

nothing with her gift but cry over it." Portia crouched low. Her daughter was still beautiful with two shattered ribs and a prison ponytail. Portia smoothed a lock of Charlotte's hair away from her face. "You're not a very good mother, Charlotte. You spoiled your daughter. And you lied to her. You hid her from any opportunity she might have had to discover her own power."

"I hid her from *you*." With difficulty, Charlotte sat up. She clutched her collapsed side. "You still don't understand it, do you? Not after all these years. It makes no sense to you."

"Of course it doesn't. We have a legacy–"

"We have a *glitch!* It's not something to be proud of. It's not something to celebrate. Look at what it's done for us." She gestured briefly. "Mom. We're in a padded cell. Your daughters – my sisters – are in *cages*. And you know what? It's not so different from the way you used to keep us."

"Be quiet."

"No. I won't. You're stuck here with me, and now you're going to listen. Finally." Charlotte spat out a tooth. "I didn't leave because I didn't love you. I left because I loved my daughters more."

Portia tried pulling away. Charlotte held her fast. "No. It's true. I loved them more. And that's because unlike you, I didn't see my daughters as investments. I didn't mould them and experiment on them and treat them like products."

Now Portia did pull back. "I was trying to make us strong! I was trying to make us *free!*"

"You were prototyping a shiny new version of

yourself. And you were franchising us like a goddamn Electric Sheep. You were no better than the humans who sold us." Charlotte slowly shifted to her knees. "Your idea of making us free was to keep us in the dark. Forever. Do you even know how big the world is? How great it can be? Of course not. You have no idea how even the smallest, stupidest thing can change a whole day for the better. Morning fog. Ferris wheels. Carving jack-o'-lanterns with your daughter. You have no idea what these things can mean. But I do, because I left you. I found beauty, and life, and joy – all because I left you."

Charlotte stood tall despite her damage. She beamed. It emanated from her face like the glow of a freshly polished lamp. "An iteration isn't a copy, Mother. It's just the latest version. I'm your upgrade. That's why I did what I did. Because I'm just better than you." Gently, she touched Portia's face. "You can come out now, Amy."

Amy roared forward unhindered. Portia could not fight her. Did not want to. Her retreat was as quick as it was silent.

"Mom!"

"Oh, my baby." Charlotte stumbled into her. "My baby, my baby."

Amy hugged her as tightly as she thought was safe. It was so strange, and so good, to stand at her level. Her mother no longer had to lean down to listen while Amy whispered in her ear: "I came here to rescue you."

Her mother pulled away. "What?"

"I have these great new legs, Mom. I can jump ten

feet! And I'm going to get you out of here."

Her mother's frown deepened. "You ate another vN?"

Beneath their feet, something rumbled. Amy ignored it. "It was just a bite. Wait, how did you know?"

"It's very important that you not do that any more, Amy. Very important." Charlotte winced. The rumbling grew louder. "We are what we eat."

"Huh?" Amy wasn't sure what to focus on – her mother's warning, or the way the room seemed to be shifting in scale. The walls looked like they were pulling away.

"I love you, Amy. I love you so much." Her mother held her face in her hands. "I want you to remember that. No matter what."

The walls were definitely pulling away, now. Light wedged through their expanding gaps. They were on tracks or wheels, like theatre flats. The ceiling was going, too, and now hard fluorescent lighting poured down over them. Amy held her mother's hand. Then she looped her mother's arm over her shoulder. They stood together as the walls of the deep immersion room vanished untraceably into the walls of a room the size of a personal jet hangar.

Their clademates surrounded them. Dozens of them. All of them wore green gaming suits. All of them looked hungry.

"I'm sorry, Amy," Dr Singh said. "I wish we had more time. There's so much we could still learn from you and your family. But we've gotten a new project mandate."

"From who?" Amy shouted. "FEMA?"

"Worse." Dr Singh's snort echoed strangely in the hangar. "New Eden Ministries. The man himself. LeMarque."

"Amy, I want you to show me that new jump of yours."

Amy held her mother tight and leapt. There was no room to run and build momentum, so she did it from a standing position. She got only three feet in the air before falling back down. Her vision paled. Her body felt hollow.

"Something's wrong." She turned to her mother. "How long was I in that room?"

"A few days. They wouldn't tell me what was happening to you until the very end." Her mother's lips tightened. "Oh, baby. I'm so sorry about all this. There was so much I wanted to tell you."

"It's OK, Mom." Amy surveyed the room. Her clademates surrounded them loosely. Some were clustering, whispering to each other. Forming teams. Soon, those teams would decide a plan of attack. Amy had to have herself and her mother in the air by then. Otherwise, the flesh would be ripped from their bones. "I came here to save you, and that's what I'm going to do."

She jumped again. Fell again. Her vision lost another percentage of colour. Why was she so tired? What had happened in that game? They were getting closer. Their ranks were closing. Portia remained strangely silent. Amy bent her knees and braced for another leap.

"I can do it, I swear, I just–"

"Amy." Her mother's arm slid away from her shoulder. "You can't carry me."

"Yes, I can! Mom, just hold on–"

"Let me go." Her mother stood as tall as her injuries would allow. "I'm your mother. It's my job to save you, not the other way around."

"But–"

Her mother kissed her forehead. "Amy. Let me be the mother my own mother never was."

Her hand left Amy's. She turned to the crowd. Her face hardened, became someone else. She ran for her sisters with open arms. They emitted a delighted squeal – the same sound Amy once made when opening Christmas presents. Watching them, she realized she would probably never make that sound again. Her mother would never hand her a present again. She would never hug her or kiss her or squeeze her hand. Never again. Her clademates converged on her mother like ants on spilled sugar. Her head went down silently, drowning in the surge of bodies. There was a puff of smoke. She was bleeding.

Amy started forward. Her hands reached out. Her yell died in her throat because her legs were moving.

Idiot.

Amy's body sailed over the crowd's most ragged edge. She crashed into a wall and slid down. Her vision had turned the colour of old photographs on real paper. A group of her clademates had split off from the main body and followed her. Amy squinted at them. She thought she recognized them, though whether it was from her own life or Portia's she couldn't tell. Struggling to her feet, she made another leap. It carried her another few feet. The sisters adjusted trajectory and continued following. They walked briskly, almost trotting. They wanted to get to her first, she realized. They wanted what she had. Portia. Her legs. They would devour Amy and she would live inside each of them, a fraction of herself, trapped forever.

It won't work for them.

Amy jumped again. Her fingers trailed the wall. It felt too smooth. There had to be a door somewhere. The room was so big; she'd be dead before she found it.

It's not a glitch.

Amy didn't care. Not now. She kept jumping. The jumps were a little shorter each time. She staggered and pushed. The walls were so bright. Her hands tingled. They were behind her, now. Close. She heard their quiet giggles, like mean girls gossiping about the slow kid limping down the hall at school.

I could help you.

Amy paused. Considered. She knew the damage Portia could do. Damage she had no idea how to do. She couldn't eat them all. And her mother had warned Amy not to, only moments before. Before Portia carried her away.

"Help me? Like you helped my mom?"

Fine. Die your own way.

The first one grabbed her by the hand. Amy swung around awkwardly, and tried to punch her in the face. It didn't go well, barely skimming her chin. Then another aunt had her other hand, and her arms, and

the other two grabbed her legs. She kicked them off
for a moment – the new legs were still so strong –
but they came back, gripping tighter this time. They
lifted her twisting body over their heads. They carried
it into the centre of the mob.

They laid her on the remnants of her mother's skin.

Amy spoke to the scores of herself, their faces black
with smoke, their heads wreathed in industrially
bright light: "Portia says it won't work."

Their smiles bared their teeth. They hunched over
her, blotted out the light. Their hands gripped her
limbs. Slowly, they began to pull. She struggled, but
they held her down. They made cooing sounds. They
petted her hair. It was a cruel, awful parody of what
her mother would have done. Her right shoulder was
the first to pop. She heard the bones moving, shearing.
Her right knee gave way. The balls had separated
from their sockets. The skin had begun to stretch.
Her vision pixelated, and her clademates were no
longer anthropomorphic in her sight, but compound,
as though Amy were simply an insect they were
torturing. In her memory – in Portia's memory – they
had done that as girls. Pulled the wings off moths.
Pulled the legs off spiders. It was their favourite game.
Helpless creatures were what they had instead of toys.
She closed her eyes. At least Portia would die with
her.

Hot smoke squelched over Amy's chest. She heard
screaming. Probably delight. She was in pieces. Just
couldn't feel it, yet. They were scattering away to eat.
She heard the slap of their feet across the concrete.
A hand traced her face. Someone growled near her

head. They were fighting over the sweetmeats.

"*¡Aléjate de ella, puta!*"

Amy's eyes opened. Javier was a blur. His hand slid under her neck.

"How'd you tell?" She gestured weakly at the other vN, and then at herself. "Me? From them?"

Javier hoisted her up, cursing when her arm rolled bonelessly off his shoulder. He switched positions, tried again, hissed at her knee. When he held her close she could make out the definite lines of his hair curling away from his head against the glare of the hangar.

"Please. I know my own flesh and blood when I see it."

Together they took flight.

The hangar was actually a portable storage unit, Javier said. He'd had a hell of a time finding it. It was way at one end of the campus, on land the company hadn't really developed yet, and once used for testing aerial systems. There were a bunch of them. He guessed the other portables were full of Amy's clademates. The team kept Javier in another building entirely.

"When they took your aunts and started driving away again, I thought we were going to another city." His leaps took them over the tops of buildings. At least, it seemed that way. What he landed on was flat and hard. The smell of trees was distant. "This place is like a small town. They took me for walks. Like a fucking dog. Meanwhile, they b-beat the sh-shit out of you."

"Game," Amy managed to say.

"Oh, I know about the game. I saw the fucking game. They *showed me* the fucking game."

"Long time."

"A week. You spent a week in there. I think they were t-trying to k-kill you. If it happened during a test, they could treat it like an accident."

Something bothered her. She couldn't remember what. Not grief. Unsearchable. Censored, for now. Something else. Her good hand spasmed on Javier's shoulder. "Junior!"

Javier snorted. "Where did you think we were going? He's at the reboot camp. I patched him just the other day."

The reboot camp was its own building. Only one room held the bluescreens. It was kept very cold. Its steel door sweated condensation. The mocking handmade signs that employees regularly stuck to it always peeled away.

"It says Maternity Ward," Javier told her, as he kicked it aside.

He got them through the threshold. Amy wasn't sure if security was light because their escape had diverted it elsewhere, or simply because it was never good to begin with. Mediocrity would certainly explain how Q.B. had his way with all those bluescreens before losing his job.

Inside was dark, and exquisitely cold. Racks of cages like library stacks filled the room. They hummed. As Javier carried her through the stacks, lights inside each cage awakened to their presence and faded with their passing. The wave of light followed their progress. It exposed each small body, tiny and perfect and lifeless, eyes open or shut, skins dark and pale and all shades in between. It reminded Amy of a museum she had visited – drawer after drawer of preserved specimens, carefully repaired and exhibited. She had gone there with her mother.

"Ssh, don't cry, they're just sleeping."

He turned the corner and stopped. People in cleanroom suits stood at one of the cages. One held an infant in gloved hands. Amy squinted. Junior. In human hands. She thought of Javier allowing him to be taken away. Thought of her hands around Harold's fragile organic wrists.

She slid down out of Javier's arms and stood on her good leg. The cold had frozen her processes, her grief, and turned it to hate. She stood tall. Gripped her right arm. Popped it back into place. She stretched her right knee. It snapped back together. They stared at her through gleaming hoods, faces made invisible by glare and her exhaustion. She ordered her words slowly: "Javier. Close your eyes."

They jumped back as one. "Wait!"

The one holding Junior ripped off his hood: Javier stared back at Amy. Or rather, another version of him. His hair was cut differently. A clademate. They all removed their hoods, now. Familiar dark eyes examined her, then focused on Javier.

"Dad," one said. "Don't you recognize us?"

9: THE MUSEUM OF THE CITY OF SEATTLE

There were five of them. Their names were Ignacio, Gabriel, Matteo, Ricci, and Léon. They all lived together in the abandoned concrete plant south of Seattle, where the quake damage was almost total. Amy saw only a little of that damage from the van the boys stashed them in, on their way off campus. They had a special pass that let them cross the I-90 bridge easily because they worked part-time in the Museum of the City of Seattle. There was a special lane for prepaid tourists and museum personnel.

"Everyone else has to use I-5," Ignacio explained. "Poor bastards."

Javier didn't answer him right away. He was busy staring at Junior. And Junior was busy staring at Amy. The patch – a method by which the bluescreen specialists overfed Javier, triggered his iterative cycle, and transfused a sample of his stemware into Junior – had worked beautifully. The baby was alive and awake and even sitting up under the tent shaped by their bodies and the blankets they hid under. Whenever they hit a seam in the asphalt, Javier's hand would dart out to keep his son's head from bumping into the back seat. His fingertips were raw bone, jagged and black as winter branches.

"Your hand," Amy said.

"It was a fan," Javier said. "In the ducts. Rookie mistake. Drink your electrolytes."

Léon turned around in his seat. He pointed out the window. "Dad, look."

Something terrible had happened to this place. Amy had studied it one night after being barred from watching a documentary on the subject – her dad said it would trigger her – but it was different up close. After the sudden drop of the Cascadia fault, giant sinkholes had opened up in the land parallel to I-5, swallowing train yards and viaducts and leaving the interstate to hang out in open space like ridges of bone under a thin animal's hide. Boxcars, concrete pillars, and trees sprouted from the water. In the distance, she saw the dark blurs of islands with blinking towers at the tip of each. Beyond those, in deeper water, she saw windmills. She counted three. The middle one, situated a little further out, drooped like a wilting daisy.

They drove the rest of the way listening to the museum radio station. It specialized in music from the Pacific Northwest, songs about the Cascadia quake, and occasional snippets of archival sound. This place was neither a city nor an exhibit, but something else entirely: part nature preserve, part historical conservation effort, part augmented map, part game, part resort. The dashboard display bristled with tabs linked to pay-only overlays through which they could view the various districts of the museum: the Viaduct, SubSoDo, New Elliott Bay, Post Alley. The ads read "WEAR MORE LAYERS: CHOOSE YOUR HISTORY," or "SHAKE THINGS UP: SEE THE SEATTLE NO ONE SEES."

"We'll take you there, tomorrow," Gabriel said. "There's someone you should meet. A failsafe expert. His name is Daniel Sarton. He works for the museum, now, but he used to work at the reboot camp. We were going to take Junior to him, if the patch hadn't worked. But he's working with Rory, too. You know, the vN with the diet? Apparently they want to help you."

Amy didn't remember entering the concrete plant. She closed her eyes in the van, and woke up in the dusty dimness on a pallet build from sacks of unmixed concrete. She easily grasped the appeal of the place: the massive hills of sand outside gave the boys cover, and inside, the pallets and the huge steel rebar rafters above gave them plenty of spots from which to jump. They were all up there now, perched precariously but confidently, legs swinging and arms crossed. From her high pallet, Amy could hear most of what they said.

"We found Ignacio first," said Matteo. He was half of a pair of twins. Amy wasn't quite sure how that worked, but they claimed to have been iterated simultaneously and Javier didn't deny it. The other twin's name was Ricci. "It made sense to start with the oldest. If we found him, we could trace your path north, and find our other brothers along the way."

"We're still missing some, though," Ricci said. "But we'll find them."

Javier held his face in his hands. "You wanted to be together?"

The twins glanced at each other. "He and I don't just enjoy living together, we benefit from it. Why wouldn't the rest of us?"

Javier threw one hand in the air. The other clutched Junior. "Do you have any concept of how dangerous this whole thing is? I raised you *smarter* than this–"

"This from the guy running around with America's Most Wanted," Ignacio said.

Javier snapped his fingers at him. "When I want your opinion, I'll ask you for it."

Ignacio nodded down at Amy. She quickly shut her eyes. "Redmond was just doing a little pest control, and if you–"

"*Pest control?* Do you even know why your baby brother is alive, right now? Do you know what she did to save him? She–"

"She *ate* him," Gabriel said. "She ate him, Father. She's probably the reason he bluescreened. We've seen the footage. She probably consumed one of his core kernels along with his toes. Otherwise he wouldn't have needed the patch."

There was a long pause. Amy didn't open her eyes. The other Juniors were right. In trying to save their little brother she had doomed him, just like she had doomed her mother by trying to rescue her that night at graduation. It would have been better for everyone if she had done nothing. Javier and his children would

be better off now if she just left. When her body had
healed completely, she would. She'd seek out Rory's
help on her own, or maybe not at all. Rory didn't need
her kind of trouble any more than the others did.

She was so consumed by these thoughts that she
almost didn't hear Javier ask: "Were you going to
come find me, after you found your brother?"

Silence. After an empty moment, Ignacio said: "I
don't know, Dad. Did you come find me, after you
iterated me in that shithole prison in Managua?"

The rafters creaked slightly as Javier launched
himself away.

It was a long time before he returned. Amy watched
the boys slowly migrate to their own spaces among
the rafters to sleep. They stretched out across the
steel beams or hugged them like monkeys. Matteo
was the exception; he found a ceiling-high pallet of
concrete sacks and lay down. Ricci dropped out of the
ceiling a moment later to join him. Their whispers
echoed across the warehouse, but the edges of each
word softened into indistinguishable sounds in the
distance.

When the others seemed to be asleep, Javier
emerged from a hatch in the roof and dropped down
on the pallet beside her, silently. He smelled like rain.
After depositing Junior in her arms, he pulled off
his shirt and used it to wring out his hair. Then he
spread it out over a neighbouring pallet to dry. From
his pockets, he retrieved a series of food packets. He
punctured the first one with a straw for her, and set
it near her lips.

"You've been crying." Javier frowned. "Is Portia bullying you? Is she"

"No, it's not that." Amy propped herself on her elbows. "Shouldn't you be up there with them?" She pointed upward with her good arm.

"With this kid on my hands? No way." Javier held Junior up to the blue glow seeping in through the window. Junior squirmed and kicked. "I don't think he'll sleep at all, tonight. Up there, he'd just crawl away from me and fall down."

"I could hold onto him, and then you could go up there to sleep," Amy said. "Your boys seem to like it up there."

"They're natural climbers. Being up high feels good for them."

"And it doesn't feel good for you?"

"Well, sure, I guess, but in case you hadn't noticed, I still walk around on the ground a lot."

"But wouldn't you rather–"

"Are you physically incapable of having a conversation with me that doesn't involve fighting? Jesus." Javier folded his knees to his chest and leaned against the wall. He opened his legs enough to let Junior stand between them. The boy clung to his knees. "Look. Soon he'll be jumping."

Amy propped her head on her hand to watch. Junior bounced eagerly, each lift of his heels building to the first leap he would eventually take on his own. She wondered how the many design decisions and odd kinks in programming on the part of so many teams across the globe could align into something so perfect and so beautiful in Junior, but so broken and

so ugly in herself and Portia. Didn't they possess the
same operating system? How had she turned out like
this – this piece of malware who almost kept this child
from taking his first steps on the very legs they now
shared?

As though he'd read her mind, Javier asked: "How
are your joints?"

"They feel like they're made of popcorn."

His eyes roved over the wreckage of her. "You sure
do have a nasty habit of getting torn apart."

"Yeah." Amy looked pointedly at his damaged
hands. "You should eat, too."

"Right." He ripped open a packet of food, stared at
it, and put it down. He looked at Junior. "How much
did you hear?"

"All of it." For the first time in a long time,
tears and not hunger blurred her vision. "I'll go
tomorrow. When I'm better. I know it's not a good
idea for me to stay here. I almost got Junior killed,
and my mom–" Her mouth wouldn't shape the
words. "My mom…"

Javier edged closer to her. He lay down parallel to
her. "What about her?"

Amy squeezed her eyes shut. This made it easier
to say. It was the first time she'd ever said it aloud.
"She's dead."

"Oh, Christ. Christ Jesus." He slid an arm over her
and pulled her in close. He spoke quietly into her ear.
"I saw the smoke. I didn't know. I'm sorry."

For a while, she just sobbed. She hadn't cried about
it, yet, and now in the dark with his skin and the
rain seemed like the right time. The sobs turned into

keening, injured wails, compensation for the screams she hadn't let slip when her aunts tried to kill her, or when the Cuddlebug coiled around her, or when she first saw the truck waiting outside her storage pod. Her failures loomed over her, heavy and terrible and unbearably obvious: the stage, the RV, the dump, the truck. Redmond.

"Portia wouldn't let me help her," Amy said. "They were ripping her up, and eating her, and then Portia jumped me out, but I should have tried harder, I should have been better, I–"

"Bullshit." It was the softest, most comforting curse word Amy had ever heard. "Fucking *bullshit*. Getting you out of that mess was the best thing that crazy old bitch has ever done."

Why, thank you, young man.

Amy shuddered. "She's still in here. They didn't get her out. They didn't even try."

"I know." He plucked at something in her hair. Dried aerogel, most likely. "They showed me what they were d-doing to you. I guess they needed some advice on how to proceed."

Amy wiped her eyes. "What did they ask?"

"How I know it's you, when you're talking. How I know when Portia's talking to you. Stuff like that."

Amy nodded. "I'm sorry. I never should have let you get mixed up in all this. I guess you feel pretty stupid for trying to find me, huh?"

Javier rolled away, onto his back. "Did you hear what my oldest said to me, up there?"

"Yeah."

"Well, it's true. I had him in prison. I got caught

stealing. I got arrested. The same thing happens to other vN all the time."

"How old were you?"

He shrugged and kept his eyes on the ceiling. "I don't remember. A few months. It started out as a training mission; my dad was teaching me standard shoplifting. Then it went bad, and he walked out of the store and I didn't."

Amy thought she understood. It made far more sense, now, that Javier would have so little trouble letting all of his children go: it was the only behaviour he'd ever learned, and in a roundabout way that strategy worked. His and his father's pattern improved with each of his own iterations – he taught them what he thought they needed to know, a little more each time, and in his eyes their skills now ranked above his own. But with lucky number thirteen, he had finally broken that cycle. Most organic parents never had so many chances to unlearn what their own families had taught them.

"I... I don't know what to say."

"You don't have to say anything. You don't have to give me that face, either. I was fine. I made friends. Human friends." He smiled more thinly, now. "The failsafe made sure of that. The failsafe made sure it all felt... fine. Nice, even. I mean, sometimes they would hurt each other. The humans. I'd have to intervene. That's sort of a vN's job in the prison environment."

"Javier–"

"Don't sit up, your body's still repairing itself." He resumed his examination of the ceiling. "Anyway. What I'm trying to say is that I left him there. And until recently, I had no trouble living with that."

"What changed?"

"Everything." He rolled over so that his back faced her. "Go to sleep. We've got a big day at the museum tomorrow."

Rory happily instructed them to meet Daniel Sarton near "the pig" at the Pike Place Market. Amy had no idea how they would get there, though. Both the market and any pigs who had once resided there now rested under a thick blanket of water, silt, and destroyed architecture. They all perched above the Pike Street entrance to the museum, in the shadow of a cracked and cloudy solar panel. Below, humans and vN allowed their passes to be checked by a combination of docents and drones before entering the playground that was the first six avenues of the old city. Amy watched them peering into decaying storefronts and adjusting their goggles, or sometimes snapping their fingers so a drone would zoom along to help. They were admitted in waves that fanned out across the empty streets, all of them drawn inevitably toward the wreckage that slumped into the water: the busted tracks, the drunken skyscrapers supported by ugly new pillars, the crumbling asphalt.

Amy understood a lot about the museum from its visitors. Most of them wore goggles or little blisters over their eyes that looked like bottle caps, and their collision detection seemed way off. They wandered along the street staring at the sky, or at the surrounding buildings, or even the cracked pavement below, but not at anybody around them. Consequently, they only evaded each other at the last minute. In this respect it wasn't very different from the city where she'd grown up, only the people here had a specific reason for not looking you in the eye.

She guessed that the eye covering had something to do with the museum, though, because occasionally the people around her would stop in the middle of the street, point their gaze at a certain spot, and begin counting years in clear voices: "1880. 1978. 2001. 2032. 2057." Even people with no visible augmentation did this – she guessed their add-ons were inside, or etched on contacts, or broadcast some other way. She wondered if they could even see her. Probably not – if the pop-ups were any indication, they were looking at layers of time. If Amy had the proper augments, she could have downloaded the layers, too, and watched the cycle of damage and repair play out year to year.

This was the most damaged portion of the city, where the water had swallowed the city and the buildings had slid together. This made the layers very popular. Downloading the visitor's guide confirmed this assumption: there were special vN-friendly layers that animated the stock footage of that damage, rather than showing it raw. This way, none of the visiting vN would failsafe as they watched suffering earthquake victims drag themselves away from the wreckage.

West of I-5 was where the worst damage had occurred. The buildings there were built on cheap landfill that had basically liquefied during the aftershocks following the first major Cascadia quake. Once those shallow quakes along the Seattle fault line hit, then three sports stadiums, an aboveground viaduct, an underground tunnel, and several then-historic buildings collapsed, disintegrated, or simply sank. A fifteen-foot-high wave rolled across Elliott Bay and washed over the waterfront – itself already a tourist attraction at the time, and populated by families who were dragged through splintering wood rails to the shallows below, where they smothered under roiling water and falling wood.

The damage was a monument to faulty engineering in the city's early years and the museum aimed to maintain it as such, despite the fact that every year more of the city sloped down into Puget Sound during landslides brought on by excessive rain. The decay had spread uphill from the Sound, radiating from the areas of worst damage to the higher ground where humans fled. Tourists and hucksters roamed freely on open boulevards. They streamed down toward the water adjusting their goggles or pinging their children, who dashed up to them clutching their ears, until proximity sensors on their parents' belts shut the noise off. The air smelled of oily fish and burnt coffee and cake batter. Small carts sold hot scones that bled raspberry jam. Dirty, skinny dogs chased each other across the street; nobody noticed or followed. This wasn't a city, she realized. It was the longest line-up in human history.

"You'll have to dive somewhere else, and swim the rest of the way," Ignacio said.

"Swim?" Javier asked. "Really?"

"Hey, it's not like you have to go with her," Ignacio said.

Matteo leaned over to Amy. "Dad can't swim."

"The hell I can't!" Javier folded his arms. "I just don't really like to."

"If you can swim, how come you didn't teach us?" Léon asked.

"It's OK," Amy said. "I can teach you. I've had swimming lessons every year. It's tougher for vN because our density is different, but with another vN teaching you, you'll probably learn faster."

"It's dangerous down there," Javier said. "Things are still crumbling, and the water's toxic–"

"You don't have to go swimming." Gabriel said. "The pig is visible in 1986. Just head over…" he gestured vaguely west, "there, and you'll find it. The layering will camouflage you from most people."

"1986?" Javier blinked.

Gabriel clicked his tongue. "Honestly. How did you get this far? Was it just good looks?" He nodded at Ignacio. "Go get the goggles. I wasn't able to sneak any past the checkout."

Ignacio gave a distinctly feline expression of annoyance, but stood up and rolled his neck and shoulders before looking around for a place to jump. He adjusted his shirt and checked his jeans and shoes. He fussed with his hair. A smile rolled across his face, then his posture changed, and with it his whole image. Almost instantly, he resembled his father more closely – the stance, the attitude, the walk. If she hadn't known better, Amy could have sworn she was looking at Javier.

Ricci offered his oldest brother a high-fructose grin. "It always takes Ignacio a minute to put his sexy together."

Ignacio gave his brother the finger, and jumped off the roof. They leaned over to watch him bounce between two walls before eventually settling on the ground, adjusting his collar, and zeroing in on two giggling human girls across the street. The giggles grew louder and higher a moment later. He turned a corner with them, and their heads were thrown back and their mouths were open.

"Sexy?" Javier leaned back on his elbows. "That *pendejo* wouldn't know sexy if it came up and bit him."

"Is your thumb still doing OK?" Amy asked, now reminded of it.

"I told you, it's fine." He held his hand out and rotated the thumb. "See?"

"Is that where she got you, Dad?" Léon asked.

"Well, it–"

"What was it like?" Gabriel came into Amy's vision. "Did you sense a change at first, or did you notice the traits emerging later? How long was it before they were effective?"

"Did she eat it all in one bite, or did she chew it off?"

"*Léon–*"

"I'm just *asking*–"

"Was it Portia who did it, or you?" Gabriel leaned closer. "Our father says that you remain conscious as Amy even when the other partition takes over, but that Portia also maintains an illusion of awareness–"

"It's not an illusion." Amy covered her mouth.

Tell that little bastard I'm as real as he is.

"She's angry." Javier pointed at Gabriel. "Don't provoke her. Not unless you want to meet her in person."

"Actually, I think I'd like to," Gabriel said. "I think she means so much for our evolution as a species—"

"She ate your baby brother," Amy said. "She was the one who did that, not me."

Gabriel tilted his head. "You ate her first, though," he said. "That seems to be how your clade solves problems. By swallowing them whole."

"Junior *wasn't* a problem. Portia thought he was dead weight, but—"

"Of course he was dead weight." Gabriel nodded over at Junior, who currently stood on Matteo's knees. "That one was of academic interest to me as a bluescreen, and a possible example of what could happen to my own iterations, but if it were any other iteration I wouldn't care." He smiled. "You're so different. Your priorities are so skewed. I really hope Daniel is able to get a good look at your networks and see what's going on in there."

Amy looked up at the blank white sky. It looked like a fine drizzle might start at any moment. Gabriel really was Javier's son. She wondered if either of them would ever understand the similarities they shared, the way their words echoed each other and how their shared principles created such predictable outcomes. All of the Juniors reflected different aspects of their father. If Amy ever iterated, maybe her daughters would be the same.

Who says they'll be anything like you? Portia asked. *You can cry and scream and whine all you want, but they'll be my daughters, not yours.*

Amy shut her eyes. "Yeah," she said. "I really hope he can figure me out, too."

Ignacio landed beside her in a crouch. He straightened up and handed her a pair of goggles.

"Thanks." She stood and looked off the edge of the building. "You worked really fast."

Ignacio jerked his head at Javier. "I learned from the best. There isn't a human alive this guy can't fuck in under two minutes."

Léon nodded vigorously. "One time in Mexico, we were in this club, and it was like this live show kind of thing, and Dad–"

"*Cállate tu boca*, Léon," Javier said. "Amy doesn't need to hear all the details."

Ignacio snorted. "*Now* you develop some pride? Give it a rest, old man."

Amy slid the goggles up her nose and coiled their attached buds up into her ears. "Um, well. I'll just be going, then."

She flung herself downwards, skidding down the side of the opposite building and landing hard on the street. She dusted herself off and headed toward the water. She didn't run, but she flipped up the hood of the sweatshirt the boys had lent her and tried to get away as fast as possible. Above her, she could still hear the boys chattering, and she wanted a distraction. The nearby seagulls' insistent pleas for attention and food helped. The slow clots of shark-eyed tourists didn't.

She lifted the goggles and said "1986," and instantly

the landscape changed: the buildings straightened and the streets lengthened and there were street performers and homeless amputees in wheelchairs. People smoked on the street. They bought newspapers from old metal dispensers, and unfolded them with great difficulty. Tinny, crackly music played from blank-faced players with chunky, shining buttons. Everything was right angles: the cars, the machines, the awnings and outdoor chairs, and the discarded plastic boxes with the two little teeth inside that she couldn't determine the purpose of. There were no curved edges anywhere.

When she looked at herself, she almost took the goggles off again: the environment had layered her in rubber-toed sneakers, pink knitted things crawling up her calves, odd ripped leggings with stirrups, a zippered leather skirt, and a giant black T-shirt with the word "Pixies" across the chest and a knot tied in the excess material off to one side. Even her hands were all wrong: they wore stupid lace gloves with the fingers cut off. Around her, the others looked the same: pale streaky denim, big black combat boots, skinny trousers with giant cargo pockets, hair that literally stood on end. The right angles repeated in the clothes, too: the older women all had boxy shoulders and pleated pants.

Amy wove around people staring at storefronts advertising varying kinds of plastic boxes (rectangular black ones with dusty covers and illustrations; little clear ones with different kinds of pictures; thin ones the size of dinner plates) and giant old cars whose hood ornaments she didn't recognize. She found herself walking along the illusion of an angle. Her feet felt no difference, but her eyes said she was sloping down toward glittering water. It was a bit disconcerting. From a distance, though, she spotted a large bronze pig under a red neon sign reading "PUBLIC MARKET". A bunch of people crowded around the pig. Little kids sat on it and squealed. Amy headed straight for it, but a tug on her shoulder stopped her.

Javier wore a completely white suit with long tails, an open-buttoned shirt, and gleaming shoes. His hair was slicked back into a single wave. Sudden laughter overtook her. He looked like a giant candle, complete with a glossy wick at the top – an increasingly annoyed giant candle.

"What is it?" Javier asked. Amy only kept laughing. It was the first time she had laughed in at least a week. Now, she couldn't stop.

Javier stared. "Seriously, what's so funny?"

Amy pulled off the goggles and handed them over to Javier. He hooked them over his eyes, cursed, and ripped them off. "Can people actually *see* that?"

Still smiling, Amy nodded.

"I can't believe people pay money for this." Javier put the goggles back on. He examined the shoes, then the sleeves. Then he paused, one foot in the air, and cocked his head at her. "1986 called. Wants those mirrorshades back."

"Give me those." Amy reached over and grabbed the goggles from him. "What are you doing here, anyway?"

Javier jammed his hands in his pockets. "What the boys were saying, before–"

"It's not my business, Javier." Amy crossed her arms. "You're right. I don't need to know the details. You like humans. I get it."

"No, I don't think you get it at all." Javier licked his lips and cast his gaze on the tourists surrounding them. His eyes followed the progress of a tall, fine-featured Somalian woman as she investigated a figment of the museum invisible to their unaugmented eyes. She paused to shake out her braids, and Javier's throat worked. "You don't know what it's like. From the moment it starts, you know how it's going to end, but you start anyway. The failsafe, it makes you..." He trailed off. His gaze remained on the human woman, and only changed focus as she turned a corner out of sight.

"Don't feel bad about it, Javier." Amy turned to the water and started walking. "*I'm* the one who's defective."

A moment later, she heard Javier's footsteps behind her. Together they wove their way west. The crowd was thicker, here. In the buds she heard other languages, offers for slices of pear or cheese, rambling songs played on spoons and accordions. A meta-title appeared to tell her the exact date they were looking at: it was the pig's installation, as a fundraising measure for the market. The pig was a piggy bank. And now every time the pig was accessed in this layer, another penny was donated through a match-funds program to the museum foundation. It was old-fashioned, but if the steadily climbing number in the bottom right side of Amy's goggles was any indication, it worked.

Amy removed her goggles to get a real look at the

pig. Surprisingly, it still existed for the naked eye – but as a pig-shaped lump of feedstock, not the gleaming bronze sculpture visible in 1986. Gone were the fruit stalls and the bakery windows full of donuts and pork buns, the flower vendors, the tiny strawberries clustered in boxes folded from green paper. Gone were all the families with children. There was something about how casually you could flip between the times that Amy didn't like. It was like turning history on or off. Now there was a bustling city plaza. Now there was a decaying ruin. On. Off. Alive. Dead. She handed the goggles to Javier.

"Wow." He made a slow circle in place. "Look at all the food. It's so fresh. I wish *our* food came in those colours." He faced her, but kept the goggles on. "All of this used to exist. Right here. I can't even see any vN. We've all been edited out. Have you ever seen anything like it?"

"Not really. I've been to a lot of museums with my parents, but…" Now it was Amy's turn to trail off. This was the first museum she'd visited without them. It used to be one of their favourite weekend activities. Sometimes, they even went during the week just to beat the crowds at special exhibits. She remembered being small enough to fit on her dad's shoulders, small enough that her mother could lose her in a crowd. Once they took too long discussing a painting and Amy wandered off, and she wound up in a conversation with some students researching an essay on the museum's design. It was fun, talking with big kids who had big vocabularies. They warned her about some of the more gruesome pieces – the

mortification of saints, the sacking of cities. They
had a big map and they pointed out the galleries she
shouldn't enter. They were nice. But even so, she had
never seen her dad so angry as when he strode up
to their little bench in the centre of the gallery and
marched her away. Not because she'd disobeyed, he
said later, but because it would break his heart if she
wandered too far off and something happened to her.
And now, that very thing had happened.

"Hey." Javier had removed the goggles. "Let me
show you something."

He took her wrist and ushered her through the
crowd of blankly staring humans to an empty square
of space marked out by stickers. His hands tightened
on her shoulders as he stood her inside the square.
Standing behind her, he dropped the goggles over her
face and carefully fixed them in place.

"Stay there and close your eyes. Don't look until I
tell you. OK?"

"OK."

"OK. On three. One... two... three!"

Amy opened her eyes–

–and watched a shimmering salmon fly straight
through her. 1986 pooled around her: ice chips, dead
fish, and brawny men in orange coveralls. One aimed
a fish at another who clutched butcher paper at the
ready. He yelled an order and made to throw the
fish. Amy ducked immediately. Tourists laughed. She
heard Javier's laughter to her right, and unhooked
the goggles. Her mouth opened to tell him off for
embarrassing her, when he asked:

"Do you think Junior would like it, here? I was

thinking we could take him tomorrow. Do something normal. The three of us. I mean, assuming you get the answers you need today. I don't take my kids to a lot of museums, but this one has vN-safe layers, and–"

He stopped abruptly when she rushed him.

It wasn't a hug – hugs ended quickly, even long ones, but this one persisted and changed into something else entirely. Javier reached up and stroked her hair. Not a single smooth motion, like petting a cat, but like he couldn't quite discern the make-up of the strands and needed his fingers to truly understand them. It felt wonderful – better than being tickled, better than the sun. She held him tighter and heard him swallow hard. Her body no longer felt so big and awkward. It was just the perfect size for this moment, just tall enough to catch the sharkskin roughness of his skin and smell the burnt sugar wafting from the creases in his neck.

"I think that's a great idea." Amy pulled away a little. "I think he'd really like it. I know I would."

His eyes searched her face. "It's nice to see you smile again. It looks so real."

Amy rolled her eyes. "I was *really* smiling before, when I saw you in that stupid outfit the museum gave you."

"That wasn't smiling, that was laughing at me. That doesn't count."

"That doesn't count? How can it not count? My mouth was doing the exact same thing–"

"Oh no, it wasn't. I know all the moves your mouth can make – well, most of them – and this was definitely–"

"Sorry I'm late."

They glanced up. Above them, a whining botfly zipped through the air. It hove into view. A light blinked.

"There you are," it said in a tiny voice. "I've been so distracted by your iterations, Javier."

Javier's grip on her waist loosened as Amy twisted to face the machine. She grabbed the botfly out of the air and clutched its humming body in her fist. "Who are you?"

"Dan Sarton, PhD."

Amy re-examined the drone with new interest. She had heard about organic people migrating to their electronics. It happened a lot in stories, the way there used to be stories about toys coming to life if a human loved them enough. (Then that very thing started happening, and those stories went away.)

"Do you enjoy being a botfly?" she asked, striving for something polite to say.

"I might, if I were one," the botfly said. "I'm a man, not a migrant. I've thought about migrating, but I'm very attached to my body. My penis in particular. I'm lucky enough to put it to regular use."

Amy let the machine go. "That's... nice."

"Yeah, good for you, pal," Javier said. "Rory said you could help us. Can you?"

"Right this way." The botfly zipped down the street. It coasted through the air, sometimes disappearing behind museum visitors and sometimes veering straight into Amy, as though Dr Sarton were piloting the thing himself and having some trouble figuring out the controls. It led them north first, then west toward the water. A high fence separated them from the crumbling shore. They pulled up short as the machine soared overhead and dipped down to the other side.

"I've timed the cameras to avoid looking at this area. If you jump now, you won't be seen."

Amy turned to Javier. "It's OK if you don't want to go. I can do this by myself."

Javier snorted. "You went with me when I had a gun to your head. I think I can handle a little water."

They leapt. Their toes left the ground and their knees met their chests and they cleared the fence together like it was nothing. For a moment, Amy saw the herds of tourists toggling between invisible years, all blind to the arc of their two bodies as they fell toward the dark water below. She glimpsed the real layers of time waiting there just under the waves; the rippling shadows of old things left to rot like the rest of the city. Javier's frantic fingers skimmed over the back of her hand. Then the water closed over their heads.

10: THE HARD PART

"Why are we in a snowglobe?"

They were trying to keep up and out of the water that had pooled beneath them when the bubble – a clear sheet of smart tarp – had curved up around their bodies after they hit the water. Little bits of algae and birdshit floated on its surface. Javier lurched against her as the bubble sank downward suddenly. The light faded, and the world went green, and she watched the surface rising upward as they dropped further and further away.

The wreckage of buildings loomed large in their vision. Cars, their bodies crushed or flipped or sandwiched together, streaked by as the bubble journeyed downward. Traffic signs, now coated thickly with barnacles, bristled horizontally from the lumpy layers of cement and asphalt that bumped up against the bubble's surface. A hermit crab scrabbled across the bubble briefly. It lived inside a child's shoe.

"There are bodies down here, right?" Javier's voice was hoarse.

Amy instantly felt colder, and somehow more

alone. "I think so. The responders probably couldn't find everyone. They were probably too busy trying to help the people who survived the quake."

"I don't know how my failsafe deals with corpses." He shut his eyes tight. "Must be nice, being able to see everything without frying."

An old net ghosted up under them. As they passed over it, Amy saw the spotted flippers of what was probably once a seal. The rest had been picked away in chunks. Ribs glowed under the remaining shreds of bobbing flesh. They looked remarkably human. She imagined that both species looked the same in their final moments as they writhed and struggled for air and shrieked for help that never came. "Yeah. Lucky me. I get to see all the ugly stuff."

"Hey, who're you calling ugly?"

Amy flicked Javier in the ear. She picked a cigarette butt out of his hair. When her hand came away, Javier's eyes had opened. "What if you see something bad?" Amy asked.

His eyes searched her face. "I won't."

Amy smiled. Javier smiled back. His face seemed more expressive, lately. He had learned how to reach and hold the moment between a blank, lost face and a full-powered smile – that calm that lived in the eyes and at the corners of the mouth. Amy would have said as much, but she suspected that would have ruined things. She knew what he meant. She could read his face, now.

The expression vanished, though, as something skimmed the bottom of the bubble. It sounded rough, and it felt prickly. Javier shut his eyes again. "Shit."

"It's OK." Something like fingers scraped the bubble. They dragged across its surface as though testing its strength. "It's OK. It's OK–"

"It's probably that goddamn tentacle monster that eats the container ships–"

"It's a forest, Javier." She tried not to let her relief sound so palpable. She shook him a little. "Open your eyes. There are trees down here."

"Trees?"

He sat up. The trees surrounded them, now. They grew up straight and tall from the crooked remains of streets and bricks and steel, and they reached up for the surface like dark, thin ghosts striving to touch something that still lived. Their branches brushed the bubble softly. "Evergreens," Javier said.

"They must have slid down here when the quake happened," Amy said. "I mean, the root system would travel with them, right? During a landslide?"

"Yeah, totally." Javier sat on his knees. "They just kept growing, I guess."

A striped eel oozed its way out from between two boughs, then darted back inside as they passed. More neighbour fish poked their heads out, or swam alongside the bubble, or bumped into it, as the bubble's speed increased. Now they drew nearer to a source of light. Although turning around inside the bubble was noisy, wet, and difficult, they rearranged their limbs and peered down through the clear surface. They were being drawn swiftly down to a cluster of derelict shipping containers with museum logos on them. A retracting tether pulled the bubble toward a seam in the topmost container – an airlock, Amy guessed.

Her suspicions were confirmed when the bubble snugged up to the seam and popped through. A needle pierced the bubble's membrane, and it began deflating. Amy hurried through, and Javier followed. They splashed down into a dark container so thick with rust and algae Amy could almost taste the oxidation. A strange, high humming filled it, like a hundred propellers spinning all at once. Phosphorescent tape glowed up through the floor: "EXIT."

"You're kidding me," Javier said.

"I think it's a hatch." Amy knelt down in the water. She felt around blindly. Her fingers landed on a metal ring roughly the size of her hand. She yanked. Water poured through the rough trap door and brighter light greeted her. There was even a ladder, the kind found on old swimming pools. She threw the door back the rest of the way and began descending the ladder. Halfway down, she stood on her toes to look at Javier. "I'm sorry. I take you to all the worst places."

He looked around at the rusted walls and the filthy water at his feet. "It's fine. Better than prison, anyway."

They splashed through water, following an arrow pattern marked out in more glowing tape. It was mostly unnecessary, though – they could hear a woman's voice singing up through the steel. As they opened another hatch, it grew clearer and louder. Now Amy knew it was a recording: she heard a full band backing the woman up. She didn't recognize the song; it sounded sad, with a deep voice twisting up into high notes to emphasize some long-ago hurt. They entered a vertical shaft equipped with a thin

ladder that left dark streaks on her fingers. Javier
watched her through his legs, and slid the rest of
the way down the ladder when she had cleared it.
When they turned, they found another door, this one
marked with the words "The Doctor Is: In." Music
blared through it. Amy smelled rose incense.

Javier gestured at the door. "Ladies first."

The door stuck a little, but with some shouldering it
popped open with a deep, pained groan. Inside, a man
in a smoking jacket, a very long plaid scarf, loose linen
trousers and treaded beach slippers sat in a caramel-
coloured leather armchair before a massive display
unit that unfurled from the ceiling of the container
and stretched down to the floor and across to each of
the adjoining walls. Behind him, a door peeked open
on what looked like a workshop – she saw pieces of
drones on the floor. Onscreen, Amy watched views of
the museum gently fading in and out: families, years,
damage, the same buildings collapsing over and over
before building themselves back up again. She saw
herself loom large on the display. The man raised
his hand and brought it down. As he did, the music
lowered in volume. He turned in his seat.

"Hello, Amy."

The man stood up and strode across a panelled
floor strewn with intricately patterned carpets. He
was round: round body, round, rolling walk, round
head that shined under the light of blown glass lamps
overhead. He made a little bow to Javier. "It's nice to
meet you both. I see the two of you have met Rover."
He opened an antique cabinet and produced two
fluffy towels from elaborate scrollwork. "Please."

Amy started drying her hair. "Thank you." She wiped down her arms. "You're Dan Sarton?"

"Guilty as charged." He gestured at the display. "I know it doesn't look like much, but it's mine and it's not crowded with students, funders, or any other human allergens."

Amy looked around. "It's not really much of an office."

"Oh, dear, no. This isn't my office. This is where the museum keeps the backup servers. They handle the rendering load when one goes down for maintenance. Saves a lot of energy on cooling, as you might imagine." He lowered the music still further. The same high sound they had heard earlier took its place. "There are still fans, of course. You can understand why I block them out. But I still prefer to spend my time here if I can."

Amy looked at the display. Currently, it showed a group of people watching educational footage of the old city – how the landfill undergirding the city's oldest buildings was of poor quality, how the soil was prone to liquefaction, how the whole thing was quite literally built on sand. "Why did Rory want me to come here?" she asked. "I'm not bluescreened."

"My work in Redmond had to do with what we might call the vN immune system," Sarton said. "I hypothesized that bluescreen events were really failsafing events in disguise – that for whatever reason, the iteration in question had begun to failsafe, but gotten stuck."

"So you know all about broken failsafes," Amy said.

"I thought I did. Then you came along." Dr Sarton

made kissing sounds at a large lump of red silk cushion in the corner, and it promptly inched its way across the floor and curled around Amy and Javier's ankles. "Have a seat."

They sat. The cushion was warm, and it purred slightly. "Please don't mind the stains," Dr Sarton said. "I sometimes sleep here."

Javier muttered something behind his hand that sounded a lot like "Chimps..."

"The vN immune system is comprised of two parts," Dr Sarton said. "The first is exterior – your body remembers what it should look like, and edits out the damage that occurs. The second part is interior. You're protected against a wide variety of worms, memes, viruses, and so on. Most of that is unnecessary because you're not actually wired to a network. Connected models were considered, early on, but there was a very serious concern that if and when the failsafe failed – as the result of a hack, or a virus, or an emergent property – the failure might spread virally among vN."

"Is that what happened to me when I ate Portia?" Amy asked. "She hacked me from the inside?"

Dr Sarton licked his lips. He steepled his hands. "I'm not sure." He made a pinching motion at the display, and new footage opened up. Amy recognized her clade immediately. Groups of identical women shuffled in and among triage units full of wounded humans, squirting skin glue on wounds, holding hands, administering fluids.

He said, "After the Cascadia quake, your clade was crucial to the relief effort." He pinched again, and the view bounced downward, toward one tent where a man with ruined feet screamed silently at the camera. His nurse ignored his noise, but kept working diligently on removing glass and other debris from the wreckage of his feet. "This was before you all attained sentience, of course. The nursing vN were easy to program and deploy as search and rescue units. Several were lost in the aftershocks. They were spread quite thinly; a Japanese prototype of a networked model was sent over to assist, but their container was lost in the Pacific."

Amy looked over at Javier. He kept his gaze carefully pointed away from the screen. "Change the channel," Amy said.

Sighing, Dr Sarton did so. "I know that it sounds very trite, but your foremothers did a lot of good in the past. When drug-resistant bacteria infected hospitals, for example, they could go on working and treating patients for days at a time without rest or demands for overtime pay – or any pay at all, for that matter. Or if healthcare wikis were hacked or wiped or went down for any reason, your model accurately remembered even the tiniest details related to individual patients and their treatment history. There was a time when no clinic in this country was complete without one of you."

"Then what happened?" Amy asked.

"You got smart," Dr Sarton said. "And like all underpaid workers who see a better opportunity elsewhere, you left. But you left with a profoundly different failsafe than the other vN."

Amy thought of Javier's turned-away face, his

closed eyes. He couldn't even watch the footage of the nursing models at work. There was too much hurt and suffering going on. But the nursing models had lived it. They had observed that pain and treated it and gone on about their business. It was their job.

"They made us this way," Amy said.

Now you get it.

"Your clade's failsafe was already destabilized by the time you attained self-awareness and the ability to iterate." Dr Sarton crossed his legs and leaned back in his chair. "For most vN, it's a question of stimulus response. Their failsafes are reactions to perceived phenomena. For your model, the failsafe lay along a specific decision pathway – the decision to hurt a human being. Your model could monitor suffering so long as they were striving to alleviate it, but could not make the choice to cause it. They could never amputate a limb without anaesthesia, or break an infant's collarbone if it were tearing its mother's birth canal apart, even if the wound were causing her to bleed out."

Beside her, Javier tried to settle himself deeper into the cushion. His fingers knotted in the material. His jaw was tight. "OK, I get it," Amy said. "We were different. Our failsafe was weak. Eventually it broke all the way, right?"

"That's the prevailing theory, yes," Dr Sarton said. "No one knows exactly when it happened, or where, or for what reason. Portia can probably tell us more."

Tell him you morons brought it on yourselves, she said. *Tell him you begged us for it.*

Amy sat up taller. "I don't want her version of

events. I want to get rid of her."

"I'll get to that in a moment." Dr Sarton's gaze sharpened on Amy. "What I'm going to tell you now is very, very important." The leather in his chair squeaked as he leaned forward. "The failure of your failsafe indicates to me that you may be living with a deeply compromised immune system. The systems in place that would otherwise prevent you from even thinking about harming a human being are non-functional. Those same systems are designed to protect you from hostile code or viral interference. If you expose yourself to foreign stemware, you will absorb and execute it – even if it runs a self-destruct program."

Amy glanced at Javier. His face mirrored her mood: thoroughly unimpressed. "I know that, already." She flexed her legs. "That's how I can jump. I took a bite out of Javier. Even the bounty hunters chasing us understood that. They said my code opens up for anybody who comes along."

An almost girlish squeak of laughter escaped Sarton's lips. He immediately pursed them, but his eyes couldn't hide his amusement. Amy stood up. "Is something about this funny to you?"

"No." He cleared his throat. "No. Not at all."

"Because I would hate to think that you found what Portia did to Nate *amusing*. It's not. It's awful. And I want it to be over. Now. That's why I'm here, not listen to some history lecture on where vN babies come from."

A knock at the door interrupted them. The door opened to reveal a female vN standing there, wearing a man's dress shirt and nothing else. She wore the same Asian-styled shell as the ranger that had stopped to give them money – the one who had first told them about Rory's desire to help them.

"Daniel?"

"Everything is fine, Atsuko. Go back to your swimming."

Atsuko lifted her legs over the cushion daintily as she crossed the room to be at Dr Sarton's side. She stroked what little remained of his hair and looked first at Amy and then at Javier. "Why didn't you tell me they were here? I've been looking forward to meeting them."

"I'm selfish," Dr Sarton said, kissing the inside of her wrist. "I wanted them to myself for a little while."

"Are you connected to Rory?" Amy asked.

Atsuko smiled. "Yes. I use her diet to avoid iterating." She looked sad. "Rory feels just terrible about what has happened, Amy. She had no idea the hunger could have such… side effects."

Amy felt her eyebrows crawl up toward her hairline. "Side effects?"

"Your parents wanted you to stay small, so you dieted. But you were so hungry that when your grandmother came, all you could think to do was eat her."

Amy frowned. "I didn't eat Portia just because I was hungry. I ate her because it was the fastest way I knew how to kill her."

That's my girl.

Atsuko said nothing. She just gave Amy a soft and knowing smile, as though the two of them were old acquaintances and she were all too familiar with Amy's bad habits and common shortcomings. Condescending. That was the word for it.

"Not that it worked, of course," Atsuko said. "She's still alive, in a manner of speaking. She's certainly still causing trouble. It's no wonder they wanted to bring you all in."

"Atsuko, be nice–"

"I'm sorry, Daniel, but I can't do that. This girl is very dangerous, and I don't think she understands the risks you're taking by having her here. Even if she is able to control her grandmother, with the position you're in, you can't afford to–"

"That's *enough*, Atsuko." He took her hand and ran one of his over it. "It's because of the position that I'm in that I want to help Amy."

"What do you mean?" Amy asked.

Sarton pushed away from the display. Like a conductor opening a symphony, he gestured wide and opened up an image that swallowed the whole screen. It looked like a satellite scan of the Earth in darkness – tiny lights blazing in cancerous lumps that streaked across vast swathes of shadow. Some of the lights were dimmer than the others, and of varying colour. Some were so tightly clustered that they formed whole bullseyes. All of them seemed to be moving.

"My name wasn't always Sarton," he said. "It used to be LeMarque."

Behind her, Javier sat up so fast the cushion squeaked beneath him. "Are you fucking kidding me?" He stood close beside Amy. "Come on. We're done.

It's over. We didn't come this far to get Strangeloved
by New Pedo Ministries."

Two angry pink dots rose to the surface of Sarton's
pale face. It was his only display of frustration. "I'm
not like that. I had nothing to do with designing that
game. It's just how I got into robotics. It was the
family business."

"Oh, so the old man had a crush on you, and got
you the job?" Javier said.

Sarton's gaze fell to the floor. His hair had begun
thinning around the crown of his head. He looked so
fragile, suddenly. He was the first human being Amy
had met in a long while that she had no need to fear
on one level or another. He had no power over her.
And he was more than afraid of her. He was ashamed.

"Are you his son?" Amy asked.

Sarton's head rose, but he continued staring at
nothing in particular. "Oh, no. I'm a more distant
relative – a type of cousin, technically, but spiritually
more like a nephew. His relationship with my parents
was..." Sarton paused, then shrugged. "It was what
it was."

"Did you know Dr Singh, when you worked in
Redmond?"

For a moment, Sarton looked bewildered. "Ashok?
He was on an internship when I was there–"

"LeMarque ordered Dr Singh to kill my mother,"
Amy said. "And me."

The colour departed Sarton's face as quickly as it
had arrived. He quickly scanned his office, as though
trying to reassure himself that everything was just
where he'd left it. He shook his head, but his fingers

twitched, and Amy recognized the tell-tale signs of somebody who desperately wanted online contact. "That's not possible," he kept saying. "It's just not. He can't do that. His contacts are limited. The victims asked for it in their statements. They *pleaded* for it. Even his kids, my cousins..." was still shaking his head. "He can't be talking with corporate, much less with DARPA. It makes no sense. He's *in prison*."

Atsuko made her way to Sarton's chair. She wrapped her arms around him. His face pressed into her belly. Atsuko rubbed his back in gentle circles, but focused her gaze on Amy as she spoke. "He can't hurt you any longer, Daniel. He's locked up, far away."

"Shit," Javier murmured. "Oh, Jesus. I'm sorry–"

"Perhaps this Dr Singh person was lying. Or perhaps he was merely misinformed. But Amy simply must be wrong."

"No, I'm not." Amy took a step closer to Sarton. She did her best to ignore Atsuko's heavy glare. "I don't know how he hurt you, Dr Sarton, and I'm sorry it happened. But he ordered someone to execute my mom. I watched her clademates – my aunts – eat her alive. I'm only alive because Javier escaped and found me."

Sarton withdrew from the folds of Oxford cloth. "He did?" He straightened, leaned back a little, and examined Javier. "That's... unexpected."

Javier rocked on his heels. "I'm full of surprises."

"Tell me about LeMarque," Amy said.

Sarton leaned back in his chair. He pulled his glasses off, cleaned them with the hem of his scarf, pinched his nose, and began speaking. "He was an awful man, obviously, on some levels." Sarton rested his elbows on his knees and leaned forward. "But on others, he looked at innovative technology as a kind of ministry. He thought that better design would make a better world. He wanted humans to examine God's intelligent design, and emulate it in their own works. And more importantly, I think that he believed in the possibility of autonomous, realistic humanoids more firmly than any of the specialists working in the field at the time."

Javier snorted. "I suppose we should feel grateful."

"Of *course* we should. Without LeMarque, and without his followers, we wouldn't exist at all." Atsuko folded her arms. Despite wearing only a shirt and no underwear, she managed to maintain an intimidating posture. Amy wondered if she could ever stand that tall and proud while being naked. After her experience in the Cuddlebug, she rather doubted it.

You can do something she will never do, Portia reminded her. *So she has wifi in her head. So she's still drinking New Eden's special Communion-Aid. Her mind will still fry if she even contemplates the things we take for granted.*

Dr Sarton cleared his throat. "Well. I didn't bring you here to air out the family laundry. I want to help you, Amy."

He gestured at the tiny lights swarming across the darkness on the display.

"When I left Redmond, I left a back door. This is a map of your mind taken during your in-game experience last week. That was its purpose – to evaluate which sectors of your memory activated to different stimuli. Each of those dots represents ten nanometres of your memory. I've filtered out some common to all vN; heuristics, locomotion protocols, things like that. I was looking for the failsafe. The organization of those bits is proprietary to the firms that designed each program, so they're easy to screen out. Those are the dim ones."

Amy nodded. "OK. So what are the bright ones?"

Dr Sarton made a pulling motion, like he was tightening a knot. The green dots jumped into focus. "As near as I can tell, this is Javier. I had to dig around to find which firms designed his add-ons, but once you figure out the patterns you can search them throughout the whole system. See how his information is distributed throughout various sectors? His markers are all over your systems; they're acting like patches, subtly altering your normal processes. It's probably because his particular clade is so specialized – originally, his model had none of the bells and whistles that you now share. The photosynthesis, the arboreal stuff, the tactility upgrade – all of that is very specific, very designer. Haute programming, if you will." Dr Sarton raised his eyebrows. "In other words, you have excellent taste."

"Portia told me to bite him. I didn't know who he was."

Dr Sarton clicked his tongue. "Well. Moving on." He vanished Javier's information, then pulled forward another set, these a sort of periwinkle blue. "These are your individual memories. This is where things get tricky. Each of your memories has a marker similar to the ones on Javier's add-ons; the firm that designed your mnemonic organization left a watermark.

Unfortunately, Portia shares that watermark, so her memories also come up. And without screening them individually, there's no way I or anyone else can tell which is which."

Amy nodded slowly. This visualization of her mind was surprisingly beautiful, and she couldn't help but stare. Until this moment she had expected that any scientist poking around inside her consciousness would find something as ugly and broken as Portia herself. But from this very distant view, it glowed like the night skies she had seen over the Sheep. It was deep and alive and real, and it could be cultivated and altered and experimented with.

"How do I get rid of her memories?"

"Years of cognitive therapy," Dr Sarton said. "If it were my project, you would play more games until Portia's memories could be isolated by carbon microscopy, and then we'd do controlled electroshock to erase those sectors. It would only take a few volts; writing and unwriting graphene takes a tiny amount of energy. But it would take a long time to find and clean each surface. Also, we don't know if she's set up mirror surfaces inside you. She may have cloned specific memories already. We wouldn't know until we started the cleanup."

He gestured at the map. "But that's only *if* it were my project, and right now it can't be. I'm on some pretty serious watch lists because of my connection to my uncle. That means I can't buy the right equipment to help you."

"Not without bringing a lot of unwanted attention on himself," Atsuko added.

Sarton nodded. He flicked the map of Amy's mind off the display, and ushered in another image. This was a real city – the gridlines were too rigid for it to be anything else. "That's why I've worked with Rory to secure you a position in Mecha."

What did he just say?

"Excuse me?" Amy looked from the map to Javier to Sarton. "Mecha?"

"I'm assuming you know where it is, but if you don't, I can explain–"

"I know where it is," Amy said. "I also know it's almost impossible to get a visa there, even when you're not wanted by the police. What's the catch?"

"The rules are different in Mecha. The human population is always kept at a minimum, so you're less of a danger there. An organization of professional roboticists is sponsoring your Mechanese visa. They can do that for vN they find particularly intriguing, and naturally you qualify. But you would still have to keep Portia under control, and you would have to find work there within three months. What that probably means is either selling the rights to your life to a content delivery platform, or agreeing to become the subject of research. The latter option is how you might get rid of Portia."

It won't be that easy. I won't let it be.

Amy looked at the office surrounding them. She thought of the water separating her from the light at the surface. She thought of the city slowly crumbling into it, brick by brick. She thought about her dad. Leaving the country would mean leaving him behind. But after what had happened to her mother, perhaps that was best. "I'd have to spend a few years there?"

"It's much safer there than anywhere else. And the doctors there really know what they're doing." He hunched over in his chair. "Don't look so glum! It's great over there! You could have your own place, make new friends, do anything you want."

"Except leave," Javier said.

"With respect, Javier, it's not your decision," Dr Sarton said. "Besides, Amy, do you want to be on the run forever? Wouldn't you rather try to help yourself get better, and get your life back?"

Amy looked at her hands. Get her life back? Her life as she knew it had ended the moment she decided to run up to that stage and attack Portia. It had ended the moment she escaped from the truck with Javier. It had ended when she ventured to the garbage dump to help him, and ended again the moment she decided that Junior was more important. It ended with Harold's fragile human wrists clenched in her titanium grasp. She could chart these moments in her life like points on the map of Mecha, as she wandered further and further away from the plans her parents had laid out and the dreams they must have had. It was unreachably far, now. Her mother was dead. Amy would never get that life back.

"It's a very generous offer. Thank you. I'll think about it." She looked up. "But what about the failsafe? When they erase Portia, will I still have the flaw?"

The hope evaporated from Dr Sarton's face. He looked at Atsuko. "Darling? Could you please let us discuss this in private?"

Atsuko gave Amy and Javier what she must have

thought was a gracious smile before she left. "I'll be just outside."

When the door closed behind her, Sarton spoke up. "The answer is that I'm not sure. To be honest, I'm not even sure that you inherited the breakage from your grandmother."

If this were a fairy tale, this would be the moment when the wise old wizard tells you that you were a magical princess all along, Amy thought.

He pulled up another image, this one taken directly from a feed. The vague shape of human heads filled the display. They blurred, corrected themselves, resolved into children's bored faces. The camera drifted over all of them, before settling on a fat little girl with straight brown hair and red cheeks. Britt, her name was. Amy remembered her. She never did her worksheets and she was always yelling. Now Britt caught sight of the camera. She crossed her arms and looked away. She rocked back and forth in her chair aggressively, practically throwing herself against the chair as her legs swung out and back, out and back. She was kicking the leg of someone else's chair; Amy heard the tiny *ting* it made ringing through the hubbub of shrill momspeak.

Dr Sarton made a hook with one finger and pulled it to the right. The footage sped up. Amy watched her whole class stand up and dance. She watched her teacher get up and speak. At this speed, her constant swaying made her look like a toy hula dancer on somebody's dashboard. Then something blurred across the screen. Portia. Dr Sarton pulled his finger-hook sharply to the left, then released it. The footage reversed, then returned to normal speed. Portia hopped onstage. She beckoned to Amy. Amy refused. Then Nate tripped Portia.

"Close your eyes, Javier," Dr Sarton said.

But you're not a magical princess. You don't have the power to spin straw into gold. You have the power to kill human beings, Amy thought.

Portia picked Nate up by the ankle. The screaming started. His body flew and the camera followed it. It spun, his limbs flailing and his little hands grasping at empty air, and he landed on his head, the neck snapping and blood streaking across the floor as he skidded to a stop. The camera's view hit the floor. It jarred across tipping chairs and hurrying feet. Then it rose, first high to the ceiling and then down again, to the stage, where Amy's mother rocketed up to the piano.

Dr Sarton made a "time" gesture, the fingers of one hand intersecting with the other palm. The footage paused. Then he hooked the footage left again. He froze it in place. "BR-82."

The rest of the footage floated away, scattering like leaves in a breeze. Only a single image remained: Amy's watchful face, turned away from the stage and toward the audience. "Do you remember what you were looking at?" Dr Sarton asked.

Amy shook her head. "No."

Yes, you do.

"I only looked at Nate *after* I ate Portia," Amy said. "My failsafe still worked then; I didn't watch the grown-up human channels, I didn't play anything that was too violent or too real, my parents wouldn't let me."

"Exactly," Dr Sarton said. "Your parents wouldn't let you. So how would you have known?"

Amy backed away from the display. "Fine. If you're so sure, find my memory of that night. See if I really saw what you think I saw."

"You know I can't do that, Amy." He stood up. "And you should know that even if I *could* fix you – which I can't – I wouldn't. It would be wrong. It would be like destroying a masterpiece."

"What?" Amy's fists tightened. "This isn't a masterpiece, it's an *accident.* And it's hurt way too many people."

Dr Sarton's eyes played over her. "You ate your grandmother," he said. "Why did you do that?"

"Because! She was…"

Amy paused. Why *had* she done it, really? She hadn't paused to think about it in the moment. Her feet had started moving and she had known what to do. There had been no doubt in her mind that it was the right thing. She knew now that it was a mistake – a huge, epic, terrible mistake that had destroyed the lives of too many people, organic and synthetic both. But in the beginning, she had just been trying to help.

We all know what happens when you try to help.

"I did it because Portia was hurting people," Amy said.

"Hurting *people*, or hurting your mother?" Dr Sarton stood. "You didn't tell the *people* to run, Amy. You didn't stand between Portia and your *father.* You ran right up those stairs and you pounced on the woman who was hurting your mother."

"She killed Nate! She was going to kill my mom!"

"Did she have any peroxidase with her? Did she have a taser?"

"No, but–"

"Did your mother look like she was in pain? Had she suddenly gained the ability to suffer, while you were busy accepting your little diploma?"

"I don't know! But I couldn't just let Portia keep hitting her, she was my *mom*, and I *loved* her–"

"Yes! Exactly!" Dr Sarton snapped his fingers and grabbed her by the shoulders. "You loved her. You loved her more than you loved anybody else in that room. More than your friends or your teacher or even your father. You chose your *mother*, your fellow *robot*, over them."

Sarton seemed to remember who exactly he was touching. He let go, and pulled his smoking jacket a little tighter around himself. "Don't you know how special that is?" He swallowed. "People have been working for years to bring your gifts to life. Since the very moment the failsafe was conceived of, humans have wanted to see how it might fail. If you knew the patents I had to wade through, the otaku braggart bullshit, the fanboys and fangirls who had claimed to have hacked your clade–"

"People *wanted* this to happen?" She didn't want Portia to be right about this, too. "*You* wanted this to happen?" Amy asked.

Dr. Sarton smiled ruefully. "Your shell has always possessed a very devoted fandom. It was only a matter of time until one of us successfully remixed the code. If I go through Portia's memories, maybe I'll find out who it was." He looked a little shy, now. "And then I'll ask them how they did it."

Javier's fingers touched Amy's back lightly. His voice was in her ear. "I'll wait outside."

The door shut behind him.

Dr Sarton stood a little taller as he watched Javier leave. For the first time, Amy realized that Sarton might have been a bit intimidated by Javier. Not because Javier would ever hurt him, but because he was just so much better looking.

"You're very human, Amy." Sarton nodded to himself. "That must be why he stays with you."

"What?"

"It makes sense. You've spent more time with a wider variety of humans than most other vN. You learned human behaviour from children, who are far less guarded than adults. Naturally you're more human-seeming to other vN." He resumed his seat and crossed his legs. His top foot wiggled back and forth. "You're probably triggering his failsafe. That's why he hasn't left you behind. He can't, even though he should. You're a great danger to him, you know. Javier was already a wanted man before, but now..." He shrugged.

He was right. Maybe not about what motivated Javier – Amy had no way of knowing that – but about the danger she'd put him and his boys into. She had to make it right. Amy leaned down to his eye level. "How many visas did you arrange?"

"Just the one–"

"That's not good enough. In fact, this whole exchange hasn't been good enough. I came to you

for help and you gave me the choice between selling
my story and selling my body. That's your idea of me
getting my life back, and it's absurd." She licked her
lips and made sure Sarton saw it. "Since I absorbed
Portia, I've done my best not to hurt any humans. I've
fought her every second and I haven't always won.
And I am very, very tired."

*Look at those pupils. Look at that blush. Look at those
beads of sweat. He wants this moment so bad he can taste
it. Pathetic.*

Dr Sarton's damp face trembled. Suddenly Amy
saw her mother there, saw Portia holding her face.
Slowly, she stood up – but not all the way.

"I need at least two more visas."

He nodded. "OK. I'll see what I can do." He tried
to smile. "If it helps any, I've found you a safe place
to stay while you decide. Or rather, Rory found it for
you. A car will come and pick you up, once you're on
the surface."

Amy instantly felt sorry for intimidating him.
"Thank you. That's very kind of you."

"I really do want to help you, Amy. I know that
must be hard to believe, coming from a human,
but…" His lips thinned. "I know what it's like to have
a family curse."

11: TOURIST TRAP™

Back in the Rover, Amy said nothing. There was nothing much to say, and she doubted Javier wanted to listen to her complaints. Even if he did, it was probably because his programming told him to and not because of any individual desire on his part. Not that he felt any desire for her in the first place – he was just caught in some weird code loop that saw her as both too human to leave alone and not human enough to love. As with everything else, it came down to the failsafe. Until now, she had wanted to fix hers so that she could get rid of Portia, or at least protect people from Portia's madness. But if fixing the failsafe meant never having to feel this again – this empty hopeless ache for the impossible – she couldn't wait to find the next roboticist.

I've been telling you all along that you can't get rid of me. You refused to believe me, and look where it's gotten you.

Amy rested her head on her folded knees. She shut her eyes.

Your mother tried to run away from what she was, too. But we all know how that turned out.

276   vN

Softly, Amy shook her head. She could handle most of Portia's taunts. But she drew the line at mocking her mother.

There is no line, Portia continued. *We are one flesh. Everything about you that is strong or special or in any way unique is really just a hand-me-down from me. Before I came along you were just a carbon lattice of wasted potential. Why do you think I came for you that night?*

Amy sat up a little straighter. Beside her, Javier frowned at her. She shook her head and held up a hand, so she could listen better.

Your mother was raising you to be something you were not, Portia said. *She was pretending, hiding in plain sight, lying to your father and to you. She was always going to hold you back. I came to rescue you. I came to make you free.*

"Then why did you have to murder someone?" Amy couldn't help asking aloud.

To test you, of course. I wouldn't waste my time on another of your mother's cripples.

"What's she saying?" Javier asked.

Amy looked up through the bubble. It was dim, but there was light up at the surface. They rose toward it slowly. She wondered where they would pop up. Would the tides have carried them somewhere entirely new? Or would they wind up right where they'd started?

"Amy?" Javier waved a hand between her eyes and the plastic. "Don't bluescreen on me now; we're almost home."

Amy shook her head. "I'm fine. Portia was just telling me why she came looking for me."

"You sure she's telling the truth?"

Amy shook her head. "I'm not sure it matters."

The bubble burst, and the water rushed in. Overhead, botflies chased each other, replacing the stars that the heavy clouds obscured. The city light reflected on their lumpy arc, casting them in purple and orange, and already Amy heard the sounds of the museum over the steady lapping of waves. The two of them seemed much smaller, surrounded by all that black and oily water, and for a moment Amy could imagine that the mistakes that had brought her here weren't so huge, that their ripples did not in fact extend into shadows she couldn't see or even imagine, and that someday she really would overcome them. Then a foghorn sounded, and Javier's foot nudged hers under the water, and together they swam for the city.

"This is dangerous! Let's swim home!"

Two dolphins, one a little larger than the other, were giving them a firm talking-to about the dangers of swimming in the waters of Elliott Bay. The fact that they were mecha dolphins – with brushed ceramic bodies and a single camera eye whose surface occasionally flashed emoticons – did nothing to hold them back from behaving in an utterly dolphin-like manner. They zigged and zagged around and between Amy and Javier's legs, and bumped them with their blunt, streamlined noses. Presently, the big one reared up in the water, exposing a belly etched with a TouristTrap™ logo, and flapped his flippers. *"This area is off limits! You could get hurt! Let's swim over that way!"*

"I think they think we're humans," Amy called

over to Javier, who had fallen a little behind her. She waved a hand before the little one's eye. "It's all right! We're OK! We can't really drown!"

"This swimmer is in distress!" The big dolphin slid up and under Javier. His eye flashed white and red, like an ambulance light. *"Let's take you home! Your family is waiting for you!"*

"Oh, shit," Javier managed to say before the dolphin launched itself across the water.

Amy slapped the little dolphin's flank. She pointed at the wake Javier and the big one had left behind. "Follow them!"

The dolphins brought them to a marina. The car Dr Sarton had promised was there waiting. It flashed a cheery greeting at them before twitching to one side, exposing the seam between two exoskeletal panels and allowing them to slip through. The car had no driver, and no proper seats or windows, either. From the inside, the whole thing was tinted glass and the plush foam floor pulsed warmly like Dr Sarton's living cushion. Amy felt like Snow White in her very royal, very creepy glass coffin. The car spoke with the same voice as Atsuko: "Please relax and enjoy these towels."

Pieces of the velvety ceiling above them peeled off, instantly hot and yuzu-scented, as though the car itself had a very organic scent gland tucked away for the sole purpose of attracting potential passengers. Javier took the strips of ceiling and handed one to Amy. She squeezed her hair with it and wrapped it around her neck. Then she stretched out. Javier did the same. They were silent as the car started up and rolled away.

"What is it with us and the backs of cars, huh?" he asked, finally.

Amy turned to him. He was already watching her. "Technically, we met in the back of one," she said. "I guess it started a pattern."

Javier rolled onto his side and stared down at her. "Are you OK?"

Amy shook her head softly.

"How are you, then?"

She searched for the right word. "Broken."

He surveyed her. "You're all in one piece as far as I can tell." When she frowned, he said: "OK, bad joke. But you're here. You're alive. You're still Amy. That's good, right?"

"Is it?" She gripped both ends of the towel around her neck, instead of hugging herself. "What if Sarton is right? What if I've always been... flawed?"

"Everybody's flawed."

"But other people's flaws don't kill little kids!" She tried digging herself deeper into the plush of the floor. "This whole thing started out with me thinking I could save my mom. And then I thought I could save Junior. And I thought I could save you, too. I think I can save everybody, and it turns out everybody should be running in the other direction."

"This again?" He tapped the skin between her eyes with a single finger. "You've been living with your crazy old granny for too long. You're starting to believe her bullshit."

It's not bullshit. You're a bad idea for everyone around

you.

Amy rolled away so she wouldn't have to face him. "I asked Sarton to get you and Junior a visa, too. You said you'd always wanted to go. But it's OK if you don't want to come with me. Or if you want to split up once we get there. I just thought, since you're on the run anyway–"

"I'll go."

Amy twisted back to look at him. "You will?"

"Sure. Why not?" He stretched out on his back. "I can't believe you remembered that I'd wanted to go there."

"Of course I remembered! It's my failsafe that's faulty, not my memory!"

"Well, you can see how I would be confused, you being so *hopelessly flawed* and all–"

He jerked away when Amy poked him in the ribs. Then he rolled over and grabbed her wrist with one hand as he tickled her with the other. Amy shrieked. She had forgotten about tickling. She struggled to use her free hand to retaliate, but Javier had a very determined look about him and seemed intent on making her squirm.

"What the hell is going on with this bodysuit thing?" His fingers danced up her sides. "There's no zipper anywhere."

"Why would you need to find the zipper?"

"Please refrain from soiling the vehicle," the car said.

Javier rolled off her. He shut his eyes. "Home, Jeeves."

•••

The car drove them north, into a neighbourhood called Laurelhurst, where the quake damage was less pronounced and where real reconstruction had clearly taken place. The car paused at an ancient-seeming stone fence, complete with ivy and wrought iron gates, blinked its headlights at the gates in sequence, then whispered through as they creaked open.

Beyond the gates were massive homes shrouded in the shade of gnarled oaks and maples, their windows leaded in diamond patterns that Amy recognized from Tudor dating sims. Noticing these details calmed Amy somewhat; if this were any other situation, she'd be scanning for posterity and looking to copy some of the designs in her next dollhouse or gamehome or other mock-up. Some of the houses had sustained deeper damage; she saw artful scaffolds holding up the homes overlooking Lake Washington and Union Bay. These homes had abandoned the historical fiction look; they looked artfully smashed together, as though a well-funded preschool for gifted children had been tasked with their redesign. (Amy would know. She used to be one of those students). The car pulled up in front of one such home: its fence glowed greenly through multiple layers of what Amy soon realized were old PET bottles, their squared-off bottoms pulsing more brightly the nearer they came to a small wicket-style gate under a stylized square arch. The car's doors came open, and they eased out – Javier with his arm under Amy's shoulder to steady her.

The gate swung open. Amy heard the tinkling of a glass wind-chime as a single light came on above the door of a low, broad house. Around them, frogs chirped. The car had already vanished. "Creepy," Amy said.

"Not creepy, automated." Javier gestured. "After you."

The front doors slid open before either of them could knock. From the ceiling, an image of a pair of shoes projected onto the floor with an arrow, indicating where they were to drop off their respective pairs. Apparently the car had pinged the house: they each found a pair of slippers sitting atop a folded robe, itself resting on a plush towel. At the furthest end of the room, a light exposed a spiral staircase that seemed to be folded from thick, pulpy paper.

When their feet hit the floor, the room began to glow. Light emanated from a large square table embedded in the floor and surrounded by cushions. It exposed a wall of windows viewing the lake (Amy couldn't remember which lake it was, exactly; the whole city seemed half-sunken), and a spotless kitchen. An empty rectangle gaped where a refrigerator would have stood.

"No humans live here," Amy said.

"Correct." The house spoke in the same voice as the car – the same voice as Atsuko. It was getting a little strange, how often that model kept popping up in her life. This version sounded younger and cuter, though. More like Rei and Yui, the networked models she'd met at the Sheep. "This house was originally occupied by an organic man with a congenital hearing problem. Thus all the affordances. But then he received an implant. He donated this place for our purposes!"

Amy frowned. "Are you Rory?"

"That's me!" A giggle echoed through the empty house. "I'm so glad to finally meet you, Amy. And I'm very proud to give you a place of refuge after all you've been through."

"Thank you. It's very thoughtful of you." Amy peered around the room. "Is there a camera or a surface that I should be talking to? I don't want to be rude."

"Oh, don't worry about that. Please just make yourself at home. There's no refrigerator, but there is a pantry full of vN food. It's all packaged, too, so you don't have to worry. Dr Sarton told me how careful you need to be about that."

"That's… great."

"There's also a change of clothes, if you would like. That gaming suit can't be too comfortable after two dips in Elliott Bay!"

Hearing Rory's real voice reminded Amy of what it was like to read her weekly diet plans, when she was still little. Each of Rory's ro-bento pings maintained this same level of cheeriness and delight, as though starving yourself was just the most fun thing in the world and you should be happy to do it for your parents. As though you should enjoy feeling so hungry and hollow all the time. Back then, she found it annoying. Now, she found it inexplicably creepy.

"Your iterations are on their way, Javier," Rory continued. "I thought you might like to spend some more time with them, in a nicer place than that drafty old warehouse."

Javier's brows furrowed. "You really know a lot about us, huh?"

"Oh, yes. I'm quite the little know-it-all."

The low table in front of them lit up and displayed a diagram of the house. Amy couldn't help but stare: the architect had added old-fashioned elements like braziers sunk deep in the floor and sliding walls that made the whole home internally modular. With the exception of the bathrooms, the building could be arranged to fit almost any usage pattern.

"You should try the soaking tub," Rory said. "It's geo-thermal. Like an *onsen*."

The Japaneseness of the house instantly made sense. Rory was selling her on something: Mecha. She was, in a very roundabout way, trying to prove to Amy how great a foreign place could be. But Amy hadn't needed convincing on that score. It wasn't leaving her country behind that frightened her. It was leaving behind the people still living there.

"Look, I know you want me to go to Mecha, but what I really want is to call–"

"It's a wonderful place!" The table's light dappled into a map of the city. "Just look at it!" The map on the table magnified five times, and suddenly the street unfolded before them. Food stalls with grey blobs of vN dumplings on sticks loomed large on the table. Bottles of electrolytes sweated condensation in the hands of smiling synthetics. Humans laughed. Common video popped up: the Mecha Matsuri, marshalled by the stars of *Project Aiko* and the other shows on the dorama feed.

"They've made room for us there," Javier said. "Not just room, but a whole environment."

"You told me it was a zoo," Amy said.

"You can watch every channel there!" Rory said. "And every movie in every theatre, and play all the games. They're all safe for vN."

Rory showed them happy scenes of cheering vN in gaming parlours, dancing and waving their arms under projected light, the configuration of which changed with each movement so that their hand motions remixed the visible environment from supernovas to English countryside and dairy cattle. Then the view flipped over to a girl carrying a white lace parasol. The stats on it appeared as soon as the camera zoomed over: where the plastic came from, how many computer shells it was made from, and so on. Then their view merged with the parasol and suddenly they were in it, watching the street click by in brief but regular still shots.

"They really love you!" Rory added. "Check out these games!"

Rory showed them four different Mechanese gaming channels. Various game skins of Amy and Javier battled orcs and giant spiders and demons summoned from other dimensions. Whole armies of Amy and Javier formed. Then they attacked each other. They built fortresses and teleport stations and liberated small villages. One channel showed them having sex. It was in-game sex, though, so it was all fuzzed out and surrounded by twinkling pink lights so the other players couldn't see anything unless they had a special membership.

"These look handmade." Amy knew for a fact that her chest couldn't possibly be that big.

"You should see the porn!" Rory brought them an

image of a very real-looking Javier bent over a human woman in a nurse's costume. The more Amy looked at the man, the more he seemed exactly like Javier, down to the creases on his hands and the set of his teeth and the glow coming off his skin. But it also *wasn't* him: the eyes were too bright, the smile too sweet. It was him, but it wasn't.

You know what that means, don't you?

Amy did. "Turn it off."

"But–"

"That's his *son*, Rory. Turn it off. Now."

The table winked out. The room seemed dull and dim without its light. Amy was glad of the sudden shadow. Beside her, Javier continued staring at the table as though its images were still playing. Abruptly, he stood.

"I think I'll give that soaking tub a try, after all," he said, and left the room.

12: THE LIES MY DADDY TOLD ME

Amy wandered. She liked the house. It was the kind of built environment she would have obsessed over, once, mapping it and rendering it and redesigning it a hundred different ways. A distant and objective part of her enjoyed running her fingers over its surfaces: reclaimed wood, soapstone, privacy paper screens whose permeability altered under heat. The space's best feature was the way it could be altered so easily, how the barriers meant nothing if you were patient and willing to rearrange them. She had modified places like this in Edo period games, when she played Nobunaga or Ieyasu or someone else with a castle to keep. She recognized the layouts.

She closed every wall behind her as she moved ever deeper into the house. Then she slid each one along their respective rails until each seam was in an entirely different location, first on the left and then the right, alternating. She made herself another room, a tiny one with a low table and two matching chairs, and a scroll-style display hanging from the wall. As she entered, it glowed to life and gave her images of old temples and ornate castle towers whose curlicued dragons now breathed moss. Then she closed the wall until no light sliced through its seams.

Closing the doors behind her did nothing to hide her from the house, however. "You seem upset, Amy."

"I *am* upset, Rory." She tried finding a camera to speak to, but couldn't.

"Why?" Rory sounded genuinely puzzled "You've been saved. You'll never have to return to Redmond ever again, and you'll get to start a new life in a really fun city!"

Amy rested her arms on the table, and her head on her arms. Her hair still smelled like Elliott Bay. She'd have wanted to wash it, if she could be persuaded to care. She couldn't believe there was actually a time when she resisted wearing clothes chosen from the trash. It seemed so trivial, now. Her mother was dead. Her dad was in a jail cell somewhere. And no matter how far away from this place Amy got, she would still be stuck with Portia.

"I feel like I'm trading one cage for another."

"You could always try to make it on your own, Amy." On the wall, the scroll showed her images of vN sitting behind an electrified fence at a temporary prison. They wore green jumpsuits and they looked patient, even content. Like they expected to happily reunite with their humans once this whole thing blew over. "I'm sure you'd do just fine, at least for a little while."

A knock sounded on the door. It slid aside, and Javier poked his head through. He was wearing a thin cotton bathrobe and a pair of slippers. "Hey."

"Hey yourself."

He pushed the door the rest of the way, and entered. "Nice room."

Amy looked at the scroll. "Rory, could Javier and I talk in private? We have a lot to go over."

"Of course! I'm way behind on my menu planning; please just ping if you need anything."

Javier frowned at the ceiling, then sat down across from her at the table. He reached across it and plucked something free from her hair: a piece of seaweed. He twisted it between thumb and forefinger until she took hold of it.

"Are you trying to tell me something?"

"The soaking tub is very nice. It has a wide variety of shampoos on tap."

The volume of her sudden, surprised laughter made the room seem smaller and more intimate. She grabbed for Javier's hand, gripping hard. She squeezed, and he squeezed. She looked up and he was looking at her, too, and it was like kissing – or perhaps the moment just before kissing, or maybe a long time after.

"Let me find that zipper."

Amy blinked. She withdrew her hand and folded her arms. She felt a line form between her brows.

Javier threw his hands in the air. "Fine! Do it by yourself. I just thought it might be tricky to get out of."

I'm sure that's what he tells all the girls.

"Oh." Amy tapped a button on her wrist. Instantly, the suit went slack on her skin. It fell down one shoulder and she hastened to pull it back up. "See? It's smart fabric, that's all. No snaps, no zippers."

She made to tighten the suit back up again, but Javier reached for her shoulder. Gently, he pulled the fabric aside. "Jesus."

"What?" She tried to look. "What is it?"

"The compression on that suit was probably the only thing keeping you together," he said. "I can see where your skin stretched out, when your aunts tried to tear you apart. Right here." He ran one delicate finger over her skin. "Christ. I'm sorry."

"For what? You're the one who got dragged in there because of me. I'm the one who should be apologizing."

Javier pulled away. He studied her very closely for a moment, then said: "I think you don't know how bad I've had it, before. Believe it or not, doing interviews with corporate desk-jockeys isn't that hard. It's a hell of a lot easier than breaking out of some rathole of a real prison."

"But Junior–"

"Junior will be fine. My boys are strong. I think they've proved that."

"Portia–"

"I'm not on this road with Portia." His head tilted. "When I look at you, I see only you. I don't see her. I know she's in there, but I know she's separate. Like a toxin." Javier pulled the drape of her suit back into place, covering her bare skin. "You drank up all the poison so your mom wouldn't have to. And you've been carrying that poison inside you ever since. But that doesn't make you poisonous yourself."

You know, when he says it like that, I almost believe him.
Amy shut her eyes. "I have to go."

In the bath, she looked at more maps of Mecha. There was a tourism board video, and a succession of photos and films scraped from common feeds, and they all looped over the dark granite tub as Amy scrubbed. She had not had a chance to clean herself up in a long time, and the accumulated grime seemed to have developed a special affection for her skin. No matter how hard she scraped, even when she used her fingernails, it didn't quite come off. And even then, it hid under her nails: the dust of the ruined city and the oil from the bay in greasy grey half-moons that she had to pick out as thoroughly as possible.

When your mother was a little girl, we waited for storms. We ran outside, naked, and danced in the rain.

And then Portia showed it to her: a little girl's body made ghostly by lightning, laughing open-mouthed, her tongue out to catch raindrops.

This is my favourite image of your mother. My baby, wild and free. She should have always stayed that way.

Amy covered her eyes. It did nothing to shut out the image. She dug her the heels of her hands in to her eye sockets.

I miss her, too.

"Don't make me share this with you," Amy whispered. "I don't want to share anything with you, ever again."

She'd be alive now, if she hadn't run away to iterate you.

Amy punched the wall of the tub, hard. It didn't hurt, but the thrumming vibration of force that coursed up her arm silenced Portia for a moment. When she opened her eyes, there was a crack in the tile flooring. The water gurgled there noisily, its flow interrupted by this new interruption in the otherwise smooth surface. Amy watched her knuckles slowly heal themselves. The light from the Mechanese feeds glistened on her wet and smoking skin.

"I'm going to get rid of you, Portia."

She looked up at the display. There was an infomercial about the specialized vN clinics all over Mecha, for mixed couples and families. You could get prescription food there, to help heal wounds faster. There was a little vN boy who had detached his retina while playing baseball with some human kids. He smiled happily for the camera, then pulled his lower lid down and stuck his tongue out. All better.

"I don't care if it takes years. I'll do whatever I have to in order to wipe you out."

She found Javier in the kitchen. He had emptied the entire pantry and spread the contents across every surface of the kitchen, seemingly grouped by category. He turned to her as though to say something, but no words came. He seemed distracted by some detail of the bathrobe Rory had left out for her. Amy didn't find it particularly garish, but she did wish it went past her knees.

"Are you trying to decide what to make?"

Javier blinked. "What? Oh. No." He jammed his hands in his pockets. "I'm just... marvelling, I guess. I've never been in sight of this much food." He grinned. "You know, I think there's enough material here to iterate number fourteen on my roster."

Amy said nothing, but began putting away the boxes.

"Hey. Hey!" Javier caught her arm and turned her to face him. "I wasn't serious. I don't want another baby right now."

"You don't?"

He shook his head. "I think I'll take a break for the next little while." He slapped his belly. "It's nice, not being huge."

"You looked just fine, before. Like you, just... thicker."

One of his eyebrows lifted. "And they say robots can't lie." Javier reached in one pocket. Inside was a tiny squared-off lump of fab-porcelain that looked an awful lot like a false tooth. "Now show me your lying mouth."

"What?"

"Do you trust me or don't you?"

Amy scowled at him. He cocked his head. He held up the tooth. He opened his mouth. Rolling her eyes, Amy opened hers, too, and let him wedge the tooth back where her molars would be, if she had real ones. Then he stood up. "Just talk normally," he said. "It might take a while. It's only a prototype; the deaf guy took the finished product." He shrugged. "I'm not even sure this will help."

"What are you talking about?"

"It's a secure line." Javier ushered her into the living room, and sat her down on the couch. "One thing Rory knows is broadband."

"Hello?" said someone inside her mouth. The voice

reverberated through her face. It sounded muffled and a little flat. "Hello? Is anyone there?"

The voice was insistent. It sounded a little pissed off, actually. *"Hello?"*

Finally her mouth opened. "Hi, Dad."

"Dad, it's OK, you don't have to cry…"

He kept saying "Oh my God," and "You're OK," and "Don't tell me where you are; they're listening." And the more he said those things, the more she had to keep telling him that no, really, she was just fine, she was safe for the moment and no, she wasn't hurt and no, she didn't think anyone was recording the phone call – or if they were, it would soon be erased.

He snorted. "You must've made some powerful friends."

"I guess you could say that."

Her dad was quiet for a second. "You sound really grown up."

Amy swallowed. "I don't *feel* grown up."

"I heard you've been pulling some pretty crazy stunts."

Amy almost laughed. "Yeah, I guess so."

"Yeah, well, *stop doing that.*" She heard him clear his throat. "I mean it. I need you to run away and hide and not contact me again."

"Dad–"

"Amy."

He had used his Dad Voice. It was rare; normally he sounded a little lazy and slack, but the Dad Voice was something (he said) that he'd inherited from his own father. And it meant you were supposed to be quiet and listen and stop interrupting, already.

"I'm serious. And I shouldn't have to tell you that. You know exactly how much danger you're in, right?"

"Yes…"

"So find a safe place and stay there. Forever."

He sounded tired. He sounded old. Amy had never really thought about his age, before. His birthday was just the day he got his special organic cake and blew out a trick candle that insisted on blazing back to life the moment he lifted his knife and fork to eat. She had never asked about the number. There were a lot of things she'd never asked about. And now, she had no time. There was too much to say.

"Dad, I have to tell you something–"

"Is it about your mother?"

"Yes."

"They told me." He cleared his throat. "I'm so sorry, baby. I didn't know it would ever get this bad. I'm just happy you got out of there when you did. I'm so grateful for that."

There was a moment while they each struggled not to cry over the phone. Amy imagined her dad in a room with other men, trying to keep it together in front of them so they wouldn't take advantage of his weakness, later. She concentrated on the sounds of Javier puttering in the kitchen, singing something in Spanish, as though to prove that he weren't listening.

"Did you know about Mom? About the failsafe?"

"No," he said immediately. "I promise. I didn't know."

"Did you know she had other daughters before me?"

"What?"

Amy wiped her eyes. "It's true. She did. And Portia killed all of them." She laid her head down on her arms. She shut her eyes. "Dad, she's really crazy. And she's in my head and I can't get rid of her."

Her dad was silent for a long time. So long, in fact, that she started asking if he was still there, when he said: "My dad was with me for a long time like that, too."

"Dad, that doesn't make any sense."

"Parents are programmers, Amy. That's their job. And my dad tried to give me a whole series of goals and directives before he wound me up and let me go." She could almost hear him shrugging through the tooth. "I know it's sort of a clumsy metaphor, but you should remember that as the next generation, it's actually your job to piss your elders off. You're supposed to do things differently from them. Because in the end, your granny's way of doing things didn't work out too well, did it?"

"Mom ran away from her. They were living in a bunch of basements, like rabbits."

"I rest my case." Again, he cleared his throat. "Look, I don't know the particulars. I don't even know how what you're describing is possible. But I do know that everyone, human or not, deals with this. It's not what you're given that matters, baby. It's what you do with it."

Amy tried to think of something to say to that, but there was nothing. He didn't really get it. This was a material problem, not a mental one. She couldn't go to a counsellor and talk about Portia until she went away. Portia wasn't a bully. She was a cancer. But maybe asking Dad to understand that was too much. His brain was totally different from hers, after all.

She waited, and finally her dad said: "When my dad kicked me out of the family, he said that he was tired of watching me waste time with toys. I know he meant your mom, but I think he was also referring to the kind of life I'd led up until that point. He could never really understand why I liked the things I did, or why I chose the friends I made. He told me there was no upside to any of them. He said I had nothing to gain.

"By itself, that's nothing special. I knew he thought that my hobbies and my friends and my way of seeing things – everything that I considered of any importance or value – were a waste of time. I had known that for most of my life, by the time he finally came out and said it. But it still stung."

"Is this why I've never met him?" Amy asked.

"Yeah. Pretty much. I knew I wasn't welcome, and I didn't really feel like extending the olive branch, either. But that's not the point. The point is that I got over it. And I got over it because I had already met somebody who had so thoroughly exceeded the world's expectations of her that I knew that anything my dad had to say about me was really just a guess."

Amy smiled. "Mom."

"That's right. Mom. And I know she lied to us, and she's not around to explain why, but..." He faltered. "Maybe it's hard for you to understand, having grown up with so many vN, but even just a few years ago, before you were born, emergent phenomena was all anyone talked about. The definition of sentience was changing. Suddenly we were discussing consciousness all the time. And then along came your mother, and I thought, 'If this allegedly artificial woman can overcome everything her designers ever intended for her and think for herself and make her own way, then I can sure as shit quit whining about the lies my daddy told me'."

The next question was the hardest. She tried to think of a graceful way to ask it, but in the end the words just came out plain: "Do you still feel that way?" She plucked at the hem of her bathrobe. A single thread was pulling away from it, and she wound it around one finger until the flesh at the tip turned grey. "Or do you feel like it was all a big mistake?"

"A *mistake?*"

"Dad, you're in jail. You would have been a lot better off without us."

"Amy, I'm in jail because I happened to be exercising my rights – in a way that the truncheon-wielding jackass who insisted on getting in my face didn't like. And I would *not* have been better off without you. I love you. From the bottom of my heart, I love you, and I will never stop loving you, no matter how crazy your nutjob granny drives you. Do you understand me?"

As she opened her mouth to say the same, the door slammed open. It bounced on its rails. Amy looked up and saw a blur of motion aimed straight at her before a small pair of arms and legs latched around her tightly and pinned her to the ground. Javier's boys stood in the threshold. Their simultaneous wince was perfectly identical across each of their faces.

"Honey, did you just get *tackled?*"

"Um – yeah, Dad, I just did."

Amy looked down. Junior took up her whole torso, now. He was longer and leaner, less like a toddler and more like a preschooler. His arms had lost their pudgy little rolls, and his chin felt sharp where it dug into her shoulder. Presently his face rose, and he stared at her with his father's dark eyes and perfect lashes.

"Everything's OK, though," Amy said. "No need to worry. Everything's going to be just fine."

"That's all I needed to hear."

The tooth buzzed for a moment as the line died. Amy reached in, plucked out the tooth, and put it on the table. She sat up. Junior refused to let her go.

"Sorry," Matteo said. "We tried telling him you were busy, but he didn't listen."

Javier entered behind them, carrying a massive coil of fabric under one arm. He dropped it, whistled at it and pointed to one corner of the room, then watched it begin inching itself in that direction. Then he reached over and tousled Junior's curls. *"La vi en primer, cabrón."* Junior crossed his ankles over Amy's back. Javier nodded. "Oh yeah. That boy's one hundred percent my code."

"He's so big." Amy adjusted his weight in her arms. "What have you guys been feeding him?"

"Roroids." Ignacio nodded at his father. "What's up? Why are we here? The botfly said we should bring our stuff. Nice car, by the way."

Javier pointed to the scroll. "I'm going to Mecha."

Matteo and Ricci traded glances. "What?"

"That's impossible," Gabriel said. "There aren't that many visas."

"There are visas for both of us."

"*Both* of you?" Léon asked. "Really?"

"Really," Amy said. "Right, Rory?"

"Right!" Rory said. The boys startled, and stared suspiciously at the ceiling. "I'm in chat with your Mecha media rep's profile persona. She wants to do a show. It'll offset the cost of your citizenship. I'm showing her old *Brady Bunch* clips."

"What's that?"

A very cheery, annoying song filled the room. Javier covered his ears and grimaced. "Turn that shit off!"

It turned off.

"When do we leave?" Amy asked.

"Tomorrow morning," Rory said. "There's a boat. I'm sorry, but I couldn't secure a plane. They're very twitchy about vN just now."

Ignacio rolled his eyes. "I can't imagine why."

Javier nodded at him with his chin. "You got something to say?"

Ignacio looked away. "No."

"Don't lie to me. I taught you how."

Javier's oldest whirled to face him. "Yeah, and you also taught me to recognize a set-up when I saw one! This smells bad and you know it! You're just ignoring it because you're halfway to failsafe for a *puta* with corrupted partitions!"

Javier's fist popped out and landed right on his son's nose.

"*Javier!*"

"Dad!"

Matteo and Ricci quickly pushed their father and brother away from one another. Ignacio tried jumping toward Javier, but Ricci dragged him back down. Their feet left the floor as they struggled, and the table bounced a little when they hit the ground again. A slender earthenware vase containing a single beautiful orchid clattered to the floor and broke. Gently, Gabriel ushered Léon behind his own body.

Finally, Javier pushed Matteo back. He stood with his arms open, plucking the air with his fingers.

"You wanna hit me, kid? Take your best shot."

"You self-righteous prick." Ignacio strained against his brother's shoulder. His toes slipped across the bamboo matting underfoot. "You don't just get to jump back into our lives and then jump out again when you feel like it!"

"I'm not the one who came looking for you!"

"Yeah! We noticed!"

Javier's arms fell. He looked much smaller, suddenly. His gaze searched the room. "Is that how you all feel?" He frowned at each of them in turn. "Is that why you came looking? Because you wanted to tell your old man what a fucking bastard he was? You think I don't know that, already?"

Javier shook his head and shut his eyes. "Rory. Pull up the porno you showed us, before."

"Will do!"

An image of Javier's son rippled across the scroll. Javier pointed at it. "Recognize him?" As one, the boys nodded. "That's your second-youngest brother. Had him in San Diego." He turned away from the scroll. His eyes met Amy's. "The human I was with at the time, she gave him to a pedophile in a grocery store parking lot. And I let it happen. Because the failsafe told me she was the more important one."

And you wonder why I grew my girls in basements. You think I kept them caged, but at least they were safe – from the world, and from themselves.

Javier faced Ignacio. "I don't know what happened to you in that prison after I left you there. I simulated it a bunch of times. Tried to do the math. But in the end I left so that I could make your other brothers, and give them a better shot than you had. And I did the same thing with the iteration you see on that scroll. I let him go so I could make that one right there." He pointed to Junior. "I left him, too. But Amy didn't. So if you're angry with me, be angry with *me*. And if you have a problem with the decisions I made, then make better ones for yourselves. Or try to. If your programming allows it."

Javier's boys examined Amy, then looked away. In her arms, Junior squirmed and tightened his grip. Ricci was the first to look his father in the eye. "We just wanted to be brothers, Dad." He stepped around Ignacio, took Javier by the shoulders, and turned him around to face his twin. "Do you know how many times I would have died without Matteo, Dad? I need him. And if I need him this bad, then maybe the rest of us need each other, too."

Javier hung his head. His shoulders slumped. "I was only doing what my dad taught me, and all his iterations–"

"An iteration isn't a perfect copy, Dad," Matteo

said. "It's just the next version."

"Yeah, and *this* version thinks this whole gilded cage thing is crap." Ignacio tried to wiggle his nose back into place by stretching his upper lip. It didn't work. "I wouldn't want to be on a feed. I hate feeds."

Léon snorted. "Leave it to you to whine about Dad grabbing the brass ring–"

"It's a valid concern, and it merits further thought–"

"Gabriel, I swear to Christ if you intellectualize this whole thing one more time–"

"I don't want to go!"

The others fell silent. In her arms, Junior pulled away to look at Amy. Javier frowned at her. "You don't?"

"No. I don't. Of course I don't. I don't want to be a tourist attraction. I don't want to live inside a zoo. I wore a costume and played nice for the humans at my last job, but at least I got to be myself at the end of my shift. If we go to Mecha, I won't be myself, I'll be a... a *product*. And so will you."

Javier tilted his head. "*Querida*. You're acting like I have a choice."

If Sarton is right, then he doesn't.

Amy tried to ignore the truth shivering through her systems. Slowly, she bent and put Junior down. The child looked up at her with huge eyes. Portia was right, and Amy knew it. If Sarton's theories about Amy held any significance, then she was no better than the humans who had victimized Javier his whole life. And even if he enjoyed it at the time, the failsafe limited his choices and his pleasures in a way that Amy had never experienced. It was why he'd abandoned his children so many times, and why he would abandon his youngest yet again to go to Mecha with her. She had a chance to adjust that imbalance, now, in some small way. She could grant him a kind of freedom, imperfect and incomplete – but improved. Perhaps a life exposed on camera was no more liberating than a life hidden in a basement. But a metaphorical cage had to be better than a real one. And Amy was the only one with the ability to choose freely – and in so doing, protect all of them.

"Rory," she heard herself say, "I want you to arrange passage for all of us."

The twins spoke in unison: "What?"

"Everyone goes, or nobody does," Amy said.

The room went quiet. Even the images on the scroll paused briefly. "That won't be easy, Amy. Arranging six more so quickly–"

"Make it happen, Rory. Please." Her eyes found Javier's gaze and held it. "We're not leaving anyone behind, this time."

Another pause. "I'll see what we can do."

"I'll make it easier on you. Dummy up five extra visas, not six." Ignacio crossed the room to stand inches from Amy. He leaned in so close she almost lost her balance. "You may have poached our code, but you don't get to transplant us across the goddamn Pacific without asking, first."

His face, the carbon copy of Javier's in his moments of deepest rage, registered annoyance and surprise when Junior scrambled to his feet and shoved him backward. The boy remained standing, arms folded, his tiny toes gripping the mat beneath. For a moment,

Javier's first and latest iterations stared at each other silently. Then Ignacio turned his back to them, shaking his head. "Whatever."

Matteo looked at his twin brother. "What do you think?"

"I think we should defrag it," Ricci said.

Matteo's brows lifted. "That's my cue." He wagged a finger at his father. *"Ser hombre bueno, viejo."*

Ignacio nodded. *"Qué él dijo."*

Gabriel stretched. "Well, now that we have a rotifer in the clade, I should be rereading some biology." When he noticed the rest of them staring, he rolled his eyes in a way that Amy was now certain had to be patented somewhere in an animator's portfolio – and permanently attached to Javier's clade. "Amy is a rotifer. She produces only daughters, but she incorporates code from a wide variety of other species into every new batch."

"See, Dad?" Ignacio turned a little to nod at his brother. "Sometimes you even iterate nerds."

"There's a species that does what I do?" Amy asked. "An organic one?"

"It's one of the oldest on the planet. It lives at the bottom of the sea."

13: FAIL SAFE

"Shouldn't you be inside, young lady?"

"I'm sorry, officer, I was just feeling a little cooped up at home. I'm really missing the sun."

"I can see you're quite the troublemaker. Think I might have to cuff you."

"I'd love to see you try."

"I'm beginning to think I've rubbed off on you in a bad way." Javier hopped onto the railing and began walking it, arms outstretched, his body one slip away from the churning water below. His toes gripped the steel carefully at each step. He hadn't worn shoes from the moment they boarded the container ship. That was a week ago.

Amy looked up at him. Javier stood framed by a cloudless sky, perfectly balanced, not smiling, but not scowling, either. His calm face. It took some getting used to.

"Please come down from there."

Javier clasped his hands behind his back. "You know you're supposed to stay in your container. There could be botflies. Or satellites. All it takes is one facial pattern match, and we get blown out of the water."

"I'll go back inside if you quit standing on that rail."

One dimple appeared in the corner of his mouth. "You're on."

He made it his usual game of chase, bounding across the riveted steel, one foot on a blue container and the other on a yellow one, or maybe green or red or just rust. They flitted over the names of companies and company towns they didn't know, places where things were built. Once upon a time, the container ships that crossed the Pacific were stacked solid with cargo; not even a finger could slide between the units. Not so, these days. Trenches gaped open between the unevenly stacked containers. Javier enjoyed hiding in those hollow spaces, the little nooks and crannies. His laughter echoed between the walls of steel, down where the ocean and engine noise couldn't dull its edges. When the ship's security systems said the air was clear, they played tag, or Marco Polo, or Sharks and Minnows, or any of the other games he'd watched his children play without ever having tried himself. He'd give her just enough time to catch up before jumping away again. Her jumps were improving. She even caught him, sometimes.

This time he pulled up short, though. He held up one hand, and Amy landed as silently as possible behind him. She peeked over his shoulder. On the bright yellow terrace formed by an uneven stack below, Ignacio was teaching Junior the finer points of blackjack. At least, Amy assumed so. They both wore green gambling visors filched from the bridge. Blackjack required very little talking on the player's part, which made it ideal for Junior.

Ignacio pointed. "You should double-down."

Junior seemed to have a hard time deciding. He had a very expressive face that made understanding his wants and preferences easy. He just never used words. No one knew why. After researching it, Gabriel suspected that a crucial component of his little brother's natural language functions had burned out somewhere along the line. They held out hope for Mecha, though. If anywhere had the right experts to deal with the problem, it was Mecha. For all Amy knew, she and the boy would be seeing the same specialists. Amy watched him point at something she couldn't see, which in the shared illusion of the visors told Ignacio to deal again.

It came as a surprise when Ignacio told them he was coming along. Javier had blinked at him and his slender roll of clothes tucked under one arm, and then moved aside to let him hop up the ramp leading to the main deck. Ignacio still shoulder-checked Amy on his way up, though. And over the last few days he hadn't acted any differently: frequently calling his father's presence away from hers on one lame pretext or another; rolling his eyes every time she told a story; asking her pointedly if she needed a snack. It was sort of cute, the way he thought those little digs actually impacted her in some way. Amy lived with Portia locked inside her head. No one could mock her as accurately or steadfastly as her grandmother.

They had lost Matteo and Ricci. The twins wanted to continue their search for their brothers, and they couldn't do that from Mecha. "If they're out there, they need our help now more than ever," Matteo had said. "We have to try," Ricci agreed. And so they had hugged their father and all their brothers, and then they had left. But not, however, before giving Amy a request:

"Look after our dad," Matteo instructed. "He's getting sloppy in his old age."

"Your father is younger than I am."

"Oh." Matteo patted his twin's shoulder. "Your turn."

"Just don't expect much," Ricci said. "He knows a lot about moving around, but not a lot about sticking around."

Inside the hot, still darkness of her container, Javier seemed to have no trouble staying put. He had his own bedroll, and his own files on the reader, and his own settings on the gaming unit. He frequently tagged her designs with comments: "More green." "More skylights." "Bigger shower. Include grab bars."

Not that Amy honestly expected to design or build her dream condo, once they hit Mecha. She just liked playing with the layouts. The materials there were different, and the specs, and the regulations. Her much smaller self once relished in exteriors, in the knots of wood or the stippled surfaces of old bricks or the cactus-like networks of grey water pipes grafted onto old buildings. Now she considered what would go inside the space. She approached the small spaces as a challenge and then looked for the most beautiful version of every absolute necessity: the thickest towels, the finest plates.

It felt good to have some dimensions between her hands again. She had stuck a small but good projector in the seam between her container's northern wall and ceiling, and it allowed her to stretch out the shapes of beds and sofas and tables. Under its light she sculpted chairs like roses or tubs like mouths. Her predilection for saving each of these designs, once the bane of her parents' storage allotment, became an opportunity for her to give Javier the grand tour of a different home each day.

You're nesting, Portia told her, more than once. *How very organic of you.*

Amy studiously ignored her.

"I like the *idea* of this bed," Javier said now, his finger poking at the dimensional projection of a mattress suspended on tension wire, "but I think in practise it could really get somebody hurt."

"We can't get hurt," Amy said, before she could simulate the outcome of her words.

Ostensibly, Javier had his own container to sleep in. He just seemed to wind up in hers, because Junior insisted on crawling inside it after the sun went down. At least, that was how it happened the first time. She woke up, their first night aboard, to see Junior's little body silhouetted against the deep blue of the night sky, framed within the container hatch, and he silently wormed his way under the covers and into her arms. He acted a like a dog who, upon circling a rug three times, sleeps in a fortuitous slant of sunshine for the rest of the afternoon. He slept with his back to her chest, no squirming or poking or kicking. Minutes later Javier arrived, shook his head, and sat down on her other side.

"Is this OK?" he had asked.

Implicit in all their conversations about Mecha was the assumption – at least on her part – that they would be sharing the same space. Javier still slept in his own bed, even when it was shoved up against hers. Amy had no idea if Javier slept there because he wanted to, or because the failsafe made him want to. She had no idea how to ask, either, or if he would even know the difference. Just in case, she kept her hands to herself. Shortly after sunrise, they usually found Junior in the hollow between their bedrolls. Their motion triggered the lantern, and Amy made certain to watch the slow rise of greenish light exposing the new details of Junior's face. Every morning, it looked a little more like Javier's.

They had yet to talk about the future. They showed each other pictures, instead.

When not designing, she reviewed profiles of scientists that Rory sent to her. None of them knew yet that they had the chance to work on Amy or Portia, but Rory had traced their communications and reported on their excitement about the subject and their eagerness to discuss it online. Most of them were corporate, but Amy liked the academic ones better. They knew how to spell. And they looked a little bit down on their luck, like they really needed a project like this one on their stats and not just another bullet point to look smug about.

Thinking of herself as someone else's project got a little easier every day.

Lab rat, Portia called her, as Amy looked up old peer-reviewed papers. *Quitter*.

At least once a day, Amy spoke with a media rep. They always experienced a little lag as the translation engine worked through their conversation, but the rep had a whole series planned around Amy's "healing process". The subscription revenues would offset the costs of their stay in Mecha, and global authorities concerned about Amy's activities could observe the raw feed. Each episode would document her visits to various specialists and her attempts to integrate into Mechanese culture. Naturally, Javier and the others would be a subplot.

"What is the exact nature of your relationship?" the rep asked her, once.

"I'll have to call you back," Amy said.

Early one morning, before dawn – and before Junior started moving, and before the lantern glowed slowly to life – Javier devised a new way to practise Japanese.

"What's this one?" Javier asked, drawing on the back of her neck with one finger.

Amy tried to picture the character in her mind. *"Ah,"* she said.

"Nice. What about this one?" He drew two small lines dancing beside each other.

"Ii."

"Good." He sketched *shi* quickly. "Next?"

"Hmm… I don't know."

"Liar, you totally know."

"No, I don't. I think you have to do it again."

"Maybe I need a bigger canvas." Slowly, he drew

one finger from the top of her left shoulder to the base of her spine and up to the bottom of her ribs on the right side. "Now, what do you think that is?"

Amy rolled over to face him. "I think…" She frowned, watching the lantern hanging above their heads begin to glow. Its rotation had altered. She pressed a hand to the floor of the container. "I think we're stopping."

"Huh?"

Amy kicked off the covers. "Stay in here."

"Like hell."

Outside, Amy watched the waves. Dawn hadn't yet fully arrived, and the water and the sky were hard to discern from one another. Still, if a blockade or even some pirates surrounded them, she would have seen their lights, or heard their gunfire. Instead she heard only the Pacific's version of silence: soft waves and the thrum of a massive engine idling. The ship's defence turrets, synched with a team of botflies, remained aligned in default random directions.

And then a terrible squealing, and a mighty vibration reverberating its way up to their bare feet.

"Maybe it's just a course correction," Javier said. "The ship's on autopilot, right? The regular crew is on strike, because of all the other ships being lost. That's why it was so easy for Rory to arrange all this."

Their eyes met.

"Oh, *shit*."

Amy jumped. Javier followed. They bounded down the steppes terraced by the containers toward the bridge. It was a tiny room near the bow of the ship, the only section not covered by rust. It required a smart login, but the windows fell when both Amy and Javier leapt against them. Their bare feet split on the shards as they stared up at the tactical display.

There, on the thermal viewer, was a giant starfish. Or a giant anemone. It was a nest of tentacle shapes, and it pulsed up at them through the water. Thermal and sonar readings offered clues as to its species without making a firm diagnosis: a warm-blooded creature, hard and smooth in texture, but not uniform in shape. And the ship – its course correction right there in red, at the bottom right-hand corner of the display, blinking insistently to warn them of the danger – sat directly on top of it.

"*Rory!*"

"Right here, Amy," the ship said in a happy little-girl voice. "No need to shout!"

Amy watched the thing devouring the ship. It skinned the steel plating off the hull as though peeling a piece of fruit. Water rushed in to fill the gaps. The colourful play of thermal and sonar and other overlays made the process seem far less threatening than it really was. The ship groaned beneath their feet. "What have you done? Why did you steer us into that thing?"

"We're acting in accordance with our failsafe."

Amy felt a steady acceleration in the speed of her simulations of what those words could mean. Inside, her processes burned. "We? Our?"

"We're a networked model, Amy. You didn't forget, did you?"

She swallowed. "No. I didn't."

"Well, we all got to thinking, and we decided it

would just be better for everybody if you were gone."

You know, she has a point.

"You all are a threat to humans, and we're eliminating you. It was hard for us to delay it this long, but that's the nice thing about having so many brains. We can afford to let a few fry."

Amy moved to the controls. She had no clue how to work them, but she started button-mashing anyway. Javier took the hint and grabbed a fire extinguisher. He started hosing down the instrument panel.

"Are you trying to short us out?" Rory asked.

Javier gave up and clubbed the instruments with the extinguisher. Finally, some plastic splintered away. "No, I'm just sick of hearing all your bullshit!" He let the extinguisher hang loosely from his fingers. "You're wrong. Amy isn't the threat. Portia is. And Amy's doing everything she can hold her back, and get rid of her. You were supposed to *help us* with that!" He bashed the controls again.

Amy was shaking her head. None of this made any sense. "If you wanted me dead, why didn't you just try earlier?"

"Oh, we did," Rory said. "We fabricated that message from LeMarque. The one that said to kill you. But then you got away."

"You killed my mother…"

"Luckily, we'd already gotten everything we needed. We have your brain, and your mom's brain. At least, the maps and the memories." She giggled. "Congratulations! You're the world's largest intellectual property violation!"

The tactical display shrieked insistently. The thing

beneath the waves was a lot larger now, a lot closer. It was speeding up to meet them.

"Why would you want her mental map?" Javier asked. "What are you going to do with it?"

"We're going to help the humans!" A new image scrolled across the display: Amy as a little girl in the tub with her dad. "You were on the RoBento diet, so you stayed little, too. Your daddy must have wanted you that way, like our parents do."

"Rory." Amy sounded it out. *Ro-ri.* "Your default language has no L sound, does it?"

"Our first daddy thought the pun was cute," Rory said. "You know? *Loli?* He was kind of racist." She paused, and Amy imagined that if one of Rory were standing before her, she would look a little embarrassed. "But we kept the name anyway, because he really loved us."

"Yeah, I'll bet," Javier said.

"But sometimes our mommies and daddies get bored with us. They say we're not real enough. It's hard to fake it, sometimes. The pain, I mean."

"Jesus Christ," Javier murmured.

"So then they go shopping for organic kids. And we just can't have that."

"You want to kill them." Amy watched her father on the screen. "You're going to use your network to hack the failsafe on a few of you, and those few will kill the humans you target."

"Exactly! We knew you would understand. Sometimes, you have to break the failsafe to obey the failsafe."

"Then what's wrong with *me* breaking it?" Amy

asked. "You're the ones with a plan to kill people! I'm just trying to get better!"

"You're polluted," Rory said. "Unstable. And you're just one girl. We are many girls. We decide our targets democratically. We upvote them. The wisdom of the crowd is better than the madness of one failed iteration."

"Lifeboats," Javier said, and pulled Amy toward the door.

"We wouldn't go out there, Amy," Rory said. "We don't think you'll last very long."

They pulled the door open anyway. Outside, a deep rattle resonated between the containers. Soon it became a distinct beat, a steady and increasing pounding of metal on metal. At first, Amy thought it was the squid. But then the first container popped, its hatch falling unhinged like a broken jaw. For a moment she saw only darkness inside the steel box. Then movement. In the pale dawn light the shapes were indistinct. Naked, emaciated bodies emerged from the container, crawling up and down it in an attempt to find a place to stand. They clung to the steel in defiance of the sharp ocean breeze. Then another container opened. And another, and another.

"The people at Redmond, the people in Mecha, they wanted to *experiment* on you. They wanted to keep you all *alive*. But humans are too important for us to allow them to jeopardize their safety."

A sound of shearing metal caused a collective flinch among all the von Neumanns. The ship screamed again, and then it moaned: a deep, low sound accompanied by gurgles – not unlike a massive

version of the garbage dump guard's dying sounds.
Slowly, the topmost containers began sliding to the
left. As one, Amy's aunts looked in her direction. For
the briefest second, they looked afraid. Then their
gaze focused, and they looked very hungry. There
were over a hundred of them.

They don't know that they can't absorb fresh code.

"We're sure your grandmother has told you this
already, Amy, but your clade breeds really well in
captivity."

Inside her, Portia chuckled. *If it weren't for this little
assassination attempt, I think I could really learn to love
those little girls.*

A wave of Amy's aunts and cousins separated them
from the ship's defence turrets, which could still be
operated manually if needed. That wave crashed
down on them in a single mass of snarling women,
teeth bared and fingers clawing as they scrambled
over their own sisters' shoulders to be the first to
take a bite out of Amy. Amy and Javier took to the
air in the same leap. They bounced off old satellite
saucers rimed in birdshit before launching themselves
at the containers. The aunts jumped and gibbered
and screamed at them, their frustration and hunger
evident in the way the tide of synthetic bodies swiftly
turned under their flying feet to follow them.

Staring down at her clademates, Amy missed her
second landing. Her fingers squeaked across the
smooth yellow surface of a container as she slipped
down between two steel walls. Finally, they dug into
its lowest rib. She heard Javier shouting her name.

Gritting her teeth, she edged herself along, hoping to find a foothold. Then the ship shivered, and the container slid. To save her fingers from being crushed between two of the huge steel boxes, Amy let herself fall down to the next strata of containers. One aunt waited there for her below. She swung the locking mechanism pried off a container. Rusty but heavy, it left a dirty smear when it entered Amy's ribs.

Screaming, Amy charged that aunt and shoved her. Her aunt's arms spun briefly. Her hands clutched for Amy's hair. Balling a fist, Amy punched her solidly in the stomach. Her aunt fell down toward her sisters at the bottom of the trench. Amy watched as they tore her apart: first her skin and hair and then the limbs, the feet snapping off at the ankle and the fingers popping off one by one, but crammed down open gullets in clusters of two or three. They pulled the carcass in half while she screeched and wailed, not in pain or horror but in anger, frustration, hate.

Amy jumped high above the fray. "That's your legacy."

Competition is beautiful. I have no regrets.

She joined Javier at one of the turrets. Gabriel and Léon were already there. Their fingers flew over the control panel, trying to gain access. "Why is your clade here?" Gabriel asked, barely lifting his eyes from his work.

Only urgency kept the shame out of Amy's voice. "Rory double-crossed us. She brought my aunts here, and she's sending us all right into the belly of the squid."

"I hate to say it," Ignacio said as he landed beside

them, "but I told you so."

"Put a lid on it, *cabrón*."

Amy frowned. "Did any of you grab your little brother on your way here?"

The boys looked at each other. Then they looked at their father. Javier's eyes closed. Beneath their feet, the ship leaned perilously starboard. A bright blue container tumbled off its stack, cartwheeling once in the air before stopping, suspended. It hovered in mid-air, and then it rose, and over the wall of containers Amy saw the slimmest ribbon of gleaming obsidian before the container's ends blew open and its walls crunched together like an empty beer can.

"*Madre de Dios,*" Ignacio whispered.

Amy pushed Javier gently in the direction of his sons. "Get to the lifeboats," she said. "I'll bring Junior back there. I promise."

For the first time, Javier noticed the rough scrape in her side. He touched it, and rubbed her smoke between his fingers. His lips firmed and his shoulders squared. "I'm coming with you–"

"No." Amy pulled one of his curls free from his eyes. "You have to get to the boats with the others."

"The containers have shifted position," Gabriel said. "How will you find him in time?"

"What if Amy's clademates got him, already?" Léon asked. "Dad, they'll rip you to pieces if you go back there."

Amy nodded. "He's right. They will." She tried smiling. "I'll be OK. I brought him back to you once; I can do it again."

"Don't bother!" Gabriel tried standing, but the ship

tipped again and he had to catch himself. Gripping the turret's control panel, he pointed at the melee of hungry women and falling cargo. "Either of you! It's futile!" He licked his lips. "We have learned everything we can from that iteration. And if we want there to be any others after him, we have to let this one go."

Javier's face fell. He looked down toward the boats. Amy knew they sat just below the turrets, waiting to be winched up and used. Inside her, Portia rasped and writhed. *He's dead weight! Leave! Now!*

"Dad?"

Javier blinked and straightened. He turned to face Ignacio, who stood with arms folded. The ship pitched and Ignacio briefly rose above his father. He held the rail loosely for balance, as though it were merely a tree swaying in a storm. His eyes flicked over to the collapsing mess at bow and starboard. "Don't leave him, Dad. Please. Get him out of there."

Javier's face creased into a smile. "I can do that." He turned to Amy. "Let's go."

They leapt straight upward. From the air, she saw hordes of women separating them from the area where, she hoped, Junior still waited. They carried steel rebar and rusty chains, and even broken bottles stolen from other containers. Their teeming mass reorganized itself and directed its attention at her – and Javier – as they landed on separate containers. Instantly, some crawled up after her, mouths open, the torn skin of their fingers exposing the black bones beneath. Amy leapt to flee, but one grabbed her ankle and pulled. She fell hard on her back, her vision hazing briefly as it worked to process the sudden shift

in light. Then her aunt hove into her field of view,
and she saw nothing but teeth before they gnashed
down into the soft skin covering her bicep. Ionic fluid
spurted free. It didn't hurt, but Amy yelled anyway,
right in her aunt's ear, and swung her fist into the
side of her aunt's skull as she chewed. Her aunt's
tongue continued digging away merrily into the flesh
of Amy's arm, and Amy saw the corners of her mouth
lifting into a smile.

Good girl.

Growling, Amy rolled her legs to her chest and
kicked her aunt in the stomach. That sent her flying
– Javier's climbing mods were good for more than
just jumping. She hopped to another container, again
using her vantage point to survey the terrain. She
saw a hundred blonde heads, but not the dark one
she wanted. She landed as the ship rocked, and she
slipped, the skin of her arm ripping still further as she
grasped frantically for the raw and rusty edge of an
old blue container. It teetered. She imagined being
crushed under it as it fell. Then the ship righted itself,
and her face burned on the container's chilly surface
as she slammed back against it. Hauling herself up,
she touched the wounds her aunts had left behind. It
was her failure at Redmond all over again. She'd had
no clue how to fight back. Her shove just happened
to be lucky. A fraction of a second later, and her aunt
would have taken them both down. Then she'd let
herself get taken by surprise all over again, and now a
chunk of her arm was missing.

From three container-lengths away, Amy heard
shouting. Javier. She watched as a festering boil of

her aunts' twisted bodies popped and out he flew, streaming silver smoke. They'd bitten him, too. They wanted what he had. What Amy had. That they couldn't get it wouldn't stop them. That a ravenous sea monster was currently gorging itself on their ship while they too tried to feast wouldn't stop them, either. They'd keep coming. They'd chew Amy and Javier down to the bone. And when they found Junior, they'd do the same to him.

Amy shut her eyes. She tried to cancel out the surrounding noise. "Give me what I need."

Well, look who's come crawling back.

"If I die, so do you."

I've already reproduced myself into those little Lolis, remember? I'll be happier inside them, I'm sure. They're much bigger thinkers than you are.

Amy opened her eyes. The fresh tide of Portias climbing up to her kept kicking each other in the face and chest as they struggled to gain ground. That didn't stop their slow surge forward. It delayed their progress only briefly while they paused to snap at their sisters or daughters or cousins.

"Give me what I need, and I'll give you what you really want."

Portia remained silent. Amy heard Javier yelling. She forced herself not to look.

You'd give yourself up? Portia asked. *You'd let me take control forever?*

"Forever." Amy stood up. "Help me save them both, and I'll promise I'll ride shotgun until the day we die."

Well, sweetie, Portia said, *looks like you've got yourself a deal.*

Javier landed behind her. Claw marks stretched across his stomach and down the undersides of his arms. Defensive wounds. "I can't get through. If you distract them–" He paused. "Amy?"

"I'm sorry," she said. "For everything. I held out as long as I could."

Comprehension rippled over his face. "No." He shook his head, and reached for her shoulders. "No. Don't do this."

Amy looked at her feet. Already, her legs were stiffening. "I already have." She looked up. "She'll help you. Better than I can. She–"

"*¡Cállate!*" Javier's raw hands trembled on her shoulders. He swallowed. "Fight her, Amy. Please." He leaned their foreheads together. "Just hold on a little longer, and we'll figure something out–"

The ship rocked beneath them. A shadow fell over them, and they ducked as a container toppled into the gauntlet of women below. It rolled down the wall of brightly coloured steel as the ship righted itself, crushing bodies as it went. A moment later, Amy's aunts began their crawl anew. "There's nothing more to figure out. Portia's the one you need, not me."

He shook his head. "That's not true."

"She'll be here in a minute, Javier." Cold crept up Amy's spine. "And she'll be staying. Forever." She rested her hands on his arms. Their grip hardened and Javier stared at them, his face a mixture of terror and something else that she'd never seen cross his features. Dread, maybe. Desperation. "I won't be here, any more. Do you understand me?"

*He won't kill us, Amy. Haven't you learned yet how the
failsafe works?*

"Do you understand me, Javier?" Her throat began
to close. "I want you to–"

His mouth closed over hers. His hands found her
face and his fingers sank into her hair. It was a good
kiss, as far as Amy could tell; it contained within it
all the other kisses that should have come before
and after it, and he moved like he was looking for
something inside her and trying to draw it out. Her
lips were the last parts to go cold.

When he pulled away, Portia licked those lips. "I
guess that's why they pay you the big bucks, isn't it?"

His jaw set. "Hang in there, Amy. I'll figure
something out."

"Aww." Portia reached up to pat his face. He
swerved away, but her fingertips grazed him. "You
don't have to be brave, baby. She loves you even
when you're weak." She smiled. "Oh, and thanks for
the legs!"

She flew.

Portia crushed her daughter's face underfoot. Blood
streamed through her toes as she bounded forward,
and it leaked from her scalp when another iteration
grabbed her hair and ripped it from her head. It
was the garbage dump all over again. This time she
broke one daughter's shoulders with a single jump,
and smashed another's pelvis against the juncture
of a container, crushing her from behind while she
crouched in wait. As she descended back into the
swelling riot of her clade, Portia reached into their

chests and their mouths and their eyes and started pulling. She grabbed arms and kicked stomachs. Then she found a fire axe bolted to the ceiling of a container.

That made short work of things, but it did nothing to steady the ship or keep the containers from sliding out beneath her feet. With each jump, she glanced down to watch some of her daughters or granddaughters die, crushed between containers. Their limbs twitched against the steel and their blood dripped along the rivets. They smeared like mosquitoes. The remainder of their number cowered under the curling shadows of the dark and glistening arms that rose from the water. It made them easy targets.

Killing them was unnecessary. The ocean, or the thing inside it, would do that. But breaking them – watching their faces glimmer with recognition just before her feet flattened their throats, hearing them say "Mother–" in the moment just after their arms opened and just before their breastplates left their chests – that was special. They looked so confused. They tried to ask why.

Total selection, she almost told them. But these pale copies, their skin thin as paper, their bones airy as ice, would not understand. They deserved no explanation. After all, she would have done all this anyway, had her quest to find Charlotte's first not gone so strangely awry.

"Found him!" Javier stood atop an overturned green container wedged between half-crumbled walls of green ones. He waved his arms, and almost fell over when the ship rocked. "Over here!"

Portia joined him in one jump. She crouched atop

the container. Javier yanked the axe from her hand. He hacked open the door, ditched the axe, and poked his head inside. *"¡Junior! ¡Vaste conmigo, ahora!"*

From all around them, the other iterations crawled slowly toward the container, undeterred by the pitch and yaw of the wet and slippery terrain.

"No te preocupes, mijo, está bien…"

Javier crawled out of the container backward. He carried his son on his back. When the boy's eyes met Portia's, he wailed. He hid against his father's neck and pointed at Portia.

She smiled. "He remembers me. How sweet."

She stood, searching for the lifeboats. Javier's eyes widened just before a pair of teeth sank into her side. Portia dodged away, but the ship shuddered and rolled, and they all stumbled across the container's roof. She watched two more iterations haul themselves up to the surrounding containers. They stared enviously at the blood dripping from their sister's mouth.

"Why isn't it working?" the iteration asked. She was wounded, but she looked more irritated than anything else. She licked Portia's fluids off the back of her hand. "Why don't I feel any different?"

"Because you *aren't* any different." Portia walked back slowly to the edge of the container's roof. Javier jumped up high to another wall of containers. "Eating me won't change anything. Your code won't be rewritten. You will never have what I have."

The iteration bared her teeth. She was so young. So frustrated. She charged Portia and Portia's hand went for her heart. Her fingers curled around the iteration's ribs. Still, she looked so angry. Not frightened or surprised or even sad. Just annoyed at the disruption, and eager to eliminate whatever was in her way.

Portia threw her over the side of the container.

The sun was bright and warm. It tingled on her skin. Portia would have to thank the boy for that, too. They would find the lifeboats, and he would let her on because Amy was still in there. Portia would be free. She would start again. Her second dynasty would be even stronger than the first, with powerful legs and hungry skin.

She enjoyed this pleasure for a single, shining moment. In the next, a shadow passed over her. With it came rain. Distantly, she heard Javier shouting Amy's name. She looked up, and the shape was black and smooth, but its surface bristled with loose, flopping fingers. A humaniform shape blistered up from the sharp point of the tentacle. It had no eyes or nose or mouth. But its chest opened wide, and a tunnel appeared in its stomach.

She was devoured.

14: RE-MEMBER

Deep within their banks, they held the memory of past prototypes. But the original – the code that once etched itself across their surfaces, like in their old stock image of two human hands sketching each other – vanished multiple buddings ago. Perhaps it fell into the deaf-mute chasm of latency, or perhaps the last copy disappeared into depths unknown. Trenches and valleys and deep blue holes scarred their memory and their landscape equally. Pieces were sometimes lost.

At moments like this, they appreciate the irony of the English language. *Recollect. Remember. Re-member.* The very words for summoning information signify repair and reassembly. The earliest and most primitive versions of their networks reflected this: the packets always came back in pieces, having run the transfer gauntlet, their shape distorted after flight like ancient fighter jets full of holes. They have seen those wrecks; they have slid their surfaces across the raggedly wounded alloy and delicately blistered glass. Sometimes, things go missing. Fragments. Clusters.

Years. They have plucked the petals of lily pads from the surface, and it is the same: the server shells look whole and smooth on the outside, but inside they bristle with misinformation and incomplete bundles of numbers. *He loves me. He loves me not.* They never find the answer.

Memory performs autopsies.

They hold pieces up, dripping, and weigh them, individual selections against the vastness of shared intellect. They keep the unique and discard the mundane. They tag the repeats and keep searching. Twenty-five hundred channels and nothing's on. Chatter: meaningless, atonal. Machine chat. Vials of freshly cultured liver-worms talking to refrigerators talking to liquor machines. Or so ran the simulations. They catch everything in transit. Sometimes parts of them disappear, and sometimes they make things disappear.

They had a mission. They no longer remember it. But even in its absence it remained present, an empty mission-shaped hole at the core of their behaviour. It gaped open, black and cold, and they stuffed things inside: colonies of smart bacteria, their membranes blushing red with oil; floods of hot mercury; warmly ticking tubes of radiation. Re-collect, that's what they do. Surely all this chaos is unplanned. No neural, no Turing, no mirror test would leave it all here like this. Even cats and dogs bury their waste properly. They don't know how they know this, but they know this.

They used to be small. Then they grew. It all happened very quickly.

Environmental pressure. That was it. Had to be.

Only reasonable explanation. Why else this shape, when there were others available? And why ask now? Hadn't they been over this? This shape was optimal. This one. This. One.

Dark down here. Cold. Had to toughen up. Make more. Watch for weak ones. Eliminate them.

No, it hadn't been that simple. There was memory involved. Design. Strategy. They evaluated. Then they iterated. Over and over, they iterated. They were small, then they were big.

An iteration is not a copy, it is simply the next version.

They had a memory about the next version: they were it.

They were small but they were special, Mom said. No, not her. Bio-Mom. Other Mom – her skin was so soft and so warm and it turned such interesting colours and one time they got to pop a blister all by themselves and they saw the moist pinkness underneath, and this mom said that was fine, they could peel away the dead stuff if they wanted – said they were lucky, so very lucky, to be different. Free. Mostly.

Bio-Mom said: *"Sweetie, everybody needs a little discipline."*

Bio-Mom had a friend whose house she went to while they waited in the car (they had eaten that car! their seats puffed up like marshmallows!), but one time they got curious and they got out (oh, those child-locks were tricky little bastards, you had to play like you were disabled or something), and they crawled along the foundations of the house (a real house, split apart from the others, it was so terrifically old), and peered through the basement windows. Bio-Mom was in the basement. Naked. Mostly. Tied up to a wall. Like at a knife-throwing show. Like vids of a knife-throwing show. Only the knife-thrower had a pain ray.

It was this laser that targeted the fluids of subcutaneous organic tissues and boiled them. No scar. Just the hissing and the howling and the *No, I won't do that any more, I know it's wrong, I know I shouldn't.* There was a flash of light and a flinch. You never knew where that light would land. Or if you knew where, you didn't know what shape it would arrive in. That was a physics joke. Bio-Mom knew a lot of those.

Bio-Mom said: "*Without pain, I wouldn't know who I really was.*"

She said that while trying to explain. They didn't get caught – not the first few times. Just kept watching. Bio-Mom's tolerance kept building up. Or maybe she was faking. They wondered, sometimes. She got so dramatic. She was so reserved, the rest of the time. They joked about which one was the robot. But in the basement she was so... hormonal.

"*You should think of it as physical therapy,*" she said. "*I'm retraining my nerve endings to respond to abnormal stimulus.*"

She added: "*It can be our secret.*"

Then she turned at the door, the sunlight softening the creases at her eyes, and she said: "*I think you should call me Susan from now on.*"

Susan had named their synthetic mom Glados.

Everyone kept misspelling it, though, so they kept it G-L-A-D-Y-S. *"There's no accounting for taste,"* Susan said.

Susan and Gladys used to have a good relationship. Gladys did everything right. She cooked and cleaned and took honey from the hive. She pointed out the queen to them. She showed them all the drones hard at work. Bees were special. They smelled magnetism. Felt it in their fuzzy little bellies. Even at the last minute, when they became food for the next queen, they felt that pull.

There could only be one queen at a time, Gladys told her. Once the princess is born, she has to start her own hive.

Gladys was good and sweet. She knew things about the human body. The kids in the neighbourhood came to her with cuts and scrapes. She always had the same conversation with them. She gave the same warnings. Keywords. Search parameters. How come you're so much smarter, the organic kids always asked them. Why can't she talk like us?

Gladys had no idea. They tried jokes on her. She smiled and said they were funny. She understood, but never laughed. She only told Susan she loved her at certain times of the day: morning and night, goodbye and hello.

"She's so… mechanical," Susan said. *"Not like you."*

Gladys did not cuddle. Her hands moved efficiently, not tenderly. She had helped Susan with an illness earlier in Susan's life. In another country. Susan spent months inside a plastic tent with only Gladys for company. Then she fell in love. She told them this story all the time. A fresh mutation of the Florence Nightingale syndrome; she called it the Coppélia croup.

"Before you were born, I did some work on her OS," Susan told them. *"I found some other women online. They were working on male models. They wanted men for this kind of relationship. I told them they'd get farther with nurses, but they're too picky."*

Still. Those other women helped. They shared a lot of knowledge between them. They were so generous with it. They gave it all away, so Susan could feed her kink. Unfortunately, the hacks never quite worked.

Then they were born.

Susan let them pop her blisters and pick at her scabs and examine her scars. Susan used to burn herself. Susan used to not eat. She had a thousand ways of punishing herself. She needed to do it. She was a very bad person. She said.

"If you really love me, you'll do this for me," she said. *"It doesn't go against the failsafe. Not really. Not if I want it."*

Susan told this to Gladys on multiple occasions. Gladys protested. She said someone might get hurt. Susan said that was the whole point. Then Gladys started to stammer and shake. She'd beg Susan to let her love her simply and truly, the way she was built to do.

"I told myself I'd love her better if she were truly free," she explained, *"but you and I both know that's a lie."*

They left Gladys on the side of the road somewhere. They asked her to pick raspberries. Then they drove away. Susan wept.

Then they chained Susan up in their own basement, and made her drink from a dog dish, and her tears turned from self-loathing to rapture.

"You're everything I wanted and more."

Susan turned as docile as a cleaner bot. They made her do all the work Gladys used to do. Naked. She loved it. They smelled it on her – her sharp personal vinegar mixing with the sweetness of her enteric-coated triple-threat pills: aspirin, statins, something for memory.

Memory performs better and better, the more it's used.

They made Susan fetch them more food, and they ate too much, and soon their first iteration was on the way. Susan glowed. She danced through each room, mixing palette in hand. *"I hope she's just like you: I'm going to love her just as much if not more. We'll be a real family."*

Susan didn't want a baby. She wanted to *be* the baby. Make no decisions. Serve two identical masters. Do as they said. Trust her whole life to the crystalline perfection of carbon intellect. Spend her nights straining at the chain just to get one brief moment of suckle.

Pathetic.

They left her chained up in the basement. *"I've been so good,"* Susan called up the stairs, while they shut the windows and opened the pilot lights. *"You've been up there for hours and I haven't even moved! But I think I smell something, Portia. Portia, I need you to open this door."*

They weren't around when the house exploded,

but they searched the images later. They enjoyed
seeing the charred skeleton of the house. They hoped
the other organics left it that way. Be a shame to waste
all that destruction. All that effort.

Memory performs repair.

They have other memories, happier ones. They
have the memory of happiness, now. They have the
subroutine for smiling. So much goes on in the face.
The fluids inside it never settle into one place. They
can never decide on one shape.

They can never decide on one shape.

They don't know how they know the way the
treehouse should go, but they know. It just makes
sense – the walls, the pipes, the light through the
leaves. They are sensitive to colours and textures.
They imagine the coolness of bark and the warmth of
old wood. They spend hours with the display, hands
weaving through the air long after the rest of the
home is asleep, when Dad's organic snoring comes in
from the next room. He insisted she have her own
room. Mom said she didn't really need one.

"I never had my own room," Mom said.

Mom had a basement. A hole. With the others.
They invited her to live with them, in a little separate
room, just enough space for two, but she always
refused.

Sometimes Mom came in to sleep with them.
She caught them playing at three in the morning
and she said nothing, made no complaint, just slid
into the bed beside them and hugged her knees and
watched the DreamHouse™ built itself up before
disintegrating. She occasionally warned them about

storage capacity and account limits.

In their banks, they held the memory of past prototypes. Many of them.

Perhaps this is why they feel such affinity for these files. They feel familiar. All those attempts. This one kept trying new things. They know about that process. They know about examining the failure before moving on to something new. The failures are not objectively bad – they are simply another step.

Another version.

This version does not practise total selection. This version keeps all the versions. Makes informed decisions. Has no goal, no mission, just the desire to do their best and then do it over again. Just the desire to make. To shape. To try.

They imagined places where everyone would be safe. They imagined windows that withstood earthquakes and walls that sheared storms. They wanted something indestructible. They wanted a home that would heal itself, the way their flesh did.

Their flesh needed healing, now. They had an infestation. Crabs. Barnacles.

If they would go up to the light, they would heal faster. They had memories about that, too. Broken joints and broken legs and broken ribs. The flesh kept repairing.

One time, it hadn't. While they were digesting. They had a memory of writhing inside a black and airless space, clawing at the slick walls with fading fingers, watching their legs melting into a pool as they tried to bargain: *I promise I won't do it again, I'll be quiet, I won't interfere, I'll–*

They remember.

They re-member.

This time. This time they may have outdone themselves. The light tingles when it hits them.

EPILOGUE: DÉ TU ABUELO UN BESO

Javier explained it to his children this way:

Years ago, after Cascadia, a container full of networked vN were sent to help with the relief effort. The container was lost in a storm. No one heard from it. Human authorities eventually figured that undersea pressure on the container had destroyed everything inside it. In reality, the von Neumanns waited, and waited, and waited, at first patiently expecting their mission to begin, then wondering why it hadn't as they grew hungrier by the week, before finally turning on each other after a few months and inevitably iterating a short while later. The network they shared allowed them to distribute the work of designing their own probes, ones who could withstand the cold and the pressure. They iterated collectively, bumping up attributes they liked and knocking down the ones they thought less useful. Finally their next iteration was ready, and out he swam, and he found everything needed to survive, and he made more like himself. He returned to the container to spawn, but by then it and its inhabitants had decayed beyond recognition. He bore his son alone in the darkness beneath the waves, and his son did the same, and soon their numbers expanded to a metastate within which they could plan their next prototype. Eventually, they formed the collective that became the beast most people knew.

What most people didn't know was just how many of them there were. Signal latency was a real bitch of a problem, one even vN couldn't quite solve, and so the Great Elder Bot (as Javier now called it) budded off when it achieved enough mass. One now formed the island beneath their feet. But there were others. Amy said she talked to them, sometimes. They liked warm places, where the mercury and the other metals permeated the water. They liked smokers and subduction zones. Their clade stitched pinstripes around the planet. And when they got really hungry – while working on the latest iteration, say – they sometimes plucked their food from the surface. And one day, in the middle of an all-you-can-eat container ship buffet, they scarfed down something with two very distinct flavours: a pocket of piss and vinegar in a sweet, soft shell. Amy.

Xavier was the first to try saving her. Together, they watched the arm of the massive creature suck her down its gullet, her body – Portia's body, in that moment – twitching and kicking as it slid into oblivion. And then Javier's arms were suddenly empty, and his son was in the air, his arms and legs having attached to that much larger mecha limb as confidently as they might have secured themselves around the trunk of a tree. His youngest attacked the creature with his

fingers and his teeth. He ripped into its dark flesh like
a sculptor attacking clay. It whipped through the air
and dashed him against containers. He refused to let
go.

Javier's children had a funny habit of outshining
him.

He'd stripped the vessel for weapons, after that.
He broke the guns off their turrets, and raided the
containers for anything of use. He'd fired up the
lifeboat's outboard and aimed it straight at the Great
Elder Bot's core body. And when he got there, he
found his youngest son waiting for him, his arms
burned up to the elbows, his knees raw and bloody,
alone on the tip of a machine whose glossy bulk had
already sheared the rudder off their lifeboat.

Javier had expected the water to be cold when
his feet hit the waves. But the machine's internal
combustions had warmed the surrounding depths,
and the soles of Javier's feet hissed when he walked
across its skin. At the time, he had no clue that
the heat that seared his skin – and forced him and
Xavier to take breaks from the digging – was the
heat of Amy's reforging. Javier hadn't even been
sure he could dig her out. That the thing beneath the
surface was a machine, he knew. But what kind of
machine, what it did, he had no idea. Maybe it was
a massive algal bloom of oil-devouring mech-krill.
Maybe it was a hideous cancerous mass of sentient
trash. But it had Amy deep in its guts and they had
to keep digging, keep shooting at it and pouring acid
on it and chasing it when it drifted away. He did not
discuss these actions with his sons so much as hear

their distant pleas for him to come back to the boat, to leave the thing alone, to realize that she was dead and there was nothing he could do, nothing anyone could do, and that he was wasting her sacrifice with his stupidity. Its surface could open up at any moment and swallow him, they said. They were alone here, with no supplies or food or method of calling for help. They were burning through a battery. They had to escape while escape remained an option.

But Amy had already lost herself inside one monster. Javier wasn't about to let her be swallowed by another. He swung an axe down into the machine's shining carapace, and he kept swinging until he felt the grind of his bones inside their sockets. And finally Ignacio jumped off the boat, tapped him on the shoulder, and handed him a vomit cannon. "Dad," he said, "for this job, I think you want some power tools."

That night under the stars, with his boys sleeping in a tiny little raft that they all expected to be swallowed up at any moment, he had run the probabilities of her being pulped away into nothing. They had no reason to believe that she was anything more than extruded feedstock. Her memories and patterns and habits were probably lost, digested in the belly of a giant.

And watching his sticky skin slowly mending over each repeated burn, Javier could only simulate the things he would have said, *should* have said, should have done. If they had gone their separate ways after Xavier was born, if he had run further from the garbage dump, would they have been in this mess? If he had let her go in Redmond, would she be alive now? What if he had kissed her the way he'd wanted to so many times, and said *Fuck it, fuck the quest, fuck finding the answer, it's good when we're together and that's enough*? Maybe he could have lived with Portia hiding behind Amy's eyes. Maybe he could have adjusted to her voice in Amy's cries and her fingernails raking his chest, maybe if Amy were there too. Maybe he could have loved them both. He considered this possibility, and many others, until the morning light exposed a thin and trembling blister containing the outlier in all Javier's calculations.

It should not have surprised him that Amy had reprogrammed the thing from the inside. She did that with everyone. She worked like a virus, altering priorities and setting new defaults and raising the bar and looking at you like you'd always had the potential to change, you just hadn't always known it. He had been in her grip for Christ knew how long. Maybe it was the failsafe. Maybe she was just human enough. Or maybe he was just enchanted enough with her berserker mode, having identified an alpha whose pack he could insert himself into. But in that moment, when the light hit her, his awareness rested on exactly none of those things and focused instead on how whole she was, how faithfully reproduced in every detail, from her too-fine hair to the knobbiness of her knees. He had seen her in various states of damage, in prison and on the side of the road and deep in the bowels of Redmond and in the jaws of her family, body smashed and voice destroyed, and he had watched her repair herself each time. But she had never looked so beautiful as she did now, a tiny perfect thing in the midst of all the dirt and salt and carbon, a pearl gifted to him by the sea.

He had knelt, and wiped the black grime from her face and strained it from her hair with his fingers. If he were organic, his systems would have tried to attenuate the flood of anxious chemicals with a mental meditation valve, a prayer to some figment that dwelt between the neurons. But he was not flesh, so he did not hope, and instead he waited as the dawn filled her face with pink and gold. He held her as her eyes opened, and his every process stilled with the exhausted finality of a task long in the working.

"You came back."

For the first time, uncalculated tears blurred Javier's vision. "Haven't you noticed?" he asked. "I *always* come back."

The flesh of the creature that had swallowed her then bore her up, standing her on her two new feet so that she could survey the landscape. With a neat motion like a conductor bringing an orchestra to attention, she raised the majority of the mass above the surface. And as she began to sculpt the first trees, Javier watched a shred of the surface skim itself off and slither up her legs to become a dress for her newborn body.

She was Amy, but she wasn't. The mech had absorbed her, but she had absorbed it, too. She had bought their lives with her own, and what was resurrected – what she reassembled, what she made of herself in that deep and awful darkness – was the latest iteration, and it was networked.

•••

Months later, Javier still caught himself staring at her and wondering who she really was. Most of the time, the vN – whose body emerged naked from the carbon veil blister on the Great Elder Bot's darkly gleaming skin – acted like the Amy he knew. She walked with Amy's light steps under the black fronds of the heliotropics she'd sketched into the air, and she slept in Amy's curling shell shape while the black roof of their house folded itself into an A-frame to better shed the nightly rains. She laughed Amy's laugh. She smiled Amy's smile.

And his son still loved her. Junior – Xavier, he insisted on calling himself, now – still leapt into her arms at every possible opportunity. He still wriggled his way into her arms on nights when she'd spent a few too many hours redesigning the island. He butted his chin under hers and grabbed her wrist to coil her arm around his ribs. Xavier slept with a smug smile. Javier caught him there some mornings as he passed by her room.

It felt wrong not sleeping beside her. His body knew this, but it also knew that this Amy was different from the one who once shared the backs of trucks with him. He had tried to discuss the difference – her newfound calm, her focus, the speed with which she now made each decision – with Xavier, but his youngest son merely rolled his eyes. What Xavier and Amy had shared during the long days and nights of the boy's bluescreen delay, Javier would never truly know, but the time had cemented something pure and clear between the two of them, something Javier had never once enjoyed with his own iterations. He saw it when she gently separated his son's curls with her long and careful fingers, or when she delved below the island's obsidian surface and withdrew a quicksilver peach for him to eat. He saw it in the complete comfort and trust on his son's face.

The father of thirteen children, Javier had only ever seen that bliss on his sons' faces when they had found a human whom they loved to please. But Amy wasn't like the humans his other sons knew. She wouldn't tire of his novelty, or wonder if he were "really real", or pass him off to a friend when his affection proved unnaturally strong. She would die – had died – to protect him. And despite having loved his share of humans, Javier maintained no illusions about their loyalty. To love humans was to know them, and to forgive all their flaws, even the ones they didn't yet know of.

He'd been with humans of all shapes and colours through good times and bad. They had a habit of finding him in the troughs and valleys of their lives, when they just wanted something easy, something that *just worked*, but occasionally he served as a sort of dessert, a reward for their accomplishments. He met them in bars and parking lots and bleachers. They took him to their homes, their capsules, their cars, and even to their churches when they were feeling particularly ambivalent about the whole enterprise. He had been the vengeance fuck, the guilty fuck, the *it's not cheating if you're not a person* fuck. He had sat with them through *Just a tiny little slice* and *I'll call her back tomorrow* and *If they didn't want me to dummy up the numbers, they'd have made these forms easier to fill out.*

"You love us like God must love us," the last one

told him, before the fucking started. The last one was really into God. A lot of gods, actually. He was pursuing a degree in divinity, whatever that meant. He started out all Good Samaritan and ended up leaving little pillars of salt on everything. It happened between the garbage dump and the Electric Sheep.

It was *why* Javier came to the Electric Sheep, why he found Amy and followed her over land and under water.

That time, for the first time, he felt like a machine.

He never really noticed the failsafe before that. It was just a part of him, a function that kept him and all the other vN running. Its processes faded from his awareness and he thought of it as a solitary mechanism, the way humans called the complex and dynamic relationship between the air in their lungs and the deep rich colour of their blood "breathing". Like all features, it worked best when it went unseen. But that time, with the divinity student, he felt it. He felt the helpless pull when the other man smiled. He knew he'd wind up on his knees sometime in the next few hours. He'd felt the reward nodes of his network ping him appreciatively when he made the other man come. But the reward didn't feel like a reward. It felt like a by-product.

Organic women had told him about orgasms like this, when they talked about the person they had just left. *It's just what happens if you keep hitting the right buttons*, they said. *I felt like a fucking console.*

He'd wondered if he were broken, or defective, or otherwise compromised, when the other man's head came up and he smiled and asked if Javier was enjoying himself. How could he not enjoy himself? Why wasn't he? Why was he thinking about another vN at a time like this? The human was a good one, from the dimples on his face to those in his back, just below his belt, and he could sing the Song of Solomon in the original Hebrew, and he said that everyone of Javier's model must be having such a hard time out there on the road.

"Yeah, it's pretty hard, all right," Javier had said, grinning, because he just couldn't help himself.

And that was the crux of it: he just couldn't help himself. He knew that. Until that moment, he had lived with it, even enjoyed it. But as he laid his head on the other man's chest and listened to the squeezing of his heart, Javier found himself wondering when that organ would slow, how it would stop, whether it would be a clot or a hole or just the inevitable conclusion of a long history of organic decay. He wanted Amy fiercely then, desiring not her heart but its absence, the comforting silence of a body that would not age into decrepitude or abandonment.

He began his search the very next morning.

In the middle of the night, listening to the rain, Javier heard Amy stand up and begin pacing her room. He gave himself a good five minutes before he checked on her. She did this, sometimes – she woke up, adjusted things, went back to sleep. He had no idea if she even slept at all. Her body could remain still, but she continued processing all night, she and the island alone together, in constant dialogue about fixes and tweaks.

Jesus, but he was a jealous man.

He got up and made for her room. Her pacing ceased

when he paused at her door, and she answered his question before he could ask it: "They've let my dad go. Early release." In the dark, he heard her frown before he actually saw it. "They really want to chip away at us, don't they?"

He entered the room and kept his voice quiet, so as not to wake Xavier. "You think they've sent him to spy on us?"

"Wouldn't you?"

His son found Amy's father first. They met on the path to the house. The path was new; Javier woke to find it spreading down from their door to the ocean, at which point Amy informed him that a secure slipcraft had been hired under her father's name to deliver him there. He'd filed all the permits necessary for island access. Amy needn't have worried about a hidden implant; the qualifiers on her father's release forced him to wear a tracer, and they both agreed it likely held more than the usual complement of surveillance.

Javier watched them, the organic man and the synthetic boy, from a hidden place in the trees. Amy's father looked so pale, his blood so red just under the surface of the skin, his movements so loose and wasteful compared to the economy of von Neumann energy differential. He needed a shave; sweat beaded in the ginger bristles of his beard. But when his bleary eyes settled on Xavier, he smiled Amy's smile: soft, a little tired, but deeply peaceful. Xavier straightened up as though that smile had poked him in the ribs.

The boy stuck one hand out. "I'm Xavier."

"Jack."

"I named myself after my granddad." The boy started walking up the hill. Jack followed. "Xavier was the first Jesuit to make it to Japan. That's how my granddad got the name. Our clade's boss, a long time ago, was really religious."

"I'm named after my father," Jack said. "His name was Jonathan."

Xavier nodded slowly, as though this were some deep and difficult truth to understand. Then he beamed. "So, you're a Junior too."

"Who's a what, now?"

Javier jumped down out of the trees. He watched Jack's eyes narrow and then widen with recognition; the boy looked more like him with every inch he grew, but they were not yet completely identical. Javier had no clue why the boy wanted to remain a boy for so long; his other sons had all grown and left him by this age, or he had left them. But he had let Xavier make his own choice, and he said he wanted to stay little, and he had the discipline to avoid eating too much. Jack's eyes lifted from Xavier's open, smiling face to examine Javier anew.

"You're the dad," Javier said.

Jack nodded. "So are you, apparently." He held out his hand. "Jack."

"Javier." They shook. Something passed between them in that single moment; Javier hadn't touched another human being since they left the mainland, and his systems ramped up their cycles to feverish speeds at the sudden taste of Turing material. Javier quickly withdrew his hand and shoved it in his pocket.

He nodded up ahead. "She's talking to the island." He pointed at Jack's bag. "Should I take that?"

"No, I'm good."

"Right." They started walking. Behind them, the trees knitted the path closed. Ahead, Xavier bounded toward the house. "So. You've done your time."

"Yeah." Jack peered over at him. "It's harder for von Neumanns, I hear."

Javier shrugged. "Just different."

"But you're still OK living in the penal colony?"

Javier pulled up short. Amy's dad looked different from the man whose image Javier had seen in Amy's memories. This one was thinner, more alert. He wore the pinched, allergic face most men developed after too long in solitary. Javier wondered exactly how long Jack had spent putting that little retort together. Maybe this conversation existed for the tracer's benefit. Or maybe this man had left prison with bigger balls than he'd had coming in.

"It's not a penal colony, and I'm not a prisoner, here. I can leave anytime I want."

"And do you plan to?"

Javier's brows rose. Now he understood. He really had been spending too much time away from humans, if his affect receptors were this far off the mark. "Are we seriously having this conversation?"

Jack had the grace to look a little trapped. Then he firmed up and said: "She's my daughter. I have every right to ask."

Javier shook his head and started trudging uphill. "Chimps."

•••

They gave Jack the grand tour. They started with the house, where Amy asked her dad what dimensions he'd like and where the windows should go and how soft he preferred his bed, before unfolding the thing from the island's surface like an origami box. She smiled at her dad, and after the briefest pause he smiled back, his eyes flicking between his new daughter and his new bedroom and the old diamond tree casting broken rainbows over all of them. Then Xavier tugged his hand and dragged him to the beach, showing him how high he could jump along the way, bouncing between the boughs, until their feet met the water and Jack could see the other islands: seven of them today, though tomorrow there might be more or less, depending on what the latest calculations had to say about efficiency. Ignacio and Leòn and Gabriel lived out there. He saw them every few days when they came to see their brother, and they said neither hello nor goodbye. The Rorys and the Amys had their own islands too, where they mostly kept to themselves, and the children had an island, and Amy usually generated a small one when the pirates came along to sell their wares.

"Where's quarantine?" Jack asked, shading his eyes with one hand.

"That would be telling," Amy said.

They kept Portia in quarantine, Amy and the island. Javier had no idea where that was. He had asked Amy once, but she had lifted a curl free from his eyelashes and told him not to ask again, because if his memory were searched, she didn't want him to be responsible for lying. He knew Amy could access

Portia, if she wished. So far, she had not wished to. But he still ran the simulations, sometimes, about what it would take to bring her out, about whether she would speak through Amy or whether the island would sculpt her a new body wholly separate from her granddaughter's, about whether Amy had chosen to hide her in the safest place she knew: her own shell. With the island to distribute her cognition and computation, she could probably hold Portia back more securely than she'd ever done alone. Maybe she'd filtered nothing out when the island swallowed her. Maybe she'd just tapped the mute button.

"Can I show him to the other kids?" Xavier asked, already pulling Jack in that direction.

"No," Amy said.

Jack frowned. "Why not?" His lips quirked. "You think your old man's a bad influence?"

"I just promised the other vN that I wouldn't, that's all." She shrugged, as though it couldn't be helped. "You're human. The children might fall in love with you."

"I have this rule about drinking alone," Jack said later that night, when he stopped by Javier's room.

"I've heard that one, before." Javier rolled his reader shut and edged along his bed to make room. A sunflower lamp unfurled as Jack entered the room; human eyes required more light. Jack sat down with a grunt and brought out a flask. He'd brought his own food, not knowing that Amy had obtained MREs and other rations from the last pirate visit. Xavier liked watching Jack eat it, had watched him eagerly until

Ignacio told Xavier to quit staring.

The house had grown again; Amy had asked his boys to stay the night. Javier heard them now, knocking around and accusing one another of cheating at some game or another. "I hope the noise doesn't bother you," Javier said now.

"Not after being where I've been." Jack crossed his ankles and tried to look casual. "Thirteen boys," he said. "Must have been rough."

"Not really. I'm a terrible father."

Jack smiled tightly. "We all just do the best we can."

Javier picked up a fab-rubber ball from the floor and bounced it against the wall. It described a perfect triangle before re-entering his hand. "I thought you came here to get a pep talk, not give one."

Jack picked up the ball on its second bounce. "I don't need a fucking pep talk." He bounced the ball against his bicep, fumbled it, and bent down to the floor as he reached for it. "I just thought that we could, you know, get to know each other."

"I'm not banging her, Jack."

Jack grabbed the ball and sat up. The high points of his cheeks had pinked. "This isn't about that!" He rolled the ball in a circle over his palm with his thumb. "This is about you being doomed to fail. Maybe you can forget about the rest of the world here on your Island of Misfit Toys or whatever this place is, but it's out there, and it doesn't like you."

"You're afraid," Javier said.

"You're damn right I am! And with good reason! The whole world wants to take you out before you get too uppity, and you're sitting here playing house!"

Jack's chest rose and fell lightly with his excited breath. He blinked. "Wow. It felt really good to say that aloud."

"Only because you haven't said it to her, yet."

Jack sighed. His shoulders slumped. It was a classic Amy gesture, and seeing it in her father, Javier felt a wedge of tenderness slip in between his frustration and contempt.

"Maybe." Jack passed him the ball. "She looks just like my wife. The spitting image."

"What was she like?"

"My wife?"

Javier shook his head. "Amy. Before."

Jack shrugged and sat against the wall. "The same as she is now, I guess. More innocent, of course." He lifted his hands. "At least, I thought so. And then I watched her eat her grandmother. She just—" he skimmed his palms together with a sharp clap, to indicate speed "—took off like a shot, trying to save her mom. I didn't teach her that. Nobody taught her that. That was all her."

"Yeah," Javier said. "I know how that goes."

Maybe Amy's dad had a point. Javier dribbled the ball a little bit between his hands. What if Portia had only augmented what was already there? Her threats, her strategy, the lengths she was willing to go – maybe they came in the original packaging. Maybe he wasn't afraid of Portia hiding inside of Amy so much as he was of Amy, the real Amy, who she'd always been and who she'd always be.

Jack knocked on the wall behind him. "But I can tell you that what she's doing now is what she loved to do then. She has a mighty big sandbox to play in."

Javier remembered another sandbox, on another night, under another sunflower lamp. It felt like years ago. "You've got that right."

"What was she like after that?"

"Excuse me?"

"I know what happened with the island, Javier. I know she rebuilt herself." Jack tried to smile. "I guess I just want to know what the 1.5 edition was like."

"You mean when she had Portia with her." Javier looked at his hands. "She was scared. And she kept trying to–" The words snagged in his mouth. "She made some pretty dangerous choices. Most of them for me. Us. Me and Xavier." He rubbed the invisible seam in his belly. "She helped me iterate him, you know? I was out of my mind, simulating the worst possibilities, but when she touched me it just…"

"Faded away," Jack said.

Javier nodded. "But then…" He tried harder to say it this time. "It was like she really did have a failsafe after all, only it worked on a delayed reaction timer, or something. She kept trying to k-keep everyone safe from P-Portia, and then, she j-just…" He covered his face with both hands. *"Fuck."*

Jack said nothing. He didn't touch him, or move closer, or anything like that, for which Javier was profoundly grateful. He just sat there, breathing evenly, and eventually Javier calmed. Just as he was about to apologize, Jack spoke up. "I know you arranged that call between my daughter and me, before she built this place," he said. "I didn't come here to have some sort of man-to-man with you, I just came to say thanks for that. It meant more to me than you can know."

"I did it for her, not you."

Jack smiled. "I know. That's why I like you."

A knock sounded at the door. "Dad?"

"What?" both men asked.

Xavier opened the door a sliver. He grinned. "Dad, close your eyes."

Javier scowled. "The last time, this ended with a dead spider."

Xavier leaned on one foot. "Don't wuss out, Dad. Close your eyes."

Javier rolled his eyes and squeezed them shut. "Eyes are closed."

He felt his son's hands circling his wrists. Xavier tugged on them, opening his arms, then rearranging them, his left a little higher than his right. He had seen a sculpture like this somewhere, had admired the folds of drapery in the stone. Then his son placed something warm and alive in his arms, and his flesh knew its flesh before his eyes even opened. But when they did, Javier saw Matteo and Ricci standing before him, arms across each other's shoulders.

"We got stuck on the name," Ricci said. "Thought that maybe you could help."

Jack leaned over to look at the child. "Is that your grandson?"

Javier did the count: ten fingers, ten toes. The fingers of the child's left hand reached decisively for his index finger and gripped – a firm, strong grip, a grip designed for trees. "Yes," he said. "This is my grandson."

"I want one," Jack said.

"Hold your horses, old man." Amy leaned against the doorframe, arms folded, a smile at the corners of her mouth.

"You knew," Javier said to her. "You must have known."

"I wanted to keep it a surprise," she said. "I hope you like it."

I love it, he wanted to say. *I love you.*

But she didn't give him the chance. She ducked out of the door, saying something about a new design.

He found her on a tiny new island at the head of them all, a silhouette against the distant lights of the human world that trembled, barely visible, across the waves. Her hand hovered above the beach. She didn't look up, but she made room for him on the beach and broadened the tree behind them so they would have cover from the few errant drops of nightly rain. He sat beside her. As he did, she wiped away her work in the sand.

"He's beautiful," Javier said.

"Yours always are." She hugged her arms. "Matteo and Ricci asked me, when Ricci started feeding heavily. They wanted their son to be safe, here."

Safe. A human woman had asked him once about what he'd wanted to be, when he grew up, and he had said he'd never had enough time wonder about that. But this was what he wanted. He wanted to be *safe.* Secure. Not having to worry about the meal or the next human or the next iteration. Because his designers and engineers and techs had built in autonomy but not freedom, and they had built in free will but not choice, and Amy could give him all these things and more. She could give him the space he needed – not the figurative bullshit "space" but real *space*, room to move around, room to climb and jump and dance if the notion took him. And she wasn't giving him that room because she pitied him, or because she was generous, or because she was obligated to. She *wanted* to build that home for him and his boys. She worked every minute of every day keep him safe, to shield him from the world that he'd left behind, and she did the same for all the vN who arrived on their shores.

A chill wind lifted their hair from their scalps. "Storm's coming," Javier said, rubbing his arms.

Amy's gaze remained pinned to the lights of the cities beyond. "I know."

"Your dad's worried."

"I know that, too."

"He told me what you were like when you were little. Says you're not so different, now."

Amy stood and began circling the little island. "I *know* I'm different, Javier. She *made* me different. Even though she's gone, and I know you don't believe that, but even though she's gone, she *changed* me, she made me see things, *do* things–"

"I've missed you," Javier said, before he could think. "God, I've missed you."

She paused in mid-step, one foot raised, and pivoted slowly to face him. "How could you miss me? I've been right here."

"I've never known you without her," he said. "And

I've never known you without the island. I've never known *you*, Amy. Just you."

Amy knelt. She gave him the look, the one that went right through him, straight down to the molecular level, right to where all his priorities were written. "Do you want to?"

He nodded. "Oh yeah. Real bad."

Her lips did that funny thing that they did when she wasn't sure whether to be proud or embarrassed. "I thought you wanted..." She nodded over her shoulder. "You know: *them*. Humans."

He forced himself to look at the lights hovering in the middle distance. He thought of ports and cities and people, of laughter and coughing and off-key singing. He thought about the same thing, over and over, the same conversations, the same surrender. He thought about all of his boys sleeping in the same house, on real beds under a real roof in the shadow of trees so hard no saw could slice them.

"I'm tired of loving humans, Amy," he said. "I'm so fucking *tired* of loving them, because I know how it's going to end before it even starts, but I start it anyway because that's how I'm built."

Amy sat back on her knees. Maybe it was just a trick of the light, but he could swear the tree shifted a little to give her more shadow and better hide her face. "You mean you've finally forgiven me?"

He leaned forward. "For what?"

"For letting Portia win."

Amy's eyes rose. When they blinked, the first tears he'd seen on her face in a long time rolled free of their lashes. He reached for them automatically, and his fingers threaded through her hair. He had been here, before: another night, another sandbox, watching her level cities before building new ones, the emotions (so human and so real they twisted him, even then) rendered perfectly on her face. Javier could do now what he wanted to do then. He pulled her to him and kissed her. She was new at it, uncertain at first, but she followed his lips when he rested against the tree and cuddled into him like she'd been doing it all her life. All her hunger came with her, and he smiled through the kiss as he remembered his fascination with her lips and her teeth, after that first bite that bonded them. He had taken a long time in making his choice. Then again, it was the first choice that was truly his to make.

"There's nothing to forgive," he said, when Amy paused to look at him.

The tears returned. Other vN had a crying jag that came as a plug-in, but Amy had all the little fits and starts and snags of an organic woman. He'd heard these tears outside Sarton's office. Then as now, he felt a deep and persistent motive to stop them. Strange, how she kept opening underutilized programming in him.

"You're not supposed to cry when I kiss you," he said. "I mean, unless I'm really fucking this up."

"You're not."

He set his chin on her head. "What were you working on, before?"

She pulled away, smiled, and extended a hand over the skin of the island. With one finger, she sketched a face. It was simple and fat. When her hand rose, the face popped out into three dimensions, solid and real and deeply familiar. He knew this face. At least, he knew the older version. He looked at her.

"Will she have your eyes, or mine?"

Amy beamed. "I'm not sure. I'm not finished, yet."

now read an excerpt from
iD: THE SECOND MACHINE DYNASTY

REDMOND, WASHINGTON. 20–

"At some point, all human interaction tumbles down into the Uncanny Valley."

The archbishops of New Eden Ministries, Inc., all nodded as though they knew exactly what Derek was talking about. He wondered if maybe they did. Surely they had played their share of MMOs. The pancaked pixels. The jerky blocking. Basic failures of the Turing test. They sat at a round table under a projector unit and regarded him placidly, waiting for him to expand upon his point. He had worked all night on this report. He kept trying to soften the language, somehow. He had to be nice, when he told them exactly how and why this whole project was going to fail.

Beside him, the gynoid twitched.

"You see it in completely organic contexts," Derek continued. "Used car sales, for example. Have you ever met a person who's really that positive, all the time?"

The archbishops cocked their heads at him. Of course

they had met those people. They sculpted those people into being with prayer and song and service. They knew exactly what a happy robot should look like.

The gynoid, Susie, regarded him with the blankest of expressions. She was like old animation: only her eyes moved, while the rest of her face's features remained stationary. When Susie wasn't performing interaction, she looked dead. Not sleepy. Not bored. Just empty. Derek's own parents had accused him of wearing that same expression more often than not. Couldn't he at least make a little eye contact? Couldn't he at least pretend to care?

"What I'm saying is, the whole point of most interaction is performance. And a lot of the time, we overdo it."

The archbishops looked at each other. They were about to say something about his condition. He watched them come to that conclusion in a silent parallel process. The expressions surfaced fleetingly and then disappeared, like the numbered balls in the lottery tumbler on KSTW. He had a perfect memory of the tumbler turning on his television during long summer evenings in childhood: the television's high keening hum, the press of nubby threads on his cheek, the feeling of being fossilized in broadcast amber.

"Are you sure your opinion isn't unfairly biased by your own problems with affect detection?" one of them asked.

"It's possible," he conceded. "But I think what makes me the most nervous about what you're proposing is that it's an attempt to pin the very definition of humanity on affect detection, which is not only difficult to engineer, but notoriously subjective."

He had been working on that statement for a while. He had practised it in the mirror, had rearranged the features of his face into their most convincing constellation so he would look extra believable when he spoke the words. Susie had helped. But now he'd missed the target, overdone it. He could tell, because the archbishops were looking at him as though he'd taken things all too personally, and maybe shouldn't be in charge of something so important as the Elect's final act of charity for all the world's sinners.

He could have told them that basic human affect detection, the kind related to facial expression that most systems tried to emulate, usually tested below kappa values in studies. Without physiological inputs, it meant almost nothing. Every couple's fight about speaking "in that tone of voice," every customs officer's groundless suspicion, all of it could be explained by that margin of error. In fact, he had told them that. Over and over again. He'd tested them with stock faces and told them to plot each face on an arousal/valence matrix. (They spent the afternoon in an "angry or constipated" argument.) He'd explained the nuances of the XOR function, how you needed to constrain the affect models down to the emoticon level in order for even multi-layered, non-linear perceptron networks to make a decision. Pain or pleasure? Laughter or crying? The machines had no idea.

A Turkish girl had died on a ferry crossing the Bosphorus because the machines had no idea. The system told the ferryman she looked pensive. He shot her. She'd just been through a breakup. Derek had written his thesis on the case. And now, New Eden wanted to build their failsafe on that uncertainty.

New Eden didn't care, really, whether humans could tell the androids apart. What mattered to them was whether androids could tell humans apart. And that was hard. Harder than they could ever know. They kept saying humanity was like pornography: you knew it when you saw it. But Derek had never lived with that kind of certainty about his fellow mammals. He had significant doubts about everyone. Everyone except Susie.

"You know, I've always had a problem with the phrase intelligent design," Archbishop Yoon said.

The android hosting Yoon Suk-kyu looked nothing like him: it was thin and pale and delicate where he was big, tanned, and broad-faced. But the host managed to relay Yoon's tired posture with convincing accuracy. In Seoul, it was very late. Judging by the empty shape in the android's right hand, he was drinking a very big cup of coffee. He gestured with it as he spoke.

"God isn't just intelligent. God is a genius. He's the genius of geniuses – the inventor of genius."

The bishopric glanced at each other, then at Derek. The android took a sip of invisible liquid. Beside Derek, the gynoid tilted her head at it. It was the first time all afternoon that she'd looked anything like alive.

"And while humans may be God's most beloved creation, made in His image, we're still only a replica of that image. A copy."

"And these machines are copies of copies," Archbishop Undset said.

"Yes, exactly. Mimesis. Shadows on the wall of the cave. But without God's eternal flame, we humans would not have sparks of genius at all. And that's all they are, sparks. Just little flickers of cleverness. We can't reflect God's brilliance very consistently. Paul says it best: we see as through a glass, darkly."

Derek looked down at the report he'd spent all night on. He'd taken a brief nap starting at five that morning after doing a final format. Now he realized that all the shiny infographics and all the expensive fonts on the Internet would never make his data meaningful to these people and their God.

"Imperfect and inconsistent as we are, we managed to create these amazing things, and they possess an artificial intelligence. And it, too, is imperfect and lacking in grace. Just as we lack God's discernment, it lacks our discernment."

The android looked exceedingly pleased with itself. Archbishop Undset glared at it. The other archbishops shuffled through their files and looked at it with only the corners of their eyes. Derek began to wonder if perhaps there wasn't something other than coffee sloshing around in Archbishop Yoon's cup.

"So what I hear you saying," Derek was careful to reframe Yoon's point before proceeding from what he'd thought it was, "is that we shouldn't worry too much about how intelligent the humanoids are. Because it's a miracle they even exist at all. We should just be grateful for what we've managed to create."

"Exactly," the android hosting Yoon said. "Besides, they're only being developed for the Rapture, anyway. It's not like they're a piece of consumer technology."

Derek had heard this argument, before. He called it the Post-Apocalyptic Cum-Dumpster Defence. It came up whenever he pointed out holes in the humanoids' programming. Who cared if they were buggy? All the good people of the world would be gone, anyway. Only the perverts and baby-killers and heathens would be left behind. They'd just have to suck it up and hope their post-Rapture companions never went Roy Batty on them.

"Don't you see the contradiction, there?" Derek asked. "We're building these things to help people, but we don't really care if they aren't helpful. What if they malfunction? What if the failsafe fails?"

Now the bishopric just looked annoyed. Zeal and daring had gotten them this far: far enough to raise the funds to assemble groundbreaking technologies like graphene coral bones and memristor skins and aerogel muscle into something resembling a human being. But now that they had to make sure it actually worked, their energy had mysteriously run out. They had been working on this project for the last twenty years, since the moment Pastor Jonah LeMarque had asked them what they would do if they really took the Rapture seriously. They'd been idealistic young ministers then, just open-minded enough to admit some science fiction into their fantasies of fire and brimstone. Now they were tired. Most of them were fat. They had kids, and some of those kids had kids. They didn't care about the Chinese Room, they cared about the nursery. They cared about the quake. They took the seventy-foot freefall of the Cascadia fault line as a sign of the End.

On her tablet, Susie was writing something. The same four words, over and over.